VERNON AREA PUBLIC LIBRARY DISTRICT
P9-DMS-398

CRIMSON BOUND

Also by Rosamund Hodge

Cruel Beauty

CRIMSON BOUND

ROSAMUND HODGE

BALZER + BRAY
An Imprint of HarperCollins*Publishers*

Balzer + Bray is an imprint of HarperCollins Publishers.

Crimson Bound

 For information address HarperCollins Children's Books, a division of HarperCollins Publishers, 195 Broadway, New York, NY 10007.

www.epicreads.com

Library of Congress Cataloging-in-Publication Data

Hodge, Rosamund.

Crimson bound / Rosamund Hodge. – First edition.

pages cm

Summary: "Rachelle must protect the king's bastard son while searching for the weapons that will save her world from endless night"– Provided by publisher.

ISBN 978-0-06-222476-7 (hardback)

[1. Fantasy.] I. Title.

PZ7.H66144Cp 2015 2014030890

[Fic]–dc23 CIP

AC

Typography by Erin Fitzsimmons

15 16 17 18 19 PC/RRDH 10 9 8 7 6 5 4 3 2 1

❖

First Edition

For my mother,
who taught me one half of how to be brave,
and my father,
who taught me the other half

THIS STORY BEGINS WITH ENDLESS NIGHT AND infinite forest; with two orphaned children, and two swords made of broken bone.

It has not ended yet.

Prologue

"In all your life, your only choice," Aunt Léonie said to her once, "is the path of needles or the path of pins."

Rachelle remembered that, the day that she killed her.

When Rachelle was twelve years old, Aunt Léonie picked her to become the village's next woodwife.

Rachelle had been to her aunt's cottage a hundred times before, but that morning she stood awkwardly straight and proper, hands clasped in front of her. Aunt Léonie knelt before her, wearing the white dress and red mantle of a woodwife.

"Child," she said, and Rachelle's spine stiffened because Aunt Léonie only called her that when she was in trouble, "do you know the purpose of a woodwife?"

"To weave the charms that protect the village," Rachelle said promptly. "And remember the ancient lore."

Rachelle thought she would like weaving the yarn through her fingers. She knew she would love learning the old tales. But she wished that woodwives still went on quests. She wanted to *live* the stories, not just tell them to the village children.

"And who was the first woodwife?" asked Aunt Léonie.

"Zisa," said Rachelle. "Because she was the first person to protect anyone from the Great Forest, when she and Tyr killed the Devourer."

"And who is the Devourer?" asked Aunt Léonie.

"The god of the forestborn," said Rachelle. "Father Pierre says he doesn't really exist, or anyway he's not a god, because there is only one God, and he made heaven and earth; he doesn't try to eat them. But whatever the Devourer was, he had the sun and the moon in his belly until Tyr and Zisa stole them and put them in the sky."

Father Pierre said that wasn't true either, but Rachelle didn't see how he could be so sure when he hadn't been there three thousand years ago. And she liked that part of the story.

"He is the everlasting hunger," said Aunt Léonie in a voice of grim resignation. "And yes, once he held all the world in darkness, and once all mankind was ruled by the forestborn, who hunted us like rabbits."

A thread of uneasiness slid through her stomach. "Tyr and

Zisa killed the Devourer," she said. "Zisa died, and Tyr became king."

"No," said Aunt Léonie. "Tyr and Zisa only bound him. And that binding is nearly worn out."

She said the words so simply, it was a moment before Rachelle understood them, before she felt the awful, sickening lurch of real fear.

Quietly, relentlessly, Aunt Léonie went on, "One day soon he will open his eyes and yawn, and then he will swallow up the moon and the sun, and we shall live in darkness once again." She met Rachelle's eyes. "Do you believe me, child?"

"Yes," said Rachelle as her heart beat, *No, please, no,* but when she met Aunt Léonie's eyes, she had to think, *Maybe.*

It's all right, she told herself. *Aunt Léonie will save us.*

But Aunt Léonie didn't plan to save anyone.

For three years, Rachelle sat obediently braiding charms in the cottage. She learned to ward off fever and keep mice out of grain, and to prevent woodspawn—the animals born in the Great Forest, suffused with its power—from wandering into the village and attacking people. But none of it mattered, because when the Devourer returned, no charm would be strong enough to protect anyone. Aunt Léonie told her so again and again.

"What can we *do*?" Rachelle always asked.

Aunt Léonie would only shrug. "Sometimes abiding is more important than doing."

Zisa hadn't abided. Zisa had fought the Devourer and saved the whole world, but apparently woodwives weren't supposed to save people anymore. They were supposed to sit in their cottages and braid insignificant charms and never, ever dream of changing the world.

Rachelle clenched her teeth and furiously dreamed. Every day the cottage felt more like a prison.

Until one day she was walking home from Aunt Léonie's cottage and she realized that something had changed. The shadows had grown deeper; the blue flowers by the side of the path had begun to glow. The wind felt like fingertips tracing her neck. Shadowy, phantom mushrooms studded the ground; a deer made out of black cloud peered at her from between the trees, its eyes glowing red.

She blinked and it was gone, but her heart was thudding and her veins buzzing. She had seen the Forest. Not just the woods around her village—she had seen a glimpse of the Great Forest, the Wood Behind the Wood. You could wander for days beneath the trees and never see it, because it was not part of the human world; it was a secret, hidden place that sat just a little to the side. But sometimes its power trickled and oozed out through the shadows of tree leaves or the hollows carved by tree roots and brought the mortal woods to uncanny life.

Usually it could only be seen on solstice nights. Aunt Léonie had told her that. But maybe those rules were wearing down, like the bonds upon the Devourer.

And then she heard a voice, like butter and burned honey: "Good afternoon, little girl."

She turned.

Between two trees stood a man, shadowed against the glow of the setting sun behind him. She couldn't see his face.

Then he took a step forward, and she realized that he was not a man. He had a human face, pale and narrow. He wore a dark, rough cloak like any villager might wear. But she could sense the predatory, inhuman power beneath his skin. When she glanced away from him, she couldn't remember anything about his face except that it was lovely.

She looked back, and his eyes met hers, glittering and alien. He was a forestborn: one of the humans who pleased the Devourer, accepted him as their lord, and were remade by his power into something not quite human anymore.

"Little girl," he said, "where are you going?"

Her heart was making desperate spasms, but Zisa hadn't been afraid, or at any rate hadn't let it stop her. They said Zisa had learned from the forestborn themselves how to defeat the Devourer.

Maybe Rachelle could do the same thing.

He was only a pace away from the path now, the path that was lined in little white stones to protect it.

"Little girl," he said, "what path are you taking?"

"The path of needles," she whispered. "Not the path of pins."

And she stepped toward him off the path. Her mind was a white-hot blur. She couldn't even tell anymore if she was afraid. She only knew that he was part of the shadow that had lain across her world all her life, and she wouldn't run from him, she *wouldn't.* So she stared into his fathomless, inhuman eyes and said, "You can kill me, but you can't hunt me."

He laughed. "Maybe I won't. What's your name, little girl?"

"Rachelle," she said. "What's yours?"

"Nothing safe for you to hear." He circled her slowly, examining her, and Rachelle's spine straightened, even though her skin prickled with fear.

"They say you were human, once," she said.

"Then why do you dare speak to me, when you are human still?"

"I'm the woodwife's apprentice," she said. "I was born to protect people from the Forest."

Again he laughed. "Oh, little girl. You were born to be prey for my kind. You were trained to sit plaiting charms against fever until you become a half-wit old woman. What you choose—is up to you."

"Why are you here?" she asked, but there was a sudden

emptiness in the air, and she knew before she turned that he was gone.

Rachelle wondered if he had come to hunt her. But when he found her on the path the next day, he still didn't try to touch her. And she still didn't run.

She met him again and again, and every time she stepped off the path. Always she kept a pace between them. Always she wore the charms embroidered on her cloak and woven into her belt.

She could never remember his face. But she could remember that he answered her questions and never tried to hurt her.

"Tell me about the Devourer," she said. "What is he, really?"

"The breath in our mouths and the hunger in our hearts," said the forestborn. "Be patient, little girl. You'll meet him yourself someday."

"Have you met him? Is that how you became a forestborn?"

"What did your aunt tell you?" he asked.

"A forestborn puts a mark on a human," she said. "The human must kill somebody in three days or die. If he does kill, he becomes a bloodbound, which means the power of the Forest is growing in him, until finally he gives up the last of his human heart and becomes a forestborn."

"That's true enough," said the forestborn. "Would you like to try it?"

"No," said Rachelle, and tensed, wondering if he would finally kill her.

But he only chuckled. "Then answer my question. What did you mean when you said the path of needles, not the path of pins?"

He remembers what I said. The realization slid through her, terrifying and sweet at once. *He thinks of me when we are apart.*

"Something my aunt told me once. She said that you always had to choose between the path of needles and the path of pins. When a dress is torn, you know, you can just pin it up, or you can take the time to sew it together. That's what it means. The quick and easy way, or the painful way that works."

That was what Aunt Léonie said, but really she had chosen the path of pins. All her aunt's charms could do was pin the world together—keep people a little bit safer, give them a little more time.

Rachelle wanted to sew the world back to safety, if she must use her own bones for needles.

It ended on a moonless autumn night, when the wind was moaning in the trees. The forestborn stood on the opposite side of a little clearing, his breath frosting the air. He looked as remote and foreign as the stars, but Rachelle was determined to have his secrets before dawn.

She asked, "Do you know how Zisa bound the Devourer?"

"Maybe," said the forestborn. "But why should I tell our secrets to one who doesn't trust us?"

"Would you tell them to somebody who did?" she asked.

"Do you trust me?" he asked.

He had never hurt her. All these days they had met alone in the woods, and he had never even tried.

"Yes," she said, and looked into the eyes that she could never remember. "I trust you."

"Then prove it," he said. "Take off your cloak. If you're right, you won't be needing it anymore."

Her red cloak was embroidered with charms to hold the power of the Great Forest away. She was never supposed to take it off in the woods, and her fingers trembled as she undid the pin, but she did not hesitate. The dark red wool slid off her shoulders and puddled at her feet.

His teeth gleamed as he smiled and stepped toward her. "Little girl," he said, "take off your belt. You won't be needing it anymore."

She was shuddering now in the cold and her fingers were numb. She gripped the belt buckle, but she could barely feel it. Aunt Léonie had spent six months braiding and rebraiding the leather before she was satisfied that the belt was strong enough protection for her apprentice.

It was too late to turn back. But she still said, "Tell me first. *Is* there a way to stop the Devourer?"

He stepped closer. "Yes."

The metal bit at her fingers as she fumbled the clasp open. And then the belt fell to the ground, and she was standing unprotected before a forestborn, and her blood was pounding hot and ready.

"So tell me," she said, and it felt like the world was whirling and creaking and falling apart around her. All her life she'd been traveling toward this moment where she wagered everything, and whatever happened, she would never be the same. "Tell me about the Devourer. All I need to know."

"All you need to know," he whispered, and his hands gently cupped her shoulders.

Then he slammed her against the nearest tree.

For a moment the pain dazed her. Then his mouth was pressed over hers and his tongue was forcing her lips open and sliding inside. It was a bizarre, helpless sensation, nothing like she'd heard kisses were supposed to be. She choked and tried to push him away, but he had her pinned.

Then he pulled back, and while she was still gasping for breath, he pressed his thumb to the base of her throat. From that one little point, fire seared throughout her body.

When she was aware again, she was lying crumpled on the snow. The forestborn stood over her, tall and remote and terrible.

"This is all you need to know," he said. "You belong to our

lord and master now. And you will kill for him before three days are up, or you will die."

Her body was numb except for the throbbing pain of the mark on her neck. She knew what it looked like: an eight-pointed black star. If she killed somebody and became a bloodbound, it would turn crimson.

"You said," she choked out, "that you would tell me how to stop him."

"Yes," said her forestborn. "The only way to stop him is with Durendal or Joyeuse, the swords of Tyr and Zisa. And those swords are lost forever."

Then he was gone.

She lasted for nearly three days.

On the first day, she hid the mark under a scarf and tried to be brave.

On the second day, she crept into the village church, clutching her rosary, and begged the Dayspring for a miracle.

On the third day, she gave up and ran for Aunt Léonie's house. The mark hurt so badly she could barely breathe. She didn't care anymore how ashamed she was; she just wanted Aunt Léonie to comfort her. Surely she could help. Aunt Léonie had always been able to make everything all right.

Around her, the woods awoke. Shadows became deeper

shadows, and eyes glimmered from their depths. Ghostly fawns leaped over tree roots and disappeared. The Great Forest was coming into being all around her, and soon she would be lost. Then she made the last turn, and she finally saw Aunt Léonie's house. She sobbed in relief as she staggered to the door.

But she was too late.

The forestborn had gotten there first.

ONCE UPON A TIME, THERE LIVED A PRINCE AND a princess named Tyr and Zisa.

You have heard this. After a fashion, it is true. The people who lived before the sun and moon built no cities, crowned no kings, fought no wars. They stole from one darkened hollow to the next, listening to the wind, dreading the day when the lords of the forest would visit them.

When the forestborn did visit their mewling human flocks, sometimes they would choose favorites. Tyr and Zisa's father was one of these: he had danced to the forestborn's music and offered them his kin. In return, they had made him ruler of the tribe that huddled beside an icy black lake.

What it gained Tyr and Zisa was this: they knelt beside him when the forestborn came to visit. Every member of the tribe but their father watched them with silent fear. And when they were sixteen years old, they painted their faces with ocher and blood, and sat obediently as the forestborn came to decide which of them would become a forestborn, and which would be sacrificed as a vessel for the Devourer.

The forestborn stood in a ring about the twins and laid a sword between them. Whichever one first cut off the hand of the other would become the forestborn. Whichever was weak enough to be maimed would become the sacrifice. If neither fought, they both would die that instant.

Zisa would have gladly lost hands and feet and eyes and tongue for her brother. But she knew that if she waited for him to pick up the sword, he would refuse and die beside her, and his death was the one thing she could not endure.

So she picked up the sword and cut off his right hand.

1

Wind gusted down the twisting nighttime streets of Rocamadour, whipping up the soft rain into a lash. Crouched atop the house's gable, Rachelle slitted her eyes against the sting and looked across the rooftops. There was no moonlight, but to Rachelle, the air gleamed with hidden currents, whorls and eddies of power unseen by normal human eyes. She could not only see the great hulk of the cathedral far off to her left, but also distinguish the silhouette of every gargoyle clinging to its spires. Three streets over, a carriage rattled homeward, and she could spot the individual spatters where the horse's hooves struck mud.

And all around her, she could see the shadow of the Great Forest.

Something happened when cities grew large enough. When the

labyrinths of their grimy cobblestone streets became as twisted as the interwoven branches of the forest canopy, the power of the Great Forest began to seep through. Ordinary humans might only have a vague feeling that there was something uncanny about the darkened streets. But Rachelle was bloodbound. Within the shadows of the buildings, she could see darker shadows cast by phantom leaves and branches. Within the whistle of the wind, she could hear the ghostly forest whispers.

It was time to hunt.

Rachelle took off running along the ridgepole. Ahead of her, the roof came to an end, and she leaped. For one moment she sliced, weightless, through the air and darkness; then her feet hit the next roof and skidded. In a heartbeat she had her balance back and was running again.

East of the cathedral, there was a neighborhood that had suffered five woodspawn attacks in the last two weeks. That wasn't just a series of random incursions; that was a pack, returning again and again to the place where they had found prey.

They were not going to hunt anyone else tonight.

Another roof, and another. Then Rachelle reached the wide, paved expanse of the Place du Gloire. She ran straight across, dropping from the rooftops to the ground.

At the center of the square stood two bronze statues of Tyr and Zisa holding the swords Joyeuse and Durendal. The bases of the statues were papered over with broadsheets—more dissidents asking how the King could dare to raise taxes when crops were failing because of the shortening days. To resist naming an heir when rumor said his health was ailing. To let the bloodbound live when everybody knew the Forest was growing stronger.

She'd been seeing a lot of broadsheets lately. Soon there would be another set of fools trying to attack the King's bloodbound. And another round of arrests.

Rachelle swarmed straight up the face of the building on the other side of the square, and put both King and rebels out of her head. Everything was simpler on the roofs. She ran and leaped, nothing to push her back but the wind itself, until she reached the neighborhood where the woodspawn kept attacking. Then she settled herself on a ridgepole to watch and wait.

And wait.

The night slowly wore on. The fire that had burned in her veins as she raced across the city was gone. Now she was cold and stiff; her eyes throbbed from lack of sleep and her fingers, still clutching the hilt of her sword, were almost completely numb. But she had promised herself she wouldn't sleep until she took care of this pack.

To keep herself awake, she stared at the glowing red string that was tied to her finger and trailed away off the roof. The string—invisible to everyone but her—was a reminder of why she couldn't stop hunting. If she looked at it long enough, she knew the scar on her right palm would start aching. That, too, was a reminder.

She would never deserve to stop hunting.

As if in answer to the thought, she heard a chorus of soft, almost musical moans.

Then she saw them on the street below: five doglike woodspawn, whippet-thin, their white bodies translucent, their muzzles bloodred. They looked like the ghosts of a court lady's lapdogs, but Rachelle had seen them tear a man to pieces in minutes.

One of the hounds slowed, lagging behind the others, and tilted its head up to sniff the air.

Rachelle drew her sword and flung herself down.

The hound had dodged before her feet hit the mud. But it didn't move fast enough to escape her sword. The blade cut through translucent flesh and bone; blood spurted, suddenly vivid and corporeal, but by the time the body hit the ground, it was already turning to mud.

The other hounds had wheeled to face her. They growled, lips curling as they faced the obscene enigma of a creature who was filled with the power of the Great Forest and yet turned against them. Then they sprang.

Rachelle grinned. Rain and wind and blood flung against her face as she whirled among them, her blade slicing. Moments later she was alone, the bodies of the woodspawn melting into the mud around her.

Gasping for breath, she listened: nothing but the patter of

the rain, the whispers of the wind, the faint shouts and clatters that filled the city air even at night. She couldn't sense anything, either.

The hunt was over, and as she realized that, all her earlier exhaustion washed back over her.

She also realized that the hunt had ended in front of a place where she could get a hot drink. Two doors down, light spilled from the windows of a coffeehouse; its wooden sign rocked in the wind. Rachelle strode through the puddles. As she reached for the door, the wind whirled up again behind her back and shoved her forward. She clattered into the coffeehouse on her toes.

Rachelle squinted against the sudden glare of the oil lamps. She'd never been in this coffeehouse before—it was well away from her normal territory—but it seemed pleasant enough. The air was warm, thick with the scent of coffee. Despite the hour, there were still eight men sitting at the tables. After the cold loneliness of the night, their presence crowded the room: the stubble on their chins, the trim on their coats, the little *human* noises they made as they breathed and muttered. Behind them, an artist more willing than skilled had painted a swirling promenade of figures from history and legend. By the counter hung a bronze foot enameled red at the ankle-stump: the Dayspring's left foot, the common devotion for tradesmen.

Glances drifted up to her and stopped. Voices fell silent. It was unusual for a young woman to walk into a coffeehouse alone—especially this late at night—but they didn't care a whit about that. They didn't even care that she was one of the rare women with permission from the King to carry a sword and a dispensation from the Church to wear men's clothing. Not when her red coat was embroidered on each shoulder with a black fleur-de-lis, symbol of the Royal Order of Penitents. The King's bloodbound.

The King's pet murderers. That was what the illegal broadsheets plastered on the alley walls called them, and all the people who met her knew it. Rachelle had long since stopped choking when she saw that name in their eyes.

But this time there was more fear than usual. And hatred. These people had probably marched in penitential processions and pasted up broadsheets that all but called for rebellion. They thought that the growing darkness was the judgment of God, brought down by the King's willingness to make use of the bloodbound's unholy powers.

She thought, *I could kill them all if I had to.*

A girl stepped in front of her. She was no older than fourteen, with big eyes and big elbows and pale, twiglike arms that Rachelle could have snapped between her hands.

"What can we do for you, mademoiselle?" she asked, her voice respectful but her gaze flickering nervously around the floor.

Rachelle could fight them all. But she didn't want to. She wanted to get a cup of hot coffee and sit in a corner, warming herself amid the human clatter while everyone looked past her, the way she could in the coffeehouse back on the rue Grand-Séverin, where the people knew her and remembered the night she had saved four children from woodspawn.

This place was warm and human but hated her, and suddenly the cold, wet night seemed more appealing.

Then she noticed the man seated in the corner, his long legs stretched out in front of him. His coat collar was turned up and his cap was pulled down, but she would know those sharp cheekbones and lush, arrogant lips anywhere. It was Erec d'Anjou, captain of the King's bloodbound, masquerading as a common citizen so he could spy out the King's enemies.

Damned if she was going to turn tail and run while he was watching.

Rachelle planted her feet a little more firmly. "I need coffee," she said.

Abruptly an older man shoved the girl aside. He had similar lines to his face—father, maybe, or uncle—and corded muscles.

"This is a respectable coffeehouse," he said, his voice low and rumbling.

"Good," she said. "I would hate to ruin my reputation."

"You don't need to trouble us," said the man. "For the love of the Dayspring, go somewhere else."

He was brave, she had to give him that. Her senses had sharpened as they always did when somebody nearby was afraid; she half saw, half heard the swift, desperate pulse in his throat. But he was staring her down as if she couldn't draw her sword, cut his neck open, and walk away. As if she didn't know what it felt like to have blood beneath her fingernails and spattered across her face.

She forced the memories back. "I'm a servant of the King. A respectable house would be honored to serve me."

"You know, you can threaten all you like," Erec said from his corner, "but they're still going to spit in your coffee." He gave her a look of bored weariness. "Why don't you come back when you've learned how to make people do what you want?"

Her throat tightened in helpless frustration. Erec always found ways to tease her when she couldn't get back at him.

Without a word, she strode to his corner and sat herself down in his lap. "What a considerate young man you are," she said loudly. "Tell me *all* about persuading people."

Nobody could embarrass Erec—it was as impossible as water running uphill—but at least she could make sure that his evening of being inconspicuous was thoroughly ruined.

He slid his hand up her cheek, hooking a thumb under her jaw. "Some things are better shown than told, hm?"

Heat blossomed across her cheeks. Two years ago, he'd found it very easy to persuade her to kiss him, back before she'd learned to tell when he was joking and when he was serious. Before she'd realized his kisses were never serious.

"I don't need to be shown anything," she said. "I already know what *you* are."

"Do you?" asked Erec, with that oblique tilt of his eyebrows that she knew so well, and her heart thudded.

Then she heard a soft chorus of clicks.

She looked over her shoulder and cursed herself for letting Erec distract her. Because there were twelve men now, and four of them were holding muskets, their wide brass mouths gleaming in the dim light.

"Step away from him," said the owner of the coffeehouse.

Rachelle's mind whirled through cold calculations. She had thought she could kill them all. She probably still could, with Erec's help, because while some fools thought that killing bloodbound was as simple as pointing the musket and pulling the trigger, human hands were slow and muskets had terrible aim.

But sometimes fools were lucky. And even bloodbound couldn't survive a musket ball in the face.

"You really should have left when I told you to," Erec murmured.

"You really should have arrested them as soon as they got muskets," Rachelle muttered back.

"I was waiting for them to implicate all their friends."

"I said *step away,*" the owner growled. "We're done with bowing and scraping to murderers."

"Well, then I should probably be leaving as well," said Erec.

"Because I'm Erec d'Anjou, captain of the King's bloodbound, and you would not believe the blood on my hands."

"I really think they would," said Rachelle.

"You traitor," snarled one of the men.

"Not to the King," said Erec, wrapping his arms around Rachelle. She knew that he was preparing to fling her in one direction while he threw himself in the other. The real risk was in the very first moment, when they were still in front of the muskets; once moving, they would be almost safe, because muskets were only as good as the hands that held them and the eyes that aimed them.

She could feel the cold-hot thrill of battle starting to hum in her veins.

If she hadn't been readying herself to fight, she might not have noticed the flicker of movement at the edge of her vision. She looked at the mural, at the wonderfully lifelike leaves painted in the background.

Then she realized they were moving. They weren't part of the painting, they were growing out of the wall, rippling in a breeze she couldn't feel.

It was a glimpse of the Great Forest like she'd had in the rain-swept streets. But that didn't happen indoors. No bloodbound, no matter how strong her second sight, could see the Forest from within a human home.

Unless the Forest was beginning to actually manifest, enough of its power seeping through to take physical form in the human world.

"Erec," she said quietly. The thrill of battle was turning into a sick expectation. "The Forest's here."

Now she could feel the sour, humming presence of the woodspawn. Right here in this room, surrounded by hateful and hostile and terribly fragile humans.

"Inconvenient," said Erec.

Suddenly he threw himself to the side, dragging Rachelle along with him. She rolled free of his grasp and back onto her feet. Where they had stood a moment before crouched another doglike woodspawn, red tongue lolling between its fangs.

The muskets went off in a deafening chorus.

"Everybody out!" Rachelle yelled, shifting her grip on her sword as she realized that she had drawn it. Then something rustled above her. She looked up.

The whole ceiling of the room was completely overgrown, and at least ten of the woodspawn crouched among the branches, staring down at her with glittering eyes.

This wasn't a chance eddy in the Forest's power. This was a full manifestation, and she hadn't seen one this bad since—since—

The rest of the woodspawn dropped. The humans, at last seeing them, started screaming. Rachelle ducked one way, Erec the other, and all thought was seared away by the glorious, white-hot delirium of movement. Human words and human fears didn't exist anymore, just simple, instinctive knowledge: lunge here, slice there. Vault the table, and there was Erec at her back as they took down another knot of the creatures.

Then, diving to avoid a lunging woodspawn, she stumbled straight into the coffeehouse girl—why hadn't those idiots gotten her out before attempting murder? Rachelle shoved her under the nearest table, and was turning when a woodspawn hit her in the shoulder and slammed her to the ground.

With a wet thud, Erec's dagger plunged into the woodspawn's head.

"Watch yourself!" he snapped, already turning away.

Rachelle sat up, pulled the blade out of the writhing creature's head, and threw it to land between the eyes of the woodspawn closest to him. She grabbed her sword and gave the twitching woodspawn beside her a final, fatal slash across the middle. It shivered and dissolved into mud.

She realized that only two of the woodspawn were left alive, and Erec was fighting both of them with a lethal grace that promised the hounds didn't have long left.

"You saved me."

The girl's voice was quiet, trembling. Rachelle looked back under the table: she was very pale. Her eyes were wide, her lips parted in fear.

No.

That was *hope* in the girl's face, and it was hope that made her voice tremble as she said, "You're not really a monster, are you? People like you—they can still be saved."

Rachelle leaped to her feet, ice running through her veins. Because she knew why this girl was agonized with hope. She knew why the Forest had manifested indoors.

And she knew what was waiting for them upstairs.

"Erec," she said, "finish them," and charged up the steps. Ivy grew down the walls of the stairwell and little red birds flashed among the leaves.

The door at the top was bolted shut. Rachelle kicked it once, twice, and then it gave way.

Inside was the Great Forest.

2

The Forest was just like her dreams. The dark, tangled growth of trees, branches, and roots woven together. The cold air, pulsing with half-heard laughter, that tasted of blood and smoke. The glint of a bonfire in the distance.

This was the Great Forest, the Forest of Dreams and Dreadful Night: the dark, primeval wood that had once covered all the world in the days before the sun and moon. She'd seen its phantom shadow a thousand times, haunting the streets of Rocamadour, blossoming around her when she met the forestborn in the woods near Aunt Léonie's cottage. She'd dreamed of it night after night.

She had never imagined that when she finally walked all the way inside, it would feel like home.

Rachelle stepped over the threshold. The cold darkness rippled over her skin, kissed her eyes, and unfurled her hair.

The longing hit her like a kick to the stomach. For just one moment, she was convinced that the distant bonfire was the only light in all the world—that the sun was a dream and the moon a delirium—and she wanted nothing but to drop her sword and run for that fire. She wanted to forget her foolish human name, relinquish it to the sweet, secret darkness, and run to that fire-lit world of dancing.

Then the mark burned on her neck, flaring to life in response to the Forest's power, and she remembered the price of that darkness and that dancing.

Around her little finger, she felt an answering burn. She looked down.

No one but Rachelle could see the phantom red string that the forestborn had tied to her finger. Even she couldn't feel it. But here, though it had no physical presence, it burned cold against her finger.

After she had . . . *after,* the forestborn had congratulated her on joining the lords of the Forest in time to rule with them. She'd dropped the knife and tried to run. He had caught her and thrown her to the ground, and she'd wondered if he was going to use her the way people said forestborn used innocent maidens. But she wasn't innocent anymore and she didn't have enough strength left to fight back. So she had lain still, but he'd only tied the red string around her finger, saying, *Leave me all you want. You're still mine.*

She had never seen him since, but he had been right. She had never again been anything but what he made her, and someday she would lose herself completely to the call of the Great Forest.

But not today.

Not like the other poor, mad bloodbound she had followed here.

She listened carefully, and there it was to her left: the soft, harsh breathing of a human driven almost past endurance. She followed the sound, picking her way through the trees.

The breathing grew louder. Rachelle moved softly and silently as smoke.

A lean, middle-aged woman crouched in the hollow of a tree. Her clothes were in rags; deep scratches scored her arms. Her eyes were squeezed shut and her hands were pressed over her ears. On her forehead was the mark, an eight-pointed star, no bigger than a thumbnail, exactly the same color as fresh blood.

It was the same mark that burned on Rachelle's neck.

Because this woman was exactly like Rachelle. A forestborn marked her and left her with a choice: die in three days, or kill somebody and live as a bloodbound, heir to the power of the Forest.

Like Rachelle, she had chosen to kill and live.

Now the power of the Great Forest had almost finished growing in her. She had fought it. She had fought until it broke her mind, until the Great Forest grew up around her because she would not run to it. But this was the end. In another moment the last scraps of her humanity would be washed away, leaving her with nothing but a senseless desire to hunt and kill.

The woman's eyes opened. Rachelle's hand tightened on her sword hilt, but the woman remained still, watching with blind wariness. Was she still human, or had the change fully overtaken her?

She was a bloodbound and therefore a murderer; like Rachelle, she deserved to die.

She was helpless and in pain. Like Aunt Léonie.

The woman's hands dropped from her ears. Her lips curled back, and a little whining snarl escaped between her teeth.

She isn't human, thought Rachelle. *She isn't human anymore.*

The woman sprang.

Rachelle's body had no doubts. Quicker than thought, she swung her sword and sliced the woman's throat open; blood sprayed as the woman sank to the ground.

Rachelle stumbled back a step. Now that it was over, she was shaking and panting like she had run up a mountain. She could see the crumpled body at the edge of her vision, but she couldn't look at it now.

She didn't need to. She knew what a human body looked like, ripped open and stripped of life. What it looked like, dead by her hands. She *knew.*

Her throat burned with the need to scream or weep.

But this time, at least, she had also saved lives. There would not be a new forestborn to plague the world. This manifestation of the Forest would end without spilling more chaos into Rocamadour.

Except it didn't end.

Rachelle had never killed a transforming bloodbound, but she knew how it worked: the fledgling forestborn's awakening called down the power of the Great Forest. Killing it would release the Forest's grip on the spot. Justine—who had killed nine mad bloodbound, six of them in the Forest—said that the Forest always vanished instantly.

But it didn't.

Rachelle waited, the dark breeze tickling the hairs against her neck, but nothing happened. Except the phantom laughter got a little louder, and perhaps the distant fire flared a little brighter.

The thread on her finger burned red-hot.

No, she thought. *No, no, no—*

Her forestborn's voice came from behind her, soft and smooth as butter. "Are you ready to join me now?"

She didn't turn around. She didn't think she could move. His voice had wrapped around her spine, her legs and arms and throat, and locked her into place. Her heart pounded with helpless, animal fear.

She should have known he would find her as soon as she stepped into his realm.

"No," she said, staring into the darkness.

The string had no physical substance. She had seen people walk through it, time and again. Yet now it felt as it were going taut, as if he were tugging at the phantom, unbreakable bond that tied them together.

"I grow impatient, little girl."

"Then learn to wait," she bit out, but she was shaking. She had sworn that the next time she saw him, she would take revenge for Aunt Léonie. So many nights, it had been her only comfort, the only way she could let herself sleep. Now she finally stood before him, and she was still the terrified, bloodstained little girl she had been three years ago. All she could think was that he was going to kill her and she *did not want to die.*

Or he was going to give that thread one more pull, and all her strength would unravel and she would walk into his arms and forget how to be human.

"I don't have to." She heard him stepping closer. "Behold, I bring you glad tidings of great joy. Our lord is almost ready to return."

"I know that." Her heartbeat was jagged in her throat.

His breath was hot against the back of her neck. "Did you know how soon? Before the summer sun makes its last valiant gasp, our lord will smile and awaken and eat the light from the sky."

Rachelle felt sick. Before the end of summer. It was one thing to know that the Devourer would return sometime soon; it was another to realize that it was starting now.

Then she shuddered as the forestborn's lips pressed against her neck in a kiss. "No pleading?" he asked.

It took all her strength to answer steadily, "I don't see the point."

"Or praying?" His voice had an extra mocking edge, and she remembered the whimpering babble that had spilled out of Aunt Léonie's lips, desperate pleas to the Dayspring and the Holy Virgin that had never been answered.

Fury hit her like a wall of flame, and her fear went up in smoke. She whirled, sword coming up—

But he was gone. There was only darkness, and the Forest, and then both wavered and blew away like smoke.

She was in a dingy little room, lit by a single lamp. In front of her, a woman was chained to the wall. Her head lolled forward; her whole chest was soaked with blood. So much blood. The floor seemed to rock under her feet, and Rachelle wobbled back a step. Strong hands caught her shoulders, and she flinched before she realized it was Erec.

"Congratulations," he said.

"Shut up," muttered Rachelle. None of the woman's blood had fallen on her, but she still felt the hot, sticky mess all over her hands and arms.

She forced herself to look away from the corpse to the tray piled with cracked chicken bones, the gouges clawed into the wall. The woman must have been up here for at least a month, teetering on the edge of madness, only iron chains and the last scraps of will keeping her something like human.

It was a mercy, she told herself, but that was no comfort.

"All right downstairs?" she asked.

"Let's see," said Erec. "Half of them are missing bits of their faces due to woodspawn. The rest are unconscious or stabbed, due to me. So everything's quite all right."

Behind them, somebody gasped. Rachelle turned, pulling free of Erec's grasp, and there was the scrawny girl from downstairs.

"Mama," the girl whispered, and burst into tears.

Behind the girl stood her father, his face pale. "Murderer," he said.

"No," said Erec. "Executioner. Your wife was the murderer. You know, don't you, the penalty for concealing a bloodbound from the King?"

The man spat. "If you'd ever loved someone, you'd understand."

Rachelle didn't realize she was moving until she had grabbed him by the shoulders and slammed him against the wall. "Do you know what *I* understand? There have been five woodspawn attacks in this neighborhood in the past two weeks. That's two people dead and one who will never walk again, all because *your* wife was sitting here, calling down the power of the Forest. If we hadn't put her down, she would have broken those chains when she finished transforming, and then she would have killed every person she could find. Starting with your daughter."

"She would never—"

"Let me guess. The Bishop promised that if you just prayed hard enough, she would stay human."

The man's mouth tightened, but he didn't say anything.

Bishop Guillaume helped people hide bloodbound from the King's justice. Rachelle and Erec knew it, they just hadn't been able to prove it yet. She still wasn't sure if the Bishop had some fantasy of building his own bloodbound army, or if he was just that deluded about the chances that bloodbound could stay sane and human. Either way, he was a hypocrite for also preaching death and judgment on them every Sunday.

"It's a lie," said Rachelle. "Nobody escapes the Forest. But if you'd given her to us, we'd have executed her before she hurt more people."

"She wasn't like you—"

"She killed. She was *exactly* like me. And like her, I will die for my sins and go to hell. But at least I'm not fool enough to think that bloodbound won't bring death all around them."

Then she shoved him away and stalked out of the room.

"Do you really believe you're going to hell?" asked Erec.

"I don't see a way to doubt it," said Rachelle, not looking down at her hand. She was still acutely conscious of the crimson thread tied to her finger.

They were finally back at the Palais du Soleil, just inside the main courtyard, where lamplight glinted off the wet blue-and-gold tesserae that covered the ground in a vast mosaic. A few minutes ago, the bells had rung out two in the morning, but on one of the grand balconies above them, light and music spilled out into the night, and Rachelle could glimpse the brilliant swirl of silken dresses.

"But you're bloodbound," he said, with a quizzical tilt to his eyebrows. Rain glistened on his cheekbones. Despite the dingy coat and cap he had worn to infiltrate the coffeehouse, despite being soaked by the rain, he still looked as elegant as a court portrait.

"I believe it *because* I'm bloodbound," Rachelle snapped. "Or did you forget how we're made?"

She remembered it with every breath.

"Did *you* forget? Bloodbound become forestborn, the lords of the forest and beloved of the Devourer, who grants them the life to dance ten thousand years and never die." He tossed off the words as if they were nothing, without a break in his long, easy stride. "And what never dies, cannot be damned."

Her feet stopped. For one moment, she was back in the Forest, listening to her forestborn gloat: *I bring you glad tidings of great joy.*

"Believe me," she said, "I do not forget. Not for one moment do I forget that if I live long enough, I will become one of the monsters that did this to me. And believe this also, I would rather be dead and damned. I *will* be."

She realized she was shaking. In the distance, the music tinkled on, as if all the world were an orderly music box and none of them were doomed.

Erec's hand landed on her shoulder. "You're a strange woman, do you know that?"

She went rigid at his touch, and for an instant she wanted to turn and strike him.

For all his knowing airs, Erec had no real understanding of the Great Forest's power. Like so many people, he thought that the Devourer was no more than a myth told by the forestborn. And unlike most people, the forestborn were the best thing that had ever happened to him. Becoming a bloodbound had raised him from being a landless bastard to the King's right hand. He could talk all he wanted about living for ten thousand years, but he'd never really thought about what that would mean.

She barked out a sudden, pitying laugh. He would have such a surprise, and so soon.

"Normal women don't survive the forestborn," she said.

"Then survive them for ten thousand years. That's the only victory for us, don't you think?"

Suddenly Erec seized her hand and pulled. She stumbled forward a step, her body automatically moving to break the grip and take him down. But he spun her effortlessly in another direction, and then another, and suddenly they were moving in time to the music.

They were dancing.

Rachelle didn't know any of the court dances Erec did. But he whirled her through the motions, and her body followed with the same unholy grace it had in a fight. Except here, for one moment—her heart beating in her ears, the courtyard lights spinning around her—that grace didn't feel like anything wicked or deadly.

The music stopped. Erec spun her out one final time, then twirled her back into his embrace.

"Ten thousand years of this," he said. "Would it be so terrible?"

It took Rachelle a moment to speak. Her heart had already been beating fast in the dance, and now she was clasped against his body, his arms warm around her waist.

"It wouldn't be like this," she said. "We'd be monsters living in the woods."

"Are you sure? Maybe the forestborn have palaces and balls as well."

Her laugh was almost fond. "If you can believe that, clearly you were marked by a different kind of forestborn than I was."

"Oh? Was yours not elegant enough to satisfy you?"

She remembered his soft voice laughing and coaxing her. She remembered rough tree bark digging into her back as her mouth was forced open.

"Would you call a rabid animal 'elegant'?"

"Maybe, if it was pretty enough." He leaned down a little

closer. "But if that's not what you crave, how about me? If you must die soon, at least you could enjoy tonight."

She knew that if she stayed in his arms another moment, he would kiss her. He would kiss her and take her back to his room and make her forget, for a little while, the blood in her past and the thread on her finger and the darkness waiting for her. If she let him.

Once upon a time, she would have been insulted by such an offer. Even when she'd first come to Rocamadour, bitterly aware that she had no honor left to lose, she'd still been furious to discover that being kissed by him made her no different from a hundred other women. But she had known him for three years now, and he'd saved her life in half a dozen fights, and he was her friend. She couldn't hate him for his games; even less could she hate him for thinking she might say yes. She was a bloodbound because she could say yes to anything.

She pulled herself out of his grip, because she didn't have any honor left, but she had a little pride. Erec was a good friend but he was incapable of falling in love; his women were pretty, shiny pieces in his collection, and Rachelle had no intention of being the latest prize.

"I am going to enjoy *sleeping* tonight. You can do as you please." She turned away but he caught her shoulder.

"If it's time for good night, then I should tell you—the King wants you at his levée tomorrow."

The levée was the ceremonial rising-from-bed that the King enacted every morning. Courtiers would scheme, fight, and bribe themselves bankrupt for a chance to attend. As one of the King's bloodbound, Rachelle had the right to attend anytime she pleased, but she had never bothered.

"Why?" she asked. Beyond accepting her into the ranks, King Auguste-Philippe had never taken any interest in her.

"Our gracious King will tell you when he pleases. Good night, mademoiselle." Erec bowed extravagantly and strode away, probably to join the party overhead. With a sigh, Rachelle turned in the opposite direction and trudged toward the cold, narrow refuge of her bed.

Whatever the King wanted with her, it wouldn't matter for long. Nothing would matter. The thought hollowed her out with cold, despairing fear, and yet it was strangely liberating.

She lay awake a long time, staring at the dim red glow of the string. After the forestborn had tied it to her finger, he had made no move to stop her when she staggered out of the house. He hadn't pursued her as she ran through the woods, stumbling because she wasn't used to the sudden strength in her limbs.

She hadn't tried to go home. If the villagers knew what she had done, they would burn her. They would tie her to a stake and her own family would light the pyre. That was the penalty for becoming bloodbound, and as much as she deserved it, Rachelle still wanted to live. She hadn't stopped running until she reached

Rocamadour, where she had begged to be made one of the King's bloodbound, her sentence of execution delayed so she could serve him.

For a little while, she'd hoped—not for herself, but for the world. The forestborn had told her that the Devourer could only be defeated with Joyeuse or Durendal, and that both swords were gone forever. But while Durendal had vanished over a thousand years ago—shattered in battle, they said—Joyeuse had been the coronation sword for the kings of Gévaudan until just three hundred years ago, when a woodwife had hidden the sword from Mad King Louis to prevent him from destroying it. Nobody knew where, and so that sword too was lost.

That was how everybody in Rocamadour told the story. But when Aunt Léonie had told it to Rachelle, she had said, *The woodwife opened a door above the sun, below the moon, and hid Joyeuse against our hour of greatest need.*

When Rachelle had asked her what that meant, she'd only shrugged. At the time, it had seemed like just another one of Aunt Léonie's maddeningly obscure sayings. But after Rachelle became bloodbound—after the forestborn had told her that Joyeuse could kill the Devourer—it had given her hope. All she had to do was solve the riddle and find the sword. Just like in the stories she'd loved as a child.

But she wasn't like any of the heroines in those stories. And though she searched the city until she had found every door and gate and fountain and mosaic that had the sun or moon upon it, though she had spent hours scrutinizing all of them for the least trace of power, she had never found anything. And nobody whom she talked to had ever heard Aunt Léonie's version of the story.

Eventually, she had accepted that she would never defeat the Devourer. She would never redeem herself. So she had sworn that the next time she saw her forestborn, at least she would avenge Aunt Léonie.

But when she had finally seen him again this night, she hadn't been able to do anything. She was still just that helpless, frightened little girl.

No. She had turned to fight in the end. If he hadn't disappeared, she *would* have fought him.

When the Devourer returned, her forestborn would certainly come find her again. And when all the world was covered in the Great Forest, there would be no disappearing into it. Rachelle would have her chance to fight then, and she would kill him. No matter the price.

She fell asleep still promising.

Her dreams were a tangled mess of blood and shuddering trees. Rachelle struggled awake with a gasp, her heart pounding in her ears. It was still before sunrise; her room was dark and silent—a simple, human darkness that would melt away with the dawn.

Soon she would lose that darkness, as well as the light. Rachelle wondered how long, exactly, she had left. Her forestborn had said, *Before the summer sun makes its last valiant gasp.* Did that mean before winter? Before autumn? Or before the summer solstice, after which the days would only grow shorter?

The power of the Great Forest was always stronger on the solstices, when the rise and ebb of the sun's light shifted. And this year's summer solstice was only three weeks away.

The thought made Rachelle feel cold and hollow and free all at once. If the world was ending in three weeks, then she didn't have to care about Erec or the King or the unrest in the city anymore. She just had to ready herself to face her forestborn.

Maybe she could make a final effort to find Joyeuse. She'd given up over a year ago, because she couldn't see any hope, and the worry was driving her mad. But now . . . well, she could bear to go mad with searching for a few more weeks or months. She could bear it, and then she could die fighting, and she didn't have to care about anything else.

In the distance, the palace bells started tolling. Rachelle counted the peals, the same way she did every morning.

Five . . . six . . . seven.

The bells stopped. And then she remembered the levée.

She didn't have to care about anything, including the King's orders, but if she wanted to make another attempt at finding Joyeuse—and she did want to, she *had* to—then it would be a good idea to avoid mortally offending him. Becoming a wanted fugitive could wait a week or two.

Rachelle sprang out of bed. The King's levée started at eight, and he was famously intolerant of people who were late for any court ceremony. An hour was more than enough time to get to the royal apartments, but if she wanted breakfast before facing an hour or more of tedious ceremony, she'd have to get to the guard's mess room, all the way on the opposite side of the palace.

Luckily, she was still in her uniform from the night before.

She buckled on her belt, not even bothering to grab her sword, and ran out the door, rebraiding her hair as she clattered down the dark, predawn hallway. She started running down the stairs, then simply vaulted over the railing to the landing below. The impact sent a jolt up her bones, jarring her enough that she stumbled to the side—

Into the young man who had been running up the stairs.

In a heartbeat, she had him slammed against the wall with her dagger at his throat. Their faces were barely a hand's span apart; she could feel his chest heaving for breath under her arm. Then her mind caught up with her body and she realized he was unarmed.

"What are you doing?" she demanded.

"Well, I was running from assassins," he said. "Now I'm being threatened with a knife."

"What?" said Rachelle, and then she heard the men clattering up the stairs after him. She turned, and saw the glint of drawn blades.

There were three of them, all with rapiers, and she had only a dagger. It would have been a wretchedly uneven fight, if she were human.

It was still a wretchedly uneven fight; it was just uneven in her favor. Rachelle took down the first with a simple kick to the head, then whirled and caught the second's blade in the hilt of her dagger. Twist, wrench, and the rapier flew out of his hand—she forgot how weak humans were, she thought as she slammed her dagger's hilt into his forehead.

The third one came at her with a rapier and a dagger, and from the way he twirled them, she could tell he was really very good. His technique was probably better than hers. But now her heart was thundering with the joy of the fight, her blood was singing in her ears, and he seemed ridiculously slow, as if he were moving through honey. Stepping inside his guard, seizing his sword arm, and wrenching it out of the socket was almost too easy. A few good kicks, and he was down.

She looked back at the man they had been pursuing. Wiry, with a square, sharp face softened by a snub nose, and tousled, pale brown hair, he couldn't be much older than her. There was nothing remarkable in his features—not like Erec's sculpted beauty—yet they felt vaguely familiar. He had sat down on the stairs to watch her fight, elbows on his knees, gloved hands resting loose, and he was watching her with an intense, guarded calm.

"Shouldn't you have kept running?" she asked.

"Were you planning to lose?" He sounded politely curious.

"No." She stepped to the nearest would-be assassin, pulled his belt loose, and started tying him up. "Does anyone?"

"You're bloodbound. They couldn't hurt me unless you let them." He shrugged. "And if *you* wanted to hurt me, I couldn't hope to escape."

Rachelle moved to tie up the second man. "You think I want to hurt you?"

"I don't know. Do you?" His voice was light and soft, but she could see the tension in his jaw, in the lines of his arms. She could feel the swift beat of his pulse beneath his calm facade.

Rachelle knew she wasn't being fair—anyone *should* be suspicious of her, after the things she'd done—but even so, for a moment she could hardly breathe through the helpless fury choking her.

She pulled out one of her knives and flung it to land quivering in the wall two finger widths from his head.

He barely twitched.

"Keep the knife," she said. "Maybe it will make you feel safer."

His eyes widened a little and his mouth started to open.

"Don't thank me," she added, finishing the knots on the third man. "Go find a guard to take care of the prisoners. I'm going to get breakfast."

She whirled and left. She made it across the rest of the palace without incident, even managing to snag a few rolls from the guard's mess room just before the clock tolled half-past. *Plenty of time,* she thought.

Then she got lost. She'd hardly ever been to the royal wing, and one huge room encrusted with gold-leaf tendrils and curlicues looked much like another. By the time she got to the anteroom of the royal bedchamber, it was well past eight and the sun had finally risen.

Rachelle could remember when summer had meant that the sun would be up by seven. People said that once upon a time, the summer sun would rise even earlier, but that was hard to imagine.

The anteroom, of course, was completely stuffed with people waiting to get in, a seething mass of brocade and lace, powdered wigs and the stench of pomade. Rachelle threaded through the crowd as fast as she could, trying not to think of how the King might punish her.

Then she saw the young man she'd rescued earlier, standing near the door with a guard on each side.

"Is he in trouble?" she asked one of the guards.

"No," he said.

"Waiting to get in," said the young man, with the same wry calm as earlier.

"You're coming in now," she said, seizing his shoulder. "With me." He could at least serve as her excuse.

"Mademoiselle—" one of the guards started.

"Trust me," said the young man, "you don't want to fight her."

Rachelle dragged him inside with her. The King was putting on his stockings, and the room was already crowded—with the King's valets, of course, but also the supremely lucky nobles who were privileged this morning to hand him his prayer book, his shirt, and his razor. Then there was a great crowd of other nobles, ministers, and secretaries, all of whom had wrangled permission to come in during one of the coveted first five entrances. Soon the King's illegitimate children would be admitted, and then the room would get really crowded. (By tradition, the sixth entrance was for the King's heirs, but he had only bothered to father one child on his actual wife, and that prince had died three years ago.)

This crowd was even thicker than the one in the anteroom. Rachelle shoved her way through—people muttered only until they saw her coat; then they looked away nervously. Let them. She just wanted to get inside, see the King, and please or annoy him enough that he never invited her to the levée again.

She broke through the crowd as the King stood, the ribbons on his shoes finally tied. Erec sat at his feet—the special privilege of the bloodbound—with his mouth quirked up smugly.

Rachelle went down on one knee, dragging the young man with her. "Your Majesty," she said.

The most high, most puissant, and most excellent prince, Auguste-Philippe II, by the Grace of God, King of Gévaudan and Protector of the Vasconic territories, looked down his famous nose at her.

"A tardy servant is of little use to me," he said after a short, brittle silence.

The back of Rachelle's neck prickled; she knew that everyone in the room was staring, waiting to see what the King would do to her.

Well, but what *could* he do? As a bloodbound, she was already under sentence of death.

"I'm sorry, sire," she said, "but I was saving this man from three assassins. I think you need to have a talk with the guard."

"Good morning, Father," said the young man beside her. "Well. It hasn't been very good so far, but I've hopes for the rest of it."

Wait. She had just rescued one of the King's bastards? Rachelle darted a look at the young man, and yes, that was why his face looked so familiar: though liberally smudged and softened by his mother's heritage, that was still the line of the King's jaw that he had inherited.

"Did she really save you?" asked King Auguste-Philippe.

"Yes," said the young man. "Defeated three armed men, tied them up in their own belts, and gave me a knife. It was most impressive."

"I see," said the King, and looked at Rachelle. "Then perhaps you are not so tardy after all."

"Sire?" Rachelle said cautiously. Erec looked like he was about to burst into laughter; whatever was going on, it couldn't be good.

The King dropped a hand onto the young man's head and fixed his gaze on the crowd. "This is Armand Vareilles, my esteemed son," he said, in a quiet voice that nevertheless carried throughout the room.

It can't be, she thought in horror, staring at Armand's gloved hands—but of course, that would explain Erec's near laughter.

Rachelle didn't keep up with the court, and yet even she knew who Armand Vareilles was. He had been nothing six months ago, but now everyone in Gévaudan knew about him: how he was the King's illegitimate son, raised in the countryside after his mother's political disgrace. How last winter, a forestborn had marked him. How he had refused to kill, and the mark remained black on his skin, yet he was alive to this day.

How, in a fury, the forestborn had cut off his hands.

It was a lie, of course. The forestborn did not forget to claim people; if they marked somebody, they would have him or see him dead. Armand Vareilles was nothing but a clever liar who had lost his hands in some accident, then tattooed himself with a false mark and made his fortune by having people pity him.

But most of the common people were convinced. They proclaimed him a saint, a living martyr, and they called for the destruction of the King's bloodbound in his name. For if he could resist the forestborn and live, what excuse did the rest of the bloodbound have?

And not just the common people loved him. Some of the nobility were besotted with him as well. So even though Armand

Vareilles had become a symbol of those who muttered against him, the King had to keep him in luxurious style. He'd even commissioned false hands made of silver for him. That was why she had never seen his gloved hands move.

"In three days," the King went on, "he will accompany me back to Château de Lune with the rest of the court. In recognition of his rank, and the heroism he has so lately shown, and on account of the malicious unrest in the kingdom, I grant him one of my own bloodbound, Rachelle Brinon, to be his bodyguard."

"What?" said Rachelle, so surprised that she didn't care if everyone heard the outrage in her voice.

She had to find Joyeuse. Failing that, she had to protect as many people as she could until her forestborn returned and she had a chance to kill him. She didn't want to spend her last days guarding a fake saint while smothered in the elegance of Château de Lune, where ancient spells ensured that no woodspawn ever came.

But if she deserted now, there was no way to keep from instantly becoming a fugitive.

Armand's mouth was flat as his gaze flickered from her to Erec and back again; then abruptly his mouth crooked up and he leaned toward her. "Not too late to use that knife," he murmured.

Rachelle glowered at him, but before she could respond, there was another muffled commotion. She looked up to see someone striding through the crowd, and her whole body tensed in revulsion.

It was Bishop Guillaume.

He was a tall, colorless man with a wispy pale beard, a mouth shriveled into a permanent frown, and beady black eyes. On his chest glinted a huge silver pendant in the shape of the Dayspring's right hand, rubies inlaid to represent the bloody stump. On anyone else it would have been a symbol of faith, but Rachelle had always thought that on him it looked like a trophy from battle.

"Good morning," said the King. "Come with your usual request? I regret to say there are still no new bloodbound whom I could assign to you."

As soon as Bishop Guillaume had arrived in Rocamadour, he had started proclaiming that since the King had no power to forgive sins, the bloodbound should not be in his care. Instead, all repentant deadly warriors should be put under the Bishop's personal command for the good of their souls.

"No," said the Bishop in his deep, silky voice. He would have been laughed out of the city as a fanatic long ago if he didn't make words sound so lovely. "I have come with a different request. Release Mademoiselle Brinon into my care."

For a moment Rachelle couldn't believe what she'd just heard. The Bishop had never paid her any notice beyond sneering at her as he did at all the other bloodbound.

People whispered as they stared at her and the Bishop. Probably they were marveling at how he had graciously condescended to be concerned with her soul.

Rachelle knew better. He must have decided he could make her into his personal weapon.

She stood. "*I* have a request," she said loudly. "Arrest the Bishop for hiding fugitive bloodbound. D'Anjou and I found one last night, surrounded by rebels who tried to kill us."

"And you think I aided them?" said the Bishop, infuriatingly calm.

"They were all madly devoted to you," she said, but of course that wasn't evidence.

She was suddenly, acutely aware of the silence as everyone in the room stared at her. None of them would believe her. People wanted the bloodbound to serve them or protect them, but they never, ever wanted to listen to them.

The Bishop gave her a pitying look. "I am sorry that they hurt you, my daughter. I would never want you harmed." His voice was full of the gentle sorrow that made ladies weep into their handkerchiefs and then drop extra money into the collection plate. "That is why I want you to come with me: so you can be reconciled with God and find peace."

"I'd rather confess to the devil," said Rachelle.

"Enough," said the King, sounding bored. "My dear bishop, I cannot give you Mademoiselle Brinon, because she is busy guarding my dearest son." He looked at Rachelle. "Do you understand your orders?"

She understood them. She had no intention of following them. It would be difficult to hunt for Joyeuse while the King's men were hunting her down for desertion. But she couldn't afford to care about that now.

She would obey the King today. She would vanish tonight.

"As Your Majesty commands," she said, bowing her head.

Rachelle's heart pounded in her ears. She was vaguely aware that a crowd had gathered, muttering and laughing, but right now it didn't matter any more than the smear of pain on her cheekbone where a punch had just landed.

Two paces away, Justine Leblanc showed her teeth. "Well?"

Now, thought Rachelle, and lunged forward into a kick exactly the same way she had the last three times. Justine dodged and blocked—as Rachelle changed direction, grabbed her shoulder, and took them both down.

The next few moments were a blur. Justine wasn't the sort of fighter who gave up when she hit the ground; she wrenched, kicked, and slammed her elbows into Rachelle with methodical efficiency. There was no time for strategy, only instant, white-hot reactions—

And then Justine had her arm twisted back. Rachelle bucked and managed to wrench out of her grip, but as she broke free, her arm twisted out of its socket with a pop and a searing flash of pain. Rachelle gasped, barely choking off a cry.

Justine gasped too. She was always worried that she might be actually hurting Rachelle.

Grimly, Rachelle rolled onto her side and slammed a kick straight into Justine's stomach. Then she collapsed onto her back.

For a few moments, neither of them moved. Rachelle's shoulder throbbed with pain; her arm only tingled, but she couldn't move it. She stared up at the golden fleurs-de-lis on the high ceiling of the sparring room and listened to the voices of the guards who had gathered to watch them fight. Normally she hated being a spectacle for anyone's amusement. But right now—despite the exhaustion and the pain in her shoulder—the delirious song of the fight still hummed in her veins. Even the thought of the Devourer's return didn't feel so terrible.

"Truce?" Justine offered breathlessly.

"Truce," said Rachelle.

"Do you want—" Justine started.

"Just do it," said Rachelle, and clenched her teeth.

With practiced ease, Justine leaned over her, grabbed her arm, and shoved it back into the socket. Rachelle choked but managed not to make any other sound, which was better than last time.

She took a couple of slow breaths and sat up. Justine still crouched next to her. Even on the ground, she loomed: she was a tall woman, nearly six feet, with big bones and a square, big-nosed face that could not have been lovely even when she was young. Now she was nearly forty, and her dark braids were dusted with silver.

"You're improving," she said. "But you still get careless when you're angry."

"You still don't expect me to grab your shoulders," said Rachelle.

Justine smiled faintly. "Has the Bishop spoken with you?"

All the joy of the fight was instantly gone. She stared at Justine. "*You* were the one who set him after me?"

Probably she should have expected it. Of all the bloodbound, Justine was the only one to take the name Royal Order of Penitents seriously: she lived in a garret worse than Rachelle's, she wore a hair shirt at all times, and she was in the chapel on her knees almost every day. Naturally, as soon as Bishop Guillaume turned up saying she was damned, she had demanded to serve him. The King had given in, since the people were enraptured with their new Bishop and it was easier to deny his requests if he'd been treated generously once already. Ever since, the Bishop had flaunted his triumph by having his lone bloodbound attend him at ceremonies.

"Yes," Justine said quietly. "Do you really prefer d'Anjou for your keeper?"

Rachelle surged to her feet, forgetting about all the people watching. "He's not my keeper. And yes, I *do* prefer him. At least he's not a liar."

Except when he was flirting, but Rachelle would take that sort of liar any day over the kind who preached that all the blood-bound should face judgment, then tried to hide them from the King's justice.

Justine stood, her mouth pressing into a line.

"Ladies," Erec called from behind them. "I hope you weren't fighting over me."

Justine ignored him. "Think about it," she said to Rachelle, and strode out of the room.

"She didn't even look at me," said Erec, his voice mock sad. "I wonder what I've done to offend her?"

"Breathing, I think," said Rachelle. "But also wearing that jacket." The black velvet construction, stiff with silver embroidery, was by no means the gaudiest thing she'd ever seen Erec wear, but it was still painful to look upon.

"It baffles me why you don't hate her as much as her master," said Erec. "Or has that changed?"

Rachelle sighed. "I can't hate her when she's always willing to spar."

More importantly, when Endless Night returned, Justine would die fighting the forestborn. She might take orders from the Bishop, but nothing would ever make her stop trying to protect people from the Great Forest.

"You could fight me, you know," said Erec.

She rolled her eyes. "And listen to your epigrams about my every mistake? I think not."

Justine didn't care about demonstrating that she was more elegant or clever than Rachelle. She didn't even really care about demonstrating that she was the better fighter. She understood that sometimes fighting in a white-hot blur was the only way to make the memories stop.

"Well, don't get too attached to her." Erec draped a hand easily over her shoulder and drew her out one of the side doors into a paved courtyard. "We need to talk about your charge."

For a wonderful hour, Rachelle had forgotten that she had a charge. At least she wouldn't have him after tonight, when she vanished into the city for her last attempt to find Joyeuse.

Right now she needed to pretend to care about him. "What is it?" she asked. "Do you know who sent the assassins?"

"Oh, that isn't so important. One of the other possible heirs, I'm sure. Probably Vincent Angevin—he's stupid enough." Erec sighed. "It's a pity that I got all the cleverness in the family."

"You'd hardly like it if he were better at something than you," said Rachelle. Erec was an illegitimate son of the Angevin family, and he never lost an opportunity to mention how much he outclassed his second cousin Vincent. And all the rest of his family. And the whole world.

"It's a pity for them, just not for me. Anyway, I doubt Vincent will suffer for this escapade, since you know how much our King likes him."

"You do realize," said Rachelle, "that most of these problems would go away if the King would just name an heir?"

The death of King Auguste-Philippe's one legitimate son had left him without a clear successor. Several generations of peculiar treaties and marriage-contracts meant that among his nearest five nephews and cousins, none was unambiguously next in line. And there was also precedent for legitimizing a bastard as heir—and the King had eight. Needless to say, all the possible heirs were ready to cut one another's throats. The rumors of the King's ailing health had only made the conflict worse.

"Yes, but that would entail admitting that he's not immortal." Erec's mouth quirked. "What I have to tell you is far more important. You have already realized, I hope, that your true mission is not to protect Armand Vareilles."

Rachelle had realized no such thing, but she was long used to pretending that she had kept up with Erec's labyrinthine thoughts. "You mean our King would lie to us? How shocking."

"Your mission is to contain him," said Erec. "Somebody is fomenting a rebellion, and that somebody will probably attempt to recruit Monsieur Vareilles soon, at which point he goes from annoyance to danger. You know the people will riot for him."

Her chest tightened with frustration. The Devourer was returning soon—before summer's end, which could conceivably mean *today*. And yet she had to stand here in the sunlit courtyard, discussing politics with Erec and pretending to care, because nobody believed in the Devourer and she had to avoid getting arrested before she found Joyeuse.

"Why don't you just throw that somebody in the dungeons," she asked, "along with everyone else you don't like?"

"Because that somebody is good enough that we're still trying to work out who he is."

"Well," said Rachelle, "I know one man who would like to see the whole court burn. In this life *and* the next."

"And much we'd all love to see him burn instead," said Erec. "Unfortunately, harming a bishop would also provoke riots. Unless we really did have proof that he was helping fugitive bloodbound. And we don't. So instead of leading a raid on the Bishop's residence, you're going to accompany Monsieur Vareilles to Château de Lune, where he won't have access to the mob every day, and you're going to ensure that he remains a court fixture until he is a harmless joke."

“I refuse to spend the rest of my life at Château de Lune,” said Rachelle.

“Look on the bright side,” said Erec. “Since you’ll have to actually attend court functions, you’ll see such a lot of *me*.”

5

That afternoon, Armand gave an audience so the people of Rocamadour could grovel at his feet. Rachelle had orders to serve as his escort, whether because the King was taking no chances or because Erec wanted to torment her, she wasn't sure.

It was just as awful as she had expected.

They held the audience in the wide square in front of the cathedral. There wasn't a scrap of shade; heat shimmered off the cobblestones. Armand sat on a little folding stool. To his left was an oriflamme banner, so that people wouldn't forget his presence was a gift from the King. To his right was a painting of the Dayspring, so that people wouldn't forget he was holy. It was hideous. Most paintings showed the Dayspring resurrected, or at least as a not-too-bloody severed head in the arms of his weeping mother. This showed the gory jumble of limbs into which he'd been hacked by the soldiers of the Imperium.

Flies buzzed as if drawn by the painted blood, but Rachelle had to stand still and tall and menacing as a vast line of people crawled forward to see Armand. They blessed his name; they wanted him to bless them. They brought babies and lame boys and blind old women, and they begged for healing. They brought rosaries and tried to touch them to his wrists, so they would have relics to protect them against the encroaching darkness.

The nobility might pretend that the shrinking daylight hours were no more than an aberration, but the common people knew. Some of them had brought clumsy little yarn weavings for Armand to touch—the fake woodwife charms sold in the marketplace. They wouldn't do a thing to protect anyone against the power of the Forest, but city folk didn't know any better. And they were desperate.

That was why they thronged to meet Armand. They hoped his holiness would protect them.

And Armand used that hope against them. He squinted against the sunlight and gave them smiles that looked brave and self-mocking at once. When an old woman begged him to pray for her health, because surely God would hear the prayers of a saint, he shook his head and said, "I'm nothing. Certainly not a saint. But I will pray for you." The old woman sobbed, and Rachelle knew she had just decided he was the greatest saint since la Madeleine.

He was playing them as expertly as a court musician played a violin. And Rachelle was helping. She was also keeping him under control so he couldn't turn his false heroism into a crown, but she was still *helping* him.

She hoped that when Endless Night fell, the forestborn hunted him first.

The audience lasted nearly two hours. By the end, Rachelle was starting to feel dizzy from the heat. Armand didn't look much better. So as soon as the guards started to push the crowd away, she hauled Armand to his feet by his collar, dragged him into the nearest tavern, and demanded a private room and a pitcher of beer at once.

There were times when being one of the King's bloodbound had its advantages. A few moments later, they were in an upstairs room that was quiet and out of the sunlight.

As soon as the door had shut behind them, Armand let out a sigh. Then in two quick, expert movements he had hooked his metal thumbs under his cuffs and pulled them up, revealing leather straps that ran up his forearms to loop around his elbows. Large metal buckles held them together in the center; in a few moments he had unlatched them with his teeth, and the hands clattered to the ground. Underneath, his stumps were covered in two little knitted socks; he pulled them off with his teeth.

Clearly he didn't intend to be the one who picked up his hands. Wearily, Rachelle reached for the nearest one. But when her fingers touched the metal, she flinched. The silver hand was shockingly hot.

"Imagine my surprise on the first sunny day that I wore them," said Armand.

She remembered the blinding glitter of sunlight on his silver hands. At the time, she'd only thought of it as one more gaudy extravagance that showed his hypocrisy.

"If they hurt that much," she said, "don't wear them."

Armand was by the pitcher; the loop of its handle was just wide enough that he'd managed to slide his stump inside. Rachelle watched in fascination as he tilted the pitcher to pour himself a cup of beer, then lifted the cup by wedging it between his wrists.

She'd seen people missing limbs before, but it still felt like stuttering when her eyes ran down the length of his arm to . . . nothing.

Her stomach twisted. She didn't believe his story. She *didn't.* But in all the times that she'd dismissed him as a liar, she'd never thought about how—whatever the truth—he had suffered *something.*

He set down the cup. "If I don't wear the hands, then they want to kiss the stumps. I'd rather burn."

"You could just not display yourself for worship," Rachelle snapped.

His mouth twisted. "Do you think the King would allow me to stop? If I weren't sitting next to his banner every week, people might start to imagine that His Majesty wasn't entirely holy."

"Maybe you should have thought of that before you became a saint."

He showed his teeth. "The way you thought things through before you became a bloodbound?"

For a moment she was back in Aunt Léonie's house, the blood hot and sticky on her hands, and she felt sick and dirty and furious.

"Do not," said Rachelle, "presume to tell *me* what it means to be a bloodbound. You haven't even met a forestborn."

He tilted his head. "You really think that?" He didn't look like someone whose secret was threatened. He looked wary but curious.

"You really think I'm fool enough to believe you?"

His mouth curved up. "You were fool enough to say yes to a forestborn."

The next thing she knew, she had slammed him against the wall. "Don't try me."

"What are you going to do?" he asked. "You can't kill me, and I'm running out of limbs to cut off."

"I don't have to kill you to make you sorry," Rachelle snapped, and then her throat closed up as she realized what she'd said.

Her forestborn hadn't had to kill Aunt Léonie either.

She let go of him and stumbled back a step. She knew there

wasn't any blood pooled across the floor, but she could still smell it. The scar on her right hand ached.

Armand was still watching her. He had to see how off balance she was, but he didn't mock her. Instead, he went on, musingly, "If you can wait until Château de Lune, you could always have a try at losing me above the sun, below the moon. Though the King and d'Anjou might have something to say about that."

Her whole body sparked with cold white fire. "What did you say?"

"Well, it's still—"

"'Above the sun, below the moon.' *Why did you say that?*"

He looked at her as if she were babbling nonsense. "Because it would be a way to get rid of me. Only nobody really believes that story, so I wouldn't actually advise you to mention it after you hide my body."

"What story?"

"The story of Prince Hugo and the missing door," he said. "You don't know it?"

"Of course I know that story," said Rachelle. "He found a way into the Forest from the Château and it ate him, and that's when they put so many protections on the spot."

Supposedly, those protections hadn't extended far enough into the gardens of the Château to keep Armand from meeting a forestborn. Actually, he was a liar, so it was probably stupid of her to listen to anything he said.

He raised his eyebrows. "Is that how they tell it where you come from?"

"Yes, Monsieur Most Educated, that's how they tell it. Now tell me your version."

"Well," he said, drawing out the word as he gave her a dubious look, "long ago, the king of Gévaudan had a son named Hugo, who could never be content unless he was adventuring. He spent so much time wandering the forest that his father began to fear he would become a bloodbound. Finally the king forbade him to leave Château de Lune for a month. At first Prince Hugo was much upset, but then he seemed to grow content. And then he started to vanish for days at a time. The king thought he had broken the ban, but when he questioned his son, Prince Hugo laughed and said that he had found his own forest within the Château's walls. He said it lay beyond a door above the sun and below the moon that would open only to his hands, and it would make him the greatest hunter the world had ever known. After that night, no one ever saw him again."

"Did they find where he had gone?" asked Rachelle.

"No," said Armand. "But the next year, in my mother's province out west—this is why I know the story—they found a skeleton with his signet ring upon its finger. If it was him, and how he came to be there, nobody knows."

When Rachelle looked at him, he met her eyes. He seemed more curious than anything, as if he genuinely didn't know why she was so interested in a single turn of phrase.

It was too convenient. The moment she was assigned to watch over him—the moment she needed Joyeuse more than anything—he dangled her lost hope in front of her? It had to be a trick.

But nobody among the bloodbound or the court had ever heard her question people about the door—she knew that, because if somebody had, Erec would have found out and teased her. Armand couldn't possibly know what this story meant to her.

And it actually seemed plausible. She had never been to Château de Lune, the country palace that lay twenty miles outside Rocamadour. But while now it was a glittering garden of delights for the nobility, once it had been a hunting lodge from which the kings of old would ride out to destroy woodspawn. Ancient charms protected the spot, but it was not impossible that the Château might also have a hidden door into the Forest. And it made sense that such a door would only open to members of the royal house, who had inherited Tyr's power against the Great Forest.

It didn't sound much like the door that Aunt Léonie had described. But even that made a sort of sense. Suppose the door didn't open directly on the Forest, but had some sort of . . . entryway. The power of the Forest would hide the power of Joyeuse from the ability of woodwives to sense it. That was *exactly* what someone hiding the sword from Mad King Louis would want, because he had used captive woodwives to hunt down and destroy charms and magical artifacts.

It was a wild guess, a slim chance. But with the Devourer's return so close, any chance was worth taking.

"Why do you care?" asked Armand, something shifting in his voice. He sounded almost suspicious.

"Because I like stories about fools who get eaten by the Great Forest," she said.

She needed someone of the royal line to open the door. But the less she told Armand, the less chance he'd have to scheme.

"And mysterious doors," said Armand.

She grinned. "Maybe I'll find it and throw you in."

The apothecary's shop always made Rachelle feel like a great lumbering wild animal. The walls were lined with shelves and cupboards full of tiny, gleaming jars. Little sprays of dried herbs hung by ribbons and swayed in the draft. Everywhere were tiny white labels written in Madame Guignon's minuscule hand. Sometimes Rachelle felt that it would all shatter if she breathed.

If she didn't find Joyeuse, it would shatter before the year was out.

"Good morning," said Madame Guignon, barely looking up from the herbs that she was sorting into piles with swift, sure movements. She was a short, gaunt woman, but somehow she still managed to seem like the tower of a castle.

"Good morning," said Rachelle. "Is Amélie here?"

"Upstairs." Madame Guignon didn't look at her again as she started another pile of herbs. She'd never forbidden Rachelle from visiting, but she didn't encourage her, either.

When Rachelle got to the top of the stairs and opened the door, Amélie was sitting at the table, fussing over a little bowl. Then her head snapped up. She was a short girl—eighteen years old like Rachelle—with mousy brown hair and a bony little face that turned beautiful when she smiled.

"At last!" Amélie jumped up, hugged her, and planted two kisses on her cheeks. "It's been weeks. I was starting to think you'd been eaten."

Rachelle patted her back awkwardly. They'd known each other for over two years, but it still felt wrong for this cheerful, purely human girl to embrace her so easily.

"Sit down," said Amélie, shoving her into a chair. "You're just in time."

Rachelle looked down at the bowl Amélie had been stirring. It was full of white paste. "Bismuth?" she asked.

Amélie made a face. "With chalk mixed in. It's too expensive otherwise, to use for practice. Just a moment, and I'll get my other brushes." She whirled away.

Rachelle's stomach tightened. "Now? I don't—"

"You're not in the middle of hunting, are you? The King hasn't dispatched you on a desperate quest? Then you can sit here for ten minutes and let me practice painting your face." With a clatter, Amélie set down a tray filled with brushes and little pots. She seized Rachelle's head by the temples and adjusted the angle. "There. Don't move."

Two years ago, Rachelle had saved Amélie from the woodspawn that killed her father. Another girl would have considered herself in debt and paid it off long ago. Amélie had simply decided that they were going to be friends, and kept insisting it no matter what anyone said.

Every time Rachelle visited, she always thought, *I should never come back.* It felt like a betrayal to let someone so innocent like her. And it would surely be the ruin of Amélie someday; the way people were turning against the bloodbound, anyone known to be friends with them would be in trouble soon. But she had never been able to stay away, because of what Amélie was doing now. She laid three fingers against Rachelle's forehead to steady her and, biting her lip, began to spread the white paint over her face in swift, sure little strokes.

Nobody touched Rachelle like this. Not since she became a bloodbound. Nobody touched her without trying to fight her, seduce her, or drag her somewhere. Nobody but Amélie.

She thought, *I am never going to see her again.*

If she found Joyeuse, she would fight the Devourer when he returned, and it didn't seem likely she'd survive killing her master. If she couldn't find it—

She would still fight. And she would certainly die.

"Look up at the ceiling," said Amélie, and the brush tickled under Rachelle's eyes.

Amélie would die too. If the sun and moon were gone, if the forestborn hunted men through the woods like foxes hunting rabbits—Amélie would never lose her gentleness fast enough to become somebody who could survive in that world.

So Rachelle *could not* fail.

"I'm going to Château de Lune in three days," she said.

"Lucky." Amélie sighed.

"I'm not going there to dance at the parties," said Rachelle. "I'm going as a bodyguard."

"For whom?" asked Amélie. Her tongue peeked out between her lips as it always did when she was painting a particularly tricky bit of Rachelle's face.

Rachelle shrugged, embararssed for reasons she couldn't fathom. "Armand Vareilles," she mumbled.

Amélie's brush stopped moving. She stared at her a moment, then let out a wild snort of laughter.

"What?" Rachelle demanded.

Amélie rolled her eyes. "You're to guard the living martyr himself. And you say, 'Oh, Armand Vareilles,' as if he were last week's laundry."

"I'd rather guard the laundry," Rachelle muttered.

Amélie's forehead creased slightly. "Why?"

He's an arrogant fraud, Rachelle nearly said, but she didn't know how Amélie felt about Armand Vareilles. They had never discussed him—or Bishop Guillaume, or the unrest in the city, or anything that had to do with what it meant for Rachelle to be bloodbound.

"Every time I turn around, there are people bowing at his feet," she said finally. "It's very inconvenient."

With another strange lurch of embarrassment, she remembered Armand's face as he said, *I'd rather burn*.

"Hm," said Amélie, leaning forward again. Her brush made tiny, feather-light strokes over Rachelle's face. Then she sat back and studied her, pursing her lips. "Done," she said finally.

"Anyway," said Rachelle, "I don't know when I'll see you again, so—"

"I'm coming with you," said Amélie.

"What?" Rachelle stared at her.

"I'm coming with you." Amélie grinned. "You don't get to look in the mirror till you say yes."

"I don't care about the mirror," said Rachelle. "But what do you think you'll do at the Château? You aren't a bodyguard."

"And you are, but you know you'll still have to dance," said Amélie. "Or at least stand in a corner at one of those grand parties, and that means you'll have to wear a pretty dress, and you know you'll look ridiculous if you don't have someone apply cosmetics and do it well, and you couldn't hire someone good if your life depended on it, so I, because I am your loyal friend, will help you."

She crossed her arms and nodded. Rachelle was about to tell her that no bodyguard who hoped to be effective would ever wear an elaborate court gown—but then she realized there was a nervous edge to Amélie's grin. And she couldn't bear to shatter it.

"All right, I probably will have to dance," she said, and realized it was true: Erec would find it hilarious, so he would make it happen. "But you don't have to come help."

She wanted Amélie there with her. She was only this instant realizing how *much* she wanted to spend her last days with the only person who looked at her with simple, undemanding affection. But they could be the last days of the whole daylight world. If Rachelle failed, Amélie would die alone, far away from her mother and surrounded by strangers. Rachelle might watch her die.

She couldn't let her do it.

"I want to," Amélie said softly, her smile melting away. "It's my only chance. To do—*this*"—she waved at Rachelle's face—"and have anyone see it." Her voice grew even softer. "My mother could spare me for a week or two, but not . . . not longer. You know."

Rachelle knew. That was why Amélie had never practiced applying cosmetics on anyone but Rachelle: because after her husband died, Madame Guignon had taken over his business of making medicines as single-mindedly as if she meant to save all the sick people in the world, though there was no saving half of them, and Amélie had taken it upon herself to help her mother, though her mother's quest would never be done.

Two days ago, giving Amélie this chance would have been all Rachelle wanted in the world.

"I can't let you," she said. "It's too dangerous."

Amélie tilted her head. "Why?" she asked. "What do you expect? A palace coup? Open rebellion?"

"Not if I have anything to say about it, but—"

"Famine? Plague? Lightning from heaven?" Amélie leaned forward. "Or ravening woodspawn in the street? Because I might remind you, Château de Lune is the one place that doesn't happen."

Rachelle's hands slammed on the table. "I can't tell you, it doesn't matter, you just *need to stay safe*."

Amélie sat back in her chair, eyes wide and startled. She was probably wondering why her friend was going mad. Rachelle wished she had never come.

"You're really worried, aren't you?" said Amélie. "That means it's serious. But you're not going to tell me why."

"No," Rachelle whispered.

"Well, I can't let you go alone into danger," said Amélie.

"I go into danger all the time," said Rachelle.

"I'm in danger all the time, too, and worse every day." Amélie's voice dropped lower. "You know the light is dying. My mother won't admit it. But *you* know."

The look she gave Rachelle was worried and solemn and

Rachelle would have given anything to wipe it off her face. But there was no changing what was happening to the world, and now that she had failed to protect Amélie from knowing, there was no way to change that, either.

"I don't understand what's happening with the darkness," said Amélie. "But I don't want to let you go alone. And I want to have this chance, whatever happens after. Please."

If Amélie was by her side, then Rachelle could protect her. That wasn't too selfish, was it? And she could send her back in just a few weeks, before the solstice. There was hardly any chance the Devourer would return before then.

"All right," she said. "We'll go together."

Amélie's smile was as bright and beautiful as the sun. "Then you're allowed to see your face," she said, and held up the little hand mirror.

A lady stared back at Rachelle.

She had Rachelle's black hair—slightly messed from the wind—her dark eyes, her narrow face. But this lady had no freckles; she had pale, flawless skin just half a shade lighter than could possibly be natural. Her cheeks flushed in two perfect triangles, and her lips glistened with rouge. One little round black beauty mark sat beneath her left eye.

She looked like a hundred other court ladies Rachelle had seen. And though Rachelle had always found the court fashions silly, for a moment she wished that the illusion was real, that it actually was possible for her to paint on a new face and become a different person.

"It's beautiful," she said.

There was no way she could ever escape herself and become the lovely, innocent girl in the mirror. But that was for the best. Because lovely, innocent girls could not ever hope to fight the Devourer.

Rachelle was going to fight him and win.

Even when she was a little girl, living in the northern forest, Rachelle had heard about Château de Lune. Everyone had. It was the glory of Gévaudan: a shimmering, elegant wonderland. And when the carriage finally drew close, Rachelle saw that it was just as lovely as the stories had promised. The Château itself was a vast, sinuous building of pale stone, glittering glass windows, and gold. For nearly two miles around, it was surrounded by impeccably ordered gardens: fountains, lawns, rosebushes, and long lines of identically trimmed trees.

But when the carriage finally drew to a halt on the wide gravel courtyard inside the main gate, when Rachelle stepped out and drew a breath of the sweet, warm air without the least trace of the city's stink—as lovely as it was, all she could think about was finding the door.

Above the sun, below the moon.

"Beautiful, isn't it?" said Erec.

"Yes," said Rachelle. "Beautiful."

The crimson thread trailed off her finger and wound across the ground, until it was lost among the feet of the servants and courtiers waiting to greet the King. Like a crack in the otherwise perfect surface of a painting.

"Almost as delightful as last time," said Armand, surveying the crowd of silk and wigs and feathered hats. Somebody was presenting the King with a monkey wearing a lace dress.

Last time he was there, he had claimed to meet a forestborn, and he had definitely lost his hands. Rachelle glanced at him. He seemed to be squinting a little in the bright sunlight; she couldn't read the expression on his face. Then Erec clapped a hand on his shoulder, and though his face didn't change, she saw Armand flinch.

"Let's hope this visit is even better," said Erec. "Monsieur, mademoiselle, come with me. I will show you to your rooms myself."

Armand squared his shoulders and marched after him.

Inside the Château was another world. Vast hallways. Patterned marble stairways. Statues in the alcoves. Mirrors that gleamed in one shining piece from floor to ceiling. And everywhere, gold and silver painted and molded across walls, ceilings, and doors, in patterns of birds, flowers, horses, fruits, and naked women—but most of all, in the patterns of the sun and moon. On the mirrors, the ceilings, the statues, the floors.

Everywhere was above the sun. Everywhere was below the moon.

The whole Château was mocking her.

Armand's room was in the royal wing, not far from the King—"An honor no bastard has yet received," said Erec—and it came furnished with not only silk-cushioned chairs and gilt-framed mirrors but also two bland-faced, obsequious valets who bustled out and started exclaiming over the state of Armand's clothes, though Rachelle couldn't see anything wrong with them beyond a few creases from sitting in a carriage all day.

Erec's hand pressed against the small of her back. "This way," he said softly, pushing her toward the door that led farther into the suite.

"I thought I was supposed to guard him," said Rachelle.

"You are, but his valets report to me and they can keep him out of trouble for the five minutes it will take me to show you your room."

So Armand could be left alone in his room sometimes? Rachelle would be happy to use that excuse to sneak out and search the Château as often as possible.

"I'm staying in his suite?" she asked.

"Not exactly. Through here."

The bedroom was dominated by the vast, gilded hulk of a canopied bed. Ignoring the entrance to the study at the opposite end of the room, Erec pushed aside one of the hangings to reveal a narrow door.

“The reason he received this suite,” he said, “is so that he could have no secrets from you.”

On the other side of the door was another bedroom, this one decorated in pale blue and silver. But Rachelle hardly noticed the luxury, because the far door stood open, and through it she could see Amélie kneeling in the dressing room amid an ocean of silk and lace.

Amélie looked up. “You’re here!” she exclaimed, and jumped up to grab Rachelle by the shoulders and kiss her cheeks.

“Yes,” said Rachelle. The warm, comforting pressure of Amélie’s hands on her shoulders nearly stole her breath away. Then she looked around the room. Several trunks sat open on the floor, and their contents had exploded across the room in great waves of shimmering, many-colored fabric.

“Where did that all come from?” she asked.

“There are one or two things beyond my power,” said Erec, “but obtaining ladies’ dresses is not one of them. You’re going to be the loveliest lady in the court tonight.”

Rachelle rolled her eyes. “Save the flattery for someone who’s in love with you.”

“Very well.” He leaned close and breathed in her ear, “You will be the lady dearest and most dreadful.”

For a moment, she almost felt the wind of the Great Forest in her hair.

“That is not a compliment,” she said quietly.

"At least it's perfectly true." He kissed her cheek. "Now I have duties to attend. Remember, you and your charge will be at the reception tonight."

Then he was gone. Rachelle could still feel the press of his lips against her cheek. She forced herself to look at Amélie, who had now seen her kissed and complimented by the most famous and unrepentant of all the bloodbound.

Amélie pursed her lips. "So that's Monsieur d'Anjou. I thought he'd be prettier." She spoke with the same half-prim, half-laughing voice she used to describe her mother's most troublesome customers. As if nothing had changed.

Rachelle laughed shakily and said, "You should tell him that. It might be the first time he's ever heard it." She surveyed the chaos of the dresses. "Do you have any idea how I'm supposed to get these on?"

"You don't," said Amélie. "You stand still and let me put them on you."

"Do *you* know how they go on?"

Amélie made a face. "More or less. There's going to be a chambermaid to help, so I'm sure we'll work it out." She paused, then said, "So Monsieur Vareilles is here?"

Rachelle sighed. "In the next room."

"You still don't like him?" Amélie's voice was soft; she didn't quite look at Rachelle, as if she knew this question might be difficult.

"I never said—" Rachelle began.

"You don't like him." Amélie picked up a dress and shook it out. Her voice was calm and matter-of-fact. "I'm not angry. I just wonder why."

There were a hundred reasons, and only one that really mattered: Armand pretended that the most terrible day of her life had been a joke. That the forestborn had never really been able to threaten her, because there had been some other way out. That if she'd just been clever enough, or brave enough, or holy enough, she could have defied the Great Forest itself and survived.

Rachelle had no illusions. She had chosen wrongly. But she knew beyond all doubt that there had been only two choices.

She could never say that to Amélie. Because Amélie had never, even once, said anything about what Rachelle had done. She had never looked at her as if she were anything evil or inhuman. From the night they met, Amélie had been hard at work pretending—as skillful a deception as she had ever painted with her brush—that Rachelle was just another girl who deserved to be alive.

"He wants everyone to know he's a saint," Rachelle said finally.

"Hm." Amélie started to fold the dress. "Well, they say he has reason."

Rachelle snorted. "There are plenty of beggars with missing hands who don't even have silver ones to replace them, but nobody calls *them* saints."

"Bishop Guillaume says that many a beggar is holier than an abbot, and we should strive to see the Dayspring in all the unfortunate," Amélie said piously. Rachelle had never been able to decipher if she was being sarcastic or sincere when she used that voice, but she had always laughed at it anyway.

This time she didn't laugh. Her body had gone cold. She couldn't stop herself from saying, "I didn't know you liked his sermons."

Amélie went still. After a moment she said slowly, "I don't like all his sermons. But sometimes he speaks kindly. And he's done marvelous things for the hospital. I've seen him—" She paused. "He's not afraid of the sick, the way some people are."

Because he's not afraid of anything, Rachelle wanted to shout at her. *He's not even afraid that God will judge him for using his sermons to gain power.*

But Amélie might not believe her. If Rachelle tried to make her pick which one to trust, her or the Bishop—she didn't want to know what Amélie would do.

She had no right to ask for more. Amélie had foolishly chosen to trust Rachelle; she couldn't complain if she trusted the Bishop just as foolishly.

IN THE DARKEST SHADOWS OF THE WOOD stands a house.

Yes. Though the sun rides high in the world outside, in the heart of the Great Forest, that house is standing still. It is carved of wood most skillfully; from every post and lintel leap a profusion of leaves, flowers, wolves, birds, and little writhing men. And mouths. And teeth.

The walls are caulked with blood. The roof is thatched with bones.

Within that bloody house lived Old Mother Hunger, the first and eldest of all forestborn. Her fingers were slender and white as bone; her hair was long and dark as night. She had danced before the Devourer when she was but a human girl, and she so delighted him that he adopted her for his own. She had helped him to swallow the sun and moon, and so bring all the world to darkness. And now it was her part to train the children of men who would become forestborn, and those who would become the Devourer's living vessel.

If Tyr was to become a fitting vessel for the Devourer, a bridge between that vast black hunger and the world, then he must forget his name. So they placed him in the deepest cellar of the house, within a little cage of bone, and they told him he was dead. Every time they brought him food, before he could eat, he must first sing a song to them:

"My mother, she killed me

My father, he ate me.

I once had a name,

But now I have none."

If Zisa was to become a true forestborn, she must destroy the human heart within her. So she was the one who brought him his food and demanded the song of him. But every time Old Mother Hunger slept, Zisa slipped down to the cellar again, and in the darkness she whispered to him that his name was Tyr and she was his sister.

Tyr's spirit wandered far away into darkness and dreaming, and for a long time he would not speak, however Zisa implored him. She studied the arts of the forestborn, until at last she crept down to Tyr's cellar and sang him a song that commanded dreams, and Tyr turned his face to her, though his eyes remained shut.

"Brother, what holds you asleep?" she asked.

He answered: "Sister, I am dreaming of the Devourer. He is a wolf, and he gnaws me until there is nothing left but bones. And that is good."

"How can that be good?" asked Zisa.

Tyr whispered, "Only the leavings of the wolf can kill the wolf."

The next time that Zisa brought Tyr his food, he sang to her,

"My sister, she killed me.

My master, he ate me.

I am but the leavings

And thus I shall slay him."

Zisa reached through the bars of the cage and wrapped her hands around his.

"It will not come to that," she said.

Rachelle managed to slip away that afternoon to hunt for the door, but she found nothing. All the search gained her were a lot of curious glances from the bustling crowds, and Amélie's worried wrath when she got back to her room too late to be dressed up for the night's reception.

"I'm not a guest," Rachelle protested.

"You would be once I finished dressing you," Amélie muttered.

The reception was held in the Salon du Mars—a vast, domed, hexagonal room that was considered one of the wonders of Château de Lune. Personally, Rachelle couldn't see the appeal. For one, it had no suns or moons anywhere, which made it useless to her. For another, it looked like someone had vomited artwork over every available surface. The six walls were practically paneled in gold-framed paintings of every shape and size.

The ceiling was just one mural, but it was such a writhing mess of billowing fabric and twisting limbs that she couldn't tell what it depicted. Around the edges of the room were alternating black and white marble statues, all of them contorted into feverishly passionate poses.

Add to that six tables of cakes, ices, and punch bowls, a group of seven musicians playing the violin, three hundred candles, and who knew how many courtiers, and the result was a room that made Rachelle feel like she was being punched in the face just by looking at it.

It didn't help that Armand had entered the room with the King, which meant that Rachelle came in a step behind them, right at the center of the panoply. The room stilled and silenced at the King's entrance; the mass of people swayed down in bows and curtsies and then rose back up again, like a wave ebbing and flowing. The low roar of conversation resumed. Instantly they were swarmed by an exquisite crowd of people—dripping silk and lace, powder and jewels—who must speak with the King or Armand. According to some set of precise, secret rules, each of them bowed low, or kissed a hand, or received a kiss on the cheek.

Then they would look at Rachelle—sometimes a swift, covert glance, sometimes an openly nervous stare. But they didn't try to talk to her, perhaps because she was in her normal patrol clothes. She wasn't here to pretend she belonged to the glittering throng.

She was here to find Joyeuse. But after some careful glances,

Rachelle was pretty sure that there was no sun or moon anywhere in the decorations. Which meant that the next few hours would be an idiotic waste of her time, and she didn't even know how much time she had left.

Then a woman spoke up from behind Rachelle: "Good evening, Armand. Who's your cheerful friend?"

Rachelle turned and saw a nearly colorless young woman. Her skin was powdered very pale, her curls were dull flax, and her dress was pure white silk. Strings of pearls rimmed the low neckline, gathered the puffy sleeves just below her elbows, and ran in a line down the center of her bodice. The only spot of color was a single large ruby hanging at her neck. Her face was narrow, flat, and not remotely pretty.

Armand's smile was crooked and far more real than anything Rachelle had seen on his face before. "Mademoiselle Brinon, may I present la Fontaine, my second cousin and already a famous poet, fabulist, and salon hostess. She has a real name but we don't bother to use it. My dear Fontaine, this is Rachelle Brinon, most excellent of the King's bloodbound and my bodyguard."

"I'm charmed." La Fontaine inclined her head. "But you're too cold, calling me just your second cousin when I'm practically your mother." Her fingers brushed the ruby at her throat. "Since His Majesty has been so kind."

She smiled as Armand turned red. Rachelle was baffled for a moment, and then remembered that a single red ruby was the gift noblemen would give their mistresses. This young woman must be the latest of King Auguste-Philippe's long line of favorites.

"I played with you when we were both four years old," said Armand with precise calm. "I am not going to call you 'mother.' "

"Pity. You'll just have to come to my salon and address me as 'goddess' instead. The famous Tollesande is back in my employ, so we'll have her cakes." La Fontaine fixed Armand with a severe look. "I warn you, I'll make you eat five of them. You've grown much too thin."

That, strangely, made his shoulders tense. "Don't mind me."

"You could come with me and eat something now," said la Fontaine.

"I'm not hungry."

"You didn't have any lunch either," said Rachelle, suddenly remembering the carriage ride to the palace.

"Maybe I'm fasting for the good of my soul."

"I thought you were already perfect."

"Nobody is perfect," said la Fontaine. "Monsieur Vareilles, for instance, has not yet asked me to dance. So I'll have to beg. My dearest little son, will you join me for a dance?"

"If you promise never to address me that way again," said Armand, "I'll do anything you want."

La Fontaine sighed as she took his metal hand. "Unfortunately, I cannot tell a lie."

She drew him toward the center of the room, where pairs of dancers wove among each other in stately rows.

"I'm surprised the saint can actually dance," said Erec from behind her.

Rachelle flinched. Normally Erec wasn't able to slip up on her like that.

"And where have you been?" she asked, turning.

"Making myself welcome." He raised his glass to her. "But where were *you* this afternoon?"

Rachelle's heart thumped, but she said calmly, "Learning the lay of the Château."

"I think you'll find that being a saint's bodyguard calls for different tactics than solitary hunting," said Erec, and though his voice was joking, the look he gave her wasn't.

"I thought you said his valets could watch him," said Rachelle.

Erec shrugged and relaxed. "Oh, they can. And between you and me, I don't think he's going to give us much trouble." He smiled to himself. "But if the King hears about you leaving his son's side, he may get angry."

Rachelle nodded, hoping that her fury didn't show on her face. So she would have to search at night. She could do that. If she had to, she wouldn't sleep until she found Joyeuse.

"I, on the other hand, will only get angry if you don't dress yourself better for the next event." Erec looked her up and down. "Whatever possessed you to enter the room in that costume?"

"I wanted all my knives," said Rachelle.

"My dear, I promise you the repartee is not *that* cutting."

"You brought me here to be a bodyguard," said Rachelle. "And I refuse to fight anyone while wearing a court dress."

"But you won't have to. I'll be here to save you."

"Yes, if you're not too busy flirting."

"I'm flirting right now." In a heartbeat he had a knife in his hand; one quick motion, and he'd flung it across the room to spear the apple sitting atop a pyramid of fruit. "And still quite capable, as you can see."

Rachelle grinned at him and reached for one of her wrist knives. A moment later it was quivering in the apple next to his.

"I am too," she said.

The apple gave a final wobble and the fruit pyramid collapsed. Apples, pears, and oranges bounced across the floor; a lady squeaked as two apples rolled under her hem, and another said something that set all the nearby people tittering. Several harried-looking servants converged on the table and started picking up the fruit.

Erec laughed and went to retrieve their knives. "For that, you win a dance," he said when he returned, holding out a hand.

Rachelle rolled her eyes, but she remembered the easy happiness when they had danced the other night, and she let him draw her out among the dancing couples. At first all she could do was watch him and watch the other women in the dance, trying to keep pace and not stumble. It was a statelier, more mannered dance than he had dragged her through in the courtyard. Instead of endless twirls, he clasped only one of her hands as they moved in a pattern of step, skip-skip, bow; step, skip-skip, turn. But even one-handed, Erec could steer her, and bloodbound grace made up the rest. In a few minutes, she could move through the steps without thinking.

"Your charge seems to be enjoying himself, despite his martyrdom," said Erec. Near the center of the room, Armand was dancing with la Fontaine.

"I don't think it counts as martyrdom when you're dressed in court clothes and dancing with ladies," said Rachelle. "Or when you've never met a forestborn."

"You think he hasn't?" asked Erec.

She remembered the pale, naked stumps of Armand's arms, and the way he had stared her down. He didn't seem like somebody who had never faced fear.

But he couldn't have faced a forestborn.

"I *know* he hasn't," said Rachelle. "You do too. What the Forest claims, it doesn't let go. If he had been marked, and if he had refused to kill, the mark would have killed him instead. That's how it works."

"World without end, amen," said Erec. "And yet here he stands, and dances."

"Because he lost his hands and didn't want pity, so he tried for sainthood instead," said Rachelle. "What else could it be? A miracle?"

"That's what everyone else calls it."

"That makes no sense." Was the music picking up its pace, or was it just her own anger that made the swirl of the dance seem faster, sharper? "Three thousand years since Tyr and Zisa. In that time, the forestborn must have marked ten thousand people, all of whom had to die or kill—and *now* God decides to spare someone the choice? What kind of miracle is that?"

"You're the one who still has faith," said Erec. "You tell me."

"I don't have faith," said Rachelle. "If I did, I wouldn't be here."

Faith was trust. People who had it never became bloodbound, because rather than kill, they would lie down and die and trust God to make everything all right.

"Really?" Erec looked down at her, and for once there wasn't amusement or condescension in his voice. "Then why are you always doing penance?"

"I'm not," said Rachelle. The only appropriate penance was her death, and she had too much fight left in her for that. "I'm just doing as you taught me."

"Oh?" said Erec. "When did I teach you to live in a miserable garret and patrol the streets without rest?"

"When I arrived," said Rachelle. "You told me there was no going back, so I should make use of what I'd become."

It was why she considered him a friend, no matter how he annoyed her sometimes. Rachelle had fled to Rocamadour because she wanted to live. But once she had gotten there—once she had been accepted as the King's bloodbound and knew she could live at least a little longer—she'd realized she had no reason left for living. She had spent whole days in bed, too dull with misery to stand; when she was dragged out to fight woodspawn, she had flung herself at their claws, half hoping for death. It was Erec who had mocked and goaded her into sword practice; Erec who had kissed her into wanting life again; Erec who had told her to make use of what she was.

And once she had realized that she *could* be useful—that her power, however wicked, could also protect—there had been no stopping her.

"I didn't mean it *that* way," said Erec.

"Well, no, of course not," said Rachelle fondly. "Too bad for you."

As she spoke, the music came to an end; Erec gave her a deep bow. "I really don't understand your scruples," he said. "Is it because of your damned soul that you like to talk about so much? If you're doomed to hell no matter what, you might as well enjoy yourself."

"If I'm damned, what's the point of pretending that I'm not?" asked Rachelle. The vast, colorful, chattering crowd swirled around them, and she felt like she was watching it from across a vast gulf. She didn't understand how Erec or any of the bloodbound could bear to pretend they had any part in this glittering, carefree world.

"You really mean that?"

There was an odd note in his voice; she looked up, and so she had a stomach-lurching half instant to realize what he was about to do before he seized her by the shoulders and kissed her.

She'd remembered that she liked his kisses, but she had forgotten how much. It felt like the Forest was growing and casting shadows inside her, vast and senseless and wild. When he finally released her, she was shaking.

"Yes, mademoiselle," he whispered. "By all means, let's avoid pretending."

And for a moment, she could see the Forest. Shadowy trunks rose through the crowd like pillars; vines wound up statues and draped over the paintings; the candelabras cast leaflike shadows. Crimson, four-winged birds fluttered among the dancers. She couldn't hear the music or the chatter of the crowd, only the soft, vast susurration of wind among infinite branches.

Then she blinked and it was gone, so quickly that she might have imagined it. She must have imagined it: Château de Lune was far too well-protected for the Forest to manifest here, and if it did, she would see it for more than a flickering instant.

That was how much power Erec had over her: he could make her think she was seeing the Forest.

And now he was smirking at her. "I don't think I've ever rendered you speechless before."

She wanted to slap his face. She had told him never to kiss her again. She also wanted to forget what she'd said and pull him close for another kiss. But either reaction would amuse him. That was the problem with Erec: everything was always a game to him, and he always won.

Instead she tried to look bored. But she knew she was blushing, and anyway it was already too late. He would be insufferable the rest of the evening.

"Thank you for the dance," she said flatly, turning away.

"Don't tell me you're leaving already."

"Good night." She hadn't actually been planning to leave the reception, but now that he had asked her to stay, she refused to give him the satisfaction.

"What about your charge?"

"I'll take him with me." The dance had started up again; she marched straight through the wheeling couples to Armand, and seized his hand out of la Fontaine's.

"We're leaving," she said, and dragged him with her through the crowd—they were all staring, but who cared?—and out a pair of great glass-paneled doors into the garden. Outside was a long, grassy walk lined by oak trees hung with lanterns.

"Where are we going?" said Armand after a few moments, as she continued to drag him down the walk.

Rachelle had not considered that, but she wasn't about to tell him. "That way," she said, and didn't slow down.

"Not that I mind the fresh air," said Armand, after another few moments, "but you do realize that everyone in there thinks you dragged me out either to kill me or to kiss me senseless?"

Then she did stop, so she could drop his hand and turn on him. "What?"

"Well, after that display. And you know what people say about bloodbound."

The anger was so sudden and furious, she was surprised she didn't strike him.

"I know a good deal better than you do," she said, "unless *you've* been called a whore to your face."

Ladies tittered and made eyes at Erec. But men of any kind only made catcalls at Rachelle, unless they were cursing her.

Armand winced. "I'm sorry," he said.

"Why? Don't pretend you think I'm an innocent." Before he could speak, she went on, "But your second cousin just boasted to us about sleeping with the King. How am *I* the shocking one?"

Armand's mouth twisted wryly. "Accepting a man's favor is elegant. Kissing in public is vulgar."

"That makes no sense."

"Welcome to the court. Also, she is mistress to the King, and you know how much royal favor can excuse."

"Such as being bloodbound?" she asked bitterly.

"But you're not really excused, are you? I was thinking more about what the royal family gets up to."

Rachelle pushed a strand of hair out of her face. The sweat had started to cool on her skin. In the distance, the wind rustled in the trees. The night was opening up around her again; Armand, his face half-lit by the flickering lamplight, looked strange and ominous.

Not that he sounded it. "Why are you spouting this nonsense?" she demanded.

"I suppose because it's easier than thinking about the fact that we're all alone so there's nobody to hear me scream."

"Do you really think I dragged you out here to kill you? I'd get in trouble for that, and you're not worth it."

He laughed. It was a curiously open laugh, his shoulders shaking and his eyes crinkling. "You're very comforting."

"No," said Rachelle, "just honest. If I were trying to comfort you, I would promise not to hurt you."

The next morning, they had to attend the King's levée. Apparently it looked strange if the King's beloved son did not attend his father at every opportunity, so after a hasty breakfast, Rachelle and Armand squeezed their way into the royal chambers along with half the court so that they could watch the Duc de Bonne fulfill his lifelong dream of handing the King his undershirt.

Rachelle found the levée boring beyond all belief, but she supposed it wasn't worse than any of the other court functions they might have been dragged to. The most trying part was watching everyone pretend not to notice the weakness in the way the King moved, in his overstudied gestures. The rumors were right: he was ill, no matter how little he wanted to admit it.

Just like the world was ending, no matter how little the entire court wanted to admit it.

A courtier stammered a joke, and the King let out one of his famous booming laughs. Everyone pretended not to notice when it turned into a cough. Rachelle sighed and looked up at the ceiling.

The royal chambers here at the Château were just as elaborate as those of the Palais du Soleil back in Rocamadour. But here, instead of the gold curlicues splattered across the ceiling, there was a huge painting of the moon, decorated with gold-and-silver traceries. It was an oddly stylized painting, and as Rachelle stared at it, she realized it wasn't much like any of the other portraits that hung framed all over the Château. It was old. She knew very little about art, but she was sure that it was much older than any of the other decorations.

Her heart started beating faster, but she didn't let herself think what she was hoping until Erec's laugh rang out above the babble of the crowd, and she glanced at him. He sat, again, at the King's feet, glorying in his position. He was dressed all in black velvet today, with black leather boots, and the tesserae of the mosaic floor glittered around him. Gold tesserae. The pattern was huge; she couldn't quite make out what it was, besides golden and swirling.

Rachelle looked down at her feet. She saw wavy golden rays against dark blue.

It was the sun. The entire floor of the King's apartments was covered in a mosaic of the sun. Below a giant moon painted on the ceiling.

She was careful to keep her body still, her face smooth, but under her skin, her blood was pulsing with excitement, because *what if the door was right here*?

It seemed like a stupid thought. Mad King Louis had nearly torn the kingdom apart when he tried to burn all the woodwives and melt down Joyeuse. Surely anyone seeking to save the ancient sword would want it as far away from him as possible. Surely, if the door were here, someone of the royal line besides Prince Hugo would have opened it already.

But it made a curious sort of sense. If the nameless woodwife had hidden Joyeuse anywhere at the Château, that meant hiding it under the king's nose. Perhaps she had simply decided to go all the way and hide the sword in the one place that King Louis would never expect a woodwife to dare go. And there were some woodwife charms, Rachelle knew, that only operated in response to the will of the one holding them. The door might open only for somebody who already knew it was there.

It was worth trying.

But she would have to wait until there were not a hundred people crowded into the room.

Late that night, when the Château had finally begun to still, Rachelle slipped into the King's chambers.

There were guards standing outside the doors, but they weren't bloodbound—or even that well trained, in Rachelle's opinion. They didn't hear a thing when she slipped in through the windows that nobody had bothered to lock.

Of course, nobody expected a bloodbound to be sneaking into the King's chamber to look for an ancient sword hidden behind a magic door.

That morning, the King's sitting room had felt like a tiny glittering cage. Now—empty of the crowd and filled with shadows—it seemed much larger. A hidden doorway felt actually *possible* in this silent, dreaming room.

Rachelle turned around slowly in a circle, looking up at the painted moon, down at the mosaic sun. It *looked* like the perfect spot, but the only doors she could see were the solid, normal doors into the bedchamber and out into the hall.

She had been thinking about the door all day. If it had remained hidden from the kings of Gévaudan for three hundred years, it had to be concealed with a woodwife charm. It probably *was* a woodwife charm, and that meant she ought to be able to sense it. But she didn't feel anything.

Wind stirred against her neck.

The windows were shut.

Rachelle went still, heart thudding. And then she saw it: shadows on the wall, in the shape of leaves rustling in the wind, even though there were no branches outside the window to cast them.

A cold breeze traced her cheek and then was still. The shadow leaves faded into simple, normal shadows. The Forest was gone—but it had been here, just for a moment. She was sure she hadn't imagined it this time. The Forest had manifested in Château de Lune, where any trace of its power should be impossible.

Perhaps the Forest was simply getting too strong for the protections on the Château. Or perhaps she was standing right next to the door into the Forest.

She still didn't sense anything. But she knew how well hidden some woodwife charms could be until they were awakened.

Rachelle stepped to the nearest wall and laid her hand against it. It was simple wood covered in paint and gilt, but she closed her eyes and *reached*.

Awakening charms had never been one of her strengths. It was a strange, sideways movement that used none of her body. For the first six months of her training, all that had happened when she tried was that she wiggled her ears. Even after she learned how to do it right, the skin on her scalp still twitched whenever she woke a charm.

Now she concentrated until her head ached, but she felt no answering power in the wall beneath her fingertips.

With a sigh, she opened her eyes and looked around the dim room. Charms had to be touched to be awoken; just standing near them was not enough. It wasn't a large room, but it would take her a long time to lay hands on every part of the wall.

She had to try. What could she lose?

Rachelle took one step forward and pressed her hand to the wall again. And again. And again. Awakening a charm was such a little thing—she wasn't even really drawing any power—and yet the effort was starting to make her dizzy. Still she kept trying, moving slowly around the room. She had to find the door, even if it meant crawling through every room in the Château.

In the hallway outside, somebody was singing—probably drunken courtiers staggering back to their rooms—but it didn't matter. Nothing mattered except finding the door.

The ragged singing stopped, which was a relief; the caterwauling made it hard to concentrate—

Then she realized that the people were still in the corridor, chattering and laughing just outside the door.

And the door was opening.

Rachelle whirled around. Light dazzled her: the corridor was lit outside, and the people carried several lamps. La Fontaine stood in the doorway, pale blue crystals glistening in her hair and on her dress. To either side of her, a small crowd of nobles stood, swayed, and leaned on each other, cheeks flushed and wigs slightly askew. They seemed to have all been laughing over a common joke a moment before.

They were all staring at her now.

La Fontaine arched one pale eyebrow. "I hope I do not intrude," she said.

Rachelle couldn't breathe. She couldn't tell them what she was doing, but if she didn't tell, would they think she was trying to assassinate the King? Would the King consider her to have disobeyed orders by leaving Armand asleep in his room? If she wasn't executed, she could be sent home to Rocamadour, and then how would she find Joyeuse—

"I don't mind if you want to try your luck with him," said la Fontaine, "but you must know that I will win. Though you will find you get further if you actually enter the bedroom."

—and Rachelle's face heated as she realized that nobody in the room suspected her of any kind of violence.

"I'm here to patrol," she said, her voice absurdly harsh and rustic in her ears. "I needed to see if the King's rooms were safe."

"I promise I am taking good care of him," said la Fontaine, which set everyone snickering.

Rachelle wanted to snarl, *I have no interest in kissing a sick old man,* but she knew that if she showed anger, la Fontaine would arch an eyebrow and make a joke of that as well.

She wondered if she could simply bolt across the room and throw herself out the window. It could hardly make things worse.

La Fontaine stepped closer. "But I really do wonder," she said more softly, the idle amusement gone from her voice, "what are you doing here?"

Then the door behind her opened, and there stood King Auguste-Philippe, wrapped in a dark red robe.

She bowed stiffly, along with everyone else. Her body was numb with embarrassment.

The King ignored everyone to look at la Fontaine. "My dear little friend," he said, "what keeps you out so late at night?"

There was an odd shift to la Fontaine. She lost none of her poise, but she looked suddenly younger and more fragile.

"My duty to your subjects," she said, extending a hand for him to kiss. "How could I leave them lonely?"

He kissed the hand and drew her close to him. The crowd at the door he continued to ignore, but he looked at Rachelle. "And, you, what are you doing here?"

Rachelle straightened her spine. She reminded herself that she had nothing to lose. She was already sentenced to death.

"I was patrolling, sire," she said. "I thought I heard something."

He looked her up and down. "I thank you for your devotion," he said. "But my dear friend"—he settled a hand on la Fontaine's shoulder—"is all I need. You may go."

Humiliated, she fled.

For the next week, Rachelle kept looking.

There was a fountain in the east gardens that had a mosaic of the sun in its basin. She sat by it for an hour while the moon shone high overhead. She trailed her fingers through the water and closed her eyes and *tried*, but she could not find any hidden charm in it.

There was a moon-shaped clock set into the ceiling in a room whose carpet was covered in little sunbursts. The King held audiences there, and at night it was locked, the windows barred; Rachelle tried to find where the keys were kept, gave up, and broke in one night. There was nothing inside, and the next day she had to help Erec hunt for the nonexistent thief.

It was maddening. Hunting woodspawn was simple: she heard where they had been glimpsed, then sat on a roof in the neighborhood until she saw them, or felt the swelling power of the Forest. Then she chased and then she killed.

But this door wasn't something that could be hunted or chased; it had to be searched out and found, and she had nothing to guide her but a cryptic riddle that every day seemed more useless. And yet she couldn't stop trying, so night after night she roamed the Château. By the time she crawled into her bed, she was nearly ready to weep from frustration as well as exhaustion.

The days were just as bad. Hour after wasted hour standing next to Armand in party after audience after court function. It was deadly boring. At first she ignored what the people around her were saying, but then she realized that while anything was better than the return of Endless Night, she didn't want to save Gévaudan from the Devourer only to have it be ruled by the Bishop. So she watched the people who approached Armand. They bowed to him, and kissed his sliver hands, and begged to have his blessing. But if there was any plotting being done amid the glittering chatter, she couldn't hear it.

Armand hardly said a word to her. He smiled and nodded and babbled an ocean of pleasantries to the rest of the court. But when they were alone, he stared at the wall and said nothing.

Amélie was always trying to persuade Rachelle to let her start applying cosmetics. "You said I could practice on you," she said. "We had a bargain."

"I know," said Rachelle. "You will. Just not yet."

She knew that if she sat down and let Amélie start painting on her face, she would relax. The awful, drumming pressure inside her chest would cease. And she couldn't bear that. She couldn't bear to let that agonized tension go when all that stood between her and defeating the Devourer was a single door and she *couldn't find it.*

Rachelle started to wonder if Armand had been lying when he told her the story about Prince Hugo.

Then one night, after hours wandering the Château, she sat staring into the darkness and rubbing at the phantom string tied to her finger.

Once she had wound yarn around her fingers every day, and it hadn't been a curse.

The memory clutched her suddenly, like hands around her throat: Aunt Léonie sitting beside her, gently untangling the snarl she had made when she tried a new pattern.

It had been a charm for revealing hidden things. The pattern itself was very simple, but once woven, it had to be awakened with careful concentration, or the power contained in it would go terribly wrong. Rachelle had given herself headaches trying, but she had never managed it, and Aunt Léonie had kept snatching the charm away from her before it went too wrong.

She'd been angry at that. She'd wanted to master the charm so she could use it against the forestborn she was meeting in the woods.

Now she wondered, *What if I used it to find Joyeuse?*

She had seen woodwife charms a few times since becoming a bloodbound, and she had been able to sense the power woven into them. She had guessed that meant she would be able to awaken a charm. But *making* one . . . that was different. In three years, Rachelle had never once tried; she'd simply assumed it was impossible, now that she was one of the things those charms repelled.

But she had nothing to lose by trying.

Amélie was puzzled, but she gave Rachelle a length of yarn from her knitting basket easily enough. That night Rachelle didn't go out wandering but sat up in her bed, twisting the yarn around and around in her fingers.

Even after three years, her hands still remembered how to move, but they were clumsy, as if they weren't quite attached to her.

Slowly, she began to form the charm: three loops twining around each other, with a knot in the center. She thought it was right. She was almost certain that it was the right shape, and as she stared at it, she thought she felt a slight flicker of power.

If it is not awakened properly, it can be very destructive, Aunt Léonie had said.

Rachelle slipped out of the bedroom. She went nearly all the way back to the Hall of Mirrors, but she stopped in a darkened corridor just short of it, because she didn't want to unleash anything *very destructive* around so much glass.

She looked down at the charm in her hand: three little loops, and two tails drooping down toward the floor.

Her pulse quickened. This could be the night that she found Joyeuse. She wouldn't have to stand in attendance on a fake saint anymore; she wouldn't have to help him deceive people into making him king. She could be *free.*

Or this could be the night that she finally did something stupid enough to kill herself. And then she would still be free.

She let out a short, quick breath and sat down cross-legged on the floor. She cupped her hands around the charm. She tried to clear her mind of distractions, the way Aunt Léonie had taught her.

She thought, *I need Joyeuse. I need it.*

I need it.

There was a curious sensation, like weight shifting and finding its balance. The air went still in her lungs.

The charm was warm in her hands.

Without meaning to, Rachelle's eyes snapped open and she stood in a single smooth motion. It felt like there was a string tied along the length of her spine, drawing her up, and now it was pulling her forward.

She walked toward the doorway. She felt like she was floating. She thought, *Joyeuse.*

But the sense of weight continued rolling, shifting, growing—

And as she stepped through the doorway into the Hall of

Mirrors, her control broke. The charm seared her hands like fire, and her vision flashed white.

She knew she was falling.

Then she knew nothing.

She woke up in the Great Forest. There were flowers and vines sprouting all around her, and the sweet Forest wind caressed her face.

Then she blinked, and realized she was still in the Hall of Mirrors—but overshadowed by the Forest.

Impossible. The Forest didn't appear in human homes unless something terrible called it forth, like a bloodbound turning into a forestborn. And she still felt human. She didn't think Erec was ready to leave the court yet, either.

Rachelle knew she should be scared, but she was still too dazed by the charm's destruction; her head felt cold and hollow. Slowly she sat up. The floor seemed to rock underneath her as she moved; she put a hand against the floor to steady herself, and gasped in pain. Her palms were raw and bloody.

One slow breath. Two. She looked around: the Hall of Mirrors was still standing, and the Forest was fading away from it as she watched. Everything was all right, despite what Aunt Léonie had said.

Then she noticed that the mirrors nearest to her were shattered.

She had to get out of the hall before she got in trouble.

Rachelle managed to stand, but she forgot and tried to steady herself with her hand again, which made her flinch and stagger away from the wall.

Somehow she got back to her room without anyone seeing her. She climbed into her bed and a moment later was asleep.

And she dreamed.

She was in a forest of dead black trees. The ground was covered in fine white dust; the sky was featureless gray. Ahead of her, through the trees, she could see a small cottage.

Everything was real: the cool wind blowing between her fingers, the dust shifting under her feet. The terrified breath rasping in her throat.

She walked forward. She couldn't stop her feet from moving, though she tried desperately, because even a glimpse of the cottage's flat walls and closed door—its roof thatched with bones—made her choke with terror. But she still took one step and then another. She knew that when she reached the door, she would be helpless to stop herself from opening it. She knew that what lay beyond the door would destroy her.

The scar on her right hand burned with a terrible cold fire, like a last warning. But she couldn't stop.

One step forward.

Then another.

Rachelle woke gasping for breath, her body screaming at her to run. But there was nowhere to go: the nightmare was inside of her, part of her.

She'd had the dream before, over and over. All the bloodbound did. Sooner or later, they all reached the cottage and opened the door. And then they became forestborn.

Not tonight, she thought. *Not tonight.*

Now that her terror was fading, she realized that her head ached terribly. And then she remembered what she had been doing the night before. And that she had failed.

What had she been thinking? Why had she imagined that a bloodbound would be able to use a woodwife charm? She was one of the things that those charms were meant to kill.

She was one of the things that Joyeuse was meant to kill, too. Maybe that was why she couldn't find it.

10

The next day, all anyone could talk about was the mysterious vandal who had attacked the Hall of Mirrors. Even Erec was—well, not worried, but he spent a good deal of the day talking to the guard about trying to find the culprit.

Rachelle's hands had healed in the night—there were benefits to being bloodbound—but she still felt a fleeting, phantom ache where the charm had burst apart in her grasp. Her head ached too, whenever she moved too quickly or saw a sudden shaft of bright sunlight.

None of it mattered beside the useless fury of knowing that there was nothing more she could do. She'd tried and tried and done her best, and none of it had helped.

Maybe finding Joyeuse had been a fool's dream all along. Maybe she should have spent the time preparing to fight her forestborn.

"What's wrong?" Amélie asked her that afternoon.

For once Armand was not required anywhere in the Château. Rachelle might have been able to slip out and search for the door without Erec hearing about it, but today she didn't have the heart to try. She would try, again and again, until time ran out and Endless Night fell and she died fighting. But right now, her heart and her bones were made of lead. So she sat still and watched Amélie knit. She stared at the fine brown hairs falling out of Amélie's braid, at the quick, deft motions of her tiny hands, and she wondered how long somebody so gentle would survive, once Endless Night returned.

"Rachelle?" Amélie was looking straight at her now, forehead creased. "Is something wrong?"

"No," Rachelle said quickly. "Nothing." Guilt tugged at her stomach. But if she couldn't save Amélie, at least she could let her live in peace a little longer. Surely there was no need to tell her the truth when it couldn't save her.

"Of course." Amélie's voice was sharper than she'd ever heard it before. "Nothing's ever wrong." She stared at her yarn; she wrapped it around the needle with a particularly ferocious gesture.

It was all wrong; Amélie was never angry. Rachelle sat up straight. "Did something happen?"

"Nothing," said Amélie, still staring at her knitting. Her needles clacked once, twice. Then her hands stilled and she sighed. "A letter from my mother. I'm worried."

"Woodspawn?" said Rachelle, and her body tensed with the need to fight. She should have known there wouldn't be enough bloodbound to patrol the city properly without her. She should have *known*, and now people were dying, and it was all her fault—

"What?" Amélie looked up at her. "No. The riot. You know."

"The riot?" Rachelle echoed stupidly.

"I suppose it wasn't quite a riot—my mother called it a 'tussle' in her letter, but of course she never tells me the whole truth—" Amélie paused, staring at her. "You mean you didn't know?"

"No," said Rachelle, feeling like the ground was rocking underneath her. "What happened? What did the Bishop do?"

"Nothing," said Amélie, looking nervous now. "It was just a crowd on the streets. There was a bloodbound—Raymond something, I think—some people say he was hurting a child, some say he came to blows with a drunkard. Whatever happened, the people turned on him. They beat him half to death."

It must have been Raymond Dubois. He was the newest of the King's bloodbound in Rocamadour. Rachelle had always disliked him, because he was never far from the prostitutes in Thieves' Alley, but when she imagined him being trampled into the mud and cobblestones by a furious crowd, her stomach turned.

"The city guard's rounded up at least a dozen people," Amélie went on, "but who knows if they're the ones who were really there." Her mouth tightened. "People are scared, and angry. Next time there may be a real riot. And Mother will never run, not even if it happens on her doorstep. She didn't even tell me the whole story in her letter; I had to get it from the other servants."

"I'm sorry," Rachelle said faintly, as she thought, *Erec knew. He must have known my city was falling to pieces. And he didn't tell me.*

He didn't tell me.

It took her nearly an hour to find him, which did not improve her mood. He was hidden away in a little-used corner of the Château, talking to a pair of the bland-faced lackeys who ran his personal errands. And while some of those errands were simply setting up assignations with ladies, a lot of them also involved spying out and arresting the enemies of the King.

He had to know everything about what had happened in Rocamadour.

"Why didn't you tell me?" Rachelle demanded as she strode into the room.

Erec looked up. "Didn't tell you what?" he asked. "I think I've mentioned that you're pretty almost every day."

"Can't you leave off playing games for even a moment? I mean what's happening in Rocamadour. The attack. It was Raymond Dubois, wasn't it?"

"I didn't know you cared so much about him. Is that why you're so cold to me?"

"I care," Rachelle growled, "about *my city.*"

Erec waved a hand. The two lackeys filed out, and she was left alone with Erec, who rose to his feet.

"Dubois was attacked. He survived. We can't prove it was plotted by the Bishop, so the incident is useless to us. What's to tell?"

"I think I have a right to know," she bit out, "when my city is getting closer to outright rebellion."

"Well, it's not your problem now, is it?" said Erec.

She stared at him. Words clogged in her throat. Maybe there weren't words for what Rocamadour was to her. It was her prison and her penalty, full of mud and stink and people who hated her—and yet it was *hers*, her city to roam and protect. Her only purpose since she had become a bloodbound.

She supposed that now her purpose was to find Joyeuse. But she seemed doomed to fail at that as completely as she'd failed at being a woodwife. And even if she never saw Rocamadour again—and she probably *would* never see it again—

It was still hers.

Erec would not understand any of that.

She turned and left him without a word.

When she got to the suite, Armand wasn't there.

She was so used to him being obedient that it took her a moment to absorb the fact that he really had vanished. Without permission.

She asked the valets where he had gone; they only blinked large, pale eyes at her and said that monsieur had gone out to meet her, and wasn't he with her?

No, thought Rachelle, *he's plotting bloody revolution and Erec is going to have your heads.*

But she didn't say that, because the next instant it occurred to her that maybe Armand hadn't slipped away to plot treason. Maybe he was just trying to snatch one moment of freedom alone.

And if that was the truth, she knew where he would go. Yesterday he had wanted to go to the library, and Rachelle had refused.

It didn't take her long to reach the library because she ran most of the way. When she got close, she slowed down and made her steps as soft as she could. She leaned close to the door.

Armand spoke up, cheerful and casual and unrepentant. "You do realize this is a terrible idea? No matter how much you're getting paid, it's not enough."

She heard the crack of somebody slapping him across the face. "Shut up," a man snarled.

"Really, you should ask your master for more money. And"—his voice caught, then went on, more strained—"you *really* don't want to press that knife any closer."

Rachelle felt terribly sure that the knife was right against his throat, and she cursed herself for not kicking down the door in the first instant. It would take only two heartbeats for her to get across the room, but Armand's throat could be cut faster.

"Why?" It was a different man's voice, younger, brasher. "Should we be afraid of d'Anjou's bitch? She isn't even here."

"No," said Armand. One soft and indifferent syllable. "You

should be afraid of *me*." The words drifted through the air, light and inevitable as feathers. "You should put down your knives and run, because if you kill me, you won't escape, and you won't like your punishment. And I really doubt that you can kill me."

It was a distraction. And by the sound of his voice, the knife wasn't so close now. It was the perfect moment for Rachelle to kick down the door and charge inside.

Or it was the perfect moment to be free of him. All she had to do was stand still for another minute, and the assassins would cut Armand's throat. Despite his bluster, he had no way to stop them. Rachelle would not have to help him deceive anyone else. She would not have to fear him stirring up a mob to kill her.

She suddenly remembered the morning they had met. *If you wanted to hurt me, I couldn't hope to escape.* She remembered his eyes, gray and calm and waiting for her to hurt him. Ever since they met, he had been waiting.

However she hated him, she didn't want to give him that satisfaction. She was going to rescue him.

Then she realized she couldn't move. The air was cold and sweet in her lungs and her limbs would not respond, no matter how she tried. She couldn't see even the shadow of a leaf, but she still felt the power of the Great Forest all around her.

At least one of the men in the library wasn't impressed. He laughed, and said, "Pretty words won't—"

And suddenly, overwhelmingly, there was silence.

Then she was loosed and staggering into the door just as she heard the thuds of falling bodies from inside.

Her hands were still slightly numb; for a moment she scrabbled at the door handle, and then she flung it open.

There had been three men in the room, and they were all collapsed to the floor. Armand sat slumped in a chair between them, and dread sliced through her body, but then he lifted his head and she saw that while he was tied to the chair, he was alive.

"You're late," he said. "You missed all the fun." He was smiling but he looked a little dazed.

Rachelle poked one of the fallen men with her boot. His chest still rose and fell with breathing, but otherwise he didn't stir.

"What happened?" she asked.

"They wanted to question me on my secret plans," said Armand. "They told me they were going to kill me, and then that they would kill me if I didn't tell them everything. They weren't very thoughtful people."

"What happened to *them*?"

He shrugged. "Maybe God heard my prayers."

"Tell me the truth or you stay in the chair. What happened?"

His lips thinned as he met her eyes; then he said quietly, "You felt it just now, didn't you? The Great Forest? I made them see it. I can do that to people, whenever I please, and if they're not strong enough to bear the sight . . ." He shrugged. "They'll recover in time."

She stared at his face—his bland, boring face—and it was more alien than the moon.

"So?" he said. "Are you going to tell d'Anjou I'm not as helpless as he thinks?"

"How can you do that?" Rachelle asked.

He stared at her for a long, suspicious moment; then he said, "Because I can see the Forest. Everywhere, all the time."

"How?"

"That's none of your business."

She grabbed his shoulders. "How can you do that?"

He stared back at her, gray eyes calm. "You are not enough to frighten me, mademoiselle."

He hadn't been marked by a bloodbound. He *could not* have been marked. But then how could he sense the Forest?

Armand let out a little sigh that was almost a laugh and looked away. "It's not a bad chair," he said. "If you'll read aloud to me, I don't think I'll mind staying."

"I'm not going to leave you here," she said.

"Taking me to d'Anjou after all?"

"No." She drew her knife. He didn't move—his eyes didn't even flicker back at her—but his sudden, wary stillness sliced through her. She was sick of being the reason that people were wary.

"You said Prince Hugo found a door above the sun and below the moon. Do you think you could find it too?"

Then he did look at her. "Why? What do you want with it?"

"That is not your concern, monsieur. But if you refuse, I'll tell Erec what you can do and that you need even closer watching. Good luck recruiting worshippers after that."

But the threat seemed to make him relax. His shoulders loosened and he smiled at her as he tilted his head back and said, "Go ahead."

11

Of course she didn't tell Erec. She couldn't, because if Erec knew that Armand had—whatever connection to the Forest it was that he had—then he would want to find a way to use it, either for the King or for himself. And then Rachelle would never get a chance to quietly drag away Armand and make him open the door for her.

She wasn't getting a chance anyway.

"I'm going to kill you," she told Armand that evening. "If you don't help me, I will kill you."

He waited a moment. And then smiled. "That's not a good enough threat, you know."

It wasn't a threat at all. Rachelle had killed once in cold blood; she couldn't do it again. Staring at Armand, she felt sure that he knew she couldn't do it again.

Rachelle was the second-strongest bloodbound in service to the King and she had nothing to threaten with, nothing to bargain with. She could fight a whole pack of woodspawn by herself and win, but she couldn't force one irritating courtier to do her will. All she could do was spend the night searching by herself, then trail after Armand, pretending to care if he lived or died.

Bloodbound didn't need as much sleep as normal humans, but it had been days since she'd slept more than four hours. Her head wouldn't stop aching. It didn't help that there were no gaps in Armand's schedule that day. He dragged her from one court function to another, where people tittered at rumors of failing crops and laughed at the suggestion of Endless Night.

By the time they ended up at the after-dinner party, where the nobles were all wagering at cards, Rachelle was starting to think that Endless Night might not be so bad. At least there would be no giggling. Screams and blood and dying, yes, but no polite little giggles.

The blood would flow across the parquet flooring and soak into the seams of the little wooden panels. The same way the blood had soaked into the floor of Aunt Léonie's cottage.

Rachelle had been hoping that the forestborn would hurt the people around her the same way her own forestborn had once hurt Aunt Léonie. She'd imagined it happening and she had *liked* it. She felt sick.

They were standing near the table where the King played—very badly—with la Fontaine and a gaggle of other nobles. At last, after a round of particularly hideous losses, he flung down his cards with a rattling cough that everyone ignored.

"I've had my fill for the night," he said. "A good game, cards. Trains the mind." He rose and patted Armand on the shoulder; Rachelle suspected she was the only one who saw Armand's wince, and for a moment she felt sorry for him.

"A battlefield of wits," drawled a tall, muscular young man with long dark curls.

Rachelle recognized him: Vincent Angevin, one of the King's nephews and very likely the person sending assassins after Armand. He was also likely the next heir to the throne, if his royal uncle ever got done pretending to be immortal.

"Such a pity you haven't the wherewithal to join us," Vincent went on, looking at Armand's hands, and then ruffled his hair. "But it would hardly be proper for a saint to gamble, would it?"

Two of the ladies at the table giggled. La Fontaine snapped her fan open. Vincent chuckled and slapped Armand's back. "Preach me a sermon when I'm done winning, cousin." He grinned at the room: the lazy, mischievous grin of somebody who knew he could get away with being cruel.

Rachelle had known a boy who smiled like that, back in her village. For years he had charmed all the adults while beating the younger children bloody. Without meaning to, she edged closer to Armand. She was sure she was the only one who saw the very slight way that his chin raised and his shoulders set.

"I haven't heard that card games are a sin," he said. "I'll play a round if Mademoiselle Brinon will hold my cards for me."

"I don't—" Rachelle started.

"Just do what I say." Armand sat himself down at the table. "Well? Will you deal me a hand?"

Vincent smiled expansively. "I can't deny you any consolation, dear cousin. Play with us, if it comforts you."

La Fontaine dealt out the cards. Rachelle picked them up. She could read the numerals well enough, but they were decorated with various other symbols and figures that meant nothing to her.

"Let me see," said Armand, leaning over her shoulder.

"Pity Raoul isn't here," said Vincent. "I seem to remember him always helping you when you got in trouble."

"Where *is* Monsieur Courtavel?" asked one of the ladies. "We all miss him."

Raoul Courtavel was another of the King's illegitimate sons. He was widely considered a contender for the throne, despite his famously not getting along with his father, because he was enormously popular with the people for fighting pirates in the Mare Nostrum. Rachelle did not much care about the pirates—safe trade routes meant nothing when the daylight was *dying*—but at least Raoul Courtavel had never called for the bloodbound to be exterminated. He'd also never tried to recruit any of them as his personal retainers, which Vincent apparently had.

"I believe Raoul is still resting at his country estate," said Armand, "ever since Father told him that he was overworking himself." He looked at the cards, then at the faces of the other players. "Put that one down," he said, pointing at the leftmost card in her hands.

Rachelle never worked out exactly what the rules of the game were, except that some of the cards could be laid down, some could be demanded from another player's hand, and some must be held on to at all costs. But what she realized very quickly was that players were allowed to lie about their hands—except when they weren't—and that successful bluffing was the only way to win.

Armand smiled politely, lied through his teeth, and in ten minutes he had won all the money that everyone else had put down on the table.

"A marvelous conquest," said la Fontaine. "Clearly fortune favors the holy."

"Or the—" Vincent Angevin cut off whatever he'd been about to say. He shoved back his chair instead and bowed stiffly. "Good evening." Then he was gone.

"I do believe that's a miracle itself," said la Fontaine. "Vincent Angevin, leaving the gambling table before dawn." She rapped Armand's silver hand with her fan. "You still have not come to my salon. You will be there tomorrow morning, I command it."

"If the King permits it," said Armand, not looking at Rachelle.

"You too, Mademoiselle Brinon," said la Fontaine. "You must be there."

"I'm his bodyguard," said Rachelle. "Of course I have to follow him."

She stared grimly at the cards scattered across the table and tried not to remember la Fontaine finding her in the King's outer chambers.

"I mean as a guest," said la Fontaine. "I'll insist to my lord, if you need a royal order."

It was probably some bizarre scheme to humiliate her. But she couldn't afford to get in any trouble with the King.

"You can call me a guest if you like," she said.

The next morning, Amélie looked her in the eye and said, "You're going to wear a dress this time. You're going to wear a dress and let me paint your face, and no, you don't get a choice about it."

"I'm not there as a guest," Rachelle muttered.

"Yes, you are," said Amélie. "A page delivered a note last night. She officially invited you, and that means a dress and cosmetics."

"She wants to humiliate me," said Rachelle. "That means it doesn't matter what I wear."

Amélie clapped her hands. "Then you'll just have to be more beautiful than her."

What does it matter? Rachelle thought. *The world is ending and I'm trapped attending parties.*

But then Amélie met her eyes and said quietly, "We had a bargain."

If the world was ending, she owed it to Amélie to keep her promise and let her do what she loved.

And that was how Rachelle ended up sitting in a chair by the table full of little pots and brushes. Amélie, standing beside her, picked up a brush and set it down again. She put two fingers on each of Rachelle's temples and slowly tilted her head from side to side, scrutinizing her face. Then she let go and bit her lip.

"Something wrong?" asked Rachelle.

"The question is," said Amélie, sounding like she had just come to the end of a long speech, "are you brave enough?"

"What?"

"I can't make you beautiful," said Amélie. "I'm going to give you the most beautiful makeup you've ever seen, but if you just sit under it and—and wilt, you'll look pathetic. It's like a sword. If you don't wield it, then it isn't any use to you. And it's all right if you want to look pathetic most of the time, but this is my one chance to show anyone what I can do, so you are *not* going to ruin it. Understood?"

"Do I usually look pathetic?"

"No," said Amélie, "but you do get a look of terror when I talk to you about dresses."

"I'm not . . . I don't know how to be a lady," said Rachelle. "If you wanted that, you should have gotten someone else."

"No," said Amélie. "I don't want anyone else. Just walk into that salon and defy them. Promise?"

"All right," said Rachelle after a moment. The words *I don't want anyone else* drummed through her head, desperately comforting. Amélie didn't know everything Rachelle had done, so it should be no comfort at all to be wanted by her, but it was.

"Good." Amélie nodded sharply. Then she raised her voice and called, "Sévigné!"

The chambermaid—a short, plump woman with a few gray hairs peeking out from under her cap—appeared at Amélie's side, and they had a short, swift discussion in low voices, Amélie frequently jabbing a brush at Rachelle's face to make a point. Then Amélie unbraided Rachelle's hair and first piled it loosely on top of her head, next pulled it all back so tightly her scalp felt stretched. Sévigné clucked her tongue, took hold of Rachelle's hair, and seemed to do exactly the same thing—but it set off another little flurry of discussion.

Rachelle didn't listen to what they said; they were speaking in half sentences about things she didn't understand anyway. She let the patter of their words wash over her. They were both talking as if she weren't there, which was something that normally drove her to distraction. But they were talking about how to use her face and body for a canvas, and it made her feel oddly treasured.

When the consultation was over, Sévigné bustled off while

Amélie went to work with the makeup. She gripped Rachelle's face, tilted it, and started painting on the foundation with quick little strokes like a cat lapping up milk.

The tension unspooled from Rachelle's shoulders and the weariness seeped out of her bones. The Forest and the Devourer stopped mattering. The world had narrowed down to just this: the warm pressure of Amélie's fingers tilting her head. The tickle of the brush. The soft sound of Amélie's lips opening—she was forever clicking her tongue and making faces while she worked, nose wrinkling or mouth scrunching to one side.

Then came the dusting of pearl powder. Then the rouge, which Amélie applied with her fingertips, rubbing it into Rachelle's cheeks. Then the burned clove brushed into her eyebrows to darken them.

"Can you cover the mark?" Rachelle asked abruptly as Amélie finished with her eyebrows.

"No," said Amélie. "If I cake on that much powder, it will just flake off. Besides, the mark matches your dress *and* the patch I'm going to put on your face." She held up a tiny black velvet star. "Did you know there's a language to patches?"

"No," Rachelle said warily. "What does a star mean?"

"Assassin."

"What?"

Amélie laughed. "Actually, it means 'courage.'" She dabbed

glue on the patch, set it on Rachelle's right cheekbone, and then pressed it in with her thumb. "I wouldn't put anything on your face that wasn't true."

"You just covered my face with nineteen kinds of paint," said Rachelle. "I don't think there's anything true left on it."

"Three kinds of paint. Look at me and open your mouth." Rachelle obeyed, and Amélie started to paint rouge on her lips. "And don't ever talk about my art that way. I'm not painting you to hide you. I'm painting you because you're beautiful." She wiped her thumb under Rachelle's lip to clear away a smudge. "There. All done." She handed the mirror to Rachelle. "This is just the beginning."

Once again, a lady stared back from the mirror. She still looked entirely false; but this time Rachelle looked at her and thought, *Amélie believes I deserve to look beautiful*.

It was a strangely intoxicating feeling, and as the preparations went on, she only felt more drunk: the same dizzy exultation, the feeling that her body was lighter than air and no longer quite attached to her.

Sévigné descended upon her, and once she had molded Rachelle's hair into suitable ringlets—muttering all the while about how there wasn't enough time—she looped it up on top of her head with pink ribbons and pearl-ended pins.

The corset was very different from the simple stays Rachelle usually wore under her shirt: not as uncomfortable as she'd expected, but far stranger. It pressed into her ribs but also straightened her spine; though it was maddeningly confining, it felt like it added inches to her height and made her float off the ground.

And then came the dress itself: deep rose silk that fell about her body in luscious folds. The puffed sleeves were slashed to show white silk underneath, and strings of silk flowers tightened the sleeves around her elbows. With all the shifts and petticoats beneath, it was the heaviest garment that Rachelle had ever worn, wrapping her like a suit of armor; yet the neckline dipped wide and low, barely clinging to her shoulders. Not only did it expose more of her breasts than anyone had ever seen, but it showed off to all the world the bloodred star at the base of the throat.

Rachelle looked in the mirror at the star and its echo on her cheek, and she thought, *Amélie says it means courage.*

"Here's your fan," said Amélie, putting it in her hand.

"Thank you," said Rachelle, and went to get Armand. The little arched heels of her shoes gave her steps a strange, rocking rhythm that she'd never felt before.

Armand was waiting in his sitting room, standing with his back to the wall, arms loose at his sides, mouth bunched in a wry half smile.

Erec stood beside him.

"What do you want?" Rachelle demanded, trying desperately not to think of how low her dress was cut and completely failing.

"My lady," he said, stepping forward and bowing. "I am here to escort you to the salon."

"You're not invited," said Rachelle.

"I think you'll find I'm invited most places." He took her hand and kissed it.

She wanted to protest, but he would only laugh. And Rachelle had decided long ago that she could bear the occasional mockery for the sake of his friendship.

"I think you turn up most places, and people can't be bothered to chase you out," she said. "But come along if you please."

12

Of course Erec had to put her hand on his arm so they could make a grand entrance together. Rachelle didn't fight him over it. Once they were inside la Fontaine's sitting room, he would doubtless find five other girls—prettier than her and more elegant as well—and forget her, leaving her in peace.

But when they stepped through the doorway, Rachelle was the one who briefly forgot him. The sitting room was impressive enough by itself: it was quite large, with a ceiling painted like the sky and walls covered in murals of rolling green hills and shepherds. (She thought they must be shepherds because of their crooks, though the lounging, silk-draped youths looked nothing like the actual shepherds she had known. But the other option was bishops, and that seemed even less likely.) La Fontaine, though, had transformed the room into a garden. There were potted trees of every kind: apple and oak, orange and palm. Roses grew among them—southern woodwives used roses in their charms, but Rachelle doubted that la Fontaine knew enough about actual country life for it to be a conscious allusion.

There were no suns or moons painted or sculpted anywhere. She was so used to checking rooms, she hardly noticed she was doing it.

The guests, sitting on little cushioned stools, for a moment really did look like they were figures from the idyllic murals come to life. Then they all turned to stare and whisper behind their fans, and Rachelle remembered that she was an intruder in this perfect, pastoral world. She was a wolf among porcelain sheep, and Erec would probably tell her that ought to make her unafraid, but her skin crawled when she saw their eyes turning to her.

The room flurried to life as five or six of the guests converged on Armand. Rachelle noticed his shoulders tense as they bore down upon him, and for one instant her own body sparked with the readiness to fight—but then he was smiling and nodding to the flock gathered around him, and she realized he had only been preparing himself to charm and lie.

She turned away, feeling sick, and found that la Fontaine had descended upon them.

"My dear Fleur-du-Mal," she said, kissing Erec's cheek, "again you give the lie to your name. Your presence is an unexpected kindness."

"I promised my lady I'd accompany her," said Erec, somehow making it sound as if Rachelle had begged him to come because she could not stand to be parted from him for an hour.

La Fontaine raised pale eyebrows at Rachelle. "And you, my dear, what are we to call you?"

Rachelle had no idea what was the correct courtly thing to answer, but she wasn't ready to admit defeat yet. "Isn't 'mademoiselle' good enough?"

"But of course not," said la Fontaine. "We are no longer in Château de Lune; we stand now in the gentle land of Tendre, where there is neither court nor title, but all dwell in harmony alike." Her voice was such a perfect blend of honey and vinegar that Rachelle had no idea if she adored the idea or mocked it. "Even I, goddess of the realm, am addressed by my name only, and anyone may sit in my presence."

"Goddess," Rachelle said blankly.

"It was my mother, la Belle-Précieuse, who brought Tendre out of nothing," said la Fontaine. "She peopled it with the most charming of this world and left it to me for my only inheritance. As daughter of the Supreme Creatrix, I believe I may lay claim to the word."

"You can certainly claim it," said Erec. "But you might face a challenge or two."

"Gladly," said la Fontaine. "I'll rout them with my beauty for an army and my wits as cavalry. But that does not solve the problem of our nameless darling. Whatever shall we call her?"

"Isn't it obvious?" said Erec. "She wields a sword to protect our people. Surely 'la Pucelle' is the only possible name for such a brave maiden." He said the words with a little ironic smile, as if the obvious difference between Rachelle and the legendary warrior saint was a very elegant joke.

La Fontaine's eyebrows arched exquisitely. "A maiden, after all that time at your side? Truly, a miracle worthy of a saint."

"And yet it would be a miracle if she favored me," said Erec. "Pity me, for even in the land of Tendre I receive no tenderness." He laid a mocking, elegant hand over his heart.

"Yes," said la Fontaine. "I like it. And just think"—she turned back to Rachelle—"you would have your own holy day, without the tiresome work of sainthood."

Rachelle looked at the colorless, glittering gems in la Fontaine's earrings and silently gave up on making Amélie proud of her ability to act like a lady.

"I killed somebody and I'm not sorry," she said, calmly and very distinctly. "I don't think you want me on your altars unless blasphemy is the custom of your kingdom."

There was a moment of grandly awkward silence in which Rachelle noticed that everyone in the room was looking at them, which meant that everybody had been listening. It gave her a certain grim satisfaction.

Then Armand—who had apparently dismissed his flock of worshippers—said cheerfully, "Well, we needn't worry about blaspheming heathen gods. So how about Zisette? Since you have also walked into the Forest and come out again."

Rachelle snorted. Walking out of the Forest was not the most important way that she was like Zisa. But when she met Armand's eyes, there didn't seem to be any hidden mockery in his face. It felt like he wanted her to smile back at him.

"If you must," she said.

"That's as kind an answer as you're likely to get from my lady," said Erec.

"Then come with us, Zisette," said la Fontaine, "and let the land of Tendre teach you kindness."

Rachelle truly doubted that the land of Tendre had much to do with kindness, but she let herself be guided to a little stool with a red silk cushion. Armand sat down at her right. To her left was a tall woman with dark hair and a face like a marble statue's. She turned languidly toward Rachelle and said, "Tell me, what *does* it feel like?"

Rachelle gave her a blank look.

"Oh, how could I be so rude?" said the woman. "Here in Tendre, I am l'Étoile-Polaire, and it is such a delight to meet you,

Zisette. Now please, I am dying to know: what does it feel like to be a bloodbound?"

"I don't know," said Rachelle. "What does it feel like to be a lady?"

There was chatter in other parts of the room—la Fontaine was raising her eyebrows and speaking to an old man—but the people nearby were staring at her, and she knew that any moment they would all start laughing.

"Not as thrilling, I'm sure," said l'Étoile-Polaire. "You have the Great Forest in your blood. Sometimes I think I envy you."

"Darling, you don't envy her," said an older woman who wore an enormous powdered wig. "She has to fight the woodspawn all night."

"Won't she be sorry when Endless Night falls," said a colorless young man with so much lace at his throat it looked like it might strangle him. "Nothing but work, work, work forever after."

"You mean *if* it falls," said the older woman. "We're supposed to keep the sun in the sky by weeping over our sins, aren't we? I think that's what our tiresome Bishop said."

"Weeping is too much trouble." L'Étoile-Polaire sighed. "I'll just have to die in eternal darkness."

All three of them burst into soft, inane laughter that made Rachelle want to scream. They were rich enough to burn lamps all night long; they didn't have to go out on errands when woodspawn were roaming the streets. So they didn't believe in the return of Endless Night. None of the nobility did.

"I don't think I could bear killing things," said a young girl wearing a dress that was the exact same pale yellow as the curls piled atop her head. "Even woodspawn."

"But you forget," said the young man. "She's already killed somebody, the naughty girl." He gave Rachelle a grin that looked like it was trying to be rakish.

"Of course, I did forget," said l'Étoile-Polaire, and once again slowly drifted her gaze back to Rachelle. "Who was it?"

Rachelle stared at them. She had expected to be mocked or scorned. That was how it went in the city: people despised her for being bloodbound, or laughed at her for being a peasant from the north end of nowhere.

She had never dreamed that the court might find her *exotic*.

"I—I don't think it's very nice to ask," said the girl in the yellow dress.

"Come, come, Soleil," said the young man. "It's not as if she's a blushing innocent. She's already said she wasn't sorry."

"And I wouldn't be sorry after killing you either," said Rachelle. "So maybe you shouldn't bother me."

Beside her, Armand let out a soft snort of laughter.

At that moment, one of the servants arrived with a tray of little cakes—the ones, Rachelle supposed, that la Fontaine had mentioned when they first met—and everyone was distracted.

"Oh," said Soleil, turning toward Armand, "aren't you going to eat any of the lovely cakes?"

"No," said Armand, who seemed to have forgotten completely about being a charming liar. Maybe he didn't think Soleil was any use to him, though she was certainly pretty enough.

"Oh, I forgot!" said Soleil. "Your poor hands. I'll feed them to you."

Armand's jaw tightened slightly. "No, thank you."

Soleil, who had already seized a little cake frosted in pink icing, paused. "But why not?"

"Because I'm not hungry." Armand's voice stayed quiet and even, but Rachelle could see his shoulders tensing slightly, and she suddenly remembered all the times she had kept her voice quiet and even while attempting to answer Erec.

"Because," said Erec, suddenly behind them—Rachelle flinched, feeling like she had summoned him—"he's ashamed that he can't feed himself."

He spoke in the light, needling tone that he used to tease Rachelle, so it took her a moment to realize that he'd been speaking of Armand, and to realize *what* he'd said of him.

It took her another moment to realize she was angry.

"But you shouldn't be ashamed," said Soleil. "I think it's so beautiful, how *much* you were willing to sacrifice—I can't imagine it, of course, but when I *try* to imagine it, then I feel like I can be strong too, and—" She bit her lip, blushing. "Please, *please* let me help you."

Armand's mouth flattened.

"Yes, let the girl do you a kindness," said Erec. "Aren't saints supposed to be meek and humble of heart?"

Seemingly encouraged, Soleil shoved the cake forward. "Won't you—"

Rachelle caught her wrist. "Did I mention I'm his bodyguard?" she said. "And I'm not a saint, so I can do what I like."

Armand sighed and reached up with his metal hand to push their hands apart.

"Mademoiselle, you're very kind," he said to Soleil. "But I did not lose my hands for the purpose of making you feel special."

Soleil had gone red, but before she could say anything, la Fontaine clapped her hands once. Everyone in the room fell silent.

"Enough chatter," said la Fontaine. "It is time for stories. And in honor of our guest, I propose that we each tell a tale from the north."

Soleil rose. "If you will excuse me, gracious goddess," she said quietly, "I am not well enough for stories." Then she fled.

"Now you've made her cry," said Erec. "Not so very saintly."

"Now you're talking when our hostess called for silence," said Armand.

"Do you have a tale to share, my dear Fleur-du-Mal?" asked la Fontaine, her voice ringing across the room like a bell.

"No, my dear Fontaine," said Erec.

La Fontaine nodded regally. "Then we shall proceed. You." She nodded at the young man who had called Rachelle a "naughty girl." He scrambled to his feet—he was trying to grin again, but now it just looked sickly—and started a rambling tale of three shepherdesses and a bumblebee who was a prince in disguise.

Rachelle didn't pay much attention. She was too busy watching Armand and thinking. He should have been sitting in la Fontaine's place at the center of the room, everyone wincing and smiling according to what he said. If he had really lied about meeting the forestborn, if he had simply decided to turn his injury into fame, then he would *want* fame. A liar might have too much pride to be hand-fed, but surely he would at least want a pretty girl to declare that he was marvelous and brave.

Unless he wasn't a liar. But what else could he be? Once marked by the forestborn, there was no way to escape. You killed somebody or the mark killed you. There was no other way.

She hoped so much that there was no other way.

The young man stammered to a close. His tale had been nothing like the fireside stories that people told in Rachelle's village, but she didn't think that was why la Fontaine looked at him when he was finished and said, "Very charming." He flinched and retired into a corner.

Then l'Étoile-Polaire stood like a weary flower. "I believe *I* can honor our guest," she said. "Once upon a time, a prince and a princess lived in a silver tower with domes of gold and parapets of diamond. Every morning they ate berries and cream, and their days were all delightful. . . ."

The story wound slowly on, with many digressions about the delights of the palace and the prince's horse and the princess's dresses. Eventually, the two children contrived to get themselves lost in the woods.

And that was when the Great Forest awoke in la Fontaine's salon.

Or perhaps, the Forest dreamed about them. It certainly wasn't a full manifestation; Rachelle hardly felt it at all, only saw it, fleetingly and from the corners of her eyes. It started with the murals: they acquired depth and shadows, the trees growing thicker, vines winding up the legs of the shepherds. Dim animal shapes lurked among the hills, and the shepherds' singing mouths seemed to be screaming.

Until she looked straight at them, and then the murals were flat, and bright, and pretty again.

She might have thought she was imagining it. But as l'Étoile-Polaire told—with a great many flourishes—how the prince and princess stumbled upon a cottage where a mad old woman put the prince in the cage but adopted the princess and set her tasks, Rachelle started to see movement. The potted plants swayed in a phantom breeze. Flowers blossomed on the tile floor. Translucent deer peeked through ghostly foliage, startled, and fled.

It was the strongest manifestation of the Forest that she had seen here yet, and her first thought was that the door must be here. She had only given the room a cursory examination when she went in. Now she scrutinized it slowly and carefully. There were no suns or moons anywhere.

But then why was the Forest appearing? Had the protections on the Château simply grown *that* weak?

Insubstantial rose vines climbed down her shoulder. Rachelle startled at the same moment Armand drew a sharp breath beside her, and then they met each other's eyes.

So he really did see the Great Forest. That was good to know.

He raised his eyebrows a fraction. She shrugged. It didn't feel like the Forest was prepared to break through and menace them—there was no least presence of woodspawn—it was simply as if the Forest were *thinking* of them.

"—and then," l'Étoile-Polaire went on, "the old woman believed that the princess loved her, and said that she might help take the prince out of his cage and bake him in a pie—"

The half-seen Forest trembled around her, and Rachelle suddenly realized what story l'Étoile-Polaire was telling. And maybe why the Forest was listening.

"No," she said. "That's not how it goes."

Everybody looked at her, including the eyes in the ghostly foliage, and Rachelle had to strangle a bizarre urge to giggle. They all thought she was shocking, when they were sitting in the middle of the Forest.

Was anybody ever out of the Forest?

"Excuse me?" said l'Étoile-Polaire.

"You're telling the story of Tyr and Zisa, aren't you?" said Rachelle.

"If you must put it so bluntly, yes."

"You're telling it wrong." Rachelle heard a soft snort from her side: Armand had a wrist pressed to his face to smother laughter.

"I grant you, the old chronicles probably mentioned the ruffles a little less," said la Fontaine, as lightly as if there were not bluebirds with heart-shaped faces sitting on her shoulders.

"Zisa didn't win the forestborn's favor by bringing them nectar from a hundred flowers. She killed her parents and cut out their hearts, and so she became a bloodbound."

Everybody was still staring at her, and Armand was still smothering silent laughter. The Forest was still listening. It was, possibly, the worst idea in the world to tell this story when the Forest was listening, but she couldn't resist. They were all so oblivious, and Armand was laughing beside her.

"Then the forestborn trusted her enough that she was able to come with them for the sacrifice. But when they had summoned the Devourer so they could offer Tyr, Zisa tricked the Devourer into letting her walk into his stomach twice and steal the sun and moon."

"How charming," said la Fontaine. The birds on her shoulders shivered and were gone.

"Zisa meant to kill him after," said Rachelle. "But before she could, the Devourer possessed her. So Tyr killed her with Joyeuse just as the sun rose for the first time. The end."

L'Étoile-Polaire's voice was icy. "Are you saying that the first of all our kings was a murderer?"

"That is the tale as they tell it in the north," Rachelle said blandly.

"Don't judge him too harshly," said Erec. He was watching Rachelle with his familiar smile; if he had noticed the Forest, he gave no sign of it. "He would hardly be a good king if he let a patricide share his throne."

"And hardly a good man if he killed his sister," said la Fontaine. "A grievous dilemma." She sounded precisely as distressed as if she'd been given cakes with the wrong sort of icing.

"But he didn't," said Armand.

La Fontaine raised an eyebrow. "You have another version to tell?"

"No," said Armand. "If her tale is true, Tyr didn't kill his sister. He struck down the Devourer that had hidden itself inside her."

Rachelle looked at him. He was no longer laughing; his elbows rested on his knees as he leaned forward, his eyebrows slightly drawn together. He seemed simply and earnestly interested in the conversation.

"Do you think that sort of detail matters?" she asked.

His mouth twitched back toward a smile. "When it comes to killing your family, I imagine every detail matters."

"Your father will be glad to hear that," said Erec, and Armand's lips flattened.

Something tightened in Rachelle's chest; she didn't know if it was envy, or amusement, or irritation. "And do you think," she asked, "that because Tyr didn't want his sister dead, somehow he didn't kill her? Do you think Zisa didn't really kill her parents, just because she *meant* to save her brother?"

Bloody-handed Zisa, they called her in the village, and said that on moonless nights she forgot her quest was done and cut out the hearts of anyone foolish enough to wander the forest alone. They whispered of the sacrifices that were offered to her in the ancient heathen days, when people worshipped her as a goddess. She had won them the sun and moon, but she had become a monster.

For a moment, the mural showed a shadowy girl with two bleeding hearts in her hands. Then Rachelle blinked and it was gone.

"To the victor, the spoils," said Erec, glancing at her in conspiratorial irony. "And also the pardon for all misdeeds."

"No," said Armand. His voice was soft but resolute. "I think Tyr was right and Zisa was wrong and neither one was lucky. Do you think that doing the right thing will always be pretty?"

For one moment, her throat clogged in reflexive fury, because what right did he have to mock her by pretending that *he* knew about darkness and hard choices—

Except he was still looking at her with that simple, open gaze. His head had tilted a little to the side, and his lips were slightly parted. He looked like she was a code he was trying to decipher.

He wasn't mocking her. He *cared* about this question. Out of everyone in the room, he was the only one who cared.

"I think sometimes there is no right thing," said Rachelle. "What should Zisa have done? Left her brother a captive waiting to be killed and left all mankind enslaved to the forestborn, just so she could pride herself on her clean hands? Or do you think Tyr would have been saved by a miracle?"

"No," said Armand.

"Then *what should she have done*?"

His mouth scrunched unhappily, but he didn't look away. Didn't laugh. Did not pretend that anything was all right.

She realized that she actually wanted to know his answer.

"I don't know," he admitted softly.

She felt like she had just flung herself off a roof and was pitching downward through the air. "So you know what's wrong but you don't know what's right? What use is that?"

"Well," said Armand, "it narrows down the options, anyway."

"That's not an answer."

"And at least I know there is an answer, even if I'm going to die without finding it."

"You're a saint. Isn't God supposed to tell you these things?"

And then he gave her the familiar, razor-gleam smile that he used to defy her. "Yes. Right after he grows my hands back."

They stared at each other a moment longer, and Rachelle realized that her mouth was inexorably twisting into a smile.

She wished, suddenly and with her whole heart, that she could make him want to help her. But whether he was a saint or a fraud, what could she ever have to offer him?

IN A CERTAIN VALLEY, BETWEEN THREE LOW hills, there was a marsh. Nothing lived or grew there: no rushes, no moss, no fish, no birds. There was only soft, dark clay, and pale tendrils of mist, and a multitude of cold little pools.

And bones. A hundred thousand bones and more. For here was where the forestborn threw the spent husks of the Devourer's vessels.

Zisa walked among the pools, bones rustling beneath her bare feet. She picked one up, and asked it, "Who are you?"

The bone sang to her:

"My mother, she killed me,
My father, he ate me.
I once had a name,
But now I have none."

And so sang every bone she asked.

Back and forth Zisa wandered the marsh, sliding into pools, clawing through the mud, and asking every bone its name. Until at last, near the very center, she found a bone that sang,

"My sister, she killed me,
My sister, she ate me.
My sister, I loved her,
And her I remember."

"Tell me," said Zisa, "what was your sister's name?"

"She was Joyeuse," said the bone. "But she offered me to the Devourer, and I do not know what happened to her after."

Then Zisa cried out, "Tell me, bones. Which one of you was named Joyeuse?"

But there was no answer.

Again, Zisa cried, "I command you, bones, to tell me: which one of you offered your brother as a sacrifice?"

From the farthest edge of the marsh, a tiny, dry voice sang out:

"My brother, I killed him,
My brother, I ate him.
My brother, he loved me,
Too late have I loved him."

Zisa found the other bone and kissed it. "Tell me, Joyeuse," she said. "What was your brother's name?"

"His name was Durendal," said the bone.

"Tell me, bones," said Zisa. "Would you like to destroy the Devourer?"

Near the end of the salon, one of Erec's lackeys turned up to whisper a message that made him rise swiftly, kiss Rachelle's hand, bow to the entire company, and leave. Doubtless it was time for him to arrest someone, or else meet a particularly beautiful lady.

So Rachelle and Armand were able to walk back by themselves, and as soon as they were away from the biggest crowds, Armand drew her into a small alcove.

"Tell me the truth," he said softly, so that the servants standing near couldn't hear them. "Why do you want to find that door?"

He was a liar. She knew he was a liar, but right now he looked as simply and wholeheartedly earnest as he had in the salon, arguing about when it was right to stab your sister through the heart.

So she decided to tell him a bit of the truth.

"To protect Amélie," she said. His eyebrows drew together. "My friend," she added hastily. "The girl who applies my cosmetics."

"I know her name," said Armand. "But that's not an answer."

She shrugged. "That's what you're getting. Help me, and you'll find out the rest."

They regarded each other silently for a few moments.

"Why haven't you threatened Raoul?" he asked.

"What?" asked Rachelle.

"Raoul Courtavel. The only member of the royal house I care about." He was almost whispering, to keep from being overheard; in the small alcove, they were standing practically shoulder to shoulder. "Why haven't you threatened him to make me cooperate?"

He was looking at her directly, defiantly, but his body was tense, as if he were bracing himself for when she attacked.

Rachelle felt suddenly sick.

"I'm a monster and murderer," she said quietly, "but I'm not going to kill your half brother to make you help me. I don't want to kill anyone. I never wanted to be a monster either. That is the *last* thing I ever wanted. But we don't always get what we want, and—and—" She managed to choke back the flow of words. She was humiliatingly certain that she had been about to beg him, to say *please, please, just help me.*

"All right," said Armand. "I'll help you."

Rachelle stared. She had been concentrating so hard on not pleading with him that it took her a moment to understand what he'd said.

"You will?" she finally said, and hoped she didn't sound too relieved.

He grinned. "I suppose I've got nothing to lose. And I don't believe I'm supposed to be anywhere else this afternoon."

Rachelle nodded, feeling dizzy. "As soon as I change out of this dress."

Half an hour later, Rachelle was back in her normal hunting clothes and they were striding down the hallway together.

"I wish the story was a little more exact than 'above the sun, below the moon,'" said Rachelle. "Every surface in this place is covered in the sun and moon. It's not helpful."

"I've been thinking about that," said Armand. "Looking at the decoration's useless because every room in the Château's been redecorated, oh, at least twice in the last hundred years."

"How do you know?" she asked.

"Everybody knows that," Armand said easily, then looked at her. "At least, everybody whose mother was banished from the court and comforted herself with creating doll-sized models of the Château," he amended. "So I can assure you that while parts of the building are quite old, none of the rooms look the same as they did in Prince Hugo's day."

"That's why you're going to use your gift," said Rachelle.

"Yes," said Armand, "but first we're going to the library."

"Why?" she asked. "You think the door is in there?"

"No," he said calmly, "but there are books in there, and a lot of them are chronicles or memoirs. There might be something that could help."

"I thought you could see the Forest."

He sighed. "Yes, but it's not hung with signs saying, 'This way to the secret door.' I would probably see something if we walked right past the door, but as you might have noticed, this is a rather large Château and it would take us a while to walk through all the rooms."

"As if reading all the books would be any faster," Rachelle muttered. Just the thought of trying to puzzle through book after book made her head hurt. Aunt Léonie had taught her to read when she became her apprentice, but she had never been very good at it. "Don't you think that if the door's location were written down, somebody else would have found it already?"

"I don't think it's written down," said Armand. "I think maybe some hints are written down, which nobody would have paid any attention to because nobody is interested in Prince Hugo except the people on my mother's estate. And you."

His words made sense. But in the end, they weren't what made her give in. It was the memory of Armand leaning forward as he argued about Tyr and Zisa. Everything he said had been foolish and sanctimonious and wrong, but he had been the only person in that room who *cared*.

"All right," she said. "If you think you can find it that way, then try. But you're doing the reading."

The library was probably the most modest room in the entire Château, or at least the most modest room that any of the nobility would be caught dead in. There were murals on the ceiling, but the bookshelves lining the walls were made of plain wood. Spurs of lower bookshelves ran out from the walls, dividing the room into seven bays on each side. Afternoon sunlight streamed through the windows.

Armand strode halfway down the room, stopped, and peered intently at the shelves. He traced his hand along the spines of the books, fingers glinting in the sunlight, and then came to a stop at a fat red book. Rachelle stepped forward to pull it off the shelf for him, but before she could, he had tipped it back with his finger and caught it—awkwardly but securely—between his forearms.

"What's that?" asked Rachelle.

"It's the diary of a lady who lived at the court a hundred years ago," said Armand. "Madame du Choissy. She was the niece of the king, but she later married a minor nobleman and disappeared into the countryside."

There was a table in the center of the room; he set the book down with a thump, and Rachelle stepped closer with the lamp.

"And how does that help us?" she asked.

"She was obsessed with legends of the Great Forest." Armand flipped the cover of the book open. "And legends surrounding the royal line. If there were any more tales about Prince Hugo in those days, she would know them."

His eyes were already tracing the text of the book; his voice had gone vague and distracted. He looked and sounded exactly like he was absorbed in looking for an answer, and the very innocence in the set of his shoulders made suspicion worm through Rachelle's stomach.

The book was handwritten in old, elaborate letters. He could claim the pages said anything he chose, and she'd never know the difference.

She leaned closer. "How convenient that you knew about that specific book just as soon as we needed help."

"Mm," said Armand.

Her hands slammed down on the table beside him. "How did you know about it?"

He looked up then. A strand of his pale brown hair had fallen between his eyes—he didn't wear it neatly curled like so many men of the court. It made him look more real, even now, when he was wearing the bland expression that she had learned was his armor.

"Because I was reading her diary last time I was at Château de Lune," he said. "Right up until I met a forestborn and got a little bit distracted."

"You went to Château de Lune and spent your time in the library?"

"Nearly every day," said Armand. "I learned pretty quickly that memorizing my mother's library hadn't actually taught me how to act in a court, and all the lessons she gave me were twenty years old. La Fontaine was the only person who didn't laugh at me."

"And then you taught them all a lesson."

His mouth quirked. "I really don't think anyone at court has learned anything. Are you done being suspicious now, or do you want to search me for deadly weapons?"

"You are a weapon," Rachelle muttered, remembering the adoration of the people at his audience and the growing resentment she saw in the streets of Rocamadour every day.

"True enough." His voice had gone colorless; he looked down at the table. After a moment, he asked, "How is finding that door going to help you? Are you having trouble getting into the Forest on your own?"

"If I asked," she said quietly and distinctly, "the Great Forest would open up to me this instant, and I could walk into it and have the forestborn finish making me into one of them."

"Then are you trying to escape them?"

He looked up at her again. Sunlight dappled his face, catching at his cheekbones and glowing through his eyelashes. She couldn't read his expression, but she almost thought he looked hopeful.

"Don't imagine," she said, "that I am anything so kind as you pretend to be."

If he really was a saint, if he was fool enough to have hope, then she was going to destroy it. The kind of hope that saints had didn't exist, and she wanted to ruin him. She wanted to drag him into darkness and crush and rend and break him, until all the hope went out of his eyes and there was nothing, nothing, nothing left for anyone to hope.

The air was sweet and cold on her skin. Like the air in the Great Forest.

She turned away abruptly. "Keep reading," she said, and strode toward the other end of the library. Her joints felt slick and shaky. The hunger for destruction was gone, but she felt hollowed out in its absence.

It was the hunger for the Great Forest. The hunger to become one of the forestborn. The hunger to become more and infinitely more like the Devourer, until there was nothing left in her that remembered being human.

Someday she would lose herself to it. She had always known

this. She had mostly stopped fearing it. But now she was almost sick with fear, because she couldn't lose herself when she was so close, when she finally had a chance to fight the Devourer and win.

Her fingernails dug into her palms. *I won't,* she thought. *I won't.*

She was at the door now. She leaned her head against the carved wood and sighed.

Somebody drew a breath from the other side of the door.

She didn't think. She flung the door open—felt it bang against the person—and lunged out into the hallway, drawing her sword. But the door blocked her view for a crucial moment, so she only caught a glimpse of somebody tall—probably a man—dodging into a side passage.

She nearly ran after him, but she couldn't very well leave Armand behind.

Armand. She whirled around, half expecting to see him surrounded by armed men, but he was still sitting at the table, looking up at her curiously.

"What was that?" he asked.

"Somebody standing outside the door to listen." Rachelle grabbed the lamp off the table and starting inspecting the library. Her back prickled, but nobody was hiding in the shadows among the shelves.

"Oh." Armand shrugged and looked back at the book.

"Probably an assassin, or somebody who wanted to kiss my feet." He sounded bored.

Rachelle reached the opposite side of the library and swept open the door on that end. Nobody there either.

"Have there been a lot of them?" she asked.

He didn't look up. "You saw the crowd at my audience."

"Assassins, I mean."

"Five attempts. No, six, counting yesterday. My cousin Vincent *really* doesn't like me."

"How do you know he's the one?" asked Rachelle. "Maybe it's Raoul Courtavel."

Armand's mouth tightened; when he spoke again, his voice was sharp and precise. "You know quite well it can't be Raoul."

"Why not?" Rachelle asked curiously. She hadn't expected him to be so offended.

He stared at her for a moment. "Raoul is the only child of the royal house who's never hated me," he said. "Before or after. He would never do that to me. And I would never do anything to hurt him. That's why Vincent wants me dead. He knows that if the King died without naming an heir, I'd throw my support behind Raoul. And unlike the King, Vincent is too shortsighted to realize that killing me would cause riots."

"You don't seem terribly worried," said Rachelle.

Again he paused, looking at her as if he were trying to puzzle out a riddle. Then he smiled and said, "Well, I'm sure you won't let anyone kill me till you have a chance to do it first."

She smacked his head lightly. "Just keep reading."

So he read, and she watched him. She had wondered how he could possibly turn the pages with blunt metal fingers that didn't move. Sometimes the pages would start to drift up on their own, and he would simply slide his fingers under to turn them. But mostly he used the little finger on his right hand—because, while the other fingers just had half-circles indented in them to look like fingernails, the little finger actually had a thin metal plate that stuck out a fraction beyond the fingertip. It was just enough for him to slide it under the corner of a page and lift it. Sometimes he caught the next five pages by accident. Then he wrinkled his nose and tried again.

He was on his third try with a page when he suddenly stopped and looked at her. "What?"

Rachelle felt vaguely embarrassed, but there wasn't much for her to do besides stare at him.

"Why's it on your little finger?" she asked.

"Because it was cheapest when I bribed the jeweler," Armand said. He tried again, and this time caught the page he wanted. "And least likely to be noticed," he went on, sounding faintly amused as he turned the page. "My father doesn't like me having useful things."

There was a butcher in Rocamadour who had lost his right hand—while chopping roasts for a duke, he liked to tell his customers—and had replaced it with a hook. Rachelle had seen him use the hook to tie up packages with string. She thought of that as she watched Armand laboriously turn the next page. Somehow she'd always imagined that he had demanded the silver hands out of vanity.

She had imagined a lot of things about Armand, and none of them seemed to be true now. And none of the things she had actually learned made sense.

He could see the Great Forest all the time. She had never heard of anyone who could do that, bloodbound or woodwife. To have that power, he must have been touched by the Forest somehow.

But if he really had met a forestborn, if he really had been marked, then how did he survive?

It took him over an hour, but he did find an answer. The bells had just tolled four when Armand looked up and said, "The wine cellars."

"What?" Rachelle turned; she had been at the other side of the room, slowly weaving through a sword form.

"Listen. 'It baffles me not that my cousin would risk her reputation in a rendezvous, but that she would attempt it in the wine cellars; for I have heard it said that the ghost of Prince Hugo still walks those corridors, searching for the way home.' "

Rachelle snorted. "Clearly the court hasn't changed in a hundred years. But just because somebody once claimed to see his ghost there, doesn't mean it's where he disappeared."

"It's a place to start, anyway," said Armand. "And it makes sense; those cellars are one of the oldest parts of the Château."

He was smiling; he seemed genuinely excited about hunting for the door. Without meaning to, Rachelle found the edge of her own mouth turning up, and a tiny shiver of excitement growing in her own heart.

It might be nothing. But it was more of a clue than she'd ever had before.

She'd try anything to find Joyeuse.

"Then let's go look," she said.

14

The problem was not getting down to the royal wine cellars. Rachelle had the authority to go most places in the Château. All she needed to do was ask a footman, and they were shown the way.

The problem was getting there without an entourage of onlookers. They got enough attention just walking through the public areas of the Château; once they stepped into the servants' corridors, nobody could look away.

Rachelle knew that they could just wait until the middle of the night, and sneak down under cover of darkness. But she didn't want to wait. Now that she finally had a hope of finding Joyeuse, she couldn't stand to wait another hour.

So instead, she resorted to telling the truth. Almost.

"Please keep everyone out of the cellars," she said to the gaping majordomo. "In order to secure the safety of the Château, I must perform an inspection."

"Of course," he said dazedly, and then seemed to notice the sword hanging at her side. "But—but why are you bringing Monsieur Vareilles?"

Armand smiled self-deprecatingly. "I promised I'd go with her, to lend whatever help I can."

There was going to be gossip. Erec would hear and doubtless tease her. But if she had Joyeuse in her hand, she wouldn't much care what happened after.

The wine cellars were long, low tunnels, their sloping walls paved in the same cobblestones as their floors. The air was cold and still, with an absolute, muffled quiet; even Rachelle's boots hardly made any noise against the floors.

"I'm surprised they obeyed so easily," said Rachelle.

"You offered to protect them from the Forest," said Armand. "Everyone's afraid of it except the nobility. And some of them are too, they just won't admit it."

"So instead they turn to treason," she said.

"Or saints. I'm sure the King will find a way to outlaw that as well, soon."

Rachelle snorted. "That was a nice little lie you spun for them. Do many people think you can bless the Great Forest away with a wave of your hand?"

"That was a nice little lie *you* spun for them," said Armand. "A pity you aren't actually trying to protect them."

She caught her breath in anger, then remembered that she had not actually ever told him that she was trying to find Joyeuse and save the world from the Devourer.

"How do you know I'm not?" she said.

"I don't know, are you?" He was turned away from her, so she couldn't see his face, but his voice was light and teasing. It shouldn't have felt like a fishhook between her ribs.

For one moment, she wanted to tell him the truth. She also wanted to slam him against the wall and scream at him to be silent. Instead, she asked him evenly, "Do you see anything?"

"Moss." The light, easy tone of his voice didn't waver. "And flowers with teeth."

"Well, the moss isn't real." She peered at the stone walls. "Maybe a little of it's real."

He laughed. "Be careful of the flowers, then."

A chamber split off from the main tunnel; they looked inside and saw the racks of wine bottles gleaming in the lantern light.

"Anything?" she asked.

Armand strode forward into the chamber and looked around. He was truly *looking*, she realized: he scrutinized the room in every direction, and his shoulders slumped slightly before he turned back to her and said, "Nothing."

No matter what he thought of her, he was trying to help her.

She hadn't met anyone that foolish since Amélie.

"Did you really mean that?" she asked. "About supporting Raoul Courtavel?"

"Are you shocked that I'd imagine there could be a king after my beloved father, or that I'd want someone on the throne besides myself?"

"I'm curious," said Rachelle, "why you even care."

Armand laughed then: sudden, wild snickers that made his shoulders hunch and shake. He laughed and laughed and laughed.

"Whatever it is," Rachelle said after a few moments, "can't be that amusing."

He had leaned against the wall now, and he looked back at her with a grin. "Believe me, it is exactly that amusing. However you interpret it." Then he licked his lips and straightened up, composing his face. "If you want to know why I'd like to see Raoul on the throne, it's because he's the only possible heir that doesn't hate me."

"The rest didn't like being related to a saint?" asked Rachelle.

"I mean when we were young," he said, turning away from her. "When I was nothing. My mother was exiled from the court, you know, but she would visit other nobles at their estates sometimes. She particularly liked to visit relatives of the King. Raoul was the only one who didn't hate me, and he was also the only one who spent more time reading the chronicles of past kings than chasing after scullery maids. And since then, he's become the only one to drive the pirates back into the Mare Nostrum. So yes, I would rather see him king than anyone else alive today. But none of that's going to matter, is it?"

"No," said Rachelle, because as much as the common folk might hope or Vincent Angevin might fear, Armand would never get any say in the next king. Not unless he raised a peasant army in bloody rebellion, and she realized—with a sudden, hollow shiver—that she didn't believe he would do that.

And the succession wouldn't matter at all if the Devourer returned to eat the sun and moon.

They went on. They kept looking. And finally they got to the end of the wine cellar.

They found nothing.

"I'm sorry," said Armand, when they stood in the last corner of the cellar, yet another rack of wine gleaming before them. "I don't see anything."

"That's not possible," said Rachelle. "There *has* to be something." But she was already remembering how fragile their suppositions had been to begin with. Because somebody a hundred years ago said that Prince Hugo's ghost might haunt the cellar, he must have found the door and died down here? It was absurd.

She didn't give up right away, of course. They went over the cellars again and again. Rachelle pressed her hands to the walls and reached for any hidden charms a hundred times.

None of it made a difference. They found nothing at all.

The next day, the King decided that he wanted to go hunting, and he must have *all* his favorite people with him, including his beloved son Armand. So they had to get up barely past dawn and join a seething crowd of people, horses, and dogs that spent most of the morning ranging through the grounds.

Rachelle hated every moment of it. The evening before, Erec had come to tease her and ask why she had needed to take a saint into a wine cellar, followed by a torrent of clever insinuations that she couldn't even decipher, so all she could do was glare at him in silence. Afterward, once the hallways were dark and empty, she had dragged Armand out to explore the Château again. But they had no direction, so they wandered for hours without learning anything. When Armand started leaning against the wall and dozing off whenever she stopped to examine a room, she had to give up for the night.

Now she was trapped again, playing the court's wearisome game. And she hated it. She hated the sunlight pounding into her eyes. She hated the laughing, chattering nobles who thought the sunlight would last forever. She hated Erec, who kept smirking at her.

Most of all, she hated Armand, because she had really believed that his idea about the library and the wine cellar might work.

Worse: she couldn't stop seeing him.

She was supposed to watch him. But now she kept noticing every detail: his embroidered cuffs shifting against his silver wrists. The sliver of pale throat visible above his collar. The peculiar way he planted himself when he stood, as if bracing for a heavy wind. Even sitting on a horse, his shoulders had the same stubborn set.

He still smiled at the lords and ladies who talked to him, but now she noticed there was something wry to the expression. Sometimes he would draw out a word a little longer or clip it off a little shorter than she had expected, as if a bit of his thoughts had bled through. As if his thoughts were something separate and lonely that had no place in the role he was playing.

At noon, there were pavilions and baskets of food and jugs of wine. The day had grown hot, so it was a relief to sit down in the shade; Rachelle overheard several ladies complaining about the heat and then giggling as they loudly wished that there really *would* be an Endless Night.

La Fontaine drew Armand away to sit with her and the King, and Rachelle would have followed, but somebody grabbed her shoulder.

There was an instant where she nearly drew her sword. Then she turned, and there was Vincent Angevin.

"Don't be afraid," he said. "I just wanted to meet you. Won't you sit down with me?"

Everyone was sitting down around them. Rachelle supposed that the next hour was going to be horrible no matter what, so she sat down next to him on one of the rugs that the servants had thrown down.

"Tell me, is it very boring to guard my cousin all day long?" he asked.

"Not as boring as I'd like," she said. "Especially with the assassins that keep attacking."

Vincent didn't seem the slightest bit disturbed by her remark. "Poor Armand." He sighed. "Nobody ever liked him much. Except Raoul, who never could stop feeling sorry for the oddest people."

"I don't like *you* much," said Rachelle, and instantly regretted being so blunt.

Vincent grinned. "You're so pretty when you're resentful," he said, and pinched her cheek.

Nobody had pinched her cheek since she was ten. For one

moment, she couldn't believe it had happened, until the pair of ladies sitting nearby started giggling. Vincent's eyes were crinkled up with laughter.

"If you could see your face," he said, in a genial voice that invited all the world to laugh with him.

Rachelle gave him her most balefully blank look. "I'm a murderer. Do you really think you ought to upset me?"

"But that's what makes it so *exciting*. Will she kiss me or will she kill me—I think every man secretly wants to play that game."

But she couldn't kill him, any more than she could have refused to accompany Armand on the hunt. She had to keep pretending she was a part of this court. She had to keep playing their game, and there was only one role for her.

The nearby ladies were giggling again, no doubt delighted that they got to watch Vincent Angevin make a conquest of a bloodbound.

Her face burned. She thought: *You murdered your own aunt. Do you really deserve dignity?*

Then one of his hands dropped to rest on her thigh.

"Excuse me," said Armand, "but I need Mademoiselle Brinon right now."

"You'll have to wait your turn," Vincent started, but Armand was already sitting down beside Rachelle.

"The sunlight has given me a terrible headache," he said. "May I rest my head in your lap?"

It was such a bizarre request, it took Rachelle a moment to believe he had really said it. "Yes," she said.

"Thank you," said Armand, and in one fluid movement, he lowered his head into her lap and closed his eyes, as calmly as if there weren't people staring and whispering.

Rachelle was caught in a kind of stupefied surprise, like the smudged colors that would hang in her vision after staring at a fire.

Vincent laughed nervously. "Of all the strange—" He reached toward her, but now Rachelle had an excuse to take action. She caught his wrist in a grip so tight he gasped.

"I'm afraid I can't let you disturb him," she said blandly. "Maybe we can talk later."

"Of course," said Vincent, sounding rather strangled. She released him and he scrambled to his feet and stalked away.

"Is he gone?" Armand asked softly.

"Yes," Rachelle muttered. "I didn't need you to save me."

"I wouldn't dream of it. But some of the ladies wouldn't stop talking about my marvelous virtue. I got tired of it."

"So you needed a little defilement?" she asked.

"I needed," he said flatly, "to be left alone."

"You didn't seem to mind their adoration before."

He sighed, and his breath stirred against her face. "I suppose the heat is getting to me."

"Do you need to take your hands off?" she asked, remembering the audience.

"No," he said.

And then they were silent. Rachelle dared a look around; a few people were still staring, but most were chatting with each other now. La Fontaine leaned against the King and fed him grapes; a quartet of musicians played violins. Erec lounged against a nearby tree; when their eyes met, he raised his eyebrows. Her face burned, and she looked away.

She couldn't look at Armand. But she couldn't ignore his warm weight in her lap. She felt him shifting slightly as he breathed; it was as unnervingly comforting as when Amélie painted cosmetics on her face.

The song ended, and there was a smattering of polite applause. Then the King said to Erec, "You look bored, d'Anjou."

"Do I, sire?" Erec asked languidly.

Armand sighed and sat up. He pushed a lock of hair out of his face, and Rachelle's fingers twitched with the impulse to smooth it back for him.

"I confess I'm bored as well. Propose an amusement for us." The King leaned his chin on his hand and surveyed the glittering crowd that waited on his every move.

Rachelle vaguely remembered Erec having once told her about the King's penchant for demanding a courtier to decide on his next amusement. It was supposed to be a test of elegance and taste. At the time, she'd just been grateful that, unlike Erec, she'd never have to attend court herself.

"A duel," Erec said promptly, and Rachelle's stomach lurched.

"I have heard that I outlawed dueling," said the King.

"Most wisely," said Erec. "But what you forbade were duels of honor carried out to the death. I propose a duel to three strikes only, myself against Rachelle Brinon. Any blood that we shed, you have already sentenced to fall."

Rachelle bolted to her feet. "Sire," she said, and then stopped. She needed a clever retort, a way to turn his suggestion into a joke that nobody would dare to take seriously enough for the duel to go forward.

"Well?" The King raised an eyebrow.

"I'm not good enough to perform before you," she said finally. That was at least flattering.

"She brawls often enough with the Bishop's bloodbound, and bests her half the time," said Erec.

"But—" said Rachelle.

"She's just shy," Erec went on. "We have a wager between us, you see, that the next time we fight, the loser must give the winner a kiss."

And he winked at her.

Rachelle's face heated. *That's not true,* she wanted to yell, but she knew that protestations would only seem like proof, and Erec would just make her look even more ridiculous.

Armand was still sitting right behind her. She didn't dare glance back at him.

"Really?" said the King. "How charming. Duel her, then, and may the best one of you enjoy the spoils of war."

Rachelle bowed numbly. "Yes, Your Majesty."

A minute later, they had cleared a wide space in the lawn and Rachelle stood a pace apart from Erec, her sword drawn.

"Why did you have to lie to him?" she demanded quietly.

"But, my lady, how can you object? Surely either way, the victory is yours."

"I hate you," she muttered, and knew instantly that it was the wrong thing to say, because his eyes crinkled with suppressed laughter.

"Excellent." He smacked her shoulder lightly. "Then you'll fight better and have the delight of disgracing me before the King."

He knew she wouldn't. He knew she had never been as good at sword fighting as he was. Her brawling with Justine was just that—wild, enthusiastic violence for the sheer satisfaction of throwing each other across the room.

Erec had all the precision and control she had always lacked. When he fought a duel, he was perfectly capable of slicing off his opponent's buttons one by one, accompanying each swipe of his sword with a witty remark. He wouldn't hurt her, but he would cheerfully slice her dignity to pieces and make the court laugh at her.

And she would have to pretend to laugh along with them, or only look more ridiculous.

They saluted each other, took two steps away, and turned back. They lowered their swords until they barely touched, half-way down the blade.

You can fight him, Rachelle thought, *if you stay calm. He's counting on you to get angry.*

The rustle and mutter of the crowd faded away. Erec filled up her world: his narrowed eyes, the glint of his sword, the way he leaned his weight just slightly to the left.

"Now," said the King, though Rachelle only realized she had heard the word a moment later, so absorbed she had been in watching Erec and trying to gauge how he would strike.

When he moved, it was barely more than a twitch of his sword. Rachelle parried too hard, and left herself wide open for the tip of his sword to slap against her chest.

"First point," he said.

He wants me angry, Rachelle thought, circling him. *He wants me angry so I'll make mistakes.*

She tried to keep calm. But he kept attacking her in swift little flurries that would just barely miss scoring points against her, not because she was blocking them correctly—she could never quite do it right—but because he had the control to stop his sword or turn it aside just a moment before it hit her.

He was patronizing her. And anyone who knew anything about sword fighting could see it.

"Come, d'Anjou," said the King jovially. "You're not giving us much of a show."

"Do you hear that, my lady?" said Erec. "Our King demands amusement." His voice had a wry slant of *you and I know this is stupid.* Having picked a fight and made her look a fool, he was now offering a truce.

"Fine," said Rachelle, and kicked him in the face.

Though he dodged at the last moment, it sent him staggering backward in a way that should have been satisfying. But he only laughed, somehow making it sound like she had done it to please him, and he approved.

Then he attacked. The next few moments were a whirl of dodges, lunges, kicks, and leaps. They were indeed putting on a show: nobody but bloodbound could have maintained this kind of speed for so long, let alone dodged each other's blades without being sliced to ribbons. Rachelle knew this, and she knew she was fighting better than she ever had against Justine.

She still wasn't fighting well enough. Erec scored a second point against her—this time a quick tap to her arm—and then redoubled his attack. Rachelle tried to match him, and she was fighting better than she ever had in her life, but no matter how fast she moved, he was faster, dancing at the edge of her reach and laughing at her with his eyes.

Laughing. Because he knew he was going to win, and this duel was going to last precisely as long as he wanted it to.

A cold pressure pounded inside her temples. Icy sweetness shivered down her veins. The Great Forest was in her blood and it wanted her *now*.

With a numb, dazed panic, she realized that she wanted it too. She couldn't want it, and she was trying so hard to resist that she stumbled, and suddenly the tip of Erec's sword was hovering an inch away from her face, mocking her because Erec could use the power of the Forest to make himself perfect and she never could.

If she couldn't win, she might at least decide when the duel ended. With a snarl, she lunged toward Erec, dropping to her knees at the last second to skid under his blade and stab upward.

He caught the blade with his bare hand. Blood leaked out between his fingers, but he grinned.

"I dub thee," he said, "the lady of my heart." And he tapped his sword to her shoulder, taking the final point and winning the match.

Rachelle stared blankly at the ground. Her heart was still pounding from the fight; tears and fury clogged her throat. Around her, she could now hear applause, laughter, and muttering as everyone admired him.

His finger tilted up her chin. "Don't forget our wager," he said.

Despite the duel, he wasn't breathing hard at all; there was barely a drop of sweat on him.

Blood still dripped from his fingers, but she was the one who now had it smeared across her chin.

Rachelle wanted to snarl, *I'd rather kiss a forestborn,* but anger would just amuse him. Would just amuse everyone, because anger was funny when it couldn't be backed up by strength, especially when it was the anger of a stupid little girl from the northern forest.

She couldn't smile and hide what she was feeling, though. Blankly submitting was beyond her too: her eyes stung, and in a moment she really would be crying.

If she had to submit to him, at least she could do that, too, on her own terms.

"I never forget," she said, and rolled abruptly to the side, swinging a leg to sweep him off his feet. Erec went down, and though he was rolling back up a heartbeat later, she was on him and pressed him back down with her sword at his throat.

"This is for you," she said, and crushed her mouth down onto his.

For one moment, it was glorious: her heart drummed against her ribs, his body was pinned beneath hers, and for once *she* was the one wresting something from *him.* Around her, the air sang with icy, approving sweetness.

But he was Erec, and he had no problem kissing her back. Nor in wrapping his bloody fingers around the blade—again—and pushing it away as he sat up, still kissing her. Her body was catching fire, but inside her chest was a cold hollow, because always, *always* he made her helpless.

Then he broke away. Rachelle caught a strangled gasp. Her body felt like it was made of sparks and no longer quite attached to her. She had to take a few breaths before she scrambled to her feet, and by then of course Erec was already standing straight and tall and smug, convinced that he had won this contest as well, because he was looking ironic and she was breathless.

Of course he had won. He always won.

Rachelle lifted her chin and looked at the King. "Are you sufficiently amused, Your Majesty?"

That was when she noticed that the crowd had gone dead silent. She remembered what Armand had said about kissing in public.

Well, if they wanted to think her an animal, let them. It wouldn't be so far from the truth. Her body was shaking with pure animal hatred.

Then she saw Armand, still sitting on the ground where she had left him and watching her with absolutely no expression.

Yes, she thought ferociously. *This is what I am. Don't forget it.*

Her body grew tenser, as if preparing to fight again. A heartbeat later, she realized there were woodspawn nearby.

"Erec," she whispered, "do you—"

Then the woodspawn attacked.

They didn't come out of the trees. They stood up from the grass, as if they had been there all along, though the space had been empty and well-trodden a moment before. There were at least ten of them: furry creatures that stood as high as her knees but were long and limber as ferrets. They would have looked almost natural except for the glowing red eyes and the long, snakelike black tongues that lashed out of their mouths.

She had fought this kind before. She knew their tongues were deadly poison.

Rachelle had killed the first two before the crowd even realized what was happening. Then they started clapping and laughing. She didn't understand what it meant—she was busy dodging the tongues of two more woodspawn—until Armand's voice rang out: "Everyone get back! They're dangerous!"

She realized: the courtiers thought this was *entertainment*.

Somebody screamed—not a shriek of fear, but a howl of pure agony. Rachelle whirled and saw one of the ladies had fallen to the ground, clutching her arm. One of the woodspawn crouched beside her.

Rachelle threw her knife; it hit the woodspawn but glanced off, and then the creature turned on her.

She charged. The creature leaped at her and ended up spitted for its troubles. Rachelle turned, discovering as she did that the thing's body was *stuck* on her sword—

And saw, in the same instant, that Erec had managed to kill off all the others but one, and that one was preparing to spring at Armand.

She sprang first. Barely. She hit its body in midair and both tumbled to the ground. Its tongue lashed up and struck her throat, burning like white-hot iron—

With a shriek of pain and fury, she seized its neck and twisted. She felt it writhing in her grip. Felt the bones of its neck snap. Felt it go still.

She felt the air rush out of her lungs. And then she felt nothing at all.

It didn't take her long to wake. What was deadly poison to humans was only pain and an hour-long fever to bloodbound. When she was able to sit up again, her throat aching and her skin shivering, people were still shouting and fainting and chattering.

Rachelle managed to escape most of the tumult by dragging Armand away for his own safety. Though by the time she got him back to his rooms, the servants had already heard and were talking about it.

On the bright side, the horror of a surprise woodspawn attack in plain daylight seemed to have stopped people from talking about the depraved antics of the King's bloodbound. Not that Rachelle could stop thinking about it; every other minute, she remembered Erec laughing at her as he scored point after point in the duel, Erec pinned beneath her but still—through the kiss—making her dance to his bidding. He had humiliated her and laughed at her and then he had still made her *want* him.

Armand didn't speak to her for the rest of the day. That was good, because she didn't want to talk to him. He had seen her kissing Erec, seen her panting with lust and bloodlust at the same time. She knew what he must think of her.

It shouldn't matter what he thought of her.

The King didn't send for them that evening, so Armand ate dinner in his rooms, grimly stabbing at his food with the fork clamped to his hand. Rachelle sat in the corner and stared. She didn't want to look at him. Looking at him made her think of this afternoon and the day before and everything that was horrible and broken and *wrong* in her. But she couldn't look away.

Finally, Armand looked up at her. "Are we still pretending you take orders from me?" he asked with a mild curiosity that burned more than any anger.

Rachelle's chest tightened. "Have we ever pretended that?"

"I would like it," he said quietly and distinctly, "if you pretended long enough to go into the other room and *stop staring at me.*"

"And let the woodspawn eat you?" she asked.

"Why not?"

"Because you're useful. For now." She stood. "Scream if you need help."

She went to her room and spent the next hour watching Amélie mix powders and trying not to cry. Which did not make any sense.

Nothing in her heart made any sense.

She could tell she wasn't going to sleep that night, so she didn't even try. She told Amélie to go to bed, and then she sat in a chair and stared at the wall. If she stared hard enough, she could make herself stop thinking, even though the confused misery in her chest still wouldn't go away.

Then Armand let out a hoarse cry. She was in his room before she had fully realized what she was doing. She didn't see or sense any woodspawn; Armand was sitting up in bed, rigid but apparently unharmed. Beside his bed, the candle had burned down nearly to a stump.

"What happened?" she demanded.

"Nothing." He stared at the wall.

"Did you see something?"

"No."

"Did you— Just look at me!" She grabbed his wrist to pull him toward her. But she had forgotten that he had lost his hands; her fingers closed over the very end of his arm, and she could feel the rounded edge of the stump.

She had heard for months about his tragically missing hands. She had seen his stumps before. But feeling the way his arms just *ended* was like a kick to the stomach.

He did look at her then, very tired and very irritated. "I had a dream," he said. "I woke up screaming. Laugh and go back to sleep."

"I'm not going to laugh," she said.

"Are you going to let go of my arm?"

She flinched and released him.

The silence stretched between them. The darkness wrapped around them. It felt like they were the only people in the world, and the tension that had choked her all day started to seep away.

"Are you going to watch me all night?" he asked. "Because I wasn't aware that your mandate included protecting me from bad dreams."

"What really happened?" she asked. "With your hands, and the mark?"

"I thought I was a liar. Now you're going to believe what I say?"

"Maybe," she said. "Are you going to tell me it was your holiness that let you live?"

He looked at her as if she were a foreign language he was trying to decipher.

"No," he said finally, slowly, softly.

Very carefully, Rachelle sat down beside him on the bed. "Then what happened?"

He pressed his lips together. "I met a forestborn," he said. "He marked me. I said I wouldn't kill anyone. He laughed, and told me I'd change my mind in three days."

"Did you?"

"No. I didn't." His voice was light and tense and strangled. "But you know the stories about the Royal Gift? That because the royal line is descended from Tyr, they have power over the Forest? It turns out it's real. At least, real enough to keep the mark from killing me. And surprisingly, forestborn don't like it when you ruin their plans."

"Why didn't he kill you?" asked Rachelle.

"Why don't you ask him?"

He did have a point. "So the forestborn cut off your hands for revenge, and you survived it because you're special—"

"Because I'm nearly bloodbound, so I heal faster. But I still wasn't well enough to conceal the mark until much too late."

"So now you hold audiences where you pretend to be the King's pet saint. Why? Because you can't bear to disappoint the multitudes?"

"Because," Armand said, biting off each word, "my half brother Raoul deserves to get the throne and every other good thing. Unfortunately the King doesn't much like him, but he knows I care about him, and if I don't let people go on thinking I'm his pet saint, he will punish Raoul on my account."

"So instead you lie to the people."

"I don't lie," said Armand. "I always tell them I'm not a saint."

"Which only convinces them that you are one. Do you think that makes a difference?"

"Maybe. Do you believe me now?"

"Maybe," said Rachelle, but she knew she meant, *Yes.*

He seemed to know it too, because the edge of his mouth turned up. "Does that mean you're going to be kinder to me?"

"Of course not. *I'm* still a heartless bloodbound."

His face cracked in a smile utterly different from the one he'd used playing cards. "Between you and me, you're not very good at it."

The flickering candlelight danced across his face. He was beautiful.

No. Beauty was something you admired from a distance. Rachelle wanted to lock her fingers in his hair and close her mouth over his and pull him down to the bed on top of her. She wanted to possess him, and more than that, she wanted him to possess her. More than anything else in the world, she wanted him to look at her with the same absolute, burning attention he had when he talked about what he believed.

Her face heated. This was lust, plain and simple. It was why she couldn't stop watching him on the hunt, why she couldn't stop noticing his every movement now. She hadn't thought she could feel this way about anyone except Erec.

It didn't matter what she felt for anyone. It wasn't love, and even if it was, she didn't have time for it. Very soon now, she would die fighting the Devourer. Or more likely, the Devourer would return and she would simply die. There was no room for love in her future.

No room at all.

Armand let out his breath suddenly—the noise was almost a laugh—and Rachelle realized that she had been staring at him. She jumped to her feet.

"Then if we don't hate each other right now," she said, "will you help me look for the door again?"

Armand seemed to hesitate a moment; then he squared his shoulders and said, "Actually, I had an idea."

"What?" asked Rachelle.

"None of the rooms look the same as they did in Prince Hugo's day. But the name of the place—that hasn't changed in five hundred years. Maybe longer. This was Château de Lune when Prince Hugo knew it."

"You mean the whole Château is the 'moon'?" said Rachelle. "Then what's the sun?" As soon as she said the words, she realized. "The *sun*," she said, answering her own question.

Armand nodded. "One of the old women on my mother's estate said that some woodwife charms only work at certain times of day. Is that true?"

The sun had set hours ago. It was, in a sense, beneath them. Now they only needed to get beneath the Château.

"Yes," said Rachelle, and hope was almost as dizzying as terror. "Let's go."

This time they didn't have to spin a story to get past anyone. Rachelle stole the keys from their hook and they slipped down together into the chill, silent darkness of the tunnels.

"Do you see anything?" asked Rachelle, as soon as they had stepped off the bottom stair.

Armand paused. "No, just— Wait. Gold."

A cold shiver slid down her spine. "Where?"

"All over the walls and floors," said Armand. "Like traces of an old mosaic. I think it gets stronger up ahead." He strode forward more quickly, and Rachelle followed him.

Please, she thought, and she hadn't dared pray in years, but now she almost did. *Please, let us find it. Please.*

They came into a wide room lined with wine racks. Armand strode right to the center of the room, stopped, and stared down at the floor a moment.

"Here," he said. "There's a great big sun on the floor."

To Rachelle, the floor looked like the same dreary gray stone as the rest of the wine cellar. But Armand sounded absolutely certain. Heart beating very quickly, she knelt and pressed her hand to the cold floor.

She closed her eyes and reached to awaken the charm.

Nothing happened.

"Am I touching it?" she asked.

"Yes," said Armand. "Right at the center."

She tried again. Nothing happened, except that her head began to ache.

"Are you—" Armand started.

"It's not *working,*" she said harshly.

Of course it wasn't working. Why had she thought that anything would start going right for her now? Why had she thought that she might possibly be able to work a woodwife charm? She was bloodbound. Nothing could change that and nothing could make it better.

She still gave it one final effort. Black speckled the edges of her vision, but nothing happened. With a sigh, she staggered to her feet.

"It's no use," she said.

"Wait," Armand said breathlessly. Then he closed his eyes.

The air changed. The simple chill of the wine cellar became the sweet cold of the Great Forest. Rachelle's heart pounded, but she couldn't move.

She saw the Forest. Tree roots wove among the wine bottles. Moss and bloodred flowers with teeth swarmed over the walls. Tiny bright blue butterflies—no bigger than her thumbnails—fluttered through the air.

And beneath her feet, she saw the worn, glittering pattern of a great golden sun inlaid on the floor, its rays flowing out to the edges of the room.

Armand shuddered and let out a breath. The Forest was abruptly gone, but the golden sun still lingered on the floor.

The strength ran out of Rachelle's legs. She sank to the floor. Her fingers touched gold.

She didn't have to awaken the charm. It awakened to her, blossoming warmth under her hands. She didn't even realize it had happened until Armand took a quick breath, and she looked up.

Before them stood two slender birch trees, their branches reaching toward each other and intertwining to form a door frame. The door that hung within it was made of polished gold; in the branches above the door hung a silver crescent moon.

Rachelle stood slowly, barely able to believe what she was seeing.

"Do you see a door?" asked Armand, sounding a little dazed. "Because I do."

"Yes." Rachelle's voice was tiny and wavering, but she didn't care. She finally had a chance. Everything she had done and suffered might finally be worth it. "I see it. Yes."

She pressed her hand against the golden door. She had expected the metal to be cold, but it was as warm as a cat's back, and humming with a vibration not unlike a cat's purr.

They had found it. They had actually *found* it, the door that had lain hidden for centuries. Just behind this door waited Joyeuse, and once she had it in her hand, all the horror of her life would be worthwhile.

But it didn't open for her.

"I think this door is for you," she said, stepping back.

Armand raised his arm and pressed it gently against the door. It started to swing inward.

And everything went dark, as if shadow had spilled out of the doorway as blindingly as light spilled in a door opened onto summer noon.

In a heartbeat, she had reached for Armand, seized his arm, and shoved him behind her.

But there was no danger she could see. Because she could see nothing—only a darkness so intense it pounded at her eyes. She could hear nothing except her short, quick breaths and Armand's. She could sense nothing except her own pounding heartbeat.

"Do you see anything?" she whispered.

"Yes," said Armand, and as if in response, four glowing lights appeared, dim and greenish-white but blinding after the darkness.

Then she realized the lights were eyes.

Snake eyes.

She could see now. They were in a copy of the Hall of Mirrors, perfect down to the last curlicue on the picture frames, except that it was all carved out of red-brown rock. In front of them and all around them lay coil upon coil of two vast, dark snakes whose bodies were almost as wide as her own arm span.

No, she realized with numb terror as she met the pale double stare. It was only one creature. A lindenworm: the legendary snake with a head on both ends of its body, whose endless hunger would stir it to unimaginable greed and make it guard treasure with a ferocity beyond imagining.

It had to be guarding Joyeuse. It would never let her take it.

Beside her, Armand let out a short, sharp little breath, as if to say, *So this is how I die.*

Rachelle hadn't been able to die for love of her aunt. She didn't intend to die for a snake, even a lindenworm.

As the nearer head lunged toward her, Rachelle leaped up, sword swinging. With bloodbound strength behind the thrust, her sword sliced through the neck and vertebrae as if they were no more than celery coated in butter. Blood gushed. The remaining head spasmed and shrieked—

As another head grew out of its severed neck.

A coil slammed into her chest and sent her flying. She hoped Armand had run.

But there was no time for disappointment or fear, because now both heads were lunging for her. All she could do was dodge and slash, and Rachelle was fighting better than she ever had in her life, but this time it wasn't enough. Every wound healed in moments.

Teeth sank into her right shoulder. For a heartbeat it just felt like a burn too hot to hurt. Then the lindenworm shook her, and she screamed. She could feel its venom seeping into the bite, and it was like molten iron.

Then it started lifting her up, coiling a lower section of its body around her legs. Darkness speckled her vision, but with her free hand she managed to pull out another knife. She stabbed blindly at its head, once, twice, and then felt the knife slide into the jelly of the eye. Thick, hot ooze seeped across her hand.

The lindenworm dropped her. Rachelle's stomach lurched as she fell through the air, and then for a few moments, she didn't feel anything. Then she realized that she was on her feet—barely—and Armand had an arm around her waist as he dragged her toward the windows. They were not glazed, like the windows in the real Château; they were empty slits looking out into darkness, but they were better than staying with the lindenworm. When Armand shoved her in front of them, she flung herself through.

17

When she hit the ground, she rolled. White-hot pain seared up her shoulder, and for a few moments, the world went away. After a while, the pain faded into a steady burn that allowed her to breathe and think. She was flat on the ground; she could see nothing, but her shoulder burned with pain.

And then it healed. With each breath she drew of the cold, sweet air, the pain grew less. She knew that the muscles and skin were knitting themselves back together; when she sat up, she knew that her wound was gone. She saw the flicker of a far-off bonfire, she saw the starlight through the weaving net of tree branches overhead. They were in the Great Forest.

A curious peace descended on her. Everything before this moment had been an illusion. There was nothing but the cold darkness around her, the swift, warm pulse of blood inside her. She felt nothing but the empty, echoing darkness in her heart. That was all she was: a shell filled with the same darkness that surrounded her.

"Rachelle?" whispered Armand in his weak human voice, and the name felt useless, irrelevant, almost obscene beside the holy strength flowing into her body with every breath.

She was swiftly adjusting to the dim light; she could see Armand now, could see the pale, resolute set of his face. He was afraid, but he wasn't going to run.

He should be weeping with fear. He was weak. Prey. Captive. She should kill him, crush him, master him. She thought this quite calmly, with an icy relish as she imagined his blood seeping between her fingers.

"Are you all right?" he asked.

The cold in her shattered like glass, and she realized what she had been thinking. She slammed a fist into the nearest tree.

I am not a forestborn, she thought. *I will not be a forestborn. Not yet.*

The scar on her right hand ached. She was so nearly a forestborn already.

"Rachelle?" Armand sounded truly worried.

"I'm all right," she said. "I'm already healed."

"Good," said Armand after a moment. "But you have a grudge against that tree?"

"I don't like this place," she said.

"I thought it was your home."

"That's why *I don't like it.*" She drew a breath. "We have to leave. Now."

"Lead the way."

But of course, there was no trace left of the stone hall they had fled. They were somewhere in the vast expanse of the Great Forest—though "somewhere" might not even be the right word, not in this ever-shifting, infinitely unmappable maze of trees.

The string on her finger glowed bright red as it flowed into the undergrowth. If she followed it, would it lead her back to her forestborn? He wanted her to stay alive until the Devourer returned; he might help her, if not Armand.

Then she heard the horns. The sweet, ferocious horns of the Wild Hunt.

No.

She didn't "hear" them; the horns sounded, and they devoured her. Her blood pulsed in time to their call, and she wanted nothing except to run after them, ride after them, to join the hunt and run their foolish mortal prey to death.

Then she glanced at Armand. He had planted himself with his chin at a stubborn angle, but she could see the fear in his rigid shoulders.

Foolish mortal prey.

They would hunt him. They would run him to death in the woods, and then they would tear him limb from limb. But they might let her live, because she was bloodbound and destined to become one of them.

She felt like a rabbit bolting across the fields with foxes at its heels. Nobody escaped the Forest. Nobody could fight the Wild Hunt. If she tried to help Armand, she would die as well. And she had a reason to live now, as she hadn't when she lifted the knife over Aunt Léonie. There were other men with royal blood who could open the labyrinth for her, but no one else knew how to find Joyeuse and stop the Devourer.

Armand looked at her with a sort of resigned fear, as if he knew it was inevitable that she would betray him and he would die tonight.

The horns sounded again, louder, closer. Rachelle shuddered and gripped his arm.

Nobody could fight the Wild Hunt. So she would just have to cheat them.

"I'm not going to hurt you," she said. "Just do as I say."

And then the Wild Hunt was upon them.

First came the hounds, their crimson muzzles dripping with blood. Then came the hunters themselves, riding horses and stags and tigers. Light clung to every member of the hunt; they were riotously arrayed in silks and jewels and silver and gold. Their faces shimmered with impossible light and their eyes were dark with unknowable dread.

Their gazes made her feel like a small, frightened animal. But she was one of them. She had to be one of them, so she remembered Erec's arrogance and her own anger and the chill, sweet bloodlust of the Forest wind, and she stood up straight.

The hunt swirled around them, parting to either side, and drew into a ring. One hunter halted before them: a tall man, clad in rags and golden chains, riding a great black stag.

"You are not yet one of us," he said, in a voice that was deep and soft and terrifying.

"Nevertheless." Her lips were dry and stiff. "I am your sister, and I am here by right."

He looked at her. And then, in a movement more terrifying than all his pride, he bowed. The stag on which he sat bowed down as well, muzzle touching the ground, and all the Wild Hunt with him.

They bowed to Rachelle. Was her heart so cruel already, that they honored her?

Or were they simply bowing to what they knew she must become?

"Do you come to hunt with us?" asked the forestborn. "There is little time left, but plentiful prey."

"No," said Rachelle. "I would. But I have business back at home. Will you take me there?"

The hunter's teeth glinted in a smile. "We would be honored."

Two slender forestborn women helped Rachelle and Armand mount a huge white horse. Their fingers burned cold against her arm and made her shiver; their eyes were worse. When Rachelle was on the horse with Armand before her, she wanted to tell him, *I won't let them hurt you,* but she couldn't. She couldn't even think it, because when the hunter looked at her, she felt like she was made of glass.

Instead, she stroked his hair like he was a pet and then said—her voice quiet but carrying—"Ride well for me, and you might live till morning."

She could see the edge of his smile. "Yes, my lady," he said, and then the horns called again and the hunt started. Armand straightened; Rachelle wrapped her arms around his waist. She could feel the movement of his ribs as he breathed.

And they rode, through the wind and through the night, the Great Forest whispering around them, the air full of hoofbeats and hunting calls and the wild, tuneless singing of the forestborn.

Far too soon, they stopped. Rachelle had so lost herself in the thrill of speed that it took her a moment to remember why they had been riding with the hunt.

"Dismount," said the hunter, and Rachelle slid off the horse's back. She staggered a moment, then straightened in time to catch Armand as he dismounted.

"Walk forward," said the hunter, "and you will be returned."

"Thank you," said Rachelle, and instantly wondered if forestborn ever thanked anyone.

"Remember me," he said, "when our lord returns."

And then the Wild Hunt streamed around them and was gone into the night.

Rachelle realized that her heart was pounding and she was gasping for breath. They had ridden with the Wild Hunt, and they had *lived*.

She looked at Armand. "Are you all right?"

He nodded. "Yes."

"Then walk," said Rachelle, and started forward, Armand following her. They were out of the Great Forest now, she realized; the darkness was flatter, the wind thin and drab.

"The forestborn were stranger than I expected," said Armand.

"Why?" she asked. "What was yours like?"

"Well," Armand said after a moment, "he had more clothes on."

"Clearly, yours was special," said Rachelle.

Or had hers been special? She could remember the faces of the forestborn they had ridden with just now; they had been terrible to look upon because of the inhuman power she could sense dwelling within them, but they had been *shaped* like human faces. She could remember the lines of their eyes and noses and mouths. The face of her forestborn had always left her memory the instant she looked away from him. Was he older and more powerful? Or did all forestborn have the ability to hide their faces, and he was just the only one who bothered?

"They're immortal children of the Devourer who have lost

their human hearts," she went on. "What would you expect them to look like?"

"What does that mean?" asked Armand. "Losing their hearts?"

"Do you know what's the difference between bloodbound and forestborn? It's not just how powerful they are. When bloodbound turn into forestborn, they lose their hearts. The power of the Forest burns them away, and they can't love or pity anyone. They can't want anything except destruction. That's why some of them go mad. The loss of their hearts destroys their reason."

In her first month at Rocamadour, she'd seen a mad bloodbound executed. He could no longer talk, and when he wasn't chained up, he would try to attack anyone in sight. There was nothing left of him but the desire for blood.

Armand was quiet a few moments. Then he said carefully, "The forestborn I met was cruel. But he wasn't mindless. Or much more inhuman than anyone at court. I don't think it's that simple."

"Then what makes them all turn that way?" asked Rachelle. "Every time?"

"Maybe it's just that, once they're so deep in the Forest's power, they don't want to remember loving anyone."

"Why are you trying to convince me that we can be saved?"

His grin sliced through the darkness. "You're my jailer. Of course I want to think you might have a change of heart."

For a little while they walked on in silence.

Then the screams started.

The hunt, thought Rachelle, and there was nothing she could do—nobody fought the Wild Hunt and lived—but she was already running forward, Armand right behind her.

There were not just screams, but shouts and crashes. Clangs. Snarls. Woodspawn, perhaps? She could fight woodspawn. She pushed herself to run faster.

And there was an open field ahead of them, with the low stone wall that all northern folk used to keep the trees back from their lands. Rachelle vaulted it in a moment, then remembered Armand, but when she glanced back, he was already over the wall.

Rachelle flung herself forward into an all-out run. At the far end of the field, she could see flickering lights from the village. Bonfire? Torches? Or had an actual fire broken out?

She was closer now. She could see human figures running between the houses—yes, one of them was on fire—and wolf-shaped creatures running among them. Woodspawn.

She caught a glint of metal and heard a clang. They were trying to fight the woodspawn with scythes and hoes. Not bad weapons. But against this many woodspawn, human hands were much too slow.

And then she was charging into the ring of houses and the flickering firelight, and there was no more time to think. She drew her sword and lunged at the nearest woodspawn; the blade slid easily into its neck, but as the creature dissolved into muck, two more sprang at her.

One of them she got in time. The other one slammed into her, knocking her to the ground. Instinctively Rachelle threw an arm over her face, then screamed when the woodspawn's jaws crunched down on her arm.

She'd dropped her sword. She couldn't see it.

So she reached up with her free hand and slid it into the woodspawn's eye socket. It was scalding hot, but she clenched her fist on the slimy mess and ripped it out.

The woodspawn howled, letting go of her arm. She rolled free, found her sword, and stabbed it three times.

Panting, she looked around. There were only two more woodspawn left. One of them was already injured and surrounded by a crowd of men with scythes; they could probably manage to kill it.

The other one was crouched atop the roof of a cottage.

Rachelle groaned. She could barely use her right arm, so she had to sheathe her sword before she clambered up the side of the house and hauled herself onto the roof—just as the woodspawn sprang at her. She grabbed it by the scruff and they went over the side of the house together. Luckily she landed on top; she felt its ribs crunch underneath, and that bought her an extra moment to grab her sword and slice its head off.

She staggered to her feet.

The first thing she looked for was the other woodspawn. It

was dead, only a puddle of dark, viscous mud left to mark its passing. The men who had been attacking it turned to face her.

Everyone was staring at her.

Something was wrong. She could hardly think past the pounding in her head and the pain in her arm, but something was wrong.

She looked for Armand: he was safe, standing to one side, eyes wide. That was good. But there was still something not right about the crowd of people staring at her.

They could see the black fleur-de-lis on her coat. They knew she was a bloodbound. People always stared at her when they realized she was bloodbound—

And then she realized. All the people staring at her—she knew them. Claude, the baker. André, the blacksmith. Jean, the hunter.

Her father.

This was her village. The Wild Hunt had brought her home to face judgment.

18

When Rachelle was seven years old, she slipped into Aunt Léonie's house while she was out. She put on her aunt's spare cloak, got into her yarn, and pretended to weave charms. When Aunt Léonie came back early and raised her eyebrows, the shame had felt like scalding-hot water poured over every bit of her body.

She felt that way now: like an idiotic child caught playing pretend. For one moment, all she wanted to do was drop her sword, strip off her coat, and slink back into her family's house and scrub the floor until she was forgiven.

Then she heard the crackle of the burning house. She remembered what people in the countryside did to bloodbound.

She was not a child anymore. There was not going to be any forgiveness.

And right now, she couldn't accept judgment.

Her head still ached. Her arm burned with pain. But she tightened her grip on her sword.

"Everybody stay back," she said. "Armand, get over here."

Instantly she realized that she had just told them whom to take hostage, but since none of them were Erec, maybe it wouldn't occur to them at once.

Armand started to step forward; she saw the people noticing him for the first time, wondering who the other stranger was.

"Here's what will happen," she snapped, because she couldn't let them pay enough attention to realize Armand was defenseless. "My friend and I will leave. You stay here. Nobody gets hurt."

"Who are you?" called out Claude, and for a moment Rachelle couldn't breathe. Of course they didn't know her, she was just another faceless bloodbound now, and if only she'd had the wit to pretend—

"Rachelle Brinon?" said André. He was a big, bluff man and confusion looked utterly strange on his face.

She saw the recognition ripple across the faces in the crowd, saw the shift in their stances as they realized she was dangerous. An enemy.

She didn't see her father anymore; he must have fled as soon as he recognized her.

She raised her sword. "I will kill you all if you give me any trouble," she declared, but inside she was shaking with terror.

She couldn't hurt these people she'd known all her life.

She couldn't die here. She still had to find Joyeuse.

Then suddenly Armand was between her and the crowd. "Nobody's fighting," he said, pressing his back against her and grabbing her arm. "Nobody is fighting anyone without going through me."

"What do you think you're doing?" Rachelle demanded.

She felt his back stiffen. "If they want to punish you for shedding innocent blood, they can hardly cut through me to do it."

"Did nobody teach you how vengeance works?"

"Besides, I doubt I'd survive walking back through the woods on my own, so if they want you dead, then this will save time, really."

"Stand back!" a woman called out. A moment later, the crowd parted.

Aunt Léonie stepped out.

For one sick, horrifying moment, that was whom she saw. Then she realized that the woman clad in white and red was too tall to be Aunt Léonie; her hair was too light, her face too pointy. It was just another woodwife.

"I will deal with them," she said.

André grabbed her by the arm. "You don't understand, it's—"

She gave him a single look and he let go. "I understand

perfectly," she said. "This is the girl from your village who murdered my predecessor and became a bloodbound. Is that not so?" She looked around at the crowd. "Then I have the right, don't I, to administer justice in this matter?"

Silence. Nobody moved as the woman strode forward toward Rachelle.

"Mademoiselle," said Armand, "she just helped save your village. And she has saved a lot of other people in the last few years. It doesn't seem right to repay her with death."

"She killed the previous woodwife of this village," said the woman. "Did you know that?"

"I knew she was bloodbound," said Armand. "The person she murdered had to come from somewhere."

"You have the right to kill me," said Rachelle. Her voice felt like a great length of rusty iron chains. "But I can't die right now. So I will fight my way out if I must."

The woman looked her up and down. "I don't intend to kill you," she said. "I know what would happen to this village if we killed the King's bloodbound. But you will come to my house and speak with me before you leave."

"I won't go back to that house," said Rachelle.

"We burned that house," said the woodwife. "Did you think anything human could bear to live in it again? They built me a new one when I came here."

The new house was closer than Aunt Léonie's had been, just on the other side of the village wall. "It's too dangerous, now, to live farther away," Aunt Léonie had said.

Rachelle was hardly paying attention at that point. Between exhaustion and the still-bleeding wound in her arm, she could barely see straight.

"I'm going to sleep," she said, and then lay down on the floor without waiting for an answer. Nobody kicked her, so she supposed it must be all right. She fell asleep almost instantly.

When she awoke the next morning, the woodwife was sitting beside her, watching her with a narrow, unyielding gaze. Behind her was the normal clutter of a woodwife's house: spindles and baskets of wool. Bunches of herbs hanging from the ceiling, and in between them many-colored charms, like woolen snowflakes. It was so comfortingly familiar that for a moment she almost felt safe.

Then she realized who was missing.

She bolted up. "Where's Armand?"

The woodwife waved a hand. "Your friend? Safe. Outside. I didn't want him hearing us."

"I remember, you said you wanted to speak with me." Rachelle paused. "Thank you for last night."

"I did not do it for your sake."

"Who are you?" asked Rachelle.

The woodwife handed her a bowl of porridge and a spoon.

"My name is Margot Dumont," she said. "I apprenticed beside Léonie and I do not intend to forgive you for her death."

Rachelle's hand clenched on the spoon. "I didn't ask you to."

"No." Margot nodded in acknowledgment. "I need to know, and on whatever honor you have left, I charge you not to lie: What did she tell you about Durendal?"

"Nothing," said Rachelle, and took a bite of the porridge. It tasted like her childhood, and her throat ached with unshed tears.

"Nothing?"

"Just what everyone knows. That it was Zisa's sword, forged from the bones of the Devourer's victims. That it was lost. That's all." One spoonful had made her hungry; Rachelle gulped down the rest of the porridge.

Margot watched her eat, then said, "Léonie knew where it was."

"What?"

"It was her duty to know where it was. She was entrusted with it by the woodwife who trained us. You were her apprentice; she must have told you."

"She never told me anything," said Rachelle. "She never *did* anything, just—"

Just, she realized, guarded Durendal. Rachelle had despised her aunt for doing nothing when she was protecting a weapon that could kill the Devourer.

The porridge turned to stone in her stomach.

Margot sighed through her nose. "Then I will continue searching," she said. "And you—what brings you back here? An errand for the King? Or did you just need to visit the sight of your triumph?"

Rachelle set the bowl down. "No," she said flatly, "I was looking for Joyeuse. You don't happen to know anything about it?"

They stared at each other for a few moments. Then Margot snorted and looked away. "No more than anyone else. Behind a door above the sun, below the moon."

"I know," said Rachelle. "I found the door. There's a lindenworm on the other side."

Margot raised her eyebrows. "Indeed."

"Do you know how to kill one?"

"I have heard it said that the blood of an innocent virgin could lull them to sleep," Margot said musingly. "But you might find that hard to obtain, and I doubt that tale anyway."

Rachelle strangled the sudden fury in her throat and said quietly, "Try to remember that killing it could save us from the Devourer."

"No human hands can kill a lindenworm," said Margot, as placidly as if they were discussing the best way to stitch a hem.

"I thought la Pucelle killed one?" Rachelle demanded.

"I believe she had angels helping her. You do not." Margot paused, pursing her lips. "Perhaps you never learned this rule: the most powerful creatures can only be touched by the most terrible charms—or the most simple. I don't believe there is a woodwife alive who could weave a charm strong enough to stop a lindenworm, but I suppose a simple charm might beguile it for a little while."

"Do you think that could work?" asked Rachelle.

"No," Margot said coolly. "I think if you fight that lindenworm, it will swallow you whole, and you will feel the flesh melt off your bones as you die. But you deserve as much and more besides, so I will not dissuade you from trying."

Rachelle stared at her. She thought, *Armand would probably laugh at that,* and then she had to smother her own urge to laugh wildly.

Margot took the bowl and rose. "I won't let the village burn you, but you'd better be off now before it gets difficult."

Rachelle nodded and rose to her feet. She went to the door, opened it, and couldn't move.

Her mother stood on the front step.

How had she changed so much? Rachelle remembered her mother as a towering, imperious figure—not this slight woman with a sagging face.

"So," said her mother.

Rachelle couldn't speak. It used to be that one glance from her mother would make her stammer and confess what she'd done wrong. Now her very existence was the confession. There would be no forgiving hug after her punishment, because there was nothing left of her but the sin.

"Your father was weeping in the loft all night," said her mother. "On and on about his darling precious daughter. He never believed you'd done it, you know; he swore the forestborn must have kidnapped you, and that was why you never came back."

After all the nights she'd spent agonizing over what her father would think, it should have been a comfort that he still loved her. It wasn't.

"You believed," Rachelle whispered.

Her mother smiled mirthlessly, her gaze drifting away. "I know quite well what daughters will do when they must." Then she looked back at Rachelle. "When he wakes, he won't believe this happened. He'll swear it was only a lying forestborn who looked like his daughter. You won't ever come back so he won't ever have to learn the truth. Do you hear me?"

"Yes," Rachelle said numbly. She couldn't tell what she was feeling. She had imagined a thousand nightmare situations that might happen if she ever went back to her village. But she had never imagined anything like this.

Neither one of her parents hated her the way that Margot did, the way the rest of the villagers did. They simply didn't want her to exist.

"You won't come back?"

"Never," said Rachelle. "I will die first. I promise."

"Good." Her mother opened her mouth, then shut it, and turned to stride away.

Rachelle's chest hurt. She took a step after her.

"Mother," she called out.

Her mother stopped. Without looking back, she said, "Yes?"

Rachelle didn't know what she was going to say until the words formed in her mouth. "Thank you. For asking me to help."

"I knew you lived," her mother said after a moment. "Any daughter of mine would be ruthless enough."

She found Armand sitting in the herb garden. The morning sunlight glowed through his hair; he looked at peace in a way she didn't think he had anywhere in the Château.

"I like it here," he said. "It's quiet. Nobody knows who I am."

And then she felt it again: the sudden, sharp awareness of wanting to touch him, of the space between them as an open wound, of her own body being jumbled and awkward and far too separate when she could be pressed against him, waist to waist and chin to shoulder and her fingers sliding into that pale brown hair—

Her face was hot. She took a step back, thinking, *He isn't yours. He will never be yours. He will never, ever want you.*

"Even they will figure it out sooner or later," she said. "When they get a look at you in daylight, for instance. Get up. We're going."

He stood. "Mademoiselle Dumont—what did she want to talk about?"

Aunt Léonie could have stopped the Devourer, and Rachelle had killed her, and now nobody would ever find Durendal.

Or maybe her forestborn had already found it and destroyed it. That must have been why he was sniffing around the village to begin with. Maybe if Rachelle had told Aunt Léonie when she first met him, they could have stopped him. They could have saved Durendal. They could have saved the world.

"Nothing important," she said, and grabbed his arm. "Come on." She started to drag him toward the edge of the trees.

"Is your family here?" asked Armand. "Aren't you going to say good-bye to them?"

She didn't know if the ache in her chest was grief or freedom. Maybe they were the same.

"I did," said Rachelle.

ZISA CARRIED THE BONES TO A GREAT YEW TREE. Beneath its roots there was a cave, and in the cave there was a forge, and chained to the forge was a man with a smile like dried blood and glowing embers.

This was Volund, the crippled smith. He had once loved a forestborn maiden, and so much did he delight her that for seven years she stayed beside him. But one night she heard the hunting horns of her people and rose to follow them. Before she had taken three steps, he struck her dead.

In recompense, the forestborn hamstrung him, chained him, and made him undying as themselves, an everlasting slave to craft their swords and spears and arrows.

"Old man," said Zisa, "I must have two swords made out of these bones."

"Little girl," said Volund, "I must obey the forestborn, but not you."

"And when I am one of them, I will remember you said that," she replied.

He laughed like a rusty hinge. "And much I have left for anyone to take from me. But you, I think, have the whole world to lose." He looked her up and down. "I will make you a bargain. Give me the delights of your proud body twice, and I will make you two swords such as the world will never see again."

There was nothing she would not do for her brother.

19

"Do you have a plan?" asked Armand as they walked into the woods. They were not in the Great Forest yet, but the shadows cast by the trees were a little longer and darker than they should be in the daytime.

"Yes," said Rachelle.

Like a trickle of blood, the thread lay on the ground before her. If she followed it, then she should find her forestborn at the other end.

He wanted her to live. So if she gave him a choice between leading her back to the Château and watching her perish in the Great Forest, surely he would help her.

But if she told Armand that, he might ask her why she was so sure that her forestborn wanted her to live.

"Is the plan 'walk into the Forest and hope to meet the Wild

Hunt again'?" asked Armand. "Because I'm not sure how likely that is to work."

"Well," said Rachelle, thinking of the lindenworm, "maybe there will be a miracle to save us. Since those always happen for people who deserve them."

"I already told you," Armand said mildly, "I don't believe that."

He had, and she couldn't stop a guilty glance at his hands.

"Then what do you believe?" she asked. "That we should all be martyrs?"

She realized that they were surrounded by darkness and the cold, sweet wind. They were in the Great Forest again. The change had felt so natural, so *right*, she hadn't noticed it happen.

"What's so bad about that?" asked Armand.

"The problem with martyrs is that they're all dead. What have they got to do with those of us who are sinful enough to still be alive? Should we just give up and want to die, because death is better than dishonor? But suicide is a sin too, so then we really are damned if we do and damned if we don't."

"I don't—" Armand started to say.

"Enough. I don't want to hear it." Rachelle strode forward faster, trying not to think about the lindenworm waiting for her, and thinking of it with every step.

The journey seemed to take hours. Days. Forever. There was no keeping track of time in that endless darkness, but they walked on and on, and Rachelle grew wearier and wearier.

All she could think of was the lindenworm. She had to try to defeat it and get Joyeuse. She didn't see a way she could win.

You deserve as much and more besides.

She didn't want to be a martyr. She didn't have a choice.

When sunlight suddenly poured down on them, Rachelle's head was hanging low. She looked up, and saw Château de Lune glittering before them. They were in the garden, among the rosebushes. Judging by the position of the sun, they had only been walking for a few hours.

"How did you do that?" asked Armand. He was looking at her, his eyes squinted against the sudden sunlight.

"Luck," said Rachelle. "Maybe."

Or her forestborn was lurking somewhere near the Château, which was a truly terrifying thought.

When they got back to their rooms, they found both Amélie and Armand's valets in a state of modified panic.

"Where have you *been*?" Amélie demanded, hugging Rachelle fiercely. "Monsieur d'Anjou kept asking and asking for you, and we had to keep making up excuses."

Which was pointless, since the valets would report it all to Erec anyway, but Rachelle was surprised and touched that Amélie had taken the trouble.

"We took a walk," said Armand. "Got lost in the trees." His valets were not hugging him, but they had peeled off his coat—exclaiming about the dust—and now seemed to be checking him for injuries.

"He was tired of being cooped up," said Rachelle. "It won't happen again."

"I've learned my lesson," Armand agreed, with a smile just for her.

Of course, she had to explain herself to Erec. The valets must have sent him a message as soon as she got back, because he turned up not long after and dragged her away for a private audience.

"I hear you went wandering with our saint," he said. "What happened?"

Rachelle decided that a little bit of the truth couldn't hurt. "It turns out the protections on the Château are worse than we thought," she said. "We went walking and ended up in the Great Forest."

"And you didn't bring me along?" he asked lightly.

"I didn't have a choice," she said. "What happened while I was gone?"

"An extraordinary amount of panic. You would think that no member of the court had ever seen a woodspawn before."

"Most of them *haven't* seen a woodspawn before," said Rachelle. "Since none of them are out on the city streets at night."

Erec shrugged. "Well, the result is, the two of us are patrolling the grounds tonight lest such a terrible thing happen again." He managed to make the assignment sound like a ridiculous joke.

It was the same game he played every time they talked about the Forest. For once, Rachelle didn't get angry, but felt a sudden stab of worried pity. He seemed so sure that the Forest would never hurt him. She hoped he would never find out how wrong he was.

Erec might not yet believe that there was anything to fear. But everyone else in the Château did. She saw it all day as she followed Armand around the court: the whispers, the half-hidden fearful glances out the windows. People weren't quite ready to admit it out loud, but they knew.

Rachelle spent the rest of the day thinking about the lindenworm. She would fight it. The thought made her feel numb with fear, but she had no other choice: there was no way to stop the Devourer but with Joyeuse, and there was no way to get Joyeuse but to defeat the lindenworm. No matter how terrible the odds, she had to try.

Attacking it with just a sword would be suicide. And yet, if it came to that, Rachelle would try it. But she still hoped she could find another way.

Margot had suggested that there might be a woodwife charm that could work against it. *The most terrible charms,* she had said, *or the most simple.*

But Rachelle remembered the charm she had tried to weave

burning in her hands. She had been able to make the door appear, but that had only been awakening a charm already woven. It was quite likely that making even a simple charm would be impossible.

Could she ask Erec to help?

Two bloodbound might not be enough. Margot had said no human hands could kill a lindenworm. Then again, Margot wanted her to die, and anyway, bloodbound were not exactly human anymore. And Rachelle and Erec were the very best. If any bloodbound could do it, they could.

But would he help her?

Rachelle knew that asking Armand to help had been a far riskier gamble. He'd had reason to want her dead, while Erec considered her a friend. But Erec was . . . Erec, and when she imagined trying to tell him everything that she knew and suspected and planned—everything she *cared* about so desperately—she felt an awful, sinking suspicion that maybe he would laugh and decline to risk his life.

She was still wondering when they met that evening to patrol the grounds. Erec seemed to be in a fine mood; he grinned, and when she asked where they would start, he said simply, "Run with me."

So they ran.

When she was a child, Rachelle had loved to run. She had loved that one perfect moment, just after she hit her stride, when it felt like the air itself was flinging her forward and the ground had lost all claim to her, when her heart was racing faster than the wind.

Now that she was bloodbound, she could run like that forever. Or close enough. The wind roared in her face but couldn't stop her. And unlike all the other powers she had gained as a bloodbound, in this one there was no lingering memory of what she had done to win it. She ran, and didn't smell blood, only the damp, sweet evening air.

Erec finally skidded to a stop in a little moonlit clearing, beside a fountain full of writhing marble mermaids and living, placidly glinting carp. Rachelle stopped abruptly enough that she had to grab at his shoulder to regain her balance, and for a moment they teetered together, gasping for breath in a way that was almost laughter.

Erec smiled at her. "Do you like me now, my lady?"

"For once," she said, "yes."

And she meant it. He was only unbearable when he remembered he was a glory of the court. When they were just Erec and Rachelle, hunting in the darkness, then he was kind. Then she was happy to be with him.

They were Erec and Rachelle right now. If she told him about the lindenworm, would he understand?

She drew a breath to speak, but she wasn't sure where to start, and for a moment her heart thudded in the silence—

"And yet you scorn me still," Erec went on, because they were still on the grounds of Château de Lune and he had still not forgotten how handsome he was.

She laughed shakily. "I scorn to be one of your five hundred women."

"But if you were the only one?" asked Erec. "Because you could be, if you only said the word. There is a ruby waiting for you."

"No," she said flatly, trying to think how to turn the conversation back. It was sliding away from her, back into the well-worn paths of teasing and disdain, where neither of them could be truthful.

He raised his eyebrows. "Are you still angry over our duel? I can't help being better than you at sword fighting."

"You could have helped forcing me into it," she said. The familiar anger was so comforting that she spoke without thinking. "Not to mention—" She cut herself off.

"What?" said Erec. "The kiss? The force of *that* was entirely on your side, I believe."

Rachelle looked away. "You made me look like an animal," she said, and instantly wished the words unsaid.

"My lady, I did you honor. I showed you to all the court as a bloodbound terrible and lovely." He stepped closer and leaned down so they were nearly eye to eye. "We're stronger and fairer and we are going to live forever. Why would you want to pretend you're a plodding daylight creature?"

And there was her answer. She hadn't even had to risk his mockery by asking.

Erec might not fully understand their destiny. But he wanted it. He would never risk his life against a lindenworm, just so Rachelle could kill the Devourer.

She put a hand on his chest to push him back a step. "I told you already. I will die first."

"Such a perverse wish." He caught her hand. "Do you know what the old heathen stories called the first man and first woman, who crawled out from the roots of the first tree? Life and Life-Desiring."

Her chest ached, but she met his eyes with her normal scorn. "Were I a heathen, I'd find that inspiring."

"I only mean that it's the oldest law we know. Life, and desiring it."

"And destroying it. That's why the heathens spilled blood to Tyr and Zisa." She wrenched her hand free. "And that's why we both did what you know *damn* well we did!"

"That's not why I did it," said Erec. "I walked out into the woods and called for the forestborn because I needed a way to be pardoned after I killed my half brother."

Rachelle stared at him. "What?"

"It's a neat loophole: plain murder will get you hanged, but murder for the sake of becoming bloodbound can win you fame and fortune."

Of course she had known that since Erec was bloodbound, he must have killed. But she had never thought that— Well, she had never thought. She had spent so much time trying not to remember what she had done, there had been no time left over to wonder about others.

"Why did you want to kill him?" she asked numbly.

"You've noticed, haven't you? That the old families always have a well-placed bloodbound or two? It's not because the forest-born care about rank, it's because the families pick someone to walk into the woods and beg for the blessing. I should have been the bloodbound, since I wasn't due to inherit, but I overheard my father complain that my brother would rather roam the woods than manage the estate. I knew what that meant. I knew who was expendable enough to be his sacrifice. And I decided I would kill him first." Erec's mouth curved in the old ironic smile, and for once she could not tell whom he was mocking. "I won't deny it gave me satisfaction. He was legitimate, and heir to everything I lacked. At the time, that seemed very important."

Rachelle was silent. She didn't know what to say.

"Later it seemed less so," Erec went on thoughtfully. "And going by my brother's last words, I don't think he intended to become a bloodbound after all."

"I'm sorry," Rachelle said.

He smiled brilliantly and touched her cheek. "Why should you be? Don't I have everything I ever wanted?"

"I don't know," Rachelle said slowly. "Do you?"

"Well, I have not yet achieved *you*, my lady."

They patrolled the grounds for several more hours but found no more woodspawn. Rachelle bid Erec a very firm good night, then slipped into the Château through a side door and strode silently through the halls. There was a party still going in the eastern wing, but most people had finally gone to bed, so the halls were almost empty.

Erec wouldn't help her. That meant she had to face the linden-worm alone, with charms or with her sword. Either way seemed doomed to fail.

Every day for the last three years, she had thought she deserved to die.

She still didn't *want* to. She wanted to live with every filthy, desperate scrap of her heart.

When she saw somebody sitting huddled in the shadows at the feet of a statue, her hand went at once to her sword. Then she realized that it was Amélie.

"What are you doing here?" she asked.

Amélie, who had sprung to her feet as if to flee, relaxed.

"First I was waiting for you to get back," she said. "Then I thought I'd take a walk. Then I got tired. Where have you been?"

"Hunting." Rachelle sighed, and sat down. Amélie sat back down beside her.

"Why were you waiting for me?" Rachelle asked after a few moments.

"I worry about you," Amélie said simply. "You're very sad. And very far away."

And she was only going to get farther, because if by some miracle she did not die facing the lindenworm, she would surely die fighting the Devourer, and Amélie would never know the reason. Perhaps she would never even know for sure that Rachelle was dead. And it was worth it, absolutely worth it all if Amélie stayed safe and innocent, but when Rachelle thought about the yawning, never-to-be-crossed gulf between them, all the strength went out of her.

"Amélie," she asked, "what do you want, more than anything else in all the world?"

"I want my father back," Amélie said promptly.

Rachelle stared at her. "Well, that's not going to happen."

Amélie shrugged. "You didn't ask what I thought likely."

"I mean . . . what do you wish for?"

"Wishes are always impossible, that's the point," said Amélie. "I wish my father were alive. I wish I could paint cosmetics all the time. I wish that you would stop crying."

"I never cry," said Rachelle.

"That's what makes it extra impossible." Amélie leaned a little closer. "Why are you wondering about wishes?"

Rachelle looked at her hands. "I used to know what I wanted," she said. "A long time ago. I don't anymore."

Amélie's hands twisted together. "My mother says it's frivolous, wanting to learn cosmetics. Vain, too, even though it's not myself I'm painting. But when I'm mixing the pigments—when I'm painting *beauty* onto someone's face—I feel at peace. As if, just with a few brushstrokes, I am . . . being what God made me. I have never felt that way doing anything else."

Her jaw was tight, her eyes fixed on the other side of the hall as if a glorious battle awaited. With a spurt of guilt, Rachelle realized that as much as she'd enjoyed Amélie's art, she had never thought it was more than a frivolous game either.

"When you practice your cosmetics on me," she said quietly, "I feel at peace too."

Amélie turned to her with a smile. "I hope you think God wants *something* more out of you than sitting still while I paint."

The problem was that Rachelle knew exactly what God wanted her to do. He wanted her to die. Three years ago, she should have died rather than kill, and every breath she took since had been stolen. Maybe that was why she couldn't find any way to defeat the lindenworm: because she was supposed to die fighting.

But she couldn't tell Amélie that.

Instead, she asked, "So painting cosmetics is what you want the most?"

"Well," said Amélie, "I'm giving it up to help my mother make medicines. So I suppose it's not."

They sat in silence for a while longer. At last Amélie said quietly, "I know . . . something's going on in this palace. If you ever want to tell me, I'll listen."

Rachelle looked at her. She noticed the careful way that Amélie leaned toward her, closing the distance between them but not ever touching. She noticed that Amélie was biting her lip, the way she always did when she was nervous. She noticed that this was, in fact, her only friend.

She still couldn't tell her anything. Maybe it was foolish, but she had spent two and a half years trying to shelter Amélie. She couldn't bear to undo that now.

But she couldn't let Amélie's concern go unanswered, either.

So for the first time since she had pulled a bloodstained, crying Amélie off the street, wrapped her in a coat, and taken her home, Rachelle put an arm over her shoulders.

"Thank you," she said.

20

The next day was Sunday. All the court was expected to accompany the King to the palace chapel, where every week he demonstrated his devotion to appearances, if not to God.

Rachelle had not attended mass since she became bloodbound, and she hadn't expected to start now. For the past two weeks, she had gotten Erec to watch Armand while he was in the chapel. But this morning she couldn't find him, so she had to follow Armand inside.

She knew that the stories about bloodbound screaming and bursting into flame on consecrated ground were false. Justine was proof enough of that. But the last time she'd walked into a church, she hadn't been bloodbound. She'd been the good little daughter of Marie and Barthélemy Brinon, training to become a woodwife and dreaming of saving the world. She'd still believed that she loved God. That chapel was everything she had lost and renounced and spat upon.

But when she actually walked inside, it wasn't so bad. The church she had grown up with was a little stone building, the walls plastered and painted with fading, clumsy portraits of the saints. The windows were narrow slits paned with cloudy, pale glass. The altar was a simple square stone with only the jawbone of a nameless martyr sitting upon it.

The royal chapel was a jewel box of a room: the floor was pure, shimmering white marble, while the walls and pillars were coated with a vast tracery of gold leaf. Between the gem-like stained glass windows hung tall paintings in equally glowing colors. Before the marble altar lay the skeleton of le Montjoie, patron saint of the royal line. Every one of his bones was completely gilded, enameled eyes set into his sockets, jeweled rings on his fingers and jeweled chains about his neck. It didn't feel a thing like the place where Rachelle had worshipped as a child, and filing into it with a mass of richly arrayed courtiers didn't feel much different from filing into the Salon du Mars.

Rachelle and Armand were seated in the lower section. That was the other thing that was different: in Rachelle's church, the people had all sat watching the priest as he stood at the altar. Here, every seat faced the back of the building, so they could spend the entire time looking up at the King sitting in his elevated red-velvet box with his chosen few. Today that chosen few did not include Rachelle and Armand, so they got the full view of the royal presence.

As the choir began to sing, Armand's jaw tightened, and then he turned around to stare at the altar.

"I think that's an insult to the King," Rachelle muttered under her breath.

"Forgive me if I don't feel like worshipping him today," Armand muttered back.

"I don't think anyone's worshipping anything in here," said Rachelle. Certainly the ladies next to them seemed a great deal more absorbed in whispering to each other and playing with a tiny dog than in paying due reverence to their King or deity. For a brief moment, she felt very sorry for whatever priest would be called upon to minister to such a blatantly impious congregation.

Then she realized who was leading the crowd of acolytes: Bishop Guillaume.

She felt hot and cold at once. *Who let him into the Château?* One glance up at the gallery convinced her that it hadn't been the King.

Well, who cared? She had never yet been forced to sit through one of his sermons, and she didn't care to start now. She stood, pushed past the other people in the pew, and walked out of the chapel. Whatever trouble she might get into, she'd rather bear it than the sermon.

Outside, leaning with her back against the wall, she knew she was a fool. It was a man she hated muttering prayers to a God she'd rejected. What did she have to fear? You couldn't get more damned than damned.

"Shouldn't you be in the chapel?" said Justine.

Rachelle's eyes snapped open. "What are you doing here?"

Justine stood a pace away, her arms crossed. Her face was grim, though as that was her usual expression, it meant nothing.

"Never mind that," Rachelle went on. "What's your precious Bishop doing here?"

"He came to preach to the King," said Justine. "I came to speak with you."

Rachelle's stomach turned. "I know what you're going to say. And I'll die before I join him."

Justine pursed her lips. "Did I ever tell you," she said quietly, "that before I was a bloodbound, I was a nun?"

Rachelle stared at her. It was the unspoken rule of the King's bloodbound that they never, ever talked about their pasts. But Erec had broken it last night, so perhaps she shouldn't be so surprised at Justine.

"I was pure as an angel and proud as a devil," Justine went on, frowning slightly as she stared into the distance. "Only, I found that neither purity nor pride was courage, in the end." Then she looked back at Rachelle. "Your pride won't be enough for you either. Give up serving the King. Ask to be made the Bishop's bloodbound."

"And then what?" Rachelle demanded. "Help put him on the throne? Do you think treason will save your soul?"

"I think I would rather serve him for the last of my days than the King. Why do you think the days grow shorter and the forestborn grow stronger?"

Rachelle threw away her caution. "Because the Devourer is awakening."

She'd expected nothing else, but it still hurt when Justine's mouth twisted with disgust. "Do you still cling to your heathen superstitions? The darkness falls because God is judging us for our sins. He has delivered us over to the woodspawn and the forestborn for chastisement."

"Our sinfulness," said Rachelle, "is in living and in letting other bloodbound live. If you were truly sorry, you would get out a knife and cut your throat. As for me, I've spent more time talking to the forestborn than you ever have, and I much prefer them to the Bishop. At least they don't pretend they're holy."

"Do as you will, then." Justine stood. "But I will pray for you," she added imperturbably, and walked into the chapel.

The doors had barely shut behind her when la Fontaine wandered into the hallway, gently fluttering a mother-of-pearl fan. She raised an eyebrow at Rachelle. "Slipped out before the consecration? Perhaps we should call you Mélusine."

"Shouldn't *you* be in there as well?" Rachelle asked sourly. She'd come out into the hallway to be alone, not to chat with every member of the court.

La Fontaine shrugged exquisitely, setting her ruby earrings swinging. "I've lived my life for one imaginary kingdom. I've no patience left for another."

Rachelle had not imagined that the court concealed many true believers, but she also hadn't expected anyone to be so blatant. Then again, if you were the King's mistress, she supposed you weren't going to impress anyone with your piety anyway.

"Who's Mélusine?" she asked.

"You don't know the story?" said la Fontaine. "And you the beloved of Fleur-du-Mal."

"He's not my beloved," said Rachelle. "And he doesn't tell me bedtime stories."

"You might like it, for it's a grim tale." La Fontaine snapped her fan shut. "Once upon a time, a certain lord lost his way as he was hunting through the woods. He stumbled upon a clearing that he had never seen before, and there on the grass sat a woman of dazzling beauty, naked as the day she was born, combing out her long yellow hair. Of course you can imagine how deeply he fell in love with her. He bore the strange lady, who said her name was Mélusine, back to his castle and married her with all due pomp and ceremony. For years they lived happily and she bore him three sons and four daughters. Only one curiosity marred their life together: the lady always found a reason not to go with him to chapel. She was too tired, or she had a headache, or she needed to be shriven. Finally the lord demanded that his wife come with him. After many protestations, she consented, but as the mass progressed, she grew more and more restless, until at last she leaped out of the pew and fled for the door. On the threshold, her husband caught hold of her, but with a great shriek, she grew tusks and wings and claws. The lord let go of her in horror, and she flew away, never to be seen by mortal eyes again. That lord's name was Marcelin Angevin, first duke of Anjou, and ever since a shadow has lain upon his line."

"And thus," said Erec, emerging from one of the side doors, "we are called the devil's children. A title even bastards can inherit."

"And yet you are not the only one who could be called the devil's child," said la Fontaine. She carefully did not look at Rachelle, and the line of her turned-away jaw was a more pointed accusation than any glare.

Since Rachelle would someday change into a creature hardly better than a demon, she could not object to the comparison.

"If you're referring to the pair of us in our capacity as bloodbound," said Erec, who had no sense of when to stay silent, "the devil's lovers might be better. I assure you, there was nothing parental in the forestborn who brought us to this state."

Rachelle winced, remembering her own forestborn's kiss.

La Fontaine saluted him with her fan. "You will never lack wit, my dear Fleur-du-Mal, not even on Judgment Day. Best hope the Dayspring finds you as amusing as I do."

"I thought you didn't believe," said Rachelle.

"I believe in making threats when it's convenient," said la Fontaine. "Doesn't everyone?" She gave them a slight curtsy, just barely treading the line between sarcasm and respect. "Give my respects to my cousin, Mélusine. I look forward to seeing him again. You, too—if convenient."

"Oh dear," said Erec, watching her skirt swish as she walked away. "She isn't jealous, is she?"

Rachelle remembered the way la Fontaine had found her and Armand at the reception, her distress when she thought Armand wasn't eating enough. "I think she's protective."

"So long as she keeps attacking with literary references, I think we can withstand her." Erec looked at Rachelle. "Did she guess correctly? Did the holy chapel make you sprout horns?"

"No," said Rachelle, "I just didn't care for the preaching. What's your excuse?"

"Myself, I don't care to worship anyone who got hacked to pieces. It doesn't inspire confidence. The Dayspring is the image of the invisible God, isn't he? Maybe that's what really dwells in the Unapproachable Light: just a pile of bloody limbs."

She was so far past damned that it didn't matter what blasphemies she heard, but Rachelle still winced. "I'm sure the Bishop would like that," she said. "A dead God who could never contradict him—that would be his dream come true."

"And you? Have you seen any sign that the world is governed by something besides hunger and devouring?"

She remembered Aunt Léonie's futile, gasping prayers as she died.

"No. But I'd rather worship bloody bones than the murderer who makes them."

"And yet instead of worshipping, you stand here gossiping with a fellow murderer."

She grinned at him. "When have I ever followed my principles?"

"Never. And far too often." He took her hand. "I wish you'd reconsider some of them."

Then she laughed out loud. "If you're asking me to be your mistress again . . . blasphemy is a terrible way to start."

"I'm only wondering if you truly regret your choices as much as you claim," he said.

She remembered his soft voice as he told her about his brother the night before, and her throat tightened.

"Do you?" she asked, and she truly wondered.

"I think it doesn't matter what either one of us regrets," said Erec. "We are going to live forever, in darkness and in dancing. Because I know you, my lady, and you don't have it in you to be a lamb for the slaughter any more than I do. The same wolfish greed beats in your heart: to have what you will, and kill for it. Or why would you be alive? And you are alive, and have your will, so what should you regret?"

It was like when Justine dislocated her arm: something familiar, swinging painfully out of place. Because Rachelle had told herself those same words, or near enough, a thousand times. She had wanted to live. She had gotten her wish. She could not claim to regret. Only minutes ago, she had snarled at Justine: *If you were really sorry, you would get out a knife and cut your throat.*

But now that she heard Erec say those words to her . . . they sounded wrong.

She thought, *I regret.*

"Speechless?" asked Erec. "Don't be ashamed. I bring all ladies to that state sooner or later."

Rachelle had always thought Erec understood her. No matter how she hated him, she had always loved him a little too, because he knew what she was in the darkest part of her soul. And yet now he really thought that she was speechless with desire for him. He really thought that she did not regret what she had done.

"Too bad for you," she said, "I'm not a lady."

He chuckled, clearly thinking that this was only another step in their dance together.

It was the most exquisite kind of freedom to realize that he could be wrong. It was terrifying too.

21

Talking with Erec had made everything more clear. She *did* regret. She *was* willing to die. And that meant there was only one path for her to take: weave a charm and try her best against the lindenworm.

It would have to be a sleep charm. Margot had said, *The most terrible charms or the most simple,* and sleep charms were the only simple charms she knew that seemed like they might be at all helpful. Yet one of the little snowflake-shaped sleep charms she used to hang over baby beds could not possibly be enough, or nobody would have ever feared lindenworms.

She decided to try weaving multiple sleep charms together, and she spent the rest of the day working out the pattern. Luckily Amélie already had a ball of yarn that she could use.

"You're going to help," Rachelle told Armand that evening.

He raised his eyebrows. "Are you planning to clamp knitting needles onto my hands? Because I don't think that will work as well as it does with forks. And it doesn't work all that well with forks either, though apparently it looks quite impressive. Several ladies have assured me that I'm very brave for managing to eat by myself."

"Well," said Rachelle, "I certainly won't tell you that."

He laughed.

"And luckily," she went on, "I don't need you to tie knots. I just need you to stay still. Here." She sat him down in a chair and had him hold up his hands. She looped the yarn through his silver fingers and started weaving it together.

It was awkward sitting so close to him—their knees were almost touching, she could hear every breath he took, and the strange desire for him was seeping back into her. She tried to concentrate on the pattern, looking frequently at her sketches and weaving in quick, short motions.

The problem was, she hadn't woven in three years. Very soon, the pattern started bunching. She had woven it too tight. So she pulled it out, and starting whirling through the pattern again with less tension—only now ungainly loops were dropping from it, because she was making it too loose. Again she pulled it out. This time it seemed to go better, but slowly the shape got more and more wrong, until at last she realized that she had left out two steps when she started the pattern. Her breath hissed out between her teeth in frustration.

"Now you know how I feel with forks," said Armand.

She looked up at him, tensing. She expected to see mockery—Erec would have said the words with a sly grin and then winked—but Armand just looked at her with a wry half smile. Come to think of it, Erec would never have mentioned that he was bad at anything.

Rachelle laughed shakily and started to unwind again. "I have bloodbound grace and speed," she said. "But it's all for fighting."

"You seemed to dance pretty well."

"That was with Erec. That counts as fighting." Her voice was rougher than she meant it to be, and she didn't meet his eyes.

"I think everything at court counts," he said.

She started weaving the pattern again, slowly and carefully. "I don't think there's enough chance of bloodshed."

He paused. "There's chance of bloodshed in dancing?"

"I repeat: with Erec d'Anjou."

He laughed, and it shouldn't have made any difference. But it did. The memory of the duel was no longer crawling right beneath her skin; it had still happened, but it felt like a much smaller and sillier thing.

For a few moments she wove in silence. Then Armand said, "I've been wondering about something. The way you fight—it's incredible. Not just your speed, but your technique. I've seen men trained all their lives who weren't that good. But you couldn't have been trained before you came to Rocamadour."

"No," Rachelle agreed.

"Did you . . . learn it from the mark?"

"Not exactly." Rachelle paused, finishing a particularly tricky bit of the pattern before continuing, "It's . . . an instinct. For any sort of fighting. It's like reading a book, I suppose. You don't know the words until you see them, but you have them as soon as you do." She remembered Amélie reading aloud a cosmetics recipe to her. "Erec trained me when I came to the city. In two weeks, I could nearly keep up with him."

"Hm."

Armand sounded pensive; she looked up. "Do you feel it?" she asked. "That instinct?"

His mouth puckered. "Sometimes. Maybe. I really hope not." He paused. "Is that how it feels to have the Forest's power growing inside you?"

"It's not . . . just that."

"What is it?"

She couldn't tell him about the strange fury that sometimes came over her, the desire to crush and destroy. Sitting here with him in quiet peace, knowing she had felt that fury toward him, however briefly—the thought was just obscene.

So she told him about the other way that the Forest crawled into her mind.

"All of us bloodbound," she said. "There's a dream we have.

You're standing on a path in the woods—barren woods, with snow on the ground—and at the end of the path, there's a house. It's made of wood, but thatched with bones. There's blood seeping between the wooden boards. And you have to walk toward it. You can slow yourself down, but you can't stop. I can't . . . I can't tell you how terrifying it is."

"And what happens when you reach it?" asked Armand.

"Nobody that I've ever talked to has reached it yet. But I think—we all think—when you open the door, that's when you become a forestborn."

Armand was silent.

"Do you dream it?" she asked finally.

"No," he said distantly. "No, I don't."

"So you have the healing, but not the dreams? That's convenient."

"I also have visions of the Great Forest all the time," he said. "Trust me, that's not convenient."

And Rachelle went back to weaving. Armand didn't speak again—unlike Erec, who could never stop talking. He seemed content just to watch her and the pattern she was weaving. When she looked up and caught his eye, he didn't feel the need to wink or smirk; he smiled faintly and went on watching.

She began to remember how weaving charms had always soothed her: the soft slide of the yarn against her fingers. The quick, repetitive motions. The slowly building pattern. Her hands found their rhythm, dancing through the pattern, looping the yarn in and out and around his fingers, and slowly the woven pattern grew between them.

Something else was growing too. She felt every breath that Armand took and every breath that she took. She felt the tiny space of air between their knees. She felt the way his head tilted, the way light glanced off his jaw, the way his eyelids flickered as he looked down at the yarn, and up at her face.

She thought it was just the same curious peace she felt when Amélie did her makeup, because like then, the world had narrowed down to her and Armand and tiny scraps of sensation. Then her hands overshot the pattern, and she nearly jerked the yarn out of alignment. She caught herself, but her wrist brushed against his, and a tiny shiver went up her arm.

Their eyes met. Her face felt hot. Her hands, though gripping the yarn, felt empty.

She thought, *This is not the way I feel about Erec.*

She thought, *I think I love him.*

The words slid into her head between one breath and the next, and she couldn't deny them any more than she could pretend she wasn't breathing.

She loved Armand. It was a simple, absolute feeling, as if her heart had turned into a compass that pointed toward him. Suddenly it didn't matter that she was dying, that she didn't get to keep him, that she didn't get to have him in the first place because he would never feel the same way about her.

He was here. She stared at the line of his jaw, listened to his breathing, and wrapped yarn around his glittering fingers. He was here, and she could drink in his presence like cool water and fresh air. For this one moment, just seeing him was a miracle, and it was enough.

"It's pretty," said Amélie.

Rachelle flinched and turned. Amélie stood behind her, next to one of the little tables, on which rested a tray bearing a silver pitcher and three cups. The warm, rich smell of hot chocolate wafted up from them.

"That's the first time you didn't notice me walking into the room," said Amélie.

"I was busy," Rachelle said stiffly. Her fingers shook as she wound the last few loops in the pattern. Then she ripped the yarn from its skein, tied it off, and pulled the piece loose from Armand's fingers. "There. All done."

"Pretty," said Armand, looking at the floor.

Amélie leaned in closer to look. "What's it for?"

Rachelle's heart thumped. "To keep Monsieur Vareilles safe," she said, because if she told Amélie about the lindenworm then she'd have to tell her about the door and Joyeuse and the Devourer—and she wanted to keep her friend free of that darkness for just a little longer.

"It's awfully big," said Amélie. "Is he that much trouble?"

"You have no idea," said Rachelle, and Amélie's grin made the lie completely worth it.

"Well, then you deserve chocolate," said Amélie, and handed her a cup.

"Do I deserve any?" asked Armand. "Even though I'm trouble?"

"I don't know, does he?" Amélie looked at Rachelle.

Rachelle looked at him as she took a deep breath of the steam from her cup.

"Yes," she said. "This time he deserves it. Yes."

The next day, Rachelle woke up and thought, *Tonight we get Joyeuse. Or die.*

The morning was busy with attending the King, and Rachelle found it harder than usual to pretend to be respectful. Armand, too, seemed tense. Finally, when the bells were tolling two o'clock, Rachelle turned to Armand and said, "I don't care if we get in trouble. I can't stand this a moment longer. If there's a place you like in the gardens, tell me now, or I'll just drag you out any which way."

Armand smiled and said, "There is a spot, actually."

Fifteen minutes later, she was following him on a narrow ghost of a path between hedges, wondering if this was an elaborate joke. Except Armand—unlike Erec—did not seem particularly interested in teasing her.

They rounded two little hills and went through a gate in a hedge—and then Rachelle stopped. Before them was a miniature lake, studded with lily pads; on the other side was a small country cottage, red tiles on the roof and dark wooden beams crisscrossing its white plaster walls. Roses cascaded over one side of the building; on the other was a low, open stable that housed no horses—but chickens wandered clucking in and out among the piles of straw. It looked like a house from her own village as described by la Fontaine; any moment, ruffles would appear on Rachelle's coat.

"What *is* that?" asked Rachelle.

"The Trebuchet," said Armand. "Built by the King's late father for his mistress Marie d'Astoir."

"Why did he name it after a siege weapon?" she asked.

"He didn't. But Marie d'Astoir only accepted him after he built it, and the Queen retaliated with an epic poem of rhymed couplets, describing the siege of Marie's virtue and calling this cottage the trebuchet that brought down her walls. Marie was humiliated and swore never to associate with the Queen again. It was the great scandal of the day."

"I can't see why that would be scandalous," said Rachelle. "Since apparently *everyone* does it."

"Oh, it wasn't her sleeping with the King that was a scandal, it was her fighting with the Queen. And yes, that doesn't make a bit of sense, and no, the court hasn't changed. Guess what the Bishop talked about in his sermon last Sunday."

"Everyone in this court is mad," Rachelle said, trying not to think about what else the Bishop might have said, or what Armand might have thought of it. But then she realized with a sudden, sick clarity that she did want to know. She was desperate to know what Armand was thinking.

They had come to the stable—if it could be called that, since on closer inspection it was clear that it had never been meant to house horses, but simply to have the same vague outline as a stable and provide a resting place for all the hay bales that were now infested with chickens. The cottage, too, was subtly different from the ones Rachelle had known—windows too large, hall too long. It was like the entire building had been sketched from somebody's nostalgic, drunken memory of a farmhouse.

"What else did the Bishop talk about?" she asked.

"Oh, you know, the sins of the court and so forth." Armand's voice was light, his face slightly angled away so she couldn't quite read his expression. "There has not been such hypocrisy since the Imperium, when they fed men to lions for amusement, yet called themselves righteous because of the sin-eaters they kept chained at their doors."

"And let me guess," Rachelle bit out, "I'm one of the sin-eaters."

"You've said so yourself, haven't you?" Without waiting for a reply, Armand strode forward into the shade of the not-stable and seated himself in a pile of straw.

"What are you doing?" she asked.

"Sitting down." He poked at the straw and slid his silver hand under an egg, cradling it neatly. "Catch."

Rachelle's hand snapped out. She caught the egg easily, but too hard; it crunched in her hands, yolk running out between her fingers.

"You," she said furiously, and then Armand looked up at her half grinning, half fearful. Memory sliced through her chest: Marc, her little brother, one morning when they were supposed to be gathering up the eggs carefully for Mother. They'd started tossing the eggs instead, and when Marc threw one too hard and it cracked against her hand, he'd looked at her just like that.

The forestborn had marked her the next day.

She stooped swiftly, grabbed an egg from among the straw, and threw it at Armand. He got his hand up in time: the egg crunched against the metal of his palm. He rocked backward with a laugh.

"What is wrong with you?" asked Rachelle.

He looked at the egg dripping down his hand. "I was wondering if you would snap and kill me."

His voice was light, but with a strange alertness. And Rachelle felt like she had been kicked in the gut as she realized that he meant it.

"What is *wrong* with you?" she repeated.

"No talent for survival, but you already knew that." He rubbed his hand awkwardly in the hay. "That will take a while to clean off."

Rachelle knelt beside him, grabbed a handful of hay, and started wiping away egg. "Did you really think I might kill you?" she asked quietly.

He went still. Then he looked up at her and said, "You're angry, but you're never vicious. You've been kind to me, and I'm very grateful. I don't think you would kill me unless you received orders."

"An assassin." Her voice was thick and rough in her throat. She shouldn't have felt betrayed, and yet she did. "You think I'm an assassin."

"Isn't that what all the bloodbound are?" His voice was very quiet. "People speak out against the King and then they vanish. Everyone knows how it works."

"I have *never* done that."

"Have you?"

"No, damn you, I have *begged* Erec to keep me away from those missions, and if you don't think that was a sacrifice, you haven't ever owed him a favor. I hunt woodspawn. I save the lives people like you are too weak to protect. That's all."

"But you are the King's bloodbound," he went on quietly, relentlessly. "You serve him and support his rule, even if you let the other bloodbound kill for you and be your sin-eaters."

"*You* support his rule," she snapped. "And wear silks and live in palaces because of it."

"So now I'm not a prisoner? That's lovely. Do you mind if I get up and leave now?"

Rachelle was drawing her hand back to strike him before she even knew what she was doing. Then she saw him bracing himself. Feeling sick, she dropped her hands. How had they come to this so quickly?

"You know what I am," she said. "You knew when we were in my village and you said—" She couldn't force the words out. "I have saved your life *how* many times now, and you still don't trust me?"

"You've said how many times that it's only because I'm useful?"

He did have a point there.

"Why are you so desperate to hate me?" she asked quietly. "Why *now*?"

His mouth tightened and he looked away from her. Then he said quietly, "Because I am terrified to trust you." He let out a shaky laugh. "I was ready for any kind of jailer but you."

And the worst thing was, she understood. She had told him, right from the start, that she was a bloodbound and dangerous, that she was his jailer and didn't want to protect him. He was only trying to listen to her. And yet now—even now, he was biting his lip and looking sideways at her.

"You shouldn't trust me," she said. "You shouldn't."

He looked suddenly distressed. "Rachelle—"

"Do you know who was the woodwife who trained me, whom I killed to save my own life? She was my aunt. I loved her more than my own mother. She told me and *told* me to be careful in the woods, but I thought I was clever enough to speak with a forestborn and outwit him. So he marked me. And I was too scared and ashamed to tell her until the last day, and when I did— When I finally ran to her for help, the forestborn had gotten there first."

Then her throat closed up, and for a moment she couldn't speak. She had spent so long trying so hard not to think of that day, but the memories were as sharp as ever and they shredded through her.

"He had taken his time with her. There was blood everywhere." She could smell it even now, and her stomach roiled. "Do you know, when people are cut up enough, they don't look human anymore? They look like . . . like dolls that were sewn by a monster. But she was still alive. She *saw* me, and she whimpered.

"Then the forestborn said he'd found a worthy sacrifice for me. I couldn't move. He said this was the bargain I had made, and she whimpered again. He said he could make her live for days longer if he wanted. I would die screaming of the mark and her agony would go on and on before he let her die. Or I could kill her quickly and live.

"So I did." Rachelle clenched her teeth for a moment, then

went on, "She still tried to escape. Do you see this scar?" She held up her hand, showing him the tiny white mark in her palm. "She stabbed me in the hand with a needle—he'd found her making charms; there was thread everywhere—but she was so weak. And so horrible. I couldn't bear to look at her. I hated her the way you hate a spider when you're killing it. I cut her throat and I hated her for being hurt by me."

She dared to look at him then. Armand looked steadily back at her, his eyes solemn, and said nothing.

"Well?" she demanded. "What are you going to say? It's all right because at least I tried to resist? Everyone tries to be good until it stops being convenient!"

"No—"

"Or are you going to tell me it was a kindness to kill her? That it wasn't so bad, because at least I ended her suffering? I was there. I know *exactly* how bad it was, and not all the suffering in the world could make it right."

She realized her eyes were stinging, and she scraped at them with the back of her hand.

"No," said Armand after a moment. "It's not all right. You should have died first."

She had been dreading those words. She had expected they would break her. But instead, she only choked on a laugh as her hand clenched around the scar. "If I ever want to be driven to despair, I'll go straight to you."

"If I'd said you'd done right, you would have throttled me," he said.

"I thought you didn't have any talent for survival."

"Maybe you're teaching me."

"And what do you want to teach me?" she asked wearily. "I already know I ought to be dead."

"No, you shouldn't," said Armand. "What good would that do?"

"At least then I'd get what I deserved. Like your precious Bishop says."

"You know," said Armand, "my mother used to say that if we all got what we deserved, we'd all be dead. And yet somehow God refrains from smiting us. Whatever you ought to have done then, dying won't undo it now. And I'm glad I got to meet you."

"You," said Rachelle, "are insane."

"You," he said, "are not the first one to tell me that. And one more thing. I don't believe you're damned."

"Then what am I?"

He let out a breath. "I think . . . you are not content. You have power and beauty and strength that others could only dream of. You could be immortal. But you are never content. Not when you're at the center of the court and not when you're riding with the Wild Hunt and not when you're cutting down your enemies with a sword. So you cannot be damned."

Her throat tightened. It was unfair—it was absolutely unfair that his voice could make her heart beat with jagged, idiotic hope.

"Pretty words," she said. "But a bit heretical. I don't recall hearing that any of the damned were content."

"They're content to stay in their sins." He grinned at her, and it felt like there was no space or barrier at all between them, like his smile was happening inside her heart. Without meaning to at all, she smiled back.

They were both fools, perhaps.

23

As soon as the sun set, they slipped back down to the wine cellar. Rachelle laid her hands on the floor, and the door appeared before them.

Armand got to his feet. "So how do we use the charm?"

"Normally we'd hang it over somebody's bed." She pulled out the charm, which had been hung like a scarf around her neck. "Or we would if this were a regular sleep charm. I suppose instead we throw it over the lindenworm's coils."

"That sounds strangely easy," said Armand.

"Well . . . this sort of charm needs to be awakened."

"And that means?"

"A lot of things that I spent years learning. But what it comes down to is that I have to hold the charm in place and concentrate for a moment." And now that she was saying it out loud, her heart was finally starting to pick up speed.

"While the two heads try to bite you?" Armand asked dubiously.

"Last time it took a moment to wake up. As long as I awaken the charm faster, we'll be all right." Rachelle hoped that the words didn't sound as stupid to him as they did to her.

Armand shrugged. "Well, I don't suppose it will be the craziest thing I've ever done." He pulled back his sleeve with his teeth and lifted his arm to the door. Rachelle shifted the charm to her left hand and drew her sword.

The door swung in. Darkness fell.

Instantly Rachelle lunged forward, flinging the charm while clinging to one end. She let herself feel the soft fibers against her skin, and inside her mind she *reached* as she tried to awaken the charm. For one moment she had it—she could feel the power humming through the charm—

Then she remembered the way Aunt Léonie had smiled at her the first time she managed it, and the way she had shuddered when Rachelle laid the knife against her throat, and the power was gone.

Four eyes opened.

There was no time to think, only move. Rachelle drew her sword and slashed, cutting off the nearest head, then dodged to the side and tried to cut off the other. But she moved at the wrong angle; her sword only got halfway into the creature's neck and then stuck. The lindenworm screamed and reared up, tearing the sword from her hands—and then the other head was already grown back and surging toward her.

Rachelle ducked just in time. At least she still had a hold on the sleep charm.

"Armand!" she shouted. "Distract it!"

She didn't notice if he did or not; all her attention was on the lindenworm's two swaying heads—and her sword, stuck in its neck. When the head with the sword lunged at her, she was ready. She rolled to the side, grabbed the sword, and wrenched it free. The next moment, she had sliced off the head, but the other was hurtling toward her—

Armand flung himself at the other head, hitting it right where the neck began and throwing his arms around it. "Do it!" he yelled.

Rachelle grabbed the charm, ducked as the head lunged at her, slammed her sword into the neck and down, pinning it to the floor. The lindenworm bucked and writhed beneath her, but she was pressing the charm against its neck and trying, trying, *trying* to awaken it—

And the charm sang in her mind, and the lindenworm went slack beneath her. Its eyes were still open, but the glow had dimmed; when she looked closer, she saw that the pale film of its inner eyelids had slid across its eyes.

It looked like the creature could still see her. But when she waved her hands in front of its nose, it didn't move. She kicked it lightly in the head, and all that happened was that its scaled outer eyelids finally shut.

Rachelle's breath shuddered out of her. She thought, *I really did it. I'm still alive.*

Then she remembered what Armand had done. She looked up.

There was more light now, she realized: torches blazed on the walls, as if celebrating the lindenworm's defeat. But she couldn't see Armand anywhere, just the vast tangle of the lindenworm's body, scales gleaming in the torchlight.

"Armand?" she shouted, climbing over the body. "Where are you?" Her heart pounded because if he was dead—if he was dead—

"Here." His voice was muffled. "I'm a little tied up."

And then Rachelle saw a foot sticking out from under the lindenworm's coils.

"Buried, more like," she said, her voice shaky with relief, and she set about untangling him. He was still gripping the lindenworm's other head; it jiggled when she started to pull him free, and in an instant she had her sword drawn.

"I think it's asleep," said Armand, letting go of the head.

Rachelle sheathed her sword. "I know that," she said. "But you, what were you *thinking*?"

"That it was going to bite you and then we'd both be dead?"

"You're an idiot."

"You are not the first to tell me that." He smiled, and it felt like ground glass in her chest, because she was sure he had smiled like that at his forestborn, and he would smile like that every other time he tried to do the right thing. And she knew what happened to good people, from the Dayspring right on down to Aunt Léonie.

"You're going to die an idiot," she snarled. "You won't last another week, and I'll have to watch you die."

And strangely, that wiped away his smile and left him looking desperately tired and sad.

"True enough," he said. "So I really have nothing to lose."

He flung an arm around her shoulders, and kissed her.

It was nothing like Erec's kisses. It was just Armand's lips clumsily mashed against hers. But she felt it through her whole body like a bolt of lightning because it was Armand, warm and alive and *wanting to touch her*—

It seemed like only a heartbeat later that he let go. It took her a moment to remember how to breathe and how to think and by then he was stepping back, smiling again.

"You," said Rachelle. "You—"

"Really," he said, "you have to be careful about telling people they're doomed. It makes them crazy."

"You were already crazy," said Rachelle. He couldn't want her. He was everything that could never want her, but he had kissed her, and now her heart was starting to beat with dreadful hope.

"So that means you need to be extra careful." Then he was

starting to climb down the coils of the lindenworm on the other side.

She caught at his shoulder. "Armand—"

"I know." He pulled free and didn't look back. "You're not here to kiss me, you're here to make use of me."

He believed it. His voice was cheerful, but she could tell he believed she had no use for him beyond opening doors, and in that moment nothing mattered except making him see that he was wrong.

Rachelle lunged after him. Her feet hit the stone floor and she seized him by the shoulders. "You are not just *useful* to me," she said. "You are . . ."

His eyes met hers, wide and suspicious and unyielding. "What?" he asked. "What am I to you?"

She couldn't speak. There weren't words for what he was. He was everything she hated, and in all the world, he was the person with the most right to hate her. But when the Forest blossomed around them in la Fontaine's salon, he'd looked her in the eyes, denied everything she said, and *understood* her. He had listened to her in the garden that morning, and denied nothing she said, and still forgiven her. What could you even call that kind of person?

Armand was the one who knew how to speak, anyway. He smiled and turned his words into knives that sliced out answers and distinctions. She was just the girl who plunged blindly ahead and doomed herself doing it.

But she thought he might actually want that girl. So she leaned forward and kissed him. Just a tiny, hesitant kiss, and it was more terrifying than any woodspawn she had ever faced. But then his arms wrapped around her as he started to kiss her back, and she still couldn't believe that he meant it, that this sweetness was for *her*—

She pulled away. "This is all I have to give you," she said. "I'm—I'm still bloodbound. You know what that means."

"Yes," he said quietly. "Yes, I do."

"But everything I have," she said, "I want to give you. Because I love you. I think I'm falling in love with you."

"I don't have anything else to give you, either," he said. "But I think I love you too."

Then he kissed her again. And kissed her and kissed her, until her heartbeat was a song and her veins pulsed with honey and fire, and his arms were around her and he was not letting go. He knew what she was and he was not letting go.

She had never understood, until now, what it would be like to kiss somebody who was not trying to use or master her. Who cleanly and simply *delighted* in her.

Finally he stopped and whispered, "Rachelle—"

"Don't say it," she said. "Whatever you're going to say. Don't. You know what I am. What I'm going to be. Not even you can change that."

"I was going to say, 'I think the lindenworm might be waking up.' "

In an instant she was out of his arms with her sword drawn. One of the lindenworm's heads lay near her; its eyes had started to open, though the pale film of the inner eyelids was still drawn shut.

Her first panicked impulse was to hack at it with her sword. Then she remembered the charm. She could just barely see one end of it, hanging off the pile of the lindenworm's coils.

She let herself panic for one stomach-churning moment. Then she dropped the sword and scaled the lindenworm in two leaps. She fell to her knees, pressed shaking hands to the charm, and thought, *Sleep, sleep, sleep.*

She thought it wasn't working, but then it did. The lindenworm shuddered and grew still underneath her. In the silence after, Rachelle could hear her own heartbeat, her ragged breaths.

That had been too close. She should never have let herself get distracted.

After gulping a few more breaths, she slid down off the lindenworm, back to where Armand waited.

"Come on," she said. "We need Joyeuse. Now."

"Is that why you dragged me here?"

He didn't sound surprised, and Rachelle stared at him. "You *knew*?"

"I guessed. There are only so many lost things that a blood-bound might be desperate to recover. I think it's right there." He pointed.

They were on the far side of the lindenworm now, and here the room was not a perfect replica of the Hall of Mirrors: there was a statue the like of which Rachelle had never seen in the Château. It was Zisa, but unlike every other statue of Zisa that Rachelle had ever seen, she was not identified by the sun or moon in her hand. Instead, she stood over the prone body of Tyr, a moment after cutting off his right hand.

She was carved of the same sandstone as the rest of the hall. But she held a sword made out of bone.

It was all bone, blade and hilt. Runes were carved up the blade; the pommel and cross-guard were delicate filigree that looked like tiny branches. She couldn't see what the grip was like because Zisa's stone fingers were wrapped firmly around it.

That was a problem. Rachelle tried to push the statue over so it would break, but it was immovable.

"There must be a trick," said Armand, poking at the statue with his silver hand.

Where he touched it, the statue started to crumble. In moments, it was no more than a pile of dust on the floor, Joyeuse lying free at the center.

"Lovely," said Rachelle, reaching down to grab the sword—only to drop it again with a hiss of pain. The sword *burned*. She shook her hand; it wasn't bleeding, but it was flushed and swollen where she had touched the hilt.

"What?" asked Armand, bending down to nudge the sword with his silver hand.

The hilt moved. It grew and stretched and wrapped like ivy around his hand, until it looked like he was holding it, though Rachelle supposed that in a way, the sword was holding him.

Darkness fell around them. The lindenworm was gone, and the strange hallway with it.

A moment later, they were in the west gardens with the moon overhead.

They were alive. Against all odds, they were alive, and Armand was holding Joyeuse. It felt like the sun in her mind, and without meaning to, she reached for it.

As soon as her finger touched the bone, she felt the burn again, and her hand snapped back.

"I don't pretend to know your plans," said Armand, "but it's going to be a problem if you can't hold Joyeuse."

"It hurts," said Rachelle, "but I can hold it if I have to."

"So you're planning to wield it?"

Rachelle looked at him: his rumpled hair, his weary, affectionate eyes. He had helped her. Against all reason, he loved her.

But it was one thing to love a bloodbound. It was another to believe that the Devourer—the ancient heathen terror denied by priest and bishop—could rise again, and in such power as to destroy the world. And Armand had lost too much for his beliefs to ever question them.

"I'm not going to hurt you with it," she said. "The rest is not your business."

"I see," he said quietly, and he sounded disappointed.

Rachelle's throat tightned, and she almost told him then and there. But she couldn't stand to find the limits of his trust. And whether he knew or not—whether he trusted her or not—wouldn't make any difference in the end.

"I told you," she said roughly, "that you couldn't change me."

He laughed softly. "That you did." He paused. "But even if you don't—"

"Please. Don't ask." The words came out more desperate than she had meant them to. If he asked her, really asked, then she wasn't sure.

Armand looked at her in silence for a moment. Then he glanced down Joyeuse. The bone tendrils unwrapped from his wrist, and the sword fell to the ground. He knelt, awkwardly scooped up the sword with his silver hands, and held it out to her.

"Wrap it in your coat," he said. "You can carry it that way."

24

The next day, Rachelle didn't know which was stranger: that she had Joyeuse itself hidden underneath her bed—or that she was *happy*.

She didn't have much time left. If she was right about the solstice, she only had three days. Then the Devourer would return, and she would fight him, and one way or another, she would die. But until then—for those precious few days, however many they were—she had nothing to fight and nothing to fear, and nothing to do but spend time with Armand and Amélie.

Something was wrong, though. Armand was quiet and grim at breakfast; Amélie chattered with a rapid brightness that didn't seem quite real. Throughout the day, as Rachelle escorted Armand from one court function to the next, she noticed him examining each room as they entered it. It was as if he were waiting for an attack.

She meant to ask him about it. But when they finally got back to their rooms at the end of the day, he smiled at her and kissed her, and she forgot everything except this one moment of feeling safe and loved. They drank hot chocolate together, and it was the most perfect evening Rachelle could remember.

Then one of Armand's valets entered the room. He handed her a note written in the messy scrawl that Erec liked to use and that Rachelle found completely unreadable.

"What is it?" she asked.

"Monsieur d'Anjou wants to speak with you," said the valet.

That was just like Erec, to summon her imperiously with a note she couldn't read. But for once it didn't make her too angry, because for now she had her peace with Amélie and Armand. And soon she would have a chance to fight the Devourer. There was nothing Erec could do to take either joy away from her.

"All right," she said, and went to find Erec.

Erec's rooms were not close to Armand's; it took her a while to get there, and when she did, his valet told her that he'd gone out for a few minutes. So she had to wait in his study for nearly half an hour before he arrived.

"Finally," she said when he walked into the room.

He raised his eyebrows. "Hardly courteous. I came as fast as I could."

"You could have waited for me to get here," said Rachelle. "Did you leave the room as soon as you sent the note?"

She saw his body tense with readiness. "I didn't send a note. I came here because I got a message from you."

And that was when the soldiers kicked the door in.

The next thing Rachelle knew, her sword was drawn and she was lunging toward the nearest soldier. There was a brief, timeless chaos. Fighting humans was not as dizzily blissful as fighting woodspawn. It was partly because her gifts did not manifest as strongly when she was facing mortal enemies instead of Forest creatures—and partly because she knew she was hacking at human limbs and stopping human hearts.

When they were finished, she was gasping for breath. She tried not to look at the bodies that lay on the floor.

"We have to run," she said. "The King—"

Erec shook his head. "They aren't from the King," he said, wiping his sword.

"The rebels," she said, and her heart lurched. Somebody was organizing a palace coup; that was why they had lured her and Erec together, so that they could be taken out together.

"Armand," she said, and realized this was the first time she had called him by his first name in front of Erec.

"Yes," said Erec, "secure him before he gets to the throne room."

She didn't bother explaining as she ran out of the room.

Armand wouldn't start a bloody revolution. He *wouldn't*, and that meant that anybody doing it would have to take him prisoner, and that meant—

And then she saw Armand at the end of the corridor, surrounded by armed men.

She didn't think about odds or tactics. Her mind flashed white fire, and then she was upon them.

She cut down two of them before they realized how dangerous she was and started to fall back. Then somebody lunged forward, and she nearly stabbed him before she realized it was Armand.

"Stop," he said. "Rachelle, stop. It's all right. They aren't hurting me."

"You don't understand," she said, "they're attacking us—"

"They're with me," he said quietly. "They follow *me*."

She could see Armand's face quite clearly in the lamplight, his gray eyes and the flat line of his mouth. She could feel the hilt of her sword gripped in her hand, and she could hear the soft moaning from one of the men she had stabbed. But she felt like she had stepped out of her body and to the side, like some important part of her just wasn't *there* anymore.

"What . . . what do you mean?"

"These are my men," Armand said steadily. "They follow me. They are going to help me take the King off the throne and—"

"You lied to me."

"No." Armand shook his head, actually looking distressed. "I've never—"

"You lied to me," she said, and her voice sounded like a pathetic, lost little thing. "All this time, you pretended to hate being a saint, when you were really plotting to get yourself on the throne."

"No," he said desperately, "I'm trying to put *Raoul* on the throne. You can help. Please, Rachelle—"

She raised her voice. "Anyone who wants to live had better start running."

Armand must have sent the message to get her in the same room as Erec. So that his men could kill them both at once.

The men with him in the hall now wanted to kill her as well. When they lunged, it was a relief. She knew how to fight. She knew how to survive fighting. Her sword sliced and whirled. Blood spattered across her face. She didn't care.

Then she turned back to Armand, and with one hand she easily gripped his collar and slammed him against the wall.

"What made you think it was a good idea to lie to me?"

He was afraid. She could see it in the way his eyes widened, his breath quickened. She could feel it with the hot, deadly instinct that throbbed in her veins. He was prey and he knew it. She was a monster, and he knew it.

"Rachelle," he said quietly, gently. As if he had ever really loved her. As if he thought he could keep on making a fool of her.

"Where is Joyeuse?" she demanded. She didn't need to ask if he had taken it: she knew he must have.

He met her eyes, his face bloodless and resolute. "I can't tell you that."

"Don't imagine I won't hurt you. Don't imagine for a moment that all your pretty kisses are going to make me spare you." She raised her bloody sword and pressed the blade against his throat. "You're only alive because the King has use for you. When the time comes, I will help him destroy you."

Whatever hope he'd had of beguiling her seemed to go out of him. "You were always loyal to them, weren't you?" he asked, his voice lifeless.

"Yes," she said, because she knew it would hurt him. "I told you I was still a bloodbound. What did you expect?"

"Well, then go ahead. Kill me whenever you want." His voice was quietly contemptuous. "It's the only thing you know how to do. Kill to please the forestborn and kill to please the King and kill for your beloved d'Anjou."

"At least I've never pretended otherwise," she snapped.

"Oh yes." His mouth curved in a thin, ferocious smile. "Your sad little lost soul that you can't stop talking about. Forgive me if I feel more pity for the people you killed."

It felt like there were fishhooks sliding under her ribs. "I never asked for your pity."

"Oh no, of course not. That would make you less special, wouldn't it, if you were just another sinner needing pity. No, you have to be the daughter of the devil himself before you're satisfied. You cry and you cry about your lost innocence, but the truth is, you love being this way. You love believing that you're damned because then you can do anything you want. Because you're too much of a coward to face what you've done and live with it."

She wanted to hurt him. She wanted to hurt him, and for a moment she imagined pressing the blade home, imagined the blood spurting everywhere, slippery and then sticky between her fingers. It was so real, she could almost taste it. And she could taste the black despair sliding down her throat afterward.

She knew that if she killed him, the next thing she would do was turn the sword on herself.

Her heart pounded with longing for destruction, with terror that she wanted it so much.

She lowered the blade. It was one of the hardest things she had ever done.

"Don't say another word." She grabbed his wrist. "If you want to live a moment longer, don't say another word."

He must have believed her. Because he didn't say anything as she dragged him away.

She took him back to Erec. By then the uprising had already been put down: it wasn't a true rebellion, just an attempt to snatch

Armand out of the Château. Half the soldiers involved had already fled; the rest were dead or captured.

Erec babbled something smug and smiled at Armand. Rachelle didn't listen. She just shoved Armand at Erec and said, "Lock him up." The words scraped at her throat.

"I'll put him somewhere safe," said Erec. "We'll discuss this in my study."

Rachelle turned and fled back to her rooms. She had to check, in case Armand had been lying about that too, but she already knew what she would find.

Joyeuse was gone.

Her only hope of stopping the Devourer. Everyone's only hope. It was all gone, because she had been stupid enough to trust Armand.

"Rachelle? What happened?"

Amélie stood in the doorway, eyes wide. An hour ago, she had been drinking hot chocolate with Rachelle and Armand, and suddenly Rachelle wanted to weep.

"There was trouble," she said, and took a step toward her. "Are you—"

Amélie flinched and took a quick little gasping breath. She didn't move to hug Rachelle the way she always did, she didn't ask if she was all right.

And then Rachelle realized: Amélie was *terrified*. Of her.

Finally, after three years, Amélie had woken up and realized what sort of monster she had decided to call a friend.

Rachelle's shoulders slumped. "Go," she said. "Just get out, now." She closed her eyes. "Go back to your mother and stay safe. It's only going to get worse."

She heard Amélie draw a little shuddering breath. She heard her footsteps run out of the room. But she didn't open her eyes until she was gone, because she couldn't bear to watch.

Numbly, she changed her bloodstained clothes. She scrubbed at her hands and face. She checked herself in the mirror: the girl who looked back was stiff and pale and clean—and felt like a stranger.

Then she left and started walking in the direction of Erec's study. Her skin felt too small for her body, like it was stretched tight over her skeleton and every joint scraped against it as she moved. She wanted to claw herself apart, limb from limb and bone from broken bone, until there was nothing left.

Forgive me if I feel more pity for the people you killed.

Even while he'd kissed her, he'd despised her. Exactly the way she'd always deserved to be despised.

I've killed a few, she thought viciously, *but he's killed us all. I'll let him see the Devourer rise, and then I'll kill him.*

She had the right to hate him for stealing Joyeuse. It wasn't any comfort.

In Erec's study, opulence pressed down like the weight of a mountain. The walls were papered in gold and red, hung with gilt-framed paintings of naked, allegorical women. The vast cherrywood desk was carved with a multitude of curlicues. Flowering marble columns held up the mantelpiece over the fireplace.

Rachelle paced back and forth. She wanted to stop thinking of Armand, but she kept remembering the soft sound of his breathing, her hands winding yarn around his fingers, his mouth against hers. If she hadn't loved him, she could forgive him. If he hadn't been *right* about her, she could forgive him. But she had and he was and now she couldn't seem to stop remembering his words to her over and over, feeling sicker each time.

Finally Erec strode into the room. "Well, I think we've put them all away," he said. "It was a very little plot. To be honest, I'd expected more of our dear saint."

"What are we doing with him?" asked Rachelle.

"Annoying as it is—if we can stop the news getting out that he was involved, we'll probably keep him the same way as before, because he's just so useful. And unfortunately, nobody has yet implicated the Bishop."

"I can't guard him again," she said.

Erec stepped closer. His fingertips brushed her cheek. "Oh, my dear lady," he said. "Did you start to trust him?"

"No," Rachelle snapped.

Start was such a short, small word for all the trust she'd given him. She hadn't realized how much she'd trusted him until now—now when he hated her, when the memories of him were stuck beneath her skin like needles and poison.

"You can't blame me," Erec went on reasonably. "I didn't tell you to be so kind to him."

"Shut up."

"I'm only saying—"

Rachelle grabbed the back of his head and kissed him, as savagely as her forestborn had once kissed her.

Erec kissed her back, and then at last the memories fled away. It was like fighting—not because of how fiercely he was kissing her, but because the world narrowed down to a single white-hot moment where she couldn't think, couldn't remember, could only feel and react. When he finally released her, she staggered back a step.

And the memories were there again. She could still see Armand looking at her. It wasn't enough.

"Eloquent, but hardly informative. What are you trying to tell me? Is something wrong?" He raised an eyebrow, unruffled as ever.

Rachelle's heart was pounding. Her body was a clanging discord of hate and grief and raw desire. She'd told herself again and again that she had too much pride to give in to Erec. But what was the use of pride? She was just the king's mad dog, kept on a leash until she grew dangerous enough to kill. She was just the scraps from the Devourer's table, useful for killing him but never beloved.

Too much of a coward to face what you've done.

It was true. She still liked to believe there was something honorable about her. There wasn't. She didn't *deserve* to have anything good.

If there was something good in her, she would tear it up right now.

"What's wrong," she said, her voice low but clear, "is that I'm wearing clothes and you've stopped kissing me."

She really must have surprised him, because he was silent a moment before he laughed and said, "Love me or hate me, you're never subtle. But you can't expect me to stop and start at your demand." He traced her cheek with a fingertip. "Maybe I don't feel like enjoying you now."

"Yes, you do," said Rachelle. "You are desperate for me." Her fingers wrapped around his. "You belong to me, just like I belong to you."

His mouth curved upward. The next moment he pinned her to the wall; Rachelle's body shivered with something not quite fear, not quite desire.

"You're right," he said. "You belong to me, and I don't let go of what's mine. But I still want to hear you say the words." He leaned down till their noses were almost touching. "Tell me what you want, my lady."

She could feel his breath against her face. He was so close, and she was so tired of pretending there was anything right about her.

"I will take your damned ruby," she said. "But I won't beg. And if you want me, you can stop talking and make me stop thinking. Or I leave now."

For a single, jagged instant, she thought he might refuse. She wasn't sure if it was fear or hope that pounded through her heart.

Then he grinned. "I will hold you to that, my lady," he said, and kissed her again.

Erec kept his word. He stopped talking, and she stopped thinking.

But later—much later, when they lay tangled in his bed—Rachelle stared out at the darkness and couldn't sleep and couldn't stop thinking. She could feel Erec's breath against the back of her neck, his arm around her waist. His skin against hers. It didn't seem real, and yet she could remember everything they had done with perfect clarity.

She had resisted him for so long. She realized now that she had thought she would somehow stop existing if she finally gave in. Certainly her mother had always given her that impression when talking about girls who lost their virtue.

But Rachelle should have known better. She was bloodbound, after all, and being bloodbound meant knowing how easily *I could never* turned into *Yes, I will.*

Once upon a time, she would have sworn that she'd rather die than make a covenant with the forestborn, because if she did such an evil thing, she wouldn't be herself anymore. Then she had discovered that her true self was quite willing to do any evil thing so long as she could live.

She had, all along, been a girl who was willing to sleep with Erec d'Anjou. It had just taken her three years to admit it. And admitting it hadn't allowed her to escape anything, because she could still remember Armand, and her eyes stung with useless, helpless tears as she remembered.

WHEN VOLUND HAD FINISHED THE SWORDS, HE laid them in Zisa's hands, and they took the form of needles. Back Zisa went to Old Mother Hunger, with the needles pinned in her skirt. There she found that Tyr's cage was gone.

"O my mother," she said, "where is the creature I once called brother? Is he not still meant for the offering?"

Old Mother Hunger laughed. The noise was like a storm of moths. "Surely you do not miss him," she said.

"What is any human to me but prey?" said Zisa. "But it is my duty to feed him."

"It is your duty to become one of us," said Old Mother Hunger, and marked her with the black star. "Bring me the hearts of your father and mother. Do so, and you will live to see your brother-that-was when you bring him to the offering."

So Zisa returned to her icy black lake, and saw her tribe bow down and worship her. But not her father: he stood tall and proud, ocher streaked across his face and gold in his hair, as he said, "I welcome you, child of mine."

"Father," she replied, "why did you offer us? Why do you serve the forestborn?"

"It is the way of the world," he said, "that the glorious rule the weak, and take what they like."

"That is true," said Zisa. "And now I am glorious."

Before he took another breath, she sliced his head from his shoulders.

The people trembled and were silent. But Zisa's mother rose to her feet. Quietly she asked, "Does Tyr still remember his name?"

"No, my mother-that-was," said Zisa. "Now come to my side."

And her mother came to her.

"He will remember it again," Zisa whispered in her mother's ear.

"Then I can die in peace," said her mother, and Zisa raised the sword to her neck.

Zisa cut out the hearts of her mother and father and put them in a silver chest, and back she went to the only family she had left.

"Now cook a soup and eat it with me," said Old Mother Hunger.

I tell you, there was nothing she would not do for her brother.

She woke up when Erec pinched her cheek. "Good morning, my lady."

She batted his hand away and started to sit up. Then she realized that Erec's servants were crowding into the room, and she was naked under the blankets. She dived back down.

"Getting up?" Erec asked.

"No," she growled.

"Don't worry," he said, ignoring the men who were pulling his shirt on over his head, "my valets know how to help a lady put her clothes back on."

"No," said Rachelle. "Send them away."

"You aren't planning to wear clothes today? My, that will cause talk."

How could he be saying these things in front of everybody?

But he was Erec d'Anjou: he wouldn't hesitate to say anything in front of anybody, especially when "anybody" was the servants whose names he probably didn't even remember.

"I am not going to display myself in front of your servants," she said.

He slanted an ironic gaze over his shoulder. "Don't tell me you've grown modest overnight."

There was nothing she could say that he wouldn't make to sound even more foolish, so she curled up under the blankets and waited until he was done dressing and the servants had gone before she got up and dressed herself.

Erec still watched her, but she couldn't very well complain. She'd chosen this, hadn't she? She had said she belonged to him. What right did she have to resent him?

"Well?" he asked her as she laced up her shirt. "Was I worth the wait?"

"No," snapped Rachelle, because contradicting him was a habit that would take more than one night to break.

"Then you shouldn't have waited so long."

She threw a boot at his head. He caught it easily, and leaned forward to kiss her.

Afterward, he hung the ruby pendant around her neck. The stone was as big as her thumbnail, a faceted, glittering teardrop that hung just below the mark on her throat.

"Now all the world can see you're mine," he said.

"Let me guess," she said. "You're already planning how to show me off."

"Surely you don't want me to hide you away." Erec's hand had rested on her shoulder; now he slid it up to cup the side of her neck. It was a surprisingly gentle gesture and she couldn't help relaxing a little.

She'd always hated the thought of being his prize on display. And yet now that it had happened . . . it was comforting to know that somebody was not ashamed of her.

"But we can hold the grand display later," Erec went on. "I have prisoners to question and you have . . ."

"Nobody to guard anymore," said Rachelle.

Erec was silent, and she raised her eyebrows. "Or do I?"

"Possibly," he said. "We're not going to reveal what he did just yet."

Because if people knew he had turned against the King, they might support him. She remembered the way Armand had looked at her last night, and she felt cold and hollow.

She would have to face that loathing again. After she left Erec, as she wended her way back through the Château to her quarters, she couldn't stop thinking about it. She had to make Armand tell her where he had put Joyeuse. So she would have to face him again, and he would rake her with another one of his disdainful glances, and she felt absolutely sure that it would take him only one look at her to know what she'd done with Erec.

He had never thought any better of her. Why should she care?

She tried to avoid talking to Armand. She spent the day hunting for Joyeuse along every possible path from his rooms to where she had captured him. But she found nothing, and she began to wonder if Armand had managed to dump it down a well. Or if he'd gotten someone to smuggle it out of the Château for him.

The thought made her want to beat her head against the wall. She had been so close, and if only she hadn't trusted him—

If only she hadn't trusted the forestborn. But how she felt had never mattered. Right now, all that mattered was making Armand tell her what he had done with Joyeuse.

That meant getting Erec to let her see him, and *that* meant keeping him happy. So when Erec told her that the King wanted to dine tête-à-tête with them that evening, she obediently went back to her room to dress.

Sévigné helped her with both the clothes and cosmetics. It was no comfort now to sit still with someone painting beauty onto her face. With Amélie, it had meant that she was loved. Now it just felt like pretending.

Amélie was gone from the Château. Rachelle had tried to avoid thinking of her all day, but now she couldn't escape the memories: Amélie's frightened eyes, the way she had flinched.

And now she could understand what she hadn't then: that Amélie had probably flinched because her friend had turned up gripping a sword and spattered with blood. Of course she'd been scared. And Rachelle had thrown her away because of it.

At least she'd be with her mother when Endless Night fell. It was probably for the best.

Erec arrived just as Sévigné finished painting her. He kissed Rachelle's fingers and said, "It's a most enchanting illusion. You look almost like a lady."

"Almost?"

Rachelle had seen herself in the mirror: the skin painted flawless, the glistening red lips, the precise triangle of blush on her cheeks. Her dress was pale blue silk embroidered with roses; there were little silk roses in her hair and a tiny black velvet patch shaped like a rose on her cheek. She looked so much like a lady, she could hardly recognize herself.

"Perhaps only because I know you," he said. "Beneath the silk and lace, you are still a forest creature."

Her face burned, and she didn't dare answer back. Because this was not like every other time they had walked together. With every movement he made, she was helplessly aware of him, of the way his body moved under his clothes, and she knew he could use that against her any time he pleased.

They dined outside, on a small terrace ringed with marble women holding lanterns. The lamps were lit, and crimson butterflies swirled about them in thick red clouds. Then Rachelle blinked, and there were only moths flitting next to each lamp.

The King arrived a few moments after them, and there were bows and curtsies and kissing of hands, and then they were seated.

"So," said the King, wheezing a little. "I hear you have been doing your duty excellently as my son's bodyguard."

Rachelle hoped she was still smiling, but the King's gaze had dropped, and she knew he must be staring at either her breasts or Erec's ruby. She didn't know which embarrassed her more.

"I have tried, sire," she said. "What is to be done with him?"

The King seemed to find this hilarious; he let out one of his famous booming laughs. "What *is* to be done with him? D'Anjou, do you have any idea?"

"Teach him manners and keep him out of sight," said Erec. "You know he'll soon be irrelevant, sire."

Rachelle hadn't known she could feel pity and revulsion at once. It was disgusting how they laughed over the night before, as if Armand betraying them and people *dying* were no more than a joke. And yet she couldn't help pitying them, because their words were more true than they could guess. Once the Devourer had returned and humans were the cattle of the forestborn, it would truly be irrelevant who had claimed to be king of Gévaudan.

The meal wore on. Rachelle could tell the food was exquisite, but she could barely choke it down. Out here on the terrace, with the evening breeze on her skin, the elegantly trimmed trees of the garden in the distance, she couldn't forget that Endless Night was coming. For all she knew, she was watching the next-to-last sunset the world would ever know.

Unless she could get Armand to tell her where Joyeuse was.

The King seemed to have lost interest in her; he spoke to Erec, discussing plans for hunting parties and dancing parties and the grand ball to celebrate the solstice night. What had made Erec think that this dinner was an honor worth sharing with her? But as she watched him, the way he smiled and exchanged little epigrams with the King, she realized that he was glorying in this moment—that while he respected the King no more than she did, being the special guest of King Auguste-Philippe actually meant something to him.

What was it he had said about his half brother? *He was legitimate, and heir to everything I lacked. At the time, that seemed very important.* Was it still important to him, to steal the glories and honors that his dead brother might have once enjoyed?

If so, it was a very foolish wish. He claimed to be ready and willing to cast all humanity aside, yet he was still trying to satisfy the longings of the child he had once been. But it made her heart soften a little toward him.

And how could she blame him? She was trying to kill the Devourer because she wanted to save Gévaudan and all the people she loved, but in truth, she was also trying to justify the dreams of the headstrong girl who had dared speak to a forestborn.

The sky was deep purple when Rachelle started to hear what sounded like people shouting very far away. She looked at Erec. He looked back at her, shrugged faintly, and went right on talking to the King.

She was just about ready to get up and investigate and damn etiquette when a blue-coated guardsman arrived and whispered in the King's ear.

The King sighed. "It seems there's some sort of rabble approaching the Château. Would you care to play cards inside, while the guard deals with them?"

"How tiresome," said Erec, rising.

"Deal with them?" said Rachelle.

The King waved his hand. "You've heard of the upset five years ago. They're quite experienced with this sort of thing."

Rachelle's stomach turned cold. Five years ago, a drought had caused food shortages and a crowd of hungry people had marched all the way to Château de Lune to demand the traditional midwinter alms. Whether the guardsmen had fired unprovoked or whether the crowd had been preparing to riot depended on whom you asked, but nine people lay dead at the end of it.

"What are they here for?" asked Rachelle.

"The same sort of foolery," said the King, rising from his chair. "They miss their saint, because they imagine that groveling before him will keep the woodspawn from their doors. And they think they have the right to make demands of their King. Come, the cards await."

Erec gave her an amused, superior look, as if to say, *I could have told you this would happen.*

He didn't seem the slightest bit worried about what might happen next.

"Sire," Rachelle began desperately, "don't you think—"

Erec's hand pressed over her mouth as one of his arms wrapped around her waist. "Yes, my thought exactly. Your Majesty, would you mind if we joined you in a moment? My darling has some words for my ears alone."

The King grinned. He clearly knew that Rachelle had been about to beg him to intervene and that Erec was intervening against her.

"Of course," he said. "Take all the time your lady needs."

When he had left, Erec released her mouth but maintained his grip on her waist. "Now, please don't hit me, my lady? You know as well as I what would happen if you gainsaid him."

Rachelle knew he was expecting her to yell at him. But she was silent, her mind working furiously. There was no point appealing to the King, that much was obvious. The Bishop might have enough influence to calm the crowd, but he probably wouldn't *want* to calm them.

"Erec," she said. "Let me have Armand back, just for this evening."

"Oh?" His voice showed only polite curiosity, but his grip dug into her arm. "And what were you planning to do with him?"

"Show him to the crowd," she said. "He's their saint, isn't he? He could make them disperse peacefully."

"You think the King would like that?"

"The King doesn't have to know until it's too late. He doesn't even have to know that I had anything to do with it. Do you honestly not care that there could be a slaughter?"

"Care? Do you forget we're both murderers?"

"No," said Rachelle, "but right now, I don't give a damn. Tell me where you're keeping Armand and let me take him out and show him to the crowd. I'll do anything you want after that. Just let me stop this."

Erec was silent. She wished she could see his face.

"Don't tell me," she said scornfully, "that you're afraid I'll find him so much more charming than you."

He laughed low in his throat. "You know too well I can't resist a challenge. Very well, lady, he's yours for now and I'll make your excuses to the King. But you must let me win you back tonight."

As he said the last words, he shifted, leaning into her, and Rachelle felt her opening. She slumped forward, one arm digging into him, one hand grasping his coat, and a moment later she had thrown him over her shoulder onto the ground.

"Maybe I'll win *you*," she said, and grinned, because she knew that he hadn't let her throw him; she had genuinely surprised him.

Erec rolled to his feet lightly and gracefully, but there was a sulky set to his mouth. He never liked being taken by surprise. Rachelle couldn't ever remember being the one who made him look ridiculous. It felt wonderful.

It suddenly occurred to her that in this situation, Armand would have laughed instead of sulking.

"Well?" she said.

"Would that I had time to spar with you properly." He sighed. "This way." He looked her up and down. "Actually, I'll bring him to you. Unless you're planning to dazzle the crowd into submission, you might want to change."

So Rachelle bolted for her room. "Faster, faster," she muttered over and over, as Sévigné undid buttons and pulled out the laces from the corset.

Finally she was free of her clothes, and in moments was pulling on her hunting gear. "Braid my hair," she said as she buttoned up her shirt, and Sévigné obeyed. A minute later, she was pulling on her coat. She took a wild glance in the mirror: the makeup was all still on her face, pearl powder, rouge, and burned clove to fill out her eyebrows, which looked bizarre with her patched-up red coat and slightly threadbare trousers, but it would have to do. There was no time, because even now Erec was knocking at the door.

"Here you are," said Erec, shoving Armand into the room. "When you're done, be sure to put him back where you found him. Monsieur, obey her and mind that you remember our talk."

"Thank you," Rachelle said numbly. Armand wasn't looking at her; he was very pale and staring at the floor. She felt invisible. She wished she were invisible, so she'd never have to meet his eyes. She'd spent the whole day hunting through the Château for Joyeuse just so she could avoid speaking to him again.

Erec grabbed her by the shoulders and kissed her quickly but fiercely. Rachelle couldn't stop being aware that Armand was just a step away from them.

Then Erec released her. "Until tonight," he said, and was gone.

Rachelle swallowed the desire to hide and weep, and she turned to Armand instead. "Listen," she said. "I know what you think of me. And you know what I think of you. But right now, there's a crowd outside the palace, and since the King doesn't intend to acknowledge their existence, they're probably going to riot, and you know how that will end. So you're going to go out there and talk to them."

"And say what?" he asked slowly after a moment.

"I don't know, something saintly. Something to make them go home so that they don't get shot. You're supposed to care about that, aren't you?"

"Back to thinking I'm a saint?" he asked, and there was a slight mocking edge to the words.

"I don't care if you're God or the devil," said Rachelle. "I want that crowd gone. Quietly. You are going to make that happen, *without* calling for rebellion, or I will cut your throat in front of them and damn the consequences. Do you understand?"

He stared at her a moment longer. "Right," he said, nodding sharply. "Which way?"

Rachelle didn't know, but that had never stopped her. "We'll find out," she said, and pushed past him to stride down the hallway.

The commotion was building inside the palace; they ran into another guard soon enough. Rachelle simply marched up to him and said grandly, "Take us to the crowd. Orders of the King."

"Of course," the guard said, bowing quickly. "Glad the old man decided to do something," he muttered.

"How many are there?" asked Armand as they walked quickly through the hallways.

"A hundred? Two hundred?" The guard shrugged. "They're holding them, but any moment—they say if they start to riot—" His voice wavered and he stopped talking. He was young, Rachelle realized, barely older than her and Armand. He had probably not been an active member of the guard five years ago. He must have heard stories about the massacre—and what kind of stories did the guards tell, she wondered? Was it a matter of shame and horror to them, or did they consider the guards to have defended themselves and the King? Nobody had even been flogged for it; there had been outrage over that too.

The crowd was gathered on the south side of the building, swarming along a narrow road and spilling over into one of the orange groves. The lawn nearest the palace was still clear, held by a line of blue-coated soldiers holding muskets.

The people knew just as well as she did what happened to the last crowd that stood outside the palace. They were desperate enough to come here anyway.

She'd feared for them ever since she'd heard the news, but now she pitied them. She was furious on their behalf. And she was afraid *of* them too, because she could feel the fury in the way they stood, the way they muttered and shouted.

"Performance time," said Rachelle.

"You might have . . . overestimated my ability," said Armand, sounding a little faint.

"As far as I know," said Rachelle, "you've lied to every person in this palace, one way or another. This shouldn't be too much harder."

"You're so kind." He squared his shoulders.

Without meaning to in the least, Rachelle took his hand. The metal was cold and slightly damp again her skin. "I'm Armand Vareilles," he called out. "I've come to hear your complaints."

"Where's the King?" somebody yelled, but a lot of the people started chanting, "Return to the city! Protect us! Return to the city!" The noise was like a living heartbeat or the breathing of a wolf, and Rachelle nearly took a step back.

"I must obey my father," he said. "I can't leave Château de Lune."

"You think *that* will calm them?" Rachelle muttered.

Armand gave her a bleak look. "Take off my hands," he said.

"What?"

"Take off my hands," he repeated, and then raised his voice. "I'm not the King. I can't defend your city. I can't even leave the Château. But I can be your saint. And more."

Rachelle pushed up his sleeves and unlocked the straps that bound the silver hands to his arms. He drew a ragged breath. The crowd was growing quieter.

"I am not a legitimate heir. But I am a child of Tyr, and I have the Royal Gift. I defied the Forest and survived. I can let you touch me. Let me be your relic. Take what protection you can from me, what healing you can from me. And then go home in peace."

There was a stillness where anything might have happened. Then an old woman, supported by a little girl, stumbled forward.

Armand stepped toward her. "You might want to leave," he said. "I suspect this is going to repulse you."

Rachelle gripped the back of his shirt. "You don't get away from me that easily, monsieur."

The woman was bent nearly in two, though whether by age or the sickness, it was hard to tell. Armand knelt to meet her, holding out his arms. She seized one and kissed the stump where his arm ended. Rachelle felt Armand's back tense, but he didn't move.

For a silent, rigid moment, the old woman was still. Then she let his arm drop.

"The pain is better," she sobbed, and suddenly everyone was cheering.

And then the crowd came. They came from all sides, desperate and reverent and needy and loving. They touched his face, his hair, his shoulders, his arms. They kissed the stumps of his arms again and again. They pressed their rosaries and their neckerchiefs and their staffs to him. He was their relic, their saint. A few seemed ready to regard him as their god.

Rachelle crouched behind him, still gripping his shirt. She felt him tense when a boy with bleeding sores staggered up to him. She felt him flinch when somebody touched the stump of his arm. She felt him shift and straighten, spine cracking, as he tried to find a comfortable position.

It seemed they had been sitting in the crowd for hours. Days. Forever.

She saw Armand's head bob as he nodded at people, heard him say, "God bless you. God bless you," in a weary voice.

There were no miracles. Some said they breathed easier, walked better; others simply sobbed when they touched him, and sobbing, crawled away. Rachelle constantly expected somebody to cry fake. Surely any moment they would realize that Armand was not healing them and they would turn on him. But the moment never came. It seemed to be enough for them simply that he would sit among them and let them touch him, despite their uncleanliness.

She realized there were tears sliding down her face. She had, perhaps, only ever wanted the same thing. She had gotten it yesterday, and then she had thrown it away.

Finally the crowd was finished. When they stopped, for a few moments Armand was still, breathing raggedly. Then he got to his feet and said loudly, "In the name of my father, King Auguste-Philippe II, I grant you permission to stay in the orange gardens this night. Please return to the city at dawn."

He turned and marched back toward the soldiers. "Get them some bread, if you can," he said to a captain. "They probably haven't eaten all day. It will help them settle down."

"Yes, sir," the captain said, and Rachelle realized that the guards, too, were staring at them with something like awe.

"Good," said Armand.

Rachelle picked up his silver hands by the harnesses. Then she grabbed him by the arm.

"We need to talk," she said.

26

As soon as they were out of the guards' earshot, Armand turned to her and said, "You wanted them to live."

She stared.

"The crowd," he said. "You didn't want them shot."

"Obviously," said Rachelle. "Listen. About Joyeuse—"

"I didn't send anyone to attack you." There was no anger in Armand's voice, just quiet intensity. "I swear to you. I arranged the letters to distract you and d'Anjou, but we were all supposed to *avoid* you two. Some of them must have wanted revenge, and I'm sorry about that. But—"

"I don't care," said Rachelle.

She did care. She believed him, too, which was surprising. But there were more important things right now.

"Joyeuse," she said. "You have to tell me where it is."

Armand let out a breath and then squared his shoulders, looking her in the eyes. "Rachelle," he said, "please. You don't have to keep following him. I know you think it's too late, that you don't have a choice anymore, but *you do*. You can change. You can stop Endless Night. If you help me. Please."

She knew she was gaping at him. She couldn't help herself. It was like the first time she had been punched in the face while sparring, and the world was bright and ringing and she couldn't move.

"You want me to stop Endless Night," she finally managed to say.

"Yes," said Armand. "I want you to stop it. And I think you will." His mouth curved up. "The girl I fell in love with would have given anything to stop the Devourer. And even though you were working for d'Anjou—I don't believe that girl was a lie. I think that's who you really want to be, deep down."

"You believe in the Devourer," said Rachelle, still dazed. She'd gotten so used to thinking no one else would ever believe her.

"Well," said Armand, "obviously." He held up the stump of his right arm.

"I don't think you told me everything about how you lost your hands," said Rachelle, and it was a little satisfying to see his expression sliding into puzzlement.

"Let me go first," she said. "I have wanted to kill the Devourer since I was twelve years old. That's why I talked to a forestborn in the woods. After he marked me, he said that only Joyeuse or Durendal could kill the Devourer. That's why I was looking for Prince Hugo's door, because what you said—"

"Above the sun, below the moon," Armand whispered. He looked exactly as dazed by this conversation as she was.

"I'd heard a story that Joyeuse was hidden behind a door like that. I'm not working for the Devourer. I'm not working for the forestborn. I *am* working for the King, but only because I want to stay alive, and I'm not planning to be alive much longer, because I met the forestborn who made me three weeks ago, and he told me that the Devourer was coming back before summer's end. So you have to tell me where you hid Joyeuse."

Armand stared at her a moment longer. Then he started laughing.

"What?" she demanded.

"Well," he said, "if you want to kill the Devourer, you're in luck. I'm going to be his new vessel."

And she remembered the stories: Tyr, and a thousand nameless sacrifices before him. Humans hollowed out and inhabited by the power of the Devourer, made the living link that allowed him to shroud all the world in the darkness of the Great Forest.

"Six months ago, I went to court for the first time. It was dazzling. It was especially dazzling to meet my father, who seemed much more interested in me than I had ever expected. He told me that he expected great things of me.

"Three days before Midwinter Night, a forestborn marked me. He said I had to kill or die. I said I would die. I meant to die. Only—I told you already, how the Royal Gift saved me. On the third day, I woke up in a secret room. The King was there, and d'Anjou, and the rest of the forestborn. They told me I was destined for a fate more glorious than any mortal had enjoyed in three thousand years. I'd passed the test, you see. Because I had the Royal Gift strongly enough to survive the mark, I could be a fitting vessel for the Devourer. I could break the binding Tyr and Zisa laid upon him long ago."

Rachelle hardly listened to that last part. "Erec was there?" she said. "Then he . . ."

Armand's mouth twisted. "Oh, yes. He's the one who cut off my hands."

He couldn't, she wanted to protest. It didn't seem possible, and not just because they had been lovers. They had hunted and laughed together. He had held her once when she cried. He had taught her to live again when she had been ready to die.

But she remembered everything he had said to her: *We're both murderers. What never dies cannot be damned. We are going to live forever, in darkness and in dancing.* She remembered his relentless drive to win. She remembered his brother.

His heart had rested in the Forest for a very long time now.

"The thing is," Armand went on, more rapidly, "to become a vessel, you have to consent. My father told me that the forestborn had agreed to heal his sickness if I would do it. He said that it was nothing, just a little pagan mummery to give extra power to their spells, and all for the glory and good of Gévaudan. I had read enough stories to know what the Devourer returning would mean, but he wouldn't believe me. He begged me. And then commanded me. And then threatened." He swallowed. "I kept saying no. D'Anjou cut off one hand and then the other. I still said no. Then the night was over, and the sacrifice can only be made on a solstice night."

Rachelle couldn't look down. She had thought he was a fraud when she met him, and once she had started to believe him she was used to him, and somehow she had never bothered to think that there had been a moment when he was bleeding and screaming. Or a moment before, when he was helpless as he watched the blade swing down.

"Why didn't you tell anyone?" she asked finally.

"Nobody believes in the Devourer anymore. I told my mother, and she thought I was mad. Before I could change her mind, the forestborn found out and killed her. Then they locked up Raoul in the Château and said that if I told anyone again, they would kill me slowly and use Raoul for a sacrifice instead. Or kill me and Raoul slowly, then sacrifice one of the other bastards."

"So you secretly organized a rebellion."

"D'Anjou is not as observant as he thinks he is." Armand's lips pressed together for a moment; when he spoke again, his voice was fast and miserable. "It was supposed to happen on solstice night, but when I saw you had Joyeuse—I had to try. I thought it was worth the risk. But I just ruined everything. At least d'Anjou hasn't gloated to me yet, so I think Raoul is still alive."

"I won't let him hurt you again," she said. "And all of this ends tonight. We'll get Joyeuse right now and get out."

Armand shook his head. "No. They'll just try again with somebody else. They don't need to use someone with the Royal Gift, they just really want to. *You* have to get Joyeuse, wait until the Devourer is alive in my body, and then kill the two of us together. I was hoping Raoul could do it, but you'd be even better."

"No," said Rachelle, remembering the afternoon when they had sat in la Fontaine's salon discussing murder. "Absolutely not."

"D'Anjou will let you into the ceremony if he thinks you're loyal."

"No," she said again.

"You have to. Don't you understand? The Devourer doesn't have a body; that's why he needs a vessel to manifest. Why do you think Tyr killed him while he was possessing his sister? It has to be that's the only way to stop him." Armand drew a ragged breath. "You have to kill me."

"Listen to me." She gripped his shoulders. "I killed somebody I loved once. I can't do it again."

"A noble sentiment," said Erec.

The shock was like ice in her blood and bones. She turned. Erec stood behind them, dressed in his favorite coat of black velvet.

"You," said Rachelle. She had wanted him, kissed him, made love to him. And he had tortured Armand. "I'm going to kill you."

"I really doubt that," said Erec, raising his hand.

Tied to his finger was a crimson thread. It fell to the floor, where it pooled in great circles and spirals.

The other end was tied to her own finger.

We are going to live forever, in darkness and in dancing.

He had always, always been telling her.

Her heart thudded, but it felt like it belonged to someone else; her body seemed to be wrapped in fire or ice or cotton wool. All she could smell was blood. All she could hear were Aunt Léonie's soft, agonized whimpers.

Erec slowly wrapped his fingers down into a fist. The string seared red-hot around her finger; the strength went out of her legs, and she dropped to her knees.

I never escaped him, she thought dully. *I never left the Forest. I never left that house.*

Erec strode forward. Forestborn followed him, appearing out of the shadows, as terrible and as glorious as the ones she had seen in the Wild Hunt.

"One tug along the string." Erec's hand dropped onto her

head, then slid down her cheek in a caress. "And you will always return to me. And now I don't even need to wear my mask."

Briefly the strange, memory-tearing vagueness flickered over his face, the same as when she had first met him. Then he smiled and it was gone.

He hauled her to her feet and wrapped an arm around her. "I hope you've enjoyed your evening, Monsieur Vareilles. It ends now. My darling needs her rest, and you need to prepare yourself for the glory you receive tomorrow night."

Armand's face was set in the same stubborn blankness she had seen before. But of course, he'd learned nothing new. He already knew all about Erec and the forestborn and the Devourer. He already knew they were hopeless.

Rachelle closed her eyes and let Erec drag her away.

27

Erec led them through the Château, and it was almost the Forest. Bleeding through the marble hallways, Rachelle saw labyrinthine paths between trees whose branches wove together overhead until they seemed like a single plant. Birds called with warbling, half-human voices. The wind dug its fingers into her hair, burned at her eyes.

Erec's arm stayed over her shoulders. It felt warm, solid, human. But in all the time she had known him, he had never been human. She felt his hand cupped over her right shoulder. He had given her the knife with that hand, he had wrapped her fingers around the hilt and told her to cut deep.

A month later, he had given her the strength to protect people when he told her to live.

The walk lasted only a few minutes; then they bowed low to pass under an arch in the roots of a monstrous tree, and on the other side was Erec's study, bizarrely bright and free of the Forest. Suddenly only one of the forestborn was with them, and now he looked like a short, pasty-faced servant who gripped Armand's arm with chubby fingers.

"Take him to a safe place and keep him there," said Erec. "My lady and I have some things to discuss."

She didn't look at Armand while he was dragged out. She didn't look because she was terrified of what she would see in his face, but also because she knew that the less Erec thought she cared for him, the better for the both of them.

"So," she said when the door had swung shut. "Is the King still human?"

Erec laughed. "Oh, he's human enough. And a very great fool. He thinks we're going to give him eternal youth and create him a bloodbound army."

"Are you?"

"We're building an army," he said. "You met one of them. Perfect, mindless hunger makes the best servants, you know. But I'm afraid the King won't live to use them."

She should have been past surprise by now, but his words still made her breath stutter.

"That woman," she said. "In the coffeehouse—"

"Escaped from us, yes, and found her way back to those idiot malcontents. But that nest, at least, we cleaned out the next day."

Rachelle didn't need to ask what "cleaned out" meant. She remembered the weeping daughter, the husband who had called her a murderer. Erec had killed them. Probably while Amélie had been painting rouge on her face.

"If you're so powerful," she asked, "why do you need the King's permission?"

"Because of the binding that those interfering children laid upon our master. We cannot mark one of the royal house without permission from another who holds the Royal Gift." He grinned at her. "A problem I did not encounter with you."

"You killed my aunt," she said, her voice scraping in her throat like broken glass.

"No, my lady, *you* did."

She flinched a step back. "Erec, why are you doing this? You can't—you can't really want—"

He had the same superior, amused expression that he always had when he managed to shock her. "What? Endless Night? I welcome it."

"But all those times we hunted woodspawn together— You taught me to *protect* people."

"No, my lady, I told you to live." His voice was gently teasing. "Protecting the sheep of this world was your heresy on my doctrine."

"And telling me to live," she said bitterly, "that was just so I'd be of use to you, wasn't it?"

"No," he said. "I do love you, my lady."

She snorted. "As a wolf loves its meat."

"Oh no," he said. "I went to your village to kill you and your aunt, because there was a rumor that you guarded Durendal. But then I spoke to you and you were brave, and I fell in love with you." He took a step toward her and she stepped back, running into his desk. "Observe how kind I have been to you. I let you choose to become a bloodbound. I let you choose to make love to me."

"And if I hadn't?"

"Might-have-beens are for poets. What matters is, you chose me. And I have chosen you to rule beside me."

She remembered his voice in the Forest: *I bring you glad tidings of great joy.*

"So you bring the Devourer back," she said, "night falls forever, and then . . . we're crowned king and queen of the forestborn? I suspect there are a few older ones who might take precedence."

"Oh, certainly. But kingship isn't what I'm after." He pressed forward, nuzzling at her neck. "First, darkness. The sun and moon are eaten from the sky, and all the plump, satisfied world screams in horror. That's what your saints dream of too, isn't it, judgment on the complacent? Next—the Wild Hunt. No more bowing and scraping to the sanctimonious, the weaklings, and the proud. No more fear and guilt. We ride the steeds of night and we hunt the human race. When we have had our fill of hunting, then will come the dances, the everlasting starlit dances. And finally—" He planted a hand on the desk to either side of her. "Finally, in the long secret silences, you and me together. World without end, amen. Is that not a paradise worth a little blood, my lady?"

Nothing she said would make a difference. The person she had—not loved, exactly, but been friends with—had never existed. All she could do was convince this forestborn that she was helpless and resigned and wait for a chance to escape.

She drew a slow breath and asked, "Why am I now your lady instead of 'little girl'?"

He grinned, clearly thinking that he was starting to win her over. "Because you were once a sheltered little girl. But you took up the knife. You were brave enough to face the darkness. And you became strong."

When she took up the knife, it was the weakest she had ever been.

"Eternity in the Forest," she said. "Did I ever make you think I wanted that?"

"I think I can make you want it."

Then he kissed her.

He was a monster. But her body still knew how to desire him. Of course it did; her body had been hollowed out and filled up and transformed by the power of the Forest. How could it help hungering after its maker?

If she wanted any chance to help Armand, she would have to play along with Erec. And it was going to be easy.

She couldn't bear to think about that. So she kissed him back and didn't think.

Then somebody knocked on the door.

With a sigh, Erec let go of her. "It's never ending," he said, and went to the door. The person outside spoke in low tones she couldn't make out, and Erec answered just as softly.

Rachelle wasn't listening very carefully anyway. She gripped the edges of the desk and stared at the floor. She felt like a bubble, a tiny gleam wrapped around nothingness.

"Alas, duty calls," said Erec, returning to her. "But first—I have a present for you. Something to keep you busy tonight, and console you for all eternity. Come."

Rachelle slid off the desk. *Tomorrow,* she thought numbly. *And forever.* If she didn't find a way to stop the Devourer, she would become a forestborn, and she would live forever with nothing but this. Pleasure and despair.

"Don't look so mournful," said Erec. "You're about to have all you ever wanted."

As Rachelle followed him through the corridors, she tried to think of a way out. If she could just talk to Armand again he could tell her where he'd hidden Joyeuse. But she didn't know where he was, and even if she did, he was under guard. She'd never been strong enough to defeat Erec, which made sense now that she knew he was a full forestborn, and the forestborn guarding Armand now were probably even stronger.

At least she hadn't had to sleep with Erec again. Tonight. If the Devourer returned and night fell forever—

No. She wouldn't live that way. If Endless Night fell, then Armand would be dead and Erec would have nothing left to use against her. She'd fight him with every breath in her body, she would *force* him to kill her, and before she died, at least she would make him bleed.

Erec took her to a little-used corner of the Château. He opened the door of a small storeroom, and suddenly Rachelle couldn't move.

Because Amélie was crouched in the corner.

She lifted her head slowly. Her eyes were swollen and she had a bruise on one cheek. On her other cheek was an ink-black star.

No, thought Rachelle, *no.*

"Are you real?" Amélie asked in a low, hoarse voice. Her cheeks were flushed.

It was the fever, Rachelle realized: it struck some bloodbound when they were first marked. Fever, cramps, delirium, as if mind and body alike were rebelling against what had happened. It hadn't happened to her, but she'd heard about it.

"Yes," Rachelle whispered. The word was barely more than a

catch in her breath, but it broke her paralysis; she lunged forward and gripped Amélie's shoulders.

A present.

"I don't feel well," Amélie whispered.

"It's all right," Rachelle said, but nothing was going to be all right again.

"Father, I don't feel well." Amélie squeezed her eyes shut, then opened them again. "It's all wrong. The flowers. They're all wrong."

Delirium, or was she starting to see the Forest?

"Lie down," Rachelle whispered, and eased her down to lie with her head in Rachelle's lap.

"She was braver than some, when she was marked," said Erec. "I think she'll do well as one of us. Make sure she kills somebody right away tomorrow—there's no telling what our lord's return will do to the mark—and if she's reluctant, help her along as I did for you."

"I'm going to kill you," said Rachelle, her voice low and rough.

"When darkness has fallen and our lord rules all the world, you will thank me for preserving your friend, my lady." She felt him press a kiss to the back of her head. "Until tomorrow," he said, and then he was gone.

"Don't go," Amélie whispered. "It hurts."

"I know," said Rachelle. "I'm sorry. I know."

Amélie clung to Rachelle's fingers, and she squeezed back. If she hadn't let Amélie befriend her—if she hadn't let her come to the Château—none of this would ever have happened.

"I'm sorry," Rachelle said again, when the delirium got worse and Amélie started whimpering. "I'm sorry."

All she could think, all night through, was: *Erec will die for this.*

A little after dawn, Amélie finally fell all the way asleep. Rachelle gently eased her off her lap and onto the ground, then smoothed her hair out of her face. The mark squatted atop Amélie's cheek like a big black spider.

Rachelle had been angry when she found out what they did to Armand. But she'd always known him as part of her world. When she thought he was a liar and when she knew he was a martyr, he'd always been somebody who belonged in this tangle of death and shadows and terrible prices.

Amélie was a simple human girl who'd been kind and brave enough to befriend a bloodbound. And for that she was going to become one of them. She'd talked so happily of how her art made her feel that she was pleasing God, and now she would have to become a murderer or die. Rachelle's throat closed up in fury.

Her eyes felt gritty and swollen. There was a pitcher in a corner of the room; she splashed water on her eyes, then realized that her face was still smeared with the cosmetics she had worn to dine with Erec and the King. Her stomach twisted, and she scrubbed furiously until her face felt clean.

She buckled on her sword. She checked all her knives.

And then she went to kill Erec.

She didn't know where he was, but that didn't matter. She simply followed the red string, and it led her through the passages of the Château, down to the practice room for the guards. She heard laughter, and the clash of steel on steel. She walked through the door, and there was Erec. He had just finished sparring against two guardsmen at once, and now he was laughing and looking smug as he clapped them on the shoulders.

"Erec d'Anjou." Her voice ripped out of her, loud and clear.

His eyes met hers and he bowed slightly. "My lady. Did you like your present?"

He knew she was angry. He found it amusing. For the first time, she didn't care. Her feet carried her across the wide space of the practice room; she heard her boots thud against the floor, but she felt like she was floating.

"Erec d'Anjou," she said as she got closer. Her fingers found the ruby's golden chain and she ripped it off her neck. "I officially resign as your mistress." The ruby tinkled as it bounced off the floor. "And I challenge you to a duel. You destroyed my dearest friend, and I demand satisfaction."

He raised an eyebrow. "Is that how it is?"

She drew her sword. "You can defend yourself. Or you can stand still as I run you through. Three. Two."

His sword whispered as he whipped it from the sheath. "One." He saluted. "You break my heart, lady."

She lunged.

Erec countered her with the same unholy speed and grace he always had. But she was no longer stumbling with fear or anticipated humiliation. Her sword met his, swirled it aside, plunged toward him. He had to give ground. Then he attacked again, and nearly touched her; she dropped to the ground, rolled, and came up with a knife that she flung at his back.

He whirled, and his sword lashed out in time to fling it aside. "That's cheating, my lady."

She didn't answer. She didn't care. She pulled out one of her longer knives and attacked again, two-handed. Their swords whirled and clattered against each other, and then her knife snaked forward and sliced open his cheek.

"One point," she said.

The grin was gone from Erec's face. He pulled out his own dagger now, and for a few moments they circled each other. Then he attacked again.

She matched him. It was like breathing. Like dancing, and now that she had found the rhythm, she didn't know how she hadn't done it before. Her heart pounded. Her body sang. It felt like the Forest was unfolding inside her, trees sprouting and reaching upward into the night, and the hunt was running through her, the wolf chasing the deer and the hound breaking the rabbit in its jaws.

Her sword stabbed into his shoulder. "Two points," she said, a wild grin tugging at her mouth, and she understood. This was why he'd always been better. He'd always been the more ruthless. Feed the Forest inside you with blood, and it would feed you in return.

Now she was ready to shed all the blood in the world.

The only sound was their ragged breathing, the thump of their feet, the clash of their swords. Erec managed to get a slice across her cheek, but then she was in close and she rammed her knife into his side.

"Three points," she said, and wrenched the knife free.

Erec grunted, stumbling back a step. "And yet," he snarled, "I'm not dead yet. You'll have to try harder, lady."

Rachelle twirled her knife. "Come at me, then."

She could see phantom trees around her. Her body was made of light, her blood was made of fire. The air was wine in her throat. And that was when she realized: she was turning into a forestborn. Right here, right now.

It felt glorious.

Erec attacked. But the duel had changed. He was angry now,

and desperate. He was starting to feel afraid. And she knew that she was going to win.

She sliced his face again. And his hand. And his shoulder. He was going to die. She was going to cut him to pieces right here, she was going to lick the blood off her knife, and yes, then she would turn into a forestborn. She remembered swearing she would rather be dead and damned, but she didn't care anymore. Amélie was going to die and the only thing that mattered was making Erec pay.

He stumbled back and raised his hand, clenching it around the thread. She felt the answering burn around her finger, but it was barely painful.

"That's not enough anymore," she said. "You'll have to fight me if you want to win."

She could see it in his face when he decided to stake everything on a final lunge. She ran him through. Then she pulled her sword out again. He was wavering on his feet; she kicked him to the ground, knelt over him, and pressed her sword to his throat.

He was a forestborn, and he would heal from all the wounds she had given him. But he wouldn't heal once she had cut off his head.

"Any final words, d'Anjou?"

He spat out blood and said, "You might . . . want to look around."

She looked up. A few paces away stood two forestborn, one of them the pasty-faced male she had seen last night. But now she could see past the human disguises, to the inhuman faces burning with terrifying power.

And between them they held Armand.

"Let him go," said the forestborn who had been with them last night. "Or this one dies."

Last night, that would have been enough to control her.

She grinned. "Go ahead. He already chose to be a martyr."

"Rachelle." Armand's voice was quiet, but it carried across the room and clenched at her heart. "Please stop."

"He marked Amélie as a bloodbound. You know what that means. And now *you* want me to spare him?"

"There must be fifty forestborn in the Château right now. You kill him, they kill you, and then there's nobody left to stop them."

"I don't care," she said. "If Amélie isn't part of this world, I don't see the point in saving it."

"You don't mean that," said Armand. "You know that you have always wanted to save everyone. And killing him won't save anyone. It's just murderous revenge."

"I've been a murderer for three years," she snarled. "And now I'm a monster. Can't you see I'm turning into a forestborn right now?"

Shadowy trees were sprouting up from the floor around her, spreading out branches and gnarling up roots. She could feel her hair drifting in the phantom wind.

"Yes," said Armand.

"You know what that means. When people become forestborn, they lose their hearts. They lose their souls."

Her head was starting to pound. Her blood was burning. She wouldn't be strong for much longer; soon the change would overtake her.

"It doesn't matter what I do now," she said. "I'll forget how to love in an hour. I will never save anyone again, do you understand?"

"I don't believe that," said Armand. "I don't believe you don't have a choice."

"There are never any choices in the Forest."

"Rachelle." He met her eyes. "I lit a candle for you in the Lady Chapel, before the statue of the Lady of Snows. So you can't possibly lose yourself."

She nearly snarled, *Do you think one prayer is all it would take to save me?* But then she realized that he was still looking at her with terrifying intensity.

Armand knew that hearing about his prayers wouldn't change her mind. And there was no reason to be so specific about where he had lit a candle—

Unless he was trying to tell her where he had hidden Joyeuse.

He was the worst fool in all creation. He *knew* she was turning into a forestborn. He knew that if the forestborn could get hold of Joyeuse, they would destroy it, and then there would be no more hope of stopping the Devourer, not ever. And he was wagering everything on the chance that she would do what no forestborn had ever done and keep her soul.

It wasn't just a wager. It was a bribe, threat, and prayer all at once. If she wanted revenge, if she wanted to save anyone, if she wanted to save her own soul, then she couldn't refuse a chance at Joyeuse. He was the most ruthlessly clever fool in all creation, and she had never loved him so much.

"Maybe you'll forget," Armand went on. "Tonight I'll become the Devourer, most likely, and God alone knows how much of my soul will be left. But you don't have to lose yourself *now.* Do you think Amélie would thank you for it?"

Amélie wouldn't thank her for becoming a forestborn either. But as soon as she thought of Amélie, she remembered her painting Rachelle's face into an artwork and saying, *The question is, are you brave enough?*

And she realized that she wasn't going to kill Erec. Not while Armand was watching her and wagering everything on her. And not while the memory of Amélie was still in her heart.

She threw aside her sword. She stood up, because a thousand leaves were rustling against her skin, and she knew that she didn't have much longer. She wanted to say good-bye to Armand. She wanted to tell him that she loved him while it still had a chance of being true.

But she'd used up all her strength laying down the sword. The leaves on her skin caught fire, and then her legs gave out.

"Rachelle!" Armand shouted, and she thought, *I love you. I love you. I will try.*

The last thing she saw was Erec leaning over her. "Sweet dreams, my lady. Your human heart has beat its last."

29

Rachelle was in the dead forest, walking toward the cottage thatched with bones.

Her eyes burned and stung with tears. Her throat ached like she had been screaming. She knew there was a reason she had fought to avoid this house, but her heart was a lump of meat in her chest and her agony had all been spent.

This is all, she thought as she stepped forward. *This is all.*

She raised her hand; she saw memories peeling away from it in translucent, gauze-like little scraps that fluttered away in the breeze. She could feel them sloughing off her hands, off her face; they were fluttering in her hair and tearing free.

Her foot landed on the wooden doorstep. The wood shifted with a creak, and she knew that the sound should send a bolt of terror through her, but there were no feelings left in her.

The door handle was cold beneath her hand.

The door swung open.

Inside was a bare wooden room spattered with blood. Rachelle saw herself lying dead at the center, bleeding from wound after wound.

And she saw herself kneeling over the body with a knife.

The other Rachelle raised her head, and now at last her heart was able to thud with terror again, but it was *too late, too late, too late*—

"You came home at last," said her other self. She rose and gripped Rachelle's wrists, and there was nothing but her dark eyes and cold and dark and cold.

Then she woke.

And she knew her heart was gone.

Rich afternoon sunlight shone on her face. She was lying in Erec's bed, atop the silken coverlet.

The Great Forest whispered in her mind, an endless, susurrating song. And yet her mind felt more clear and strong than it ever had before.

She could feel the little sweet-salt absence inside her, where her heart used to be. She could feel the gap, but it wasn't real. Nothing she had ever felt as a human, none of her guilt and grief, had ever been real. She was free of it all now, and it was wonderful.

There was nothing but the absence where her heart had been.

Nothing but the tiny, beautiful, *infinite* absence that would make her weep and scream if she had any tears or screaming left.

No. It was only humans who wanted meaning and hope. She was a forestborn, and she did not need those illusions.

Rachelle got out of bed and stretched, ready to run, and dance, and kill, and sing.

Her left hand ached, and she looked at the tiny white scar. For the first time she could remember, it didn't make her want to weep. The hurt that she felt was purely physical and completely irrelevant.

But then the ache turned into a stab of pain that drove her to her knees. Worse, her eyes stung with senseless tears. She scrabbled frantically for the easy despair of a moment before. This was nothing, it meant nothing—

Amélie's brush stroking makeup onto her face. Armand with yarn woven between his silver fingers. Aunt Léonie kissing her cheek.

The memories wouldn't stop. Her mind was like a whirling top that repeated *nothing nothing do not care* over and over, but now the top had fallen off balance and was wobbling wildly, back and forth between indifference and frenzied, grieving love.

You don't have to feel this. You don't have to love them.

The thought came into her head as clearly as if someone had spoken to her. Rachelle straightened up, the storm in her mind calming. She was suddenly very conscious of having one last choice.

She couldn't feel any more longing to love the people she had known. But she remembered Armand's voice: *Maybe it's just that, once they're so deep in the Forest's power, they don't want to remember loving anyone.*

Her hand clenched around the pain of the scar.

It was like trying to swallow broken glass or make her heart beat backward. But she thought of Aunt Léonie, Amélie, Armand. She remembered smiling at them, caring for them, *what would they think of me now—*

And it was over. There were tears on her face and she was gasping for breath, crouched on the floor beside Erec's expensive bed.

I love them, she thought, and the words felt numb but true. *I am a forestborn, and I love them.*

She could still hear the Great Forest singing at the back of her mind, triumphant and hopeless and unafraid. If she listened to it, wanted it, she knew she could let it sweep away her mind again.

With a slow breath, she got to her feet. Her blood pulsed, ready for a fight.

I am Rachelle Brinon. I didn't listen to my aunt when she told me to stay on the path and save my own life. Damned if I'll listen to the Forest now.

She didn't feel the slightest bit weak or unsteady as she strode to the door. Then she pushed it open and saw Erec sitting in his study.

He looked up. There was no time for fear. Rachelle thought of how the sunlight had poured drunkenly across her skin, and she let it give a swing to her steps as she strode out into the room.

He was on his feet in an instant. "My lady."

She smiled back at him. "My lord."

He crooked his finger, and she felt the compulsion he sent along the string that bound them, but she walked forward of her own will into his arms.

"Are you reconciled to your fate?" he asked.

"Yes," she said, and it was not a lie. She knew what her fate was and how she was going to use it, and not one part of her rebelled against it.

"You led me a merry chase." His fingers traced over her face. She could still feel her old lust for him. She could feel, also, the draw of the bond between them. Now that she could tell the difference, they were both less terrifying.

"Would you be satisfied with less?" she asked. "What do you need me to do?"

"Kiss me," he said, and she gave him a quick kiss on the cheek.

He laughed. "I'm glad you haven't lost your defiance."

"I'll make you gladder still tonight," she said. "Right now, I'm going to run through the gardens."

She expected him to object. To demand further submission out of her first. But he only smiled and said, "As you wish," and a moment later she was running lightly down the hallway.

Of course she didn't head for the gardens. She went straight for the Lady Chapel, which was dedicated to the Holy Virgin. It had been built in fulfillment of some king's vow a few hundred years ago, but since then it had become not just a chapel but also the repository of sundry royal treasures. So unlike the main chapel, there were guards.

Rachelle walked up to them without fear; they knew her, so they wouldn't attack until she gave them cause.

Sleep, she thought. *Darkness.* And power blossomed in her palms, forming great night-black flowers that only she could see. "Good afternoon," she said as they drew to attention.

"Good afternoon, mademoiselle," one of them said, and then Rachelle struck, her hands whipping out to slam the invisible flowers over their faces. They dropped instantly, and she stepped over their bodies and strode inside.

The Lady Chapel had no gaudy excesses of gold leaf and writhing cherubs: only white marble pillars, and slender silver traceries inlaid on the marble floor. It was a place of silence and blue shadows, which made the painting over the altar all the more jarring. It was like the gory portrait of the Dayspring that had been hung over Armand's audience, but even worse. Not only did it show the Dayspring as a hacked-apart pile of limbs; the limbs were bleeding, twisted, deformed. The hands writhed, tendons bulging. The face was twisted in agony. The pieces were laid out in a spiral, like a scream given shape.

But Rachelle had a different goal. She turned to the side altar, where sat the statue of the Holy Virgin. Here she was depicted as the Lady of Snows, dressed all in white, with the great eagle wings she had been given to fly to the mountains and hide from the Imperium's soldiers while she gave birth to the Dayspring. At her feet sat a multitude of candles, along with flowers, gold chains, bracelets, and earrings—whatever people saw fit to leave as offerings.

There was no sword.

Rachelle wasted several minutes looking in all the corners and crannies nearby and in trying to pry up paving stones. Then she remembered how Joyeuse had shifted and changed shape to let Armand hold it.

In the stories, Joyeuse had been made from a single bone.

She bent closer to the pile of offerings, squinting at the candlelight. And then she saw it: a little white finger bone, wedged in between two candles. She put on her leather gloves and reached for it.

Even through the glove, it was like touching hot iron. Her hand sprang away before she had even fully realized what she was feeling. It occurred to her that if she hadn't knocked the guards unconscious, perhaps she could have bullied or bluffed them into moving the bone for her. But she supposed she would have had to touch it sooner or later.

She held her hands out over Joyeuse for a long moment—hesitated—and then seized it.

It shifted in her grasp, turning back into the sword. Red-hot agony seared up her arms. Still she turned and managed to walk halfway to the door before her hands simply wouldn't grasp anymore. Joyeuse clattered to the ground, and after a moment of wavering, Rachelle fell to her knees.

She realized there were tears trickling down her face—tears of pain, but also frustration. She had, against all odds, survived the transformation into a forestborn with her mind and heart intact. She had fooled Erec and gotten to Joyeuse. And now she was going to fail and all the world would fall to darkness, just because she wasn't strong enough.

She thought of Armand six months ago, bleeding alone and still able to hold back the Devourer, and she reached again for Joyeuse.

Bishop Guillaume's voice rang out: "What business does a bloodbound have in the house of God?"

In an instant, she was on her feet. For there in the doorway stood the Bishop and Justine.

"Not a bloodbound," said Justine, her face pinched with loathing. "A forestborn."

Everything she had felt for him before, she felt ten times more now: the bone-deep revulsion and mistrust. Her fingers tensed with the desire to kill.

As if in answer, Justine's hand went to her sword.

And Rachelle remembered why she was there, and that if she fought them, Erec and the other forestborn would probably notice. They would wonder what she was doing in the chapel, and that would be the end of everything.

The problem was that the Bishop and Justine were surely going to fight *her*. She was a forestborn in the house of God. Who wouldn't try to stop her?

The Bishop took a step forward, and Rachelle did the only thing she could think of. She dropped to her knees and said, "Bless me, Father, for I have sinned. It has been three years since my last shriving."

There was a short, brittle silence. She saw the horror flicker across his grim face. *I think he just got more than he asked for,* she thought with bleak humor. *I suppose now I find out if he really believes what he preaches.*

Her stomach curled. What had she been thinking? She was on her knees before the man who hated her and whom she had always hated. She was going to *die* on her knees, because who would believe a monster? And who would refuse to strike it down?

Erec would laugh.

Then the Bishop exchanged a look with Justine. She nodded

and stepped back, out of the chapel. And he took the last step forward and dropped his hand on the top of Rachelle's head.

She flinched. But he said, "May the Lord be in your heart and on your lips."

Her heart lurched. Her lips wouldn't move.

It was the worst mockery of repentance to speak these words simply so he would trust her. It was the worst mockery of Aunt Léonie to think she could ever be sorry enough to win forgiveness. Who did the Bishop think he was, to act as if he knew she could?

And then she thought, *Admit it. Most of all, you're humiliated to speak your sins in front of someone you've despised.*

So she made herself look up at him.

His hand had not fallen from her head. Rachelle could, if she wanted, seize his wrist, throw him down, and break his neck before Justine could intervene.

His mouth was a hard line; his nostrils were flared. She realized that he, too, was afraid.

"I confess—"

The words were like two boulders grinding together. She closed her eyes. *Speak your sins to God,* the village priest had once told her. *The priest is just his messenger.* So she spoke to the God in the painting behind her, as ugly as her own soul and as tormented as Aunt Léonie.

"I confess to almighty God and to you, Father, that I accepted a forestborn's covenant to become a bloodbound."

Her face burned. Her words were boulders and she was being ground between them.

"This morning I tried to murder someone who had hurt my friend, and—and then I accepted the transformation into a forestborn."

The words were ragged, insufficient. They made everything she'd done sound so stupid. But also much smaller, and the words started to tumble out faster and faster.

"I have lied, and on my way to Rocamadour, I stole both food and money. I slept with Erec d'Anjou. I have not attended chapel in three years. I killed a woman who had gone mad when transforming into a forestborn. I have killed the enemies of the King, but always with good reason. I have said very cruel things. To seal my covenant with the forestborn, I killed my own aunt. I cut open her throat and I killed her. Because she was terribly wounded and I wanted to spare her, but also because I wanted to live. I killed her."

Then there was no sound but her breathing.

"For your penance," the Bishop said finally, "say three rosaries, one for each year of your sinful life, and offer them for the people you have harmed."

"That is not remotely enough," she snapped.

"Do you need also to confess doubts about the power of God to forgive sins?"

"Yes," she admitted after a few moments.

"In that case, for your penance, say only one rosary."

Rachelle couldn't say anything to that. Her throat was too tight with three years of unvoiced keening, and her eyes burned with unshed tears. It felt like every inch of her was raw and bleeding.

But now they were at the part of the ceremony where she wasn't supposed to speak. The Bishop laid a hand on her head and said swiftly, "The Dayspring who bid the sin-eaters rise and walk now bids you rise from your sins. In his name and by his power I command and adjure all unclean spirits to depart from you, and I release you from every penalty of excommunication and bond of interdict, and I absolve you from all your sins, in the name of the Father and of the Dayspring and of the Paraclete. Amen."

All of her sins, gone like that. She didn't feel relieved or joyful; she felt dizzy and confused, and the Forest still hummed in her veins. She had groveled and begged and told the most horrible truths. And nothing had happened, except that a man who once hated her had said she was forgiven.

She opened her eyes and climbed to her feet. The Bishop was still watching her, his shoulders tense, and she realized that he still was not entirely sure she wouldn't attack him.

And yet he had absolved her.

"Thank you," she said.

He regarded her another moment. "I believe Mademoiselle Leblanc was right about you." He knocked on the door, and Justine slipped back in.

"Well?" said Justine. "Reconsidered your ways?"

"The King has made an alliance with the forestborn," Rachelle blurted out, "of whom Erec d'Anjou is one. Tonight, they're going to awaken the Devourer by offering Armand Vareilles as a sacrifice to be possessed. I'll try to stop them, but I don't know if I can. Joyeuse can kill the Devourer once he's possessing a human body again, so you have to get it out of here. If I can't stop the sacrifice—I don't know what they'll do to the Château—Joyeuse has to be out of their grasp so someone can try to kill Armand. When he's the Devourer. Did I mention, you have to get out? Also, Raoul Courtavel is locked up somewhere in the Château as a hostage against Armand Vareilles."

The two of them stared at her a moment.

Then the Bishop said, "The Devourer is just a heathen—"

"He's real. I'm a forestborn, I *know*. And he's coming back tonight unless we stop him." She squashed a sudden impulse to say, *I had a vision and the Lady of Snows told me so.* "Listen, you know what Erec d'Anjou is like. Even if you don't believe that the Devourer is returning, believe that Erec thinks he can summon him back, and that he'll destroy anyone who stands in his way."

The Bishop looked at Justine. "That is something I would wager on," she said.

"You believed in my sins," said Rachelle. "Please. Believe me in this."

The Bishop stared at her for a long moment. At last he said, "Very well."

30

Rachelle strode down the halls of the palace. She cupped her hands, and thought, *Armand. Find him.* Mounds of tiny blue flowers glimmered in her hands; she blew on them and they spiraled up into the air where they drifted for a moment before eddying to the left.

She followed them. And she realized that she had known exactly how to use the power of the Forest to find someone. A little chill went down her spine, but she kept walking.

She had half expected some sort of dank dungeon, but the flowers led her to the east wing, where the less important nobles were housed; the hallways were narrower, and the rooms ranged from small to barely larger than a cupboard.

And then she saw the forestborn with the plump fingers standing outside a door. Again Rachelle thought, *Sleep,* and again the large, dark flowers blossomed in her hands. She took a step toward him—and he turned, his human appearance falling away as he drew his sword. The face that remained behind was human in shape, but filled with a horrible, beautiful power.

Rachelle ducked and rolled just barely in time to avoid the blade slicing off her head. *I should have known he'd sense it,* she thought, ripping her sword out of its sheath. He lunged at her again.

It felt like lightning seared down her spine. Her whole body lashed out, so fast that she didn't even see her sword cut into his neck. But she saw the blood spurt. It seemed to take forever, and though her body was now as sluggish as cold honey, she made it arc out of the way. Blood spattered against the floor.

Then time was normal again, and she was standing by herself in the hallway, a beheaded man at her feet. She'd dodged the blood while it was flying, but now it was pooling around her boots.

Rachelle sucked in a strangled breath. Her body was shaking, but she didn't feel afraid or disgusted; her mind was wrapped in the cold, dark calm of the Forest. She imagined that cold wrapping around her body, stilling it, and then she tried the door. It was locked, so she kicked it open and strode inside.

The room was small and completely bare except for the once gaudy, now fading red wallpaper. At the center stood Armand. And beside him, holding a knife to his throat, stood Erec.

"Good afternoon, my lady," said Erec. "I was starting to hope you would never come."

"What are you doing?" asked Rachelle. She couldn't look away from the glinting metal pressed against Armand's throat. Such a tiny weapon, and it would take such a tiny motion to slice through the skin and let the blood come pouring out. The Forest's dark calm couldn't stop her from shaking anymore, because this was what the Forest did: it made her watch the people she loved die.

"You need to get better at lying," said Erec. "I could tell you were still clinging to your human heart, and I knew you would come here to rescue him. Or are you going to claim you're here to serve the Devourer?"

"I—"

"Don't bother. I can see you're tracking our kinsman's blood into the room," said Erec. "You're not truly one of us yet."

"Isn't killing kin a forestborn specialty?" said Armand. "Shouldn't that make her—"

Erec seized a handful of Armand's hair and yanked his head to the side. "As for *you*," he said, his voice low and deadly calm, "had I known what you would do to my lady, I would have cut out those pretty eyes weeks ago and sliced that clever tongue in two."

"Stop it," Rachelle snapped. "Stop hiding behind him and face me. Or are you afraid I'll beat you again?"

"It's flattering when you have eyes only for me," said Erec, "but please take note that you're in no position to demand anything."

A hand dropped onto her shoulder, burning cold. Rachelle whirled—but her arm had already gone numb, and the sword dropped from her fingers. Behind her stood three forestborn, hooded and cloaked in blue, and behind them, the painted wall had begun to fade into the Forest.

Her knees gave out. The nearest forestborn—the one who had touched her—caught her by the shoulders. The hood fell back from the forestborn's face: it was a tall, dark-haired woman as lovely and lifeless as the moon.

"My son is intemperately fond of you," she said, "but I am not."

Rachelle tried to break free, but the last strength was leaving her body. The woman clasped her tight and sat down, laying Rachelle's head in her lap so that she could see Armand.

And then she pressed a knife against Rachelle's throat.

"I can't have my lady escaping," said Erec to Armand, "and none of us can allow *you* to escape. So here is what will happen. You have carried the shadow of our lord for six months. You already hold a little of his power, and I know you've learned how to use it enough to raise an image of the Forest. You are going to let one of us borrow that power to summon the Forest itself in a ring around the Château, so that nobody can get in or out."

Rachelle's mouth was numb and sluggish, but she managed to say, "Don't—"

And then the tip of the blade dug deeper. The power that held her in place dampened most of the pain, but she could still feel the stomach-turning intrusion of metal into her throat, and the blood dribbling down her neck.

"She'll heal from this much," said Erec. "And from a bit more. But not if we take her head off."

Armand's eyes had gotten very wide. "You're bluffing."

"I believe you thought that when I said what would happen to anyone you told. Your mother discovered you were wrong."

"You love her—"

"And therefore I will not let her be taken from me."

Armand said nothing. His expression was unreadable. *He won't,* thought Rachelle, *he can't, he won't—*

"Such a pity," said Erec, turning away.

"Wait!" Armand's voice was raw and desperate. "Wait. I'll do it. Just don't hurt her."

"Oh?" Erec turned back to him. "And where was this compliance when your dear mother's life was at stake?"

Armand's mouth pressed together.

Rachelle tried to shout, *Stop,* but between the knife and the paralysis, all she could do was make a soft choking noise. Armand shuddered and met her eyes.

"I'm sorry," he said.

One of the other forestborn stepped forward: she had the face and the form of a fourteen-year-old girl, but an awful sense of age and power clung to her face.

"Grant me your power for this deed," she said.

"I do," he whispered.

And she sang, if it could be called singing: one low note, haunting and unearthly, that made Rachelle's skin burn and shudder. She did not exactly see, but she more than felt the Forest growing up in a ring around the Château, shadows unfolding, dark flowers blossoming, ready to trick and maze and kill anyone who attempted to pass through it.

Slow the vision faded. She realized that the forestborn had stopped singing. The knife was gone from her neck; and she lay by herself on the floor. She blinked. Armand had gone.

That made her bolt upright. Erec caught her by the shoulder; he was the only one in the room now.

"Careful," he said. "Our little song seems to have taken you quite strongly."

Rachelle tried to speak, choked, and then hacked up a giant clot of blood.

"I think the knife had something to do with it," she said afterward.

"You'll need to take less heed of such things, if you're going to survive as a forestborn," he said, kneeling beside her.

"Who says I'm going to survive?" asked Rachelle.

The Forest had been summoned so quickly. The Bishop and Justine couldn't have gotten out fast enough. Were they still hiding somewhere in the grounds of the Château, or had they been lost in the Forest itself?

"It's true," said Erec. "I remember somebody telling me she would be dead and damned first. But she seems to have been mistaken about a lot of things. The same way our Monsieur Vareilles was mistaken when he told me over and over and *over* that he would never help us in the slightest."

"What happened to him?" asked Rachelle.

"He will be watched every moment from now until the offering," said Erec. "He's not essential to us, but he is precious. To be a vessel, there's a certain idiot abnegation required, and he is very good at it. Do remember, though, that we only need him alive. Not anything more. You know in what condition I can keep him alive if I please."

Rachelle swallowed.

"And I will please," he went on quietly, "if you ever rebel against me again."

"Erec," she said desperately, "you love me, don't you?"

His finger traced her lip. "More than you can imagine."

"Then don't do this."

"Why? Because I *love* you so *very* much?" His voice turned the words into a mockery.

"Because then you'll have me. We'll go away together, and I

swear, I'll do everything you want. I'll *be* everything you want, forever and ever. I'll love you. I'll forget I ever loved anyone else but you. I will live and die and breathe for you. Just don't help them. Don't let them bring back the Devourer."

"Oh, my lady." He kissed her forehead. "I wouldn't love you so much if you weren't so brave. But you've forgotten one thing. If the Devourer returns, I will still have you, and all the kingdoms of this world besides."

"I'll fight you," said Rachelle. "Threatening Armand won't work past tonight. Threatening Amélie won't work for more than three days, because I know she'll never take your covenant. And then I'll fight you forever."

"There will always be another innocent life or twelve to threaten. Besides, then you will have nothing left but the Devourer and me." Erec put his arm around her. "And you are marvelously skilled at surviving. You'll learn to love us both."

Rachelle didn't fight the embrace. "Maybe I'll just learn to kill you."

He grinned. "I'm willing to take that wager."

31

When Rachelle was able to stand again, Erec took her by the hand and led her back to her room.

"I'm leaving you here," he said, "only because I trust you to imagine what I will do to your favorite saint if you disobey."

"I know," said Rachelle, and sat down on one of the chairs. She would fight him again that evening. She knew she would find the strength to fight him then, but for now she felt empty and exhausted.

Afternoon sunlight blazed through the window; it glittered off the embroidery on Erec's jacket as he bowed to her and left.

This is the last sunlight, she thought. *The last time any of us will ever see the sun.*

No. No, the Bishop and Justine were still free—they must

be, or Erec would have gloated—so maybe they would be able to intervene tonight. Or tomorrow, or next year. The world had lain under Endless Night for thousands of years before Tyr and Zisa defeated the Devourer. If he returned tonight, he could still be defeated later, and daylight restored.

But if the offering took place, whoever wanted to save the world would have to kill Armand. She was suddenly, wretchedly glad that she couldn't hold Joyeuse.

She remembered Amélie gluing the patch on her face and telling her it meant first "assassin" and then "courage."

Amélie. She had left her to wake up a bloodbound.

Rachelle surged to her feet, meaning to run back to the little storage room and find her. But then somebody coughed softly behind her. She turned.

Amélie waited in the doorway. She stood stiffly, mouth a little tense; her hair was wrapped up in a neat bun, but one little strand escaped. She had pasted a large velvet patch over the mark on her cheek.

"Rachelle," she said, and Rachelle realized she was afraid.

"I'm sorry," she said. "I'm so sorry—"

Amélie flung her arms around her. "You're all right."

"Yes. No, what are you talking about?" Rachelle realized that she was hugging Amélie back just as fiercely. Warm, human arms that she would soon never feel again, and she just wanted to curl up and go to sleep forever in that embrace.

"I woke up and you were gone. I thought—I didn't know what to think."

"I tried to kill Erec and then I— You can tell, can't you?"

Amélie looked up from her shoulder. "I'm not a fool and it seems I'm also not entirely human anymore. Yes, I can tell you're a forestborn. I don't care any more than I did when you were bloodbound."

"I'm sorry," said Rachelle. "It's all my fault. That he hurt you."

"No," said Amélie.

"You don't understand. He said you were a *present*—"

"My mother runs a printing press," Amélie interrupted her. "You can buy anything, you know, if you just say it's ingredients for medicine. That's why I could never leave her to become a cosmetician. She needed my help mixing ink and setting type. And nobody ever looked twice at me when I carried pamphlets across the city."

"You," Rachelle said blankly.

"When I heard you were going to the palace with Monsieur Vareilles, I knew I had to come. I was the one who took his messages to the other rebels. I helped arrange the coup. Your d'Anjou caught me when I was trying to escape the Château afterward. He didn't like it." She shrugged. "Maybe he would have marked me whatever I did. But that isn't what happened. I'm going to die because I tried to resist an unjust king. Not because of you."

Rachelle stared at her. "Then why . . . if you were one of them, why did you ever become my friend?"

"I told you why." Amélie looked steadily back at her. "Mother said I was crazy. But you saved my life, and you were—you were so kind, when you thought nobody would notice. Maybe we should have told you earlier, but it wasn't just our secret and it didn't seem fair to burden you—"

Rachelle started laughing, raggedly and almost hysterically. *All this time, she was protecting my innocence,* she thought, and had to sit down, she was laughing so hard.

"But if I'd known it would make you smile, I would have told you years ago," said Amélie, kneeling beside her. She reached out a hand; Rachelle took it and squeezed her fingers.

She should have told Amélie so many things, so long ago.

When she had gotten her breath back, she said, "Did Erec tell you anything when he marked you?"

Amélie shook her head. So Rachelle told her everything.

"With so many forestborn," she said, "I don't see how I can stop the ceremony. I think—I think the only thing to do is let the Devourer awaken and then try to kill him."

"You think you can?"

"No. I'd need Joyeuse for that. But the Bishop hasn't been captured—that I know of—and neither he nor Justine will hesitate." She swallowed. "To kill the Devourer, somebody needs to be possessed. But it doesn't need to be Armand. I won't let it be Armand if there's any other way. I won't."

Amélie pulled Rachelle's hand to her lips and kissed it.

"I would scold you," she said after a moment, "but I'm planning to die as well."

Rachelle thought she had never loved her so much as in that moment.

"If the Bishop kills the Devourer fast enough," she said, "it might set you free."

"Maybe," said Amélie. "The great physician Albert le Magne believed that at the moment people receive the mark, both blood and bile are poisoned, and that is why they die in three days if the Devourer does not strengthen them. My mother thinks—" Her voice faltered and she fell silent.

"I'm sorry," Rachelle said again.

"I told you, it's not your fault."

"I brought you here. If I hadn't asked you—"

"If we really are doomed," said Amélie, "if the Devourer returns and we can't stop him and night falls forever—I am sorry I can't be with my mother. But I'm glad I can be with you."

"I wish there were something I could do for you," Rachelle whispered. "But there's something I'd ask of you. Tonight, for the ball. Will you . . . will you please make me beautiful?"

"You are always beautiful." Amélie smiled. "But I will make you as glorious as the sun."

Amélie kept her word. Rachelle's skin had never shimmered so flawlessly; her cheeks had never flushed so perfectly. Her lips were painted pure, warlike bloodred. There was a patch on her left cheekbone—a tiny crescent moon—and on her right, a little swirling design painted in gold.

"Does *that* mean 'assassin'?" asked Rachelle as the tiny brush tickled over her cheek, leaving gold tendrils behind.

"No," said Amélie. "For a noblewoman I would paint her house's coat of arms here. But since you're not . . ." She trailed into silence as she worked on a particularly tricky portion. Then she went on, "I found this design in a book. It was painted on the wall of a cave in northern Gévaudan. There." She laid down the brush and handed the mirror to Rachelle.

"It looks almost like writing," said Rachelle.

"Well. I might have added my initials to it."

Sévigné was gone—"She saw the mark," said Amélie, "and she's probably halfway to the Archipelago by now"—but Amélie contrived to put Rachelle's hair up easily enough. It was the dress that was a problem, because Rachelle didn't want Erec to suspect she was planning anything, but a ball gown was hardly suitable for fighting. They compromised by lacing the corset as loosely as possible and strapping four knives to Rachelle's legs.

The dress itself was magnificent. It was crimson silk that turned to gold at the hem, with golden roses embroidered on the skirt. The sleeves were slashed with white and ringed with little gold silk roses. The neckline bared her shoulders and her collarbones like a declaration of war. When Rachelle saw herself wearing it in the mirror, she felt beautiful. And glorious. And like a warrior who had a chance to win.

And none of that mattered next to knowing that every inch of her body had been decorated by somebody who loved her.

"Thank you," she said, turning to Amélie, who had been fussing with the back panels of her skirt. "You're amazing."

"This is my last performance," said Amélie. "It had better be good."

"I mean," said Rachelle, "thank you for everything, ever since we met. Without you . . . I don't know if I'd be strong enough to keep fighting."

Amélie smiled and took her hands. "I have never regretted being your friend," she said. "Make me proud tonight."

32

Erec came to fetch her. Rachelle had expected him to come looking for punishment or vengeance, but when she opened the door and saw him standing on the other side resplendent in black velvet and silver, he only smiled at her, the same as always.

"Good evening," he said. "I think you will enjoy tonight."

She raised her eyebrows. "Have you forgiven me, then?"

"Still so human, my lady?" He laid his hands on her shoulders. "You misunderstand our nature. We don't need to hate or forgive what belongs to us." He kissed her neck, and she shivered. "Someday you'll understand that."

Rachelle thought of when she had first learned what he was, and how desperately she had wanted to disbelieve it. Even now—even after what he had done to her, to Armand, to Amélie, to

Aunt Léonie—some part of her wanted to forget it all, just so that they could be Rachelle-and-Erec again, fighting woodspawn in the streets of Rocamadour.

But that had only been a game to him, when it had been salvation to her.

"Humans are not so far from forestborn as you think," she said.

He smiled. "You'll sing differently when we ride to hunt the humans for sport."

Night had fallen; as they walked through the hallways of the Château, the light from the chandeliers glittered off the glass windows. Shadowy rabbits raced beside their feet, and translucent flowers sprouted from the picture frames. The air was thick with the Forest's longing.

The Midsummer Night festival was in the Garden of the Four Fountains: a wide, square lawn, enclosed by trees, with a great fountain at each corner. Lanterns hung on every tree, and candles sat around the rims of the fountains, setting the water alight as it leaped into the air. In one corner, a score of musicians played; in another were tables nearly buried under food and wine; and in the center, almost the whole court milled about, talking and laughing and dancing.

"Is it not glorious?" said Erec into her ear. His arm was tucked into the crook of hers. "Like peacocks, rounded up for slaughter."

"Peacocks aren't raised for meat," said Rachelle. Her heart was beating fast but steady. She felt the vast magical power gathering in the air the same way she felt the exact space between Erec's body and hers. But she was not, for now, overpowered by either feeling.

"They've appeared on the King's table a time or two. Besides, it's for their feathers they are killed." Erec surveyed the glittering crowd. They wore dresses and coats of every color, with feathers in their hair and jewels at their necks. The little heeled shoes that men and women alike wore gave most of them a delicate, mincing gait quite like birds picking their way through grass.

"They're so very human," said Erec. "Laughing and dancing and civilized only because of their ignorance. If they knew what was coming, they would tear each other to pieces to escape. But that's the human way, I suppose."

"Too bad you're killing them all," said Rachelle. "When night falls, to whom will you feel superior?"

"Oh, they won't all die. We shall keep them as our King keeps peacocks on his lawn. And hunt them as we please, like foxes."

"Hardly challenging prey, in those shoes and without claws," said Rachelle, scanning the crowd. "Did you drag Armand out for a final show, or is he staying somewhere safe?"

"Quite safe," Erec began, but just then the King called out merrily, "D'Anjou!"

They turned, and there was the King bearing down upon them, dressed in cloth of gold, curls waving in the breeze. A step behind him, face solemn and still, came Armand.

Rachelle's heart slammed against her ribs. His face was pale and grim, but he was alive. He was alive, and he was not harmed, and he met her eyes.

"Your Majesty," said Erec, and bowed. Rachelle curtsied awkwardly a moment after.

"I thought it well for appearances if my son were here, this final night," said the King. "After all, the announcement we make tonight closely concerns him, does it not?"

"Of course," said Erec, and Rachelle knew that she was the only one who could hear the suppressed annoyance in his voice.

"I'll leave him in your care and Mademoiselle Brinon's," said the King, giving Armand's shoulder a light slap, and then returned to the dancing.

"Well, well, well," said Erec. "Monsieur Vareilles, whatever shall we do with you?"

"Let him dance with me," said Rachelle.

"You'll plot," said Erec.

"Yes," she said, "but what can we do? You have your forestborn everywhere in the crowd."

"That does not explain why I should let you."

"Because you'll take me away again at the end of the dance," she said. "And you would love to show how you can give me and take me away."

He bowed to her. "You have answered my riddle. Dance, then, while you still can."

Armand didn't move, so Rachelle stepped forward, took his hands, and drew them into the dance.

"Are you real?" he asked softly once they were dancing.

"What?" said Rachelle.

"Ever since I let them raise the Forest, the visions are worse. Everything feels like a dream."

"I'm real," said Rachelle. "I'm real. I promise." She wondered what had happened in the past few hours; he looked nearly at the edge of his endurance. If only she had been able to get him out instead of running straight into Erec's trap.

"I'm sorry," she said.

"You?" He laughed bitterly. "*I'm* sorry. I've done everything wrong. First the coup, then giving in when they wanted to raise the Forest. Now everyone's trapped—"

"I forgive you," she said. "And it's all the same once the Devourer returns."

His gaze flickered from side to side, probably checking for spies. "Did you see my candle?" he asked finally.

"Yes," she said. "And I told the Bishop you were praying. So don't worry. Just—when the time comes, say no for as long as you can."

"How will that help end things?"

"I have a plan," she said. "But I can't tell you the rest."

"Because I wouldn't like it or because it wouldn't be safe for me to know?"

"Because I need you to trust me," said Rachelle, her stomach knotting. She knew this was a betrayal, but he would accept the Devourer this instant before he let her take his place. "Can you trust me?"

"I do," he said. "If we somehow live through this—"

"Armand." Her voice felt thick and sticky in her throat. She couldn't tell him, but she couldn't let him believe— "You have to understand. Whatever happens tonight—I don't think you'll get to keep me."

He pressed his lips together. When he spoke again, his voice was tightly controlled. "You said you had a plan. Is there a chance we could survive?"

"Yes," she lied helplessly. "But have you forgotten already that I'm a forestborn? When we defeat the Devourer . . . I don't know what that will mean for me."

It was as close as she dared come to the truth.

"We don't know what that will mean for me either. Rachelle, I'm just saying—"

"And even if I live through it, you can't just take a demon home and keep house with her! Didn't you ever hear the story about the Duke of Anjou and Mélusine?"

"Yes," said Armand. "But he let go of her when she transformed, didn't he? Whatever creature you turn into, whatever form you take, I won't let go of you."

"You think that holding hands can make me human? That's idiotic. You don't even have human hands."

She regretted the words a moment after, but his lips only sliced into a grin. "All the better to hold you with. Since, as you keep reminding me, you aren't even human."

There was no reply she could make to that. So they danced. The music swayed and rocked back and forth, dragging them around in minor-key circles as light as leaves in air, as ponderous as the planets. The other dancers swirled around them, lovely and heedless as peacock feathers. Armand's silver hand rested in hers, and that insignificant touch sent a thrill up her arms.

This is the human way, she thought. *On the edge of destruction, at the end of all things, we still dance. And hope.*

The music wound down to a pause. Rachelle looked around and didn't see Erec anywhere nearby, and she wondered for a moment if they might get a second dance.

"Come," said a calm voice that made her skin crawl. It was the dark-haired woman who had held the knife to Rachelle's throat.

She laid a hand on Armand's shoulder.

Swiftly, he leaned forward and pressed a kiss to Rachelle's lips. Then he let himself be drawn away.

"I love you," Rachelle whispered, staring after him as he vanished into the crowd.

"So he has another darling?" asked la Fontaine. "Or is she one of your friends?"

Rachelle started and turned to the left. La Fontaine stood beside her, dressed in shimmering, pure white silk; the only bit of color on her figure was the ruby at her neck and the bloodred fan that she fluttered in front of her face.

"She's not my friend," said Rachelle.

"Indeed? She's friendly enough with your beloved d'Anjou." La Fontaine gave her a glance that seemed to divine all her secrets. "I'm not so ignorant as you might think. Nor yet so merciful, if you are planning to harm my cousin."

Did she know something? Or suspect? Rachelle opened her mouth, but she had no idea what she was going to say, and then a voice called out, "Silence for the King!"

The crowd parted in the center of the lawn, and there stood the King, resplendent in gold and white, with Erec at his side.

"Dearly beloved children of my realm," said the King. "On this night, I proclaim to you a new future for our kingdom. Many of you have feared what will happen to Gévaudan without a legitimate heir. But I tell you now that you will need no heir."

There had been silence for the King's speech, but now a nervous mutter was rising, and in another moment, Rachelle saw why: behind the King, men were marching through the trees in lines. Their eyes shimmered in the dark with reflected lamplight, like a great horde of hungry rats, and then they grew closer, and Rachelle realized that each one bore a bloodred star on his forehead.

"I am your King and your King I shall remain forever, through the offices of my dear friends." The King gestured at the forestborn gathered behind him. "Too long we have feared the Forest—"

"Too long, O King, you have made your peace with sin!"

The Bishop's voice cracked across the garden as he came striding out of the trees, Justine at his side, and a troop of soldiers behind him.

"King Auguste-Philippe II, I accuse you of betraying your kingly consecration by making an abominable covenant with our enemies, the forestborn. Kneel down and beg God for mercy before this accursed foolishness goes any further."

"Such idealism," said the King. "But I think you'll find it comes too late. D'Anjou?" He turned to Erec. "Tell them."

"Indeed, sire," said Erec. "It is much too late to care who rules this kingdom."

In a heartbeat, his sword whipped out to slice the King's head off his shoulders.

Nobody moved. It was too sudden, too unreal, for anyone to believe what had just happened.

"You have looked on the last daylight," cried Erec, his voice ringing through all the garden. "Now begins the rule of the Forest again."

SO ZISA WAS FOUND WORTHY TO TAKE HER brother to be sacrificed on a hill of raw, dead earth. Here on a throne of black rock sat the previous vessel with flowers on his head. His ribs still moved with each breath, and his skin still stretched across his face. In this sense he was alive, but no other.

"O my daughter," said Old Mother Hunger, "tell our lord he has a new body."

"With gladness," said Zisa, "but first I would dance before him."

So Zisa unbound her hair and danced. When she had finished, the Devourer hissed through the lips of his vessel and said, "I once granted your mother a wish in return for her dancing. Would you have the same of me?"

"Yes, my lord," said Zisa. "I wish to see you face-to-face."

The Devourer breathed upon her, and she vanished from the hill. Let us say that she walked into his stomach. To her, it seemed that she walked through a wood where the trees wept blood, and among the roots of a tree covered in ice, she found what looked like a glowing pearl, and she knew it was the moon. She cupped it in her hands and stole back the way she had come.

Back onto the dead hill she stepped, and she held high the moon. Old Mother Hunger screamed and leaped for Zisa, but it was too late: the moon flew out of her fingers and up into the sky, and as its light dropped down upon the eldest of all forestborn, she withered and faded and fell to ash.

"Farewell, Mother," Zisa whispered.

But while the light of the moon had killed Old Mother Hunger, it restored to Tyr his name and his wits, and he opened his eyes and saw his sister.

"You have found a way to destroy him?" asked Tyr.

"Yes," said Zisa, "but there is something else I must do first." She turned to the Devourer's vessel and said, "I still have not seen your face, my lord."

He hissed, but then he breathed upon her. This time she wandered the bleeding forest until she found a tree charred black from root to twig. Beneath it lay a kernel of golden light. When Zisa stepped back again onto the hill, the seed flew up into the sky and became the sun, and the world filled with light.

"Now for the final stroke," said Zisa, and from her skirt she took the two needles and gave one to Tyr. In their hands, the needles became swords, Durendal and Joyeuse.

Brother and sister were ready to strike; but the Devourer said, "O my daughter, have you wondered what befell the souls of your mother and father?"

"They are dead," said Zisa. "You can trouble them no more."

"The souls of those my servants kill are mine by right," said the Devourer. "Lay down your sword, come face-to-face with me, and perhaps I'll give them back to you."

She had hated her father; she had loved her mother. But Tyr, the fool, had loved them both; so she could not resist. Though Tyr begged her to say no, she laid down the sword and let the Devourer's vessel breathe on her a third time.

Zisa hunted the bleeding forest without success until she came to a desert. When she stepped upon the sand, a voice behind her said, "Turn around and face me, little girl."

She turned and saw his face and, seeing him, knew he held no souls that did not willingly turn to him.

But seeing him, she belonged to him. And on the hill, the old vessel crumbled to dust, and the Devourer opened Zisa's eyes and said to Tyr, "You never yielded to me. So you cannot touch me."

Tyr looked at his sister whom he loved more than life and who loved him more than reason.

And that is when he stabbed me in the heart.

Finally people started screaming. Justine drew her sword and charged toward Erec.

And the bloodbound attacked.

They had stood in such orderly rows that Rachelle had assumed they were the same as she had been: infected with the power of the Forest but still able to speak and think, obedient to the King because they had chosen obedience over death. But now they burst into wild, wordless screams and flung themselves on the crowd, wielding swords and knives with desperate, animal ferocity.

The world slowed to a crawl. It seemed to take forever for Rachelle to pull up the hem of her skirt and grab the knives. By the time she had finished, the closest bloodbound was nearly upon her—but he was moving slowly too, and it was the easiest thing in the world to whirl and kick. He dodged back, but a little off balance, and she was able to lunge forward and slide the blades into his ribs.

He had been human once. But his eyes were filled with the same sightless madness as the woman she'd killed in Rocamadour.

Then time was moving normally again. The soldiers were trying to pull the nobles into a group that could be protected. Justine was fighting two bloodbound at once, her sword whirling—the Bishop was fighting too, wielding Joyeuse, and his childhood must have included fencing lessons at some point because he had the stance of an aristocrat—

But there were still too many of the mad bloodbound. There were far too many.

"Stop," she said, as she whirled to slice another bloodbound across the face. But none of them seemed to hear. Then she thought of the Forest and she filled her lungs with the cold, sweet air, and she said, *"Stop."*

And they stopped. They dropped their weapons and straightened to attention, glazed eyes staring blindly ahead of them.

She felt them, a vast, dragging presence like a thousand dull little pebbles in her head. How could Erec have controlled them so easily?

"Kneel," Rachelle said, and they knelt.

She could hardly breathe.

"Sleep," she whispered, and they fell to the ground and her mind was free again.

From the other side of the garden, Justine looked at her with raw surprise.

Something cold burned against the back of Rachelle's neck. She whirled and staggered, falling to her knees in the grass. There behind her stood la Fontaine, her makeup smudged. In her hands, she held three roses, their stems plaited together in a knot that looked vaguely familiar.

"I grow more and more curious," said la Fontaine, "whether I should call you Mélusine or Zisette."

Rachelle realized that there were three more roses lying on the lawn around her in a triangle.

"Where is Armand?" asked la Fontaine.

"D'Anjou took him," said Rachelle. "I have to stop him."

"And what are you?"

"I'm a forestborn," said Rachelle. "What are *you*?"

"Did I not tell you?" said la Fontaine. "I am an almighty goddess."

Rachelle stared at the flower she held, and remembered how charms were worked in the south. "You're . . . a woodwife?"

"Why do you think I filled my Tendre with roses? My mother and I are the only reason this Château wasn't overrun by woodspawn years ago."

"The whole Château is surrounded by the Great Forest now," said Rachelle. "If we get the people inside, can you protect them?"

"A little," said Fontaine. "I am still not sure if I should kill you first, though."

"I'll vouch for her," said Justine, arriving from behind Rachelle. "And the Bishop will vouch for me."

"I am not sure I trust your bishop either," said la Fontaine, but she lowered the plaited roses and Rachelle was able to scramble back to her feet.

Beneath the simple nighttime rustlings, the air shivered with a not-quite-audible breath.

"They've started," said Rachelle. "Where's Joyeuse?"

"Here," said the Bishop, also arriving. Behind him, Rachelle could see the courtiers still huddled together behind the line of soldiers, looking unable to believe the danger was over.

The danger was just beginning.

Rachelle turned to the Bishop. "You carry the sword. Justine, come with us to help hold the forestborn back. La Fontaine, get the people into the palace and keep them as safe as you can."

"Bring my cousin back," said la Fontaine. "And tell me this tale in my salon."

"I'll try," said Rachelle, though dread curdled in her stomach. She would have to fail at one of those charges.

Then the three of them raced into the dark. Rachelle didn't worry about finding her way; she simply followed the glowing red trail of the thread that bound her to Erec. As they ran through the trees, the darkness between the trunks thickened and roughened until it was no longer air but dark, damp stone, and they were walking down a tunnel.

At the end of the tunnel was a door made of metal flowers, and it hummed with a power that forbade humans to open it.

Luckily, only one of them was human.

"I'm going inside first," she said softly. "I'll leave the door ajar. When I call, charge inside. Or when you hear screams and fighting." She took a deep breath and realized that despite everything, she was still afraid.

Justine smacked her shoulder lightly. "Be careful."

"Go with God," said the Bishop.

Rachelle nodded. "Stand back," she said, and touched the door.

The petals licked her fingers with soft affection, and the door swung open, and she slipped inside.

Her first thought was to worship.

Not thought. Instinct. And not hers. The pressure crushed her from every side, as if the very air were made of it: this place was sacred to the Devourer. In this place he had been worshipped, loved, feared, and reverenced. Hunger was his glory and destruction his delight. Worship him. Worship. Worship.

She realized that she was standing in a round, domed room hollowed out of black rock, and that the floor was carved with a labyrinth, the lines wide as a hand's span and just as deep, lined with white marble that glowed in the darkness. Forestborn stood in a ring around the labyrinth. They were singing: a low, whispering chant that had no words Rachelle could recognize. And yet she knew the song; it came from the recesses of her heart. It was the same song that had stirred on the cold, sweet winds of the Great Forest.

Our master, she thought. *Our lord. The hunger of hungers, delight of delights,* and her body stumbled, swept by another wave of desire to kneel and worship. She was a tiny candle flame, guttering in the wind before it went out.

Hands caught her shoulders, lifted her up. Erec looked into her eyes and said, "Sometimes I wish you weren't so worthy of me." His face was fondly affectionate, but his fingers had tightened on her arms as if he wanted to break them.

"I haven't come to stop the Devourer," she whispered.

"That's good. Because I brought a hostage." He glanced toward the side of the room, and there she saw one of the forestborn sitting with Amélie. Her body was rigid, her eyes wide; when she looked at Rachelle, it seemed to take her a moment to recognize her. Then her lips pressed together and she nodded fiercely.

I'm planning to die as well, Amélie had said to her, and she was brave enough that she had meant it.

Erec was not always so clever as he thought.

"I won't stop the sacrifice," said Rachelle. "I promise."

"Good," said Erec. "Then come and see."

He dragged her forward.

While they spoke, the walls of the room had faded away. Though the cold, raw stone was still beneath their feet, now vast, ancient tree trunks reared up around them, taller and thicker than cathedral towers. They were in the Great Forest.

The chanting swelled in her ears, her lungs, her blood. There was almost no difference left, she realized, between the human world and the Great Forest, between simple darkness and eternal night. The only wall that separated them now was the fragile human sitting, head bowed, at the center of the labyrinth.

The chanting ceased. The forestborn lady who had held the knife to Rachelle's throat said, "Are you ready to accept our lord?"

Armand raised his head. He met Rachelle's eyes. And then he said, "I will not."

Erec strode forward, drawing his sword, and pointed it at the base of Armand's throat. "You have one more chance. Then we use another."

Rachelle could feel the Devourer—could feel the vast, ancient power rising and waking and turning slowly toward the world again, ever hungry and ever yearning. It was like a rising black tide, and her heart stuttered because surely Armand would be drowned in it. Surely anything human would have to drown.

Armand smiled up at Erec and said, "No."

"Now!" Rachelle yelled, and then she moved. It seemed to take a very long time: hours to shove a hand against Erec's arm, jolting his sword point aside. Hours to lunge forward, slide, and crash into Armand. She had meant to shove him out of the center, but he hung on to her and they end up tangled together.

She had time to notice that the black tide had risen above them in a vast wave, cold and seeking and desperate. She had time to feel the weight of Armand's body against hers, his elbow jabbed into her side. And she had time to think, *He is never going to forgive me for this,* before she opened her mouth and said, "Yes."

The Devourer was falling too swiftly and greedily to turn aside from any willing sacrifice. The dark wave crashed down on her and filled her up. Her body shuddered and writhed under the weight. There was no sound in her ears but the screaming of the nighttime wind. Her vision blurred; she saw Justine and the Bishop charge into the room, saw the forestborn turning to fight, but it was like watching distorted shadow puppets on a faraway wall.

In one flash, she saw Armand's gray eyes, wide with panic. She couldn't see Amélie, but she knew that she was somewhere in the room. There was still a chance that both of them could live, and she thought to the darkness inside her, *Yes, yes, yes.*

Then nothing mattered, nothing besides the raw fury that she had been tricked, that *this was the wrong vessel.* This one still stank of human foolishness, but it was not human, and her lips drew back in a snarl of helpless rage.

"Rachelle? *Rachelle!*" Someone was shaking her shoulders and screaming.

She blinked open her eyes at the worthless traitor sacrifice—

"In the name of Tyr and Zisa, let her go!"

Her body shuddered. "Armand," she gasped. She could feel his fingers digging into her shoulders, but the feeling wasn't quite connected to her.

She remembered sitting with Amélie in the darkness and talking about peace. *Just a few brushstrokes,* Amélie had said.

"What did you do?" Armand demanded.

Two steps. One word. *A certain idiot abnegation,* Erec had said, and it was easier than he had ever guessed.

"Joyeuse," she said. "The Bishop has it."

She saw Armand understand, saw him shatter with the knowledge.

"Please," she whispered, because the dark tide of the Devourer was pouring over her again, into her eyes, her nose, her mouth, drowning her and refashioning her, and she knew that he was trying to burn through her and absorb her so he could take another vessel. So he could rule.

Armand looked like a broken window, desolate and razor-sharp. He stood—he shouted useless human words—and then he had the abomination, the blasphemous sword created to defy her. He was going to kill her when he should worship her, he was *vile ungrateful faithless—*

She blinked, and she loved him again. Joyeuse was clinging to his hand, and his face was set in the trembling, absolute resolution that had held the Devourer back for six months.

He had never been so beautiful. She had never loved him so much.

There was blood and battle all around them, but they were the only two people in the world.

"I'm sorry," he said, and then the blade was between her ribs, and it didn't hurt, but it burned like fire and ice, like the sun and the moon and the host of stars.

And then there was night.

She was in a forest.

But it was not the Great Forest. That forest, as dark and terrible as it could be, was riotously alive. This was the forest of her dreams, and it was dead. Leafless trees stretched writhing, naked branches toward the sky. Dark red blood oozed from the cracks in their rough black bark, the only color in the bleak world. For the ground was covered in powdery white dust, while the sky was gray. Not the mottled, damp gray of overcast clouds, but a flat, featureless gray that no sun would ever burn away. The air itself was dry and dead; her breath rasped in her throat, and every breath stole away a little more of her strength.

But she didn't need to be strong now. Rachelle dropped to her knees. Black speckled her vision and *it didn't matter.* She had been eaten by the Devourer and she had been killed with Joyeuse. She had, she hoped, killed him along with her. Was this lifeless world a last flickering dream before she fully died, or was it the beginning of her eternity?

She started to fall forward and caught herself on her hands, sending up a wave of dust that made her cough and gag. It didn't matter. She had done what she could, made what amends she could, and all the rest was beyond her.

Almost all the amends she could. She'd never said the rosary that was to be her penance. She tried to form the words, but her mouth was too dry, her breath too short. Besides, penance was for those who had a hope of heaven, and she wasn't at all sure that God could hear or find her in this place.

But that was all right, wasn't it? She had first talked to the forestborn—to Erec—because she wanted to save the world. She had known she was risking her soul, but she had gone ahead anyway, and she had gotten her wish. She might have repented, but she couldn't quite regret.

This was her home. This, her inheritance.

She hardly felt it when she crumpled to the ground. Her vision was swiftly going dark. She thought of Armand and Amélie; she could take those memories, at least, into the darkness.

There were worse endings.

BUT IT IS NOT THE END.

It is not the end because even death is not the end of fighting. I am dead, and I know.

But even beyond death, there are endings, and mine is almost here. Now it lies to you, my daughter, my sister, my pride. Wake up. Finish my story.

Wake.

34

"Wake."

It was the voice that had spoken to her just now, telling her the story of Tyr and Zisa. She had been dreaming then, as she listened—she had thought she was dreaming—but now she heard the voice's final words with her own ears.

And Rachelle opened her eyes. Beside her knelt a girl her own age. Tangled dark hair fell about her round, bony face; in the center of her forehead was an eight-pointed red star. Her dress was made from fold after fold of black silk; it took Rachelle a moment to realize that her chest was slick with blood.

Rachelle's mouth was dry and stiff; when she tried to speak, she started coughing. Finally she managed to swallow, and said, "You're Zisa."

"Yes," said the girl.

Her voice was soft but clear, sad yet resolute. It was exactly the way she had sounded when telling the story of how she and Tyr had fought the Devourer and both failed and won.

Rachelle sat up. They were still in the bleeding forest, though perhaps the gray sky was a shade darker.

"If I'm dead," she said, "where are all the others the Devourer has eaten?"

"Did you not hear? Even after death, there are endings. They all faded from this place long ago."

Rachelle's hand went to her chest. She felt cold, sticky blood, but no pain.

"Stand up." Zisa got to her feet. "We do not have much time."

Her body felt heavy and foreign, but Rachelle still clambered to her feet in a few moments. She was surprised to find Zisa a head shorter than her.

"Time for what?" she asked.

"To kill the Devourer," said Zisa. Despite her height, she seemed to look down at Rachelle. "Did you not give your heart for that?"

"I tried. I did."

"You did as I did," said Zisa. "You accepted the Devourer into your body and died with him. Now he is bound to you in your death, as he was to me, and as long as your ghost can linger, he will be trapped here with you between life and death. But you cannot linger forever. Nobody can. And when you fade away, as soon I will, another must die in your place, or else yield the world to darkness. And in the meantime, the Forest will grow at the edges of the world, and the woodspawn will infect your cities, and the forestborn will harry you."

It was not a bad bargain, Rachelle thought. But it was not a victory.

"Only the leavings of the wolf can kill the wolf," said Zisa. "That is the ancient truth. Only a child of the Devourer can strike him down. That is why I failed: I did not have the sword when I needed it, so the duty fell to Tyr. And he was much too innocent."

"But what else can I do?" asked Rachelle. "I did the same thing. I left the sword behind."

"Have you forgotten what you carry in your right hand?"

Rachelle stared at her.

Zisa tilted her head. "Or have you never known?"

Her hand throbbed. Rachelle looked down at the tiny white scar on her palm. For years she had hardly thought of it because it was so painful, but she had confessed it already to Armand, so she let herself remember again: Aunt Léonie, choking on her own blood. When Rachelle had bent over her, crying, Aunt Léonie had suddenly struggled against her, arms flailing. She must have been surprised while she was sewing, for she was still clutching a needle, and she stabbed it into Rachelle's hand all the way down to the bone.

Rachelle had choked on a scream. Choked on her tears. And then she had lowered the knife.

"I told you what Durendal and Joyeuse were made from," said Zisa. "Did you think they could not take that form again?"

Two slivers of bone.

In a sudden frenzy, she clawed at the palm of her hand. The needle twitched in answer; then with a sudden, sharp pain, its tip burst through her skin.

With shaking fingers, Rachelle pulled it free: a tiny bone needle, covered in blood. Durendal.

As she thought the name, the needle grew and lengthened in her hand, until it became a sword entirely made out of bone, a perfect twin to Joyeuse.

"Do you know what its name means?" asked Zisa.

"No," said Rachelle, cautiously hefting the sword. It had once been a bone in the body of a sacrifice to the Devourer's hunger: a boy who had forgotten self and name, but not the sister he loved.

"Endurance. It is the sword that hopes all things, bears all things, believes all things, endures all things." Zisa sighed. "In the end, I could not use it." Her voice grew softer. "I believe you can."

She looked up just in time to see Zisa fading away. Her last words were less than a whisper: *My time is over now. Good luck.*

And Rachelle was alone in the forest of bleeding trees.

Slowly she walked forward, her feet whispering in the soft white dust; little clouds puffed up where she stepped. Many of the trees, in the crooks where their branches split and twisted, were growing teeth.

Her skin crawled. The forest felt less dead by the moment, and she walked faster.

Suddenly a shape loomed between the trees. It was the cottage from her dreams—the house of Old Mother Hunger, just as Zisa had described it. The eaves and lintels were carved with a profusion of figures who at first seemed to be dancing, but on second glance were devouring each other. The walls oozed blood between their planks. The roof was thatched with bones.

The door yawned open.

Rachelle walked quietly to it, her heart beating in her throat, and peered inside. She saw only a single room paneled in wood. There were no carved decorations, but the walls and floor alike were covered in doors, large and small, with barely an inch between them.

She stepped in. The air was cold and still, spiced with the tang of wood smoke and blood.

To her right, the nearest door was tall enough for her to walk through. She flung it open.

Pure, absolute darkness looked back at her, so stark that her eyes watered. No breath of air came through the doorway. But she realized there was a very, very faint murmuring sound, like the wind in very distant trees. Was it coming through the doorway? Or had it been here all along, and she'd only just noticed?

Next was a row of four little cupboard-sized doors, one atop the other from floor to ceiling. She opened them all: the same darkness. Faster and faster, she started opening doors. They all revealed absolute shadow.

The rushing noise was getting louder. It almost sounded like breathing. Rachelle's body was wound tight and all her limbs jangled with the need to flee, but there was nowhere to run. The nightmare was her world now; there was no way out but fighting it.

The doors in the walls were all open now; she no longer stood in a room with four walls, but in a latticework cage of door frames, with darkness everywhere looking in. That was what it felt like: not an absence, but a ponderous shadow pressing in upon the walls of the room, ready to crush it at any moment.

She knelt and opened one of the doors set in the floor. More darkness.

"My dear little traitor."

Her head snapped up. Erec stood in the doorway, so unexpected that for a moment he seemed more like one of the wood carvings come to life than the person she had known and trusted and hated.

"Whatever shall I do with you?" he asked, stepping inside.

She raised Durendal. "Stay back."

The shock on his face sent a little curl of satisfaction through her stomach.

"How did you get that toy?" he asked.

"How did *you* get in here after me?"

He raised his hand where the crimson thread shone. "We are bound in every world, my lady."

"You are desperate to believe that, aren't you?" she said, looking around the room. If it came to another fight, she would probably win, but she didn't have the time to waste.

There were still at least ten doors left unopened in the floor, but she was starting to think that there wasn't a right door. Something else was the answer.

"As you are desperate to deny it." He lounged against the door frame, but she could tell he was readying himself to spring at her.

In the very center of the floor, between the corners of three other doors, there was painted a little red star. Nothing else in the house led anywhere; maybe this did. As Erec lunged forward, she lifted Durendal and plunged it down into the star.

Cracks ran through all the wood. The whole house shuddered. And then it shattered into a thousand pieces.

Erec grabbed her arm as they plunged into darkness. They only fell a few moments, but the darkness was so heavy that it choked her. Then they both hit the ground and rolled, ending in a tangle of limbs, dust flying up around them.

Rachelle drew a breath full of dust and choked. It was not really dust: it was salt and ashes. As she gagged, Erec rolled on top of her and pinned her arms to the ground.

"Listen to me," he said. "It's not too late. We can still escape. Believe me, I know, for I once explored this far. We can go back, and give your burden to Vareilles as he deserves. I will make you my queen. We will rule together."

His words were breathless, desperate. She realized that he was afraid. He was afraid of losing her, afraid of this place, and yet he was being brave. For her.

"I'm dead," she told him.

"Your blood is still steaming," he said. "The power of the Forest could still draw you back."

She didn't struggle against his grip. She looked up at him and said quietly, "Even if I could, do you really think I would go with you?"

"Where else? To your precious Armand?" A little of his old arrogance returned to his voice. "Do you think he would dare half as much for your love as I have?"

"No," she said. "He never could. That's why I love him."

"You were desperate for me."

"Desperate. Not happy." And in that moment, despite all he had done, she truly pitied him. "You can never, ever make me happy. My heart will *never* rest in you."

His mouth twisted into something that was half a smile, half a snarl. "And Vareilles, is he your rest?"

She remembered Armand saying, *You are never content.* She remembered the jagged lines of the Dayspring's body in the painting, remembered whispering her sins into a listening silence.

"No," she said. "I really don't think he is." Then she pulled her legs in and kicked viciously upward, throwing Erec off her body. She rolled to her feet, seized Durendal, and looked around.

They stood on a field of the white ash-and-salt powder that had covered the ground in the forest. It stretched out, flat and featureless, all the way to the horizon, beneath a dome of pure black sky in which floated fragments of the forest: a broken tree, a ragged circle of ground, a triangular shard of iron-gray sky.

"Don't look back," Erec rasped, sitting up. "That's the rule in this place, don't ever look over your shoulder. It sees you if you turn around."

So of course she turned and looked.

And it saw her.

It was the only appropriate word; no human pronouns could encompass the vast swirl of destruction that filled her vision. The dust spiraled around and around as it sank into the center, down and down toward . . . nothing. That was what made her heart hammer, her chest feel like it was paper wrapped over a despairing void. She knew this thing—the Devourer—had forsaken itself to plunge into deeper and deeper *nothing,* seeking the final abnegation where it would be utterly alone and therefore omnipotent. All its bloodbound and forestborn and vessels, all its mastery and devouring, the power at the heart of the Great Forest, the stomach that swallowed the sun and moon—they all were no more than foam in the wake of its hurtling ruin.

She saw a human figure floating upside down in the center of the whirlpool. She knew it was an illusion, something her feeble human mind had created to shield her from the heart of this vast destruction.

And as soon as she saw it, she could hear it: a great howling wind—no, a voice, screaming and singing at once. It sang pain-hate-loss-fear, but most of all it sang *hunger,* the vast and devouring emptiness of a creature who had once tasted bliss beyond what any mortal mind could comprehend, and now must keen unbearable loss forever after.

It sang, and she sang with it. Her throat ached and burned from the sounds that ripped out, but she couldn't stop. She felt that this sight had unlocked every secret of her life and made sense of them all. Surely she had always been singing this song in her heart. Surely this was her home. This, her inheritance.

Erec slammed her to the ground. "You belong to me, lady," he snarled, "not that thing." And he kissed her ferociously, biting her lip.

Rachelle bucked against him. "What—"

"You are *made* of that creature. That's why you can't fight it."

She realized there were a thousand red strings running through the white dust all around them, down into the maw of the Devourer. As she watched, the strings slowly slid forward. She felt a tug on her own hand.

"Yes," said Erec. "Inch by inch, he eats us all."

There was no escape. Rachelle was no longer looking at the vast swirl of the Devourer, but she could feel the icy despair starting to rise again in her heart. She was eaten. Finished. Done. There was no way she could turn and face that creature with Durendal. She doubted that it would matter even if she could. Swords were made for killing, and having seen the Devourer, she did not think that death was a concept that even applied to it.

Suddenly she remembered Aunt Léonie's fingers weaving a charm as she said, *The path of needles or the path of pins.*

Durendal's other form was a needle.

There were threads all around her.

Rachelle's heart thudded with sudden hope. She hadn't had to kill the lindenworm, only beguile it. Maybe it would be enough if she didn't kill the Devourer, but only bound it. Maybe the simple, boring charms that Aunt Léonie had taught her years ago had always been enough.

"Rachelle," Erec breathed into her ear. "Come with me. Please."

And she realized that he did love her. With all that remained of his heart, he loved her. And she pitied him.

"Erec," she said, "I came here to destroy the Devourer. If you do not let me try, I will look at him and lose myself. You won't be able to stop me, I swear it. The only way you'll have a chance to take me home is if you let me fight him now."

His face tightened. "What do you think you can do?"

"A little woodwife charm. That's all."

"You think that can stop our master?"

"So let me try and fail, and then we'll go home together."

He stared at her a moment longer, then laughed softly. "I wouldn't love you if you were any weaker," he said, and let go of her.

Rachelle sat up, grasped Durendal, and willed it back into the form of a needle. Then she gathered up a great loop of the string tied to her finger, and she started to knot it around the needle.

The most terrible charms, Margot had said, *or the most simple.*

And it was a very simple charm that Rachelle started to weave—one of the first she'd ever learned, a little knot pattern that would soothe and bind the things beneath it. Usually it was just one step in a larger charm, something to keep the barn doors shut against woodspawn or the wrong seeds from sprouting. Now she knotted it over and over, twisting in upon itself. She picked up other strings and knotted them into it as well.

She was doomed to be devoured, was she? Then she would make of herself—of all the bloodbound and all the forestborn—such a morsel as would choke the Devourer forever.

The roaring grew louder. The dust shook at her feet.

"What are you doing?" Erec demanded.

The pattern had taken life. As the strings dragged through the dust toward the Devourer, they wiggled and bunched and tied themselves into the little knots, again and again. She could sense the power in them, like a thousand voices whispering *close-shut-fall-forever.*

"It's falling," she said. "For all of time, it's been falling, and dragging us along with it. I'm setting it free."

The strings were made of the Devourer's power, and now they were twisted into patterns that continually turned the Devourer in on itself, collapsing it away from the human world. From any world.

"What have you *done*?" Erec demanded.

"I think," said Rachelle, "I've taught it to devour itself."

She stood. She still remembered what he had done. She would still hate him, when they returned to daylight. But she had seen the Devourer now, the limitless hunger and despair, and she couldn't wish for even him to become part of that.

"Come with me," she said, and took his hand.

A tremor passed through his face. He didn't say anything, but he gripped her hand in return.

Around them, the dust shuddered again, then started running toward the Devourer in little waves that crashed and broke against their legs. Rachelle staggered and marched forward, leaning against the pull of the Devourer, which sucked at her like an inverse wind.

"What do you think remains for us?" Erec demanded. "Are we going to beg and grovel before your precious saint and bishop?"

"We might die first!" Rachelle shouted back over the growing roar of the Devourer. She was actually pretty sure they would die, even if they weren't sucked in. The light had faded; she could see no way out, nothing but darkness.

She barely heard him when he said, "No, my lady. That fate is not for me."

She didn't see him look back. But she knew that he did, because she felt his hand crumble to salt and ashes in her grasp.

A scream ripped out of her throat. But there was no time for grief or rage. The pull was getting stronger; so was the song, and it took all her strength to remember that she must not turn around, must not look back and be swallowed up by the cataclysm of swirling despair behind her.

She willed Durendal back into the form of a sword, gripped it two-handed, and plunged it into the ground. Then she knelt and clung to it as the flying dust scoured her face, as the thread burned on her finger, as the Devourer screamed into her mind.

She thought of the long-forgotten boy killed to make the bone that Zisa would steal to make Durendal, and she thought, *Help me. Please.*

The hilt warmed beneath her hands. Then it grew hot, and then it burned with a fire that far surpassed that of the string on her finger. Rachelle sobbed, but she hung on. This was the sword that endured all things; she felt sure that if she did not let go, she could endure along with it.

Suddenly there was a great, rending scream that seemed to split the air in two. A flash of light.

And then, silence. And darkness.

And she was not holding a sword, but warm and human hands.

She opened her eyes.

Aunt Léonie looked back at her.

She was the same as when she died. Blood still dripped down the side of her face and soaked the front of her dress; the hollow gash was still cut into her throat. And yet there was no pain and no fear in her eyes. She was smiling, and that smile—the very way she breathed—was more alive, more *real* than Rachelle had ever seen her when she lived. Her spattered blood was transfigured into a lovingly crafted decoration. She possessed the wounds, as they had once possessed her.

"You—" Rachelle said, and her throat closed up. She did not feel afraid, only ignorant and helplessly ashamed.

"You're dead," she whispered finally. "I know you are with God, so *why are you still bleeding*?"

"Because," said Aunt Léonie, "how else could I forgive you?"

There were tears running down Rachelle's face, salty as the wasteland that had swallowed Erec. "That makes no sense."

"You were never the cleverest child," said Aunt Léonie. "But you had a good heart. That's why I chose you to guard Durendal." She laid a hand, sticky with blood, against Rachelle's cheek. "And you did. You fought very hard and you were very brave."

"And wicked."

"That too. And now you have a choice."

"What?" Rachelle asked warily.

"Look at your hands," said Aunt Léonie.

Rachelle looked down. There was a skein's worth of glowing white threads, tied to all her fingers and wending away into the darkness ahead of her like a river.

"If you want to go back," said Aunt Léonie, "you may."

"Back." The word was dry and hollow in her mouth. "You mean . . ."

"I mean you will live again."

"But I'm dead."

"Yes."

"People who are dead don't just get to . . . to *choose* to come back to life. Or why didn't you?" Her voice shook with fury. "Why didn't *you*?"

Aunt Léonie just smiled fondly. "Do you think I'm here to answer that? I'm here to remind you that you have only ever had one choice: the path of needles, or the path of pins."

Rachelle looked again at the strings bound to her hands. She knew, already, what she would do. What she must do.

"I miss you," she said quietly. "I miss you so much."

Aunt Léonie smiled and ruffled her hair. "It's not that long to wait, you know."

Rachelle stood. Durendal lay beside her on the ground; she picked it up with one hand. In the other, she clutched the threads, tiny and delicate and everlasting.

"I love you," she said to Aunt Léonie, and then she followed the threads away into the darkness.

35

And then she woke. Her body felt strange, at once heavy and empty. Her hand was still curled around Durendal, which had become a needle again; it didn't hurt much, but she could tell it was half-buried in her hand and would have to be dug out.

She was lying on somebody's lap, a heavy metal hand resting on her shoulder. It was Armand, she realized, and she heard his voice, dull and lifeless: "Leave me alone."

Justine replied, "You won't feel that way when she starts to rot."

Rachelle's breath hissed in.

Instantly Armand went tense. "Rachelle?" he said, his voice soft and raw.

She opened her eyes and saw glory. The whole world was

veined with silver threads, twisting and twirling and dancing. Then she blinked, and it was gone. She was in one of the groves of the Château. The morning sunlight had just begun to pick its way between the trees, Armand was looking down at her in desperate relief, and that was enough glory to last her a lifetime.

"Thank God," he breathed, and he started to lean down as if to kiss her.

Then he stopped, looking terribly unsure.

"Rachelle!" Amélie screamed the next moment, and pulled her up out of Armand's lap.

Amélie was not a bloodbound anymore. Rachelle knew because she pushed her back and checked before embracing her. And then Rachelle realized why she felt so strange: the power of the Forest was entirely gone from her, no longer strengthening her limbs, whispering in her ears, filling the world around her with half-seen depths. She was human once more, and it made her body feel like a heavy, foreign thing.

But it also meant that Amélie could hold her without fear. She hugged her even tighter.

"I still can't scold you," Amélie whispered, "but you are *never* allowed to do that again."

"What happened?" asked Rachelle

"You lied," said Armand, but he didn't sound angry. He didn't sound *anything*, just quiet and blank.

"I didn't lie," said Rachelle. "I just didn't tell you everything."

He smiled faintly. He wasn't exactly looking at her, and that was wrong, all wrong—

"We slaughtered a lot of forestborn," said Justine. "D'Anjou disappeared into thin air, which I suspect you can tell us more about. Then the rest of them fell down dead, and we were back in the Château grounds. All the bloodbound fell dead or were no longer bloodbound."

"And you were dead," said Amélie. Her arms were still around Rachelle. "The wound had healed, but you were still dead."

"So was the King," said Justine. "Permanently. Since most of the nobility were in hysterics, the Bishop took control. He's sent men to find the room where d'Anjou hid Raoul Courtavel."

"We'll have a just king by next week," said Amélie. "But what happened to *you*?"

Rachelle looked at her hand, saw the bloody mess of the half-impaled needle, and winced. "Durendal." She sighed. "And my aunt."

As soon as Amélie saw the wound, she clucked, seized Rachelle's hand, and started carefully drawing out the needle.

"I'm going to go tell the Bishop you're alive," said Justine. She smiled, briefly, and left.

Armand stood. He was still not exactly looking at any of them. "I need to go back," he said.

Rachelle gripped Amélie's shoulder and used it to push herself to her feet. "Then I'm coming with you," she said.

The three of them walked back to the Château together. The gardens were a mess: the ground churned up and stained with blood. Not all the bodies were cleared away yet.

The Château was in chaos. Most of the surviving guests from the party had gathered in the Hall of Mirrors. Some were being treated for their wounds. Some were drinking coffee brought by harried-looking servants. And some were simply huddled into themselves, staring into empty air.

Almost all of them turned to look when Armand walked in.

"Cousin!" Vincent Angevin's voice boomed across the hall, and Rachelle turned to see him striding toward them. Unlike many of the dirty, frightened nobles, his coat was clean and crisp, his curls perfectly arrayed. If he'd been at the celebration the night before, he'd found time to clean up afterward.

"I'm glad to see you're alive," he said with a hearty laugh that made him seem very like his late uncle.

"Thank you," Armand said blandly.

Vincent slapped him on the shoulder. "It's a sad day, but I'm sure good will come of it. And I know I'll have your support in the days ahead, as I take up my dear uncle's mantle."

Armand pressed his lips together for a moment as he looked at Vincent.

"No," he said, his voice quiet and carrying. "I won't help you."

Clearly it had not occurred to Vincent that Armand might

refuse him to his face in public. It took him a moment to respond. "You know my uncle wanted me to—"

"The King, my father, handed me over to the forestborn who cut off my hands," said Armand, his voice growing louder. "He forced me to help him while he was alive, but now that he's dead, I don't give a damn what he wanted. Or what you want."

"I don't either," put in Rachelle. "And I have a sword."

Vincent huffed. "I would advise you not to speak that way to your future king—"

"I would advise you," said Armand, in a voice that was entirely calm but reached every corner of the hall, "not to threaten somebody who has faced the Devourer twice. One of us walked away. It wasn't him."

He met Vincent's eyes, and there was no hint of hesitation anywhere in his body. Every eye in the hall was on him, and though Vincent still had his chest thrust out, Rachelle could tell he was uneasy.

Nobody but Rachelle had ever seen Armand when he wasn't playing the part of obedient saint. Even she hadn't ever seen him when he wasn't having hostages used against him.

Armand looked around the hall. He seemed to be measuring up the people around him and finding them just barely sufficient. "The King had Raoul Courtavel imprisoned in the Château as a hostage against me. I will require some guards to free him."

Vincent spluttered, clutching at the fragments of command. "You can't just—"

"I'm afraid you've made a mistake, monsieur." La Fontaine was approaching them with a set of palace guards at her back. "Last week, our dear, late king made a will that legitimized Prince Raoul and named him heir. I saw him sign it. I have the documents."

"You're lying."

"I also," la Fontaine continued pleasantly, halting just a step away from him, "have proof that you conspired to assassinate your cousin Armand Vareilles. And the captain of the guard believes me." She smiled. "I would advise you not to land that blow, monsieur."

Vincent hastily lowered his hand, his gaze flickering from side to side. He had clearly never considered that anyone would seriously contest him so quickly—especially not Armand or la Fontaine—so he had brought no supporters with him. He tried a smile; it looked rather sickly.

"I'm afraid," he said, "that grief for my uncle has caused you to start engaging in wild fantasies—forging a will in my uncle's name—"

And here came the Bishop, his dark cassock swinging. "I have seen the documents," he said. "I am satisfied."

Rachelle wondered if anyone else noticed that he hadn't said the documents were genuine.

It didn't matter. She could see it in the faces of the guards, of the nobles gathered around them. The Bishop and la Fontaine had helped save their lives last night. Armand was their saint. They trusted them now.

"Think what you want," said Armand. "I'm going to free my brother and my king."

He strode away without looking back. And so, of course, the guards and Rachelle and la Fontaine followed him. Vincent stayed behind, his mouth hanging open.

He would never be able to command anyone who had stood in the Hall of Mirrors this morning. Rachelle took a vicious pleasure in the knowledge.

Armand led them through little-used corridors to a set of small, lightless rooms. Rachelle knew them: Erec had shown them to her, and told her that they were for keeping prisoners. He hadn't told her who was held captive behind the most well-guarded of the doors.

There were no guards now. Rachelle wondered if they had been given orders to kill their prisoners if things went wrong, and if they had obeyed those orders. But Armand strode forward as if doubt and fear belonged in another world and had no power to touch him. He had always been desperately, terrifyingly human to her, but now she could see why people bowed before him and called him saint.

"This one," said Armand, halting in front of a door.

The guards broke it down on his command. And on the other side—there was Raoul Courtavel. Rachelle might not have recognized the tall man with the ragged beard. But when he pulled Armand into a desperate, wordless embrace, there was no mistaking him.

This was why Armand had led an armed rebellion. When Rachelle had killed his followers, this was what she had nearly destroyed.

She turned away, feeling sick. She found la Fontaine looking at her, no pride or courtly polish left anywhere in her face.

"Thank you," said la Fontaine, looking straight into her eyes, and the words sounded more sincere than anything la Fontaine had ever said to her.

Rachelle knew she didn't deserve them.

For the next two days, Rachelle was beside Armand almost every moment. And she barely said a word to him.

She knew why he kept her close, and she was desperately, stupidly thankful. Everyone knew her as one of the King's bloodbound, as the friend—or mistress—of Erec d'Anjou. By making sure that everyone saw her as his trusted bodyguard, Armand was freeing her of suspicion. Nobody knew exactly what she had done the night of the summer solstice—neither she nor Armand had provided many details—but everyone knew that she had helped the saint to vanquish his foes.

Unlike all the other bloodbound, she would be loved forever after. It was a debt she could never repay.

One of the many, many debts.

Something held Armand back from speaking to her during the

few, scattered moments when they were alone together. Rachelle didn't speak either, because she didn't have the right.

She'd had his love, if it had really been love. He had kissed her and said that he loved her, but he had thought he would be dead within days. It had been impossible for him to have any intention of sharing his life with her. And since then, she had thrown him away, killed his followers, slept with the man who had maimed him—and saved his life and mattered enough to be used as a hostage against him, but that wasn't love. Exactly. Maybe.

Now Armand was not only going to live, he was the favorite half brother of the new king. He could have anything that he wanted, and if he didn't want Rachelle . . . after the way she had treated him, it was only fair.

A lot of things were fair: the strange, uneasy looks that she got from most people in the Château, who didn't know whether to fear or honor her. The dull heaviness and infuriating *weakness* of her body, now that she was fully human again. The loneliness of standing next to Armand and saying nothing.

Just because things were fair, didn't make them easy.

Amélie went home on the second day. Rachelle wanted to beg her to stay, but she couldn't, because she had held Amélie when she woke up sobbing the night before. She deserved a chance to go home to her mother.

"I am not leaving you forever and ever," said Amélie, glowering as she fussed with the clothes in her trunk. "Even if *you* try to leave *me.* I will hunt you down and find you." She snapped the lid of the trunk down. "I can do it. You're not so much stronger than me, now. So *stop looking that way.*"

Rachelle choked on a laugh. "You were always stronger."

"You," said Amélie, "were always foolish enough to think that mattered." For a few moments, she studied Rachelle, her mouth puckered. "Don't leave me," she said quietly. "Promise you'll come visit."

Rachelle let out a shaky breath. Amélie's determination was like solid ground beneath her feet after she'd spent days falling.

"All right," she said. "I'll come, I promise."

Amélie grinned and pulled her into an embrace.

"I wouldn't be here without you," Rachelle said when Amélie released her. "You know that, don't you? I would have given up and lost myself to the Forest years ago."

"I think you're underestimating yourself," said Amélie.

"No," said Rachelle. "I'm not. That night we met—when I was too late to save your father, I thought that at least I got to save you. But it was really you who saved me."

Amélie smiled at her. She looked fragile and beautiful and terribly strong. "Thank you," she said.

The evening after Amélie left, Rachelle went out running in the gardens. The Château's bells had just finished ringing nine o'clock, and yet the sun still lingered on the horizon. Rachelle had never imagined the world could be so full of light.

She had never imagined, either, what it would be like to run as a human.

It was still a delight. The air was still cool and sweet in her throat, even if it was not the magical, inhuman sweetness of the Great Forest. The pounding of her heart was still a drug. But soon—so very soon—her legs burned and her chest ached. She had to lean against a tree, gasping for breath. Sweat slid down her back.

Once she could have run forever. Once the wound on her palm would have healed in minutes; now, after two days, it was a scabbed mess that ached and stung when she flexed her hand.

She was grateful—so very, very grateful—to be human again. To be free. And yet she missed the strength and speed and grace she'd had as a bloodbound. She missed them bitterly.

A breeze stirred against her face. She looked up.

In the spaces between the trees, other phantom trees stretched out their translucent branches, like indentations in the air.

The breeze stirred again. It sounded like it was laughing to itself. Dimly, between the shadows of the trees, she saw something that looked like a white deer with red eyes. A woodspawn.

She blinked, and the vision was gone. She was the most alien thing among the trees once more.

But the song of the wind still trembled in her blood. The

Forest had been here—it was still here, right now, even if she couldn't see it. Though the Devourer had gone, the Great Forest was living still. And it no longer had the same feeling of heartless menace as it had before.

She supposed it made sense. The Devourer did not seem like a creature that could create anything, much less the terrible beauty of the Great Forest.

Uncounted ages ago—not just before the daylight, but before the Devourer swallowed the sun and moon to begin with, before it enmeshed itself in the human world at all—the Great Forest had stood tall. How it must have delighted the people who lived then. And then the Devourer took it from them.

Now, perhaps, they would have it back.

Erec, you fool, she thought. *There was a whole world waiting for us.*

And there, surrounded by the shadow of the Forest that could have been, that would be now—dark but no longer so dreadful—she cried for Erec.

Eventually she dried her eyes. She stood and walked back toward the Château, out of the trees.

Back toward Armand. He stood by one of the fountains, staring at the falling water that glittered in the sunset light.

Her heart thudded. She meant to slip past him silently, but then he looked up at her and said, "Rachelle."

And she couldn't move. She could only stare at him, drinking in the curve of his cheek, the line of his mouth, wishing that he was still hers to touch.

"Are you all right?" he asked.

She shrugged. "Well. I'm human. And nobody seems to want me executed."

He wasn't happy. She could tell that from the way he had planted himself, shoulders braced, but she couldn't read anything on his face. That was what hurt most of all, that he was *biding* from her.

"I killed you," he said suddenly. "I'm—really very sorry."

It was the last thing she had expected him to say.

"You didn't kill me, you killed the Devourer inside of me," she said after a moment. "Isn't that what you said at the salon?"

He choked out a small laugh, his face coming alive again. "I did. But—that was when I thought I couldn't possibly be the one holding the blade. I spent so much time pretending to be a saint, I think I fooled myself as well."

"It's true now, isn't it?" said Rachelle. "You were ready to die twice to stop the Devourer. You helped save Gévaudan."

"I did everything wrong," he said. "Those men who helped in the coup, they trusted me to lead them, and I ruined our chances—"

"I was the one who killed them. Some of them." Rachelle's heart thudded when she said the words, and for a moment she couldn't look at him.

When she dared a glance, he was looking annoyed. "You thought we were planning to slaughter you," he said. "Because *I* didn't tell you, because I couldn't make up my mind if you knew what the forestborn were planning or not."

"It was a reasonable suspicion," said Rachelle.

"And then I let them raise the Forest when they threatened you. And then I killed you. I'm sorry."

"You do realize," said Rachelle, "that you just apologized for saving my life *and* for ending it?"

His mouth curved wryly.

She took a step closer. "It's true. You did wrong, and you should have died first. But I forgive you for it. I've heard that God will too."

He laughed then, sudden and raw and real. "You're not going to let me forget anything I ever said, are you?"

"Never." Her mouth curved up as her eyes met his, and it felt *right*, it felt like—

Why did she feel as if they had a long history of easy happiness between them? They had never been anything but enemies or else uneasy allies. Jailer and prisoner, sinner and saint. The kisses in between had hardly changed a thing.

"I'm not sorry I lied to you about the offering," she said.

"That's good," said Armand, "because I still don't forgive you for it." Abruptly his lips pressed together in a flat line. After a moment he went on, his voice expressionless, "But that doesn't matter anymore. If you feel like you owe me something . . . you don't. You can leave."

She'd expected the words, but they still hit her like a kick to the chest. Armand wasn't looking at her anymore; he'd started to angle his body away, his head bent down to stare at the grass. As if he didn't want to be any closer to her than he had to be.

Then she realized how utterly lonely he looked.

"What are you doing now?" she asked.

He did look up at her then, and smiled faintly. "Do you know, I haven't the faintest idea. For six months, I was a dead man walking. I don't remember what it was like to have a future."

"I don't either," said Rachelle.

There was another moment of silence, but this one wasn't quite so awkward. Then Armand drew a breath. "Rachelle," he said. "I know—what was between us—we were about to die. We didn't make any promises. If you want to leave, you have every right. And I have no idea what I'm going to do with myself now. But I would like you to be there while I find out."

The words were exactly what she'd wanted to hear him say, ever since she'd woken up in his arms. And yet now—

"The Forest's still alive," she said. "I saw it, just now."

Armand didn't even blink at the change of subject. "I know."

"Do you still see it all the time?" She was horrified to realize that she hadn't even wondered how much had changed for him.

He shook his head. "Just sometimes. But enough." He paused.

"It's different now. I almost don't hate it."

"Oh." She stared at the water. "I saw it for a moment today. I missed it so much. And then I cried for Erec."

Armand was silent. She didn't dare look at him.

"I haven't told anyone else this, but I think you deserve to know." Rachelle drew a breath. "Erec isn't just dead. He's worse than dead. He went with me into the stomach of the Devourer, and he chose to stay there for all eternity." She paused. "I tried to save him. I am sorry for all I did with him, you have no idea how much—and you have no idea how much I hate him, either—but I did want to save him. I still wish I could have."

"I guessed as much," said Armand after a moment.

She finally looked at him. "You're not angry?"

He gave her a wry smile. "Well, I did ask you not to kill him."

"That's not an answer."

He sighed. "For the last six months, every moment of every day, I could feel the Devourer sleeping in the back of my mind. There were some mornings I woke up and I could barely breathe for his hunger and despair. I know what fate d'Anjou chose. I can't wish that on anyone. Other, very painful fates, maybe. But not that one."

"I wished it on myself, sometimes," she said. "It doesn't seem fair that I was spared."

"It seems perfectly fair to me," he said. "But I am hardly impartial."

"What I'm trying to tell you," said Rachelle, "is that I'm not . . . I haven't stopped being . . . I don't know what I am."

"I wake up some mornings and for a moment I can't tell if I'm the only one inside my head," said Armand. "I don't think either of us knows what we are."

Rachelle looked at him. She knew she could leave. She could go back to Rocamadour and live with Amélie and maybe find some peace.

She had never, in her whole life, been satisfied with peace.

The back of his neck was warm under her fingers as she pulled him into a kiss.

"Yes," she said. "I'll stay. As long as you hold on to me. Yes."

Acknowledgments

There are a lot of ways that this book was nearly never finished, and so there are a lot of people to thank for its existence.

My agent, Hannah Bowman, has been an unfailing source of support from the first moment I said, "Wouldn't it be cool to combine *Little Red Riding Hood* and *The Girl With No Hands*?" It's difficult to imagine what this book would have been like without her. Thank you!

I would also like to thank my two editors: Sara Sargent, who worked with me on the difficult early stages, and Kristin Daly Rens, who helped bring the project to completion. The entire HarperCollins team has continued to be great, and once again, thanks to Erin Fitzsimmons for an astounding cover.

Bethany Powell, Natalie Parker, Brendan Hodge, and Marieke Nijkamp all read various drafts of the novel and provided valuable feedback.

There are many people whom I asked for advice or help of various kinds while writing this book, and any attempt to name them will surely miss somebody—but Sherwood Smith, Stephen Maddux, Adam Posadas, Stephanie Oakes, Mindy Rhiger, and Corinne Duyvis all responded very kindly to a very desperate author.

Gévaudan is almost entirely unlike seventeenth-century France (and I can only beg the forgiveness of any historians who have read this far), but I do owe the period a debt of inspiration, and I would like to acknowledge *The Splendid Century* by W. H. Lewis, *Princesse of Versailles* by Charles Elliott, and *Versailles: A Biography of a Palace* by Tony Spawforth as being particularly helpful. (Also: the letters of Liselotte von der Pfalz.)

Two major artistic inspirations were Tim Powers's short story "The Hour of Babel" and Patricia A. McKillip's novel *The Alphabet of Thorn*. Less major, but no less delectable, were the Old Norse poems *Völuspá* and *Völundarkviða*. All four works are marvelous, and you should try them.

I suspect it is not easy to be friends with a writer under deadline. Sasha Decker, Tia Corrales, and Megan Lorance all deserve ten thousand thanks for the best friends that any writer could hope to have.

Finally, I would like to thank everyone who read my first novel, *Cruel Beauty.* Writing has always been my dream, and you helped it come true. Thanks!